Brave New Love

Also available

Truth & Dare: 20 Tales of Heartbreak and Happiness
Edited by Liz Miles

Corsets & Clockwork: 13 Steampunk Romances
Edited by Trisha Telep

Brave New Love

15 Dystopian Tales of Desire

Edited by Paula Guran

RP | TEENS
PHILADELPHIA · LONDON

Constable & Robinson Ltd
55–56 Russell Square
London WC1B 4HP
www.constablerobinson.com

First published in the UK by Robinson,
an imprint of Constable & Robinson Ltd, 2012

A copy of the British Library Cataloguing-in-Publication
Data is available from the British Library

UK ISBN: 978-1-84901-601-8 (paperback)
UK ISBN: 978-1-84901-768-8 (ebook)

1 3 5 7 9 10 8 6 4 2

First published in the United States in 2012 by Running Press Book Publishers,
A Member of the Perseus Books Group

Books published by Running Press are available at special discounts for bulk purchases in
the United States by corporations, institutions, and other organizations. For more information,
please contact the Special Markets Department at the Perseus Books Group, 2300 Chestnut Street,
Suite 200, Philadelphia, PA 19103, or call (800) 810-4145, ext. 5000, or e-mail
special.markets@perseusbooks.com.

US ISBN: 978-0-7624-4220-1
US Library of Congress Control Number: 2011937815

9 8 7 6 5 4 3 2 1
Digit on the right indicates the number of this printing

Published by Running Press Teens
an Imprint of Running Press Book Publishers
A Member of the Perseus Books Group
2300 Chestnut Street
Philadelphia, PA 19103-4371

Visit us on the web!
www.runningpress.com

Printed and bound in the U.S.A.

For the young people who hold the future
in their hands and hearts.
I have faith in you.

Contents

Introduction

PAULA GURAN

History is not one long stretch of a single civilization, but humans have managed to maintain various civilizations for five thousand years or so. Thousands of years may be difficult for us to conceive but when you consider dinosaurs dominated the planet for over 160 million years, five millennia is only a blink of Time's eye. And during that blink, many civilizations have collapsed—sometimes cataclysmically, more often after a period of decline—and new ones arisen.

The inhabitants of any fallen civilization who survived found themselves having to adapt to a "new world." It was seldom an easy undertaking.

In the ancient world one civilization might disappear while another was emerging elsewhere. Each may have been unknown to the other. The Roman Empire declined while Mayan city-states reached their zenith. The Anasazi thrived as Europe climbed out of the Dark Ages. Similarly, a civilization like that of the Egyptians could decline for a time, recover, eventually collapse, and then be conquered by others.

In the twenty-first century civilization is far more singular, interconnected, and global than ever before. No civilization, in all of human history, has been as dependent on technology and the resources that support it as we are today. We've never lived so clustered together in cities that can quickly be rendered unlivable by relatively minor cataclysms. Yet we still face, perhaps more than ever, all the factors that radically changed or ended our ancestors' ways of life: climate change, war, economic collapse, environmental problems, irrationality, disease. But in the modern world the weapons are more destructive, disease can spread more quickly, irrationality and hatred can be disseminated more widely and immediately, discontent is growing, and we seem to be able to create new problems much faster than we can provide solutions, which sometimes turn into new threats.

Perhaps we'll adapt, and our civilization will not only survive but flourish. We still can't help but wonder: What would life be like if the world as we know it ended? Who would survive and how? Would we find ways of individually and collectively coping or would we find ourselves living under a repressive system of social control? Would we devolve into a feudal society or something more primitive? Would there be strange new forms of humanity to deal with? Would we—or our descendents—remember what life was like in 2012? Would we even recognize the world of tomorrow? Would it seem like some dark fantasy or something utterly surreal?

For *Brave New Love* we asked authors to wonder about what would happen if the world as we know it ended. We also asked them to consider what love—perhaps the most basic of all human emotions—would be like in that world. Love is, after all, what makes us want to survive, to strive, to hope, to dare to dream.

Most specifically, we asked them to consider what love would be like for the young. For, no matter what tomorrow brings, it is always the newest generation—those growing out of childhood and accepting or being forced to bear the burdens of adulthood—on whom the responsibility for any future rests. And, for the young, love sometimes really is all you need.

Their diverse answers are the stories of *Brave New Love*.

Paula Guran

Hidden Ribbon

JOHN SHIRLEY

Los Angeles, 2044

The wind shrieked through Giorgio's long hair as he fought for balance on the rope bridge thirty stories over the street. The swaying bridge stretched from the acid-etched high-rise behind him to the top of the support buttress on the high tower of the old BP building. There'd been some acid rains recently, he remembered—which meant that if the protectant were wearing off, the footbridge cables could snap. He took another three steps into a shadow-draped part of the bridge . . .

The sun was beginning to set beyond the BP building. It would be dark soon.

The teenager took seven steps more, then the rope bridge yawed sickeningly in the wind and he clutched at the twined, scavenged cables as the thick, muggy air-current roared past, bellowing like a living creature. He staggered to the left, close to pitching over the cable. He held on, and the wind died down a little. The rope bridge sagged back, swaying, to its centerline. Only good thing about this, he figured, was that he'd be a hard target to hit with a rifle. If Limmy were back there aiming at him he'd probably miss.

After a few moments the swaying eased and Giorgio decided

to run for it, jogging the last hundred yards along the unsteady treadway of random slabs of mismatched wood to the open window at the BP building. With a strong sense of relief he leapt from the end of the rope bridge on to the top of the steel buttress—just as a bullet cracked into the concrete by his head.

Heart thudding, he ducked through the window, into the entry hall—pressing himself to one side of the opening to be out of rifle range. He craned his neck a little to look cautiously back out the window. He couldn't see the shooter but he knew it was Limmy or one of his gang.

Giorgio was pretty high up—he could see a lot of Rooftown from here. The gigantic improvised shacktown built over old rooftops stretched above Southeast LA like tree branches made from junk extending from the trunk of the old BP building. The branches were made up of shacks, several stories of them, some elaborate, others little more than tree-house-type structures. After Santa Monica and a lot of other coastal towns had been flooded by the rising waters of global warming, and the big famine caused food prices to rocket up, a lot of people lost their homes. With the Dissolve Depression destroying a good many banks and insurance companies, there was no money to replace them. Some people had built squat homes atop abandoned buildings creating Rooftown, high above the worst of the social chaos below, and the rising waters that would someday lap this far inland. They were even above some of the worst air pollution.

Of course, there were luckier people. People who'd had more money, better resources—they'd bought their way into one of the dome communities.

Me, I'm not lucky. Catching his breath just inside the window, hoping to get through the day without being shot, Giorgio thought: *That's an understatement, hodey.*

"Hey—kid!" called a gruff voice.

Giorgio turned to see Banker glaring from the other end of the hall. Banker was a hulking man in a sleeveless shirt, his beefy arms covered with amateur tattoos. He called himself Banker because he collected the "Live Here Money" from people squatting in—and on—the old BP building.

"Ya can't come in this building, here, ya bringin' gunfire down on us! We don't take in no lost teenagers nohow!"

"He's not gonna shoot at the building anymore, Banker—I'm inside now—"

"He's gonna shoot from *inside* ya chump—look!" Banker pointed out the window.

Giorgio looked out to see Limmy running across the rope bridge, his rifle on a strap over his shoulder—the shock-haired gangster stopped when the wind rose and clutched at the rope. Another figure was behind him, a ways back—looked like Roman, Limmy's second in command.

Giorgio had hoped the gangster wouldn't risk coming to this side of Rooftown—not over him balking at a hundred-WD protection pay-off. But there they were, like they had something to prove.

"Kid?"

Giorgio turned to see Banker pointing a large-caliber automatic pistol at him.

Giorgio sighed. "Well, crap. Seems like I'm the only guy around here without a gun."

"Don't get cute—just get out. The way you came!"

Giorgio thought about trying to dart past Banker—maybe Banker'd miss his shot, maybe even choose not to fire. But Banker wasn't likely to do either one. There wasn't a whole lot of mercy in Rooftown, any way you cut it.

"Okay, fine, but you're going to miss a really good joke I was gonna tell you, Banker!"

"Get out before I—"

The threat was lost in the roar of the wind as Giorgio stepped back out onto the top of the buttress. A narrow walkway without a railing was to his right. The walkway of sheet-metal-covered wood, about three-feet wide, clung precariously to the sides of the building, but that was his only route—unless he went straight down head first.

Giorgio sidled quickly as he dared onto the walkway—just as a bullet whined off the building behind him. A split second later he heard the sound of the gunshot echoing. Living in Rooftown, this wasn't the first time he'd been shot at. But it never got easier.

Giorgio made the mistake of glancing to the left, where an abyss yawned—a long, long fall to a hard, hard street shrouded in brown-gray smog.

Suddenly dizzy with vertigo, he almost lost his balance—but he'd lived in Rooftown for the last two years, and experience enabled him to shift his attention forward, focusing on the corner of the building ahead.

Just keep moving, he told himself.

A few steps more and Giorgio reached the corner, slowing so momentum didn't propel him off the walkway. He turned the corner—just as another bullet shrieked by overhead. They wouldn't keep on missing.

Up ahead, on his left, was an unfathomable drop to a quick death; on his right were six windows. As he worked his way carefully past them, leaning toward the wall with the wind prying at him, he found that window after window was boarded up from the inside—impassable. Beyond them, at the next corner, the walkway ended. It didn't turn the corner.

Two more windows—they looked to be unblocked. There was nowhere else to go except down, so his choice was to get in through one of the two windows . . . or die.

Somewhere behind him, Limmy would be reaching the end of the rope walk, would be working his own way along the walkway . . .

Giorgio moved so he was between the two windows—and had to grab at the nearest sill as the wind rose again, almost peeling him off the walkway. He winced at the ache in his fingers as he clutched at the windowsill—the wind seemed to be deliberately trying to pull him off into the void.

Then it abated—and he slipped through the shattered old window, scraped by broken glass as he went. He found himself in what appeared to be a small, empty old office—with a closed door to the corridor.

He thought: My only hope is if they think I've gone somewhere when I haven't . . .

If he could get them tangled up with Banker it might keep them busy till he could figure something out. Crunching debris with every step, he reached the door, and tried it. It felt locked.

Giorgio looked around, found an old crowbar on the floor. Demolition of the building had been started but, after the Dissolve Depression, never completed. He hefted the crowbar, then swung it like a baseball bat as hard as he could, smack into the doorknob. The knob punched through the door, falling out the other side, leaving a hole. He reached through, pressed the internal lock mechanism, and the door clicked. He shoved the door hard with his shoulder and it gave way into the debris-choked hallway, open just enough to let someone squirm through. Only, he wasn't going through.

Carrying the crowbar, he went back to the window, looked

carefully out. Limmy and his pet thug hadn't come around the corner yet. They'd be coming slowly, with that wind on the walkway, inching their way along so they wouldn't fall.

Giorgio climbed cautiously out on to the walkway, holding the crowbar close to the wall so it wouldn't overbalance him the wrong way. He went as quickly as he dared to the second window.

This window was intact, glass and all. He glanced inside—it seemed to be someone's squat, with an old mattress in the corner, a few decorations. He used the crowbar, levered the window frame, hoping it wasn't locked, that the window wouldn't break. It slid reluctantly up, and he eased into the room as quickly as he could. He turned, closed the window and locked it—hearing Limmy's voice from down the walkway.

Giorgio found an old bureau, pushed it up against the window, put a vase, a framed picture, other odds and ends on top, trying to make it look as if they'd always been there.

Then he ducked back, out of sight, pressed against the wall.

The faint light filtering through the window made a square on the opposite wall—he saw Limmy's shadow, his rifle poking up behind it, appear in that square. Limmy was trying the window, finding it locked.

Giorgio knew he could probably knock Limmy off the walkway—but he'd never killed anyone before, didn't like the idea, and didn't want to make enemies of every roof-gangster associated with Limmy. Besides, there was Roman—who would be watching Limmy. Roman had that pistol handy. A crowbar wasn't much use against a pistol.

He heard Limmy's voice, muffled, through the window. "Thing's locked. What? Nah, if I try to break the glass I could fall—What makes you think he's in that one? Oh yeah?"

Limmy's voice got fainter as he moved down the walkway. "Well go on *in* then, dumbass! I'll be right behind you."

Limmy and Roman had taken the bait, for now anyway.

Giorgio turned to look around—and saw a gun pointed at him. "I swear," he muttered. ". . . everybody but me has one . . . I got to get one of those."

A girl about his age was pointing a rusty-looking revolver at him. She was a mix of Asian and Hispanic—that was Giorgio's guess—wearing cutoff jeans, sneakers that didn't match, a torn blue sweatshirt. She was compactly built, but with curves, had long, shiny black hair. But the expression on her face was no more welcoming than her revolver. She said, "Move that stuff away from the window and climb back out, *now*. I'm gonna give you to a count of twenty."

"Look, there's a couple of bangers after me, just because I told them my uncle didn't have to pay their protection money . . ."

"Seven, eight, nine . . ."

"And they've already tried to shoot me twice and all I really want is just to hide for, like, twenty minutes . . . for reals!"

"Fourteen, fifteen . . ."

"And . . . look." He put the crowbar gently down on the floor. "I wouldn't hit you anyway. My name's Giorgio, what's yours?"

". . . twenty." She made a show of aiming the gun at his head and slowly cocking it. "That's it. Get out or I pull the trigger."

"You know what? Before you shoot me, I'm going to just sit here on the floor, and say to myself, 'If I have to die—'" He sat down and crossed his legs. "'—I'd rather this really cool, good-looking girl killed me than that creep Limmy.'"

She stared at him over the top of the gun.

"Not that I want to be shot by *anybody*," he added quickly. "I'd rather skip it."

She licked her lips, and almost smiled. "Wait—Limmy, you said? *That* guy? You've got *him* after you? Well that's just really tight. That means he's going to come in *here*. And I don't want him coming in here."

"Naw, I got 'em following a false scent, like."

They might well come back here looking for him, he supposed. But he decided not to mention that.

"Well, you still can't stay here," she insisted. "Get out!"

"I will! Eventually! But for right now I'm gonna hope you don't kill me. If I stay, and wait till he gives up *and* you don't kill me—it'll be easier for me to leave. I mean, if you shoot me, I'm a big heavy messy old body to drag outta here. So . . ." He shrugged and closed his eyes, made a face as if expecting the bullet. But he was pretty sure she wasn't going to shoot him. Not *completely* sure, though.

He cracked open an eyelid a little, glimpsed another flicker of a smile on her face. She lowered the gun—and he opened his eyes.

"I'm an idiot to trust you," the girl said. Then she frowned and pointed the gun at him again. "I'm not going to trust you. I don't know you. I'm going to keep the gun between us. But I won't shoot you for . . . um . . . half an hour."

"Half an hour! Okay! Thirty minutes! I appreciate the extension. Sorry about moving your stuff around. I don't like people messing with my stuff either. I live in Rooftown too, east side, the Rag-ass Branch. I know how hard it is to get stuff up to your place. Man, getting a mattress up there, when I first came up—big draggle. You all alone here?"

She sighed and sat down, cross-legged like him, on the futon at the opposite end of the little room. It had once been an office; she'd converted it to an apartment of sorts. She lowered the gun so its butt was supported by one knee, but she kept it pointed in his general direction.

She uncocked it, though. That was encouraging.

Giorgio kept his voice just loud enough for her to hear him as he spoke, now and then glancing toward the window. "Yeah, my uncle was out of money and they came around demanding that east side pay-up. I said, 'Naw, you got to wait, and we'll get you what we can.' And the guy tried to slap me with a pistol and I pushed him over . . ."

"That was dumb."

"Yeah, true dat. And uh—he started acting like he was going to shoot me, I slammed the door—place has a big metal door, must've been even harder to get up there than a mattress. He started yelling for his homeys. I went out the back window, across the roofs to the bridge . . ."

She nodded. "Should've tried bartering something."

"All out of stuff to barter. I got a street clean-up job coming if the Indigent Bureau comes through but that's not for months and—"

Giorgio broke off at shouts from the hall. He put a finger to his lips. She nodded, as he got on his hands and knees, crawled to the door, pressed his ear against it.

"*I don't care who your low-hode ass is connected to!*" someone shouted, out in the hall. Banker, likely. "*We got our own organization here, they set me up as collector and that means you want to pass through you pay what I tell you to pay and you leave the guns!*"

Giorgio chuckled to himself. It was working.

Then there were two gunshots. A voice yelled, "*He got me, Limmy, he got me—*"

13

Another gunshot, and the voice cut off—real suddenly.

The distinctive boom of a rifle, then a responding gunshot. Another . . .

Then a shout, *"I'm going, damn it, hold your fire!"*

Giorgio sat up, and smiled at her. "Looks like they took the bait, went through the wrong door, and ran into Banker. Sounds like Limmy scratched outta there . . ."

"What're you gonna do?"

"Well . . ." He took out his little instacell. He'd bought the disposable phone from a vending machine a week before, in one of his rare forays out of Rooftown. "Only got a minute or so left on this."

He called his uncle Tonio, afraid he wouldn't answer . . . or maybe one of Limmy's bangers would answer. Which would mean they'd killed his uncle and taken his phone. But a weary Tonio answered. "That you, boy?"

"Yeah, uh—you okay, Tonio?"

"I borrowed some money from my sister. I paid 'em the hundred."

"Okay, that's good, I guess. Probably they won't come after you, since they'll think you're gonna be a source of money. But uh—I kinda pissed them off . . . I don't think I should go back there."

"You got that right, boy. I appreciate you were trying to take care of me but . . ."

"Look, I'm gonna go to one of the youth shelters, down on the ground, till I get my job. When I get it going, I'll send for you, we'll get a groundhog house . . ."

"Kid? Don't do that. I'm gonna die up here, in my own good time."

Uncle had gone all cold on him, seemed like. He'd been

drinking a lot lately and they'd been arguing about that. "Okay, whatever. I'll call, see how you're doing. I just—"

"This unit's phonetime has expired . . ." a robotic voice interrupted. Followed by a click, a buzz, and silence.

Giorgio tossed the disposable phone aside, and slumped back against the wall. "Anyway, he's safe."

He glanced at the girl and saw she'd put the gun aside. She was still sitting cross-legged but was now holding on to her ankles and staring at the floor. He noticed she'd taken off her sneakers, too. Embarrassed to have two different kinds, he guessed. She had small feet, silver-painted toenails.

"My half hour up yet?" he asked.

"No. Anyway . . ." She looked at her silver-painted toenails. "I . . . you can stay until you're sure they're not coming back. 'Cause if you try to go back across that bridge . . . or try to get past Banker . . . I mean, you can't stay too long, but . . . awhile."

"Yeah. Thanks. So—you know my name . . ."

"Um . . . okay. I'm Felice. You want some instajuice? I don't know what the flavor is, some fakey fruit punch, but . . . It's in that cooler."

They drank instajuice, and sat across the room from one another, talking as the light dimmed outside and the room got gradually darker. Something about the room getting darker around them as they talked about where they'd come from, how they'd ended up in Rooftown, was strangely relaxing. It was as if the friendly shadows were something they were sharing, along with the juice.

He mentioned that he'd been to a roof concert of thugjuggers—contemporary jug-band/rapper crossover—and it turned out she'd been there, too. They were both fans of thug-juggers, especially of Jerome-X. That commonality seemed to flicker like a candle between them, and Giorgio started to feel as if he'd known her forever. She told him a funny story about her brother, who was in the Orbital Army now—if he were still alive—and a prank he'd pulled on a cop. She told it really well and he marveled at her sense of humor, living alone in this place—alone in Rooftown. There wasn't much self-pity in her, He liked that.

They talked thug-juggers some more and she recited a Jerome-X lyric she liked, and he finished reciting it with her, because it was one of his favorites too.

Woke up in this world,
didn't recognize a thing
Living for years, that bell just never rings
And I still don't recognize a thing, just don't recognize a thing.

They both felt that way: that the world had been made for someone else, they couldn't find a place to connect with it . . .

They talked on and on, feeling a kind of high from it—the isolation they'd both felt for a long time finally punctured, the wall cracking open. *There's someone who feels like I do . . .*

Felice told him how her parents had died in the first wave of tropical diseases that had hit LA; how she'd gotten sick too, but survived. She was living on a little bit of money her half-brother sent to her, sometimes, but it wasn't enough to pay for a groundhog apartment. She had to pay Banker for the right to squat here, so cheap it was almost free. Every other day she was going to the bus-school—the bus that came around to the base of the building with a classroom inside, protected by heavily armed security guards.

16

He told her he did odd jobs, tried to read books when he could till he could get back in school. Told her about how his aunt had died two months before, in her sleep, and how they'd given her the "Burial at Sea"—which in Rooftown meant rolling her up in a rug and dropping her off the edge of a roof for the robocleaners to find in groundhog land down below.

She told him about a place she'd always dreamed of going, she'd seen it in a holomagazine. A place called Missoula, Montana. Global warming hadn't affected it much. The land was wide open. The air clean. Then she sighed and said, "But I'll never get there."

They talked a lot about how life made them feel. Somehow the darkness in the room made that possible, too. He had never unburdened himself this much. There was something magical about it . . .

During a momentary silence Giorgio winced when his stomach growled audibly. "I heard that!" Felice said, laughing softly. "Under the red plastic in the cooler, there's some quick'n'hots."

He found the quick'n'hot packets, broke the seal that made them heat up on their own, and they ate the spicy meat paste slowly, not talking.

Not talking—for about five minutes. Then they started up again. Talking, talking into the night . . .

• • •

It must've been near dawn when Giorgio woke up on the floor. He sat up stiffly, stretching, looking around in momentary disorientation.

Oh, yeah. The squat. Felice. In the blue-gray pre-dawn glow coming through the window he saw that she'd gone.

How'd she leave without waking him? He'd been lying right in front of the door.

He went to the window, looked carefully out. No sign of Limmy. Maybe he should leave now. His being there put Felice at risk.

Giorgio went to the hallway door, put his hand on the knob—then another door opened, at the back of the room—she had hidden it behind a curtain. Felice pushed through and looked at him in surprise. "I go off to the bathroom and check out the halls, see if it's safe—and you're already buggin' out . . ."

"I just . . . thought I ought to. They might, you know, come back. I mean, Limmy, anyway. He might let my uncle go but not me. He lost a man because of me. And if you're with me when he comes . . ."

"Yeah. I know. But . . . I just . . . I was hoping you'd help me decide about something. I mean—I don't have anyone else to talk it over with. I can't get hold of my godmother directly . . ."

"What?" Giorgio was relieved to have an excuse to stay awhile longer. Anything just to be around Felice a bit more.

"I got a text from my godmother—she's in Dome Bel Air."

"Dome Bel Air! You're kidding me!"

"I'm not kidding. She says I can go there and live with her, she's got permission for me to come . . . But I don't think I want to."

"What? Why not! That's, all, like, *luxury* in there! You don't have to worry about getting caught in an acid rain or a black wind—no crime, air's clean, plenty of food from the hydro-farms. And you don't want to go?"

She made a face like she'd tasted something bad. "She got me in for a visit once. It's just . . . I can't relate to those people.

They're—Oh, god." She stared past him, and pointed. "There's someone at the window!"

He turned around, saw Limmy grinning at him from the window, which was only partly blocked by the dresser. Limmy's grin was strained, his cheeks twitching. He was on synthameth, for sure, Giorgio figured, had probably been up all night getting tweaky. Limmy's left hand gripped the window frame; he raised the automatic pistol in his other hand into view. Grinding his teeth, he pointed it at Giorgio—

Dive for the floor, dumbass. But Giorgio felt rooted to the spot.

But then something boomed behind him, and the window glass exploded outward, taking Limmy with it—he pitched backward off the walkway. He was gone. Giorgio could hear his receding scream.

Felice was coughing—he turned to see her with the revolver in her shaking hand—coughing in a cloud of gray gun smoke. "God, I never knew these things were so smoky. Never fired one inside before . . ."

"You *killed* him . . . !"

"Did I hit him?"

"I'm not even sure but that shot knocked him off the building. That's one dead banger."

He turned back to the window—again saw someone there. But it wasn't Limmy—it was a face peering cautiously from the side. A banger he remembered from the east side, a round face scribbled with blue tattoos. Guy they called Gremlin.

And Gremlin was staring past Giorgio at Felice.

When Gremlin saw Giorgio looking at him he pulled back, out of sight—knowing he could get knocked off the building as easily as Limmy.

Giorgio felt sick. "Oh, great. Limmy's little scumbag buddy

Gremlin saw you . . ." He walked over to Felice, casually took the gun from her hand. She didn't seem to care. He wanted it so he could protect her—he knew that, given what'd happened, that didn't make much sense. She'd been protecting *him*. But that's what he wanted.

She sat down, groaning, on the edge of the futon. "Me and my stupid . . ."

"I . . . Felice . . ." It was hard to express. He was stunned that she'd shot Limmy to save him. But in another way, it felt right. They had a bond now. Even though it felt as if the bond had been there even before they'd met—meeting, and talking, just made them *feel* it. It was as if they'd had a hidden ribbon connecting them all their lives. "Thanks, Felice. Another second and he'd have shot me."

"But—what do we do *now?*"

"I know what *you* have to do, Felice. You have to go somewhere safe. Tell your godmother yes. You've gotta move to Dome Bel Air."

• • •

Getting out of the BP building was fairly easy—Felice went out, checked the halls. Banker had gone inside his apartment and his only guard was sitting on the floor, slumped snoring against the wall where the corridors intersected.

Carrying a backpack of some of Felice's things, the gun in his waistband, Giorgio followed her, the two of them slipping silently past the snoring fat man in the greasy T-shirt. They went down the fire-exit stairs, taking the back way to the street. It took a long time to get to ground level. On the way they passed through several squat communities where drunks argued, jug bands chugged rough-edged music, and grubby children played. A squint-eyed guy in a flak jacket, one of Banker's men, tried to stop Giorgio—but they dashed past him, rushed quickly down the stairs. He didn't bother to pursue.

At last they pushed through a graffiti-coated metal door and out onto the street. The dull morning air was thick and acrid and made it hard to breathe, but they'd both survived heavier levels of pollution on other occasions. Giorgio took the lead this time, and checked outside for Limmy's gangsters. They saw nobody and nothing around but a passing robosweeper and a pack of wild dogs chewing at a dead homeless guy. Chances were the gang was probably still looking for them up in Rooftown.

They went carefully past the scruffy, bony dogs, Giorgio with the pistol at ready, but the animals were busy with their carrion.

Giorgio and Felice reached the corner where a self-driving truck was slowing for the corner. It seemed to be heading in the direction they needed to go, its open truckbed piled with a heap of old porcelain toilets from some demolition. They jumped on to it before it accelerated, Giorgio helping Felice to scramble up, and they each sat on a covered toilet, laughing about it.

The truck went within a quarter-mile of the dome.

• • •

The dome was centered over Bel Air but extended past the old gated community, cupping much of Beverly Hills. Encompassing five square miles, the blurrily transparent thick plasglass construction, almost a quarter-mile high in the center, enclosed several hills still covered with fine old houses occupied by the Dome's ruling class. Apart from a couple of small parks and maintenance facilities, the rest of the space under the dome—the part that wasn't underground—had been turned into blocky condo housing.

The acid rains had pitted the plasglass, and black winds had streaked its lower edges—once a year the dome was re-glossed, but it didn't last long. There were dozens of domes like this in California, usually housing moneyed families with outsourced businesses in the Third World. The staff lived in sub-bubbles of concrete and steel, scabrous extensions on one side of the domes.

Giorgio tucked the gun into Felice's backpack, he then leaned the pack against the plasglass wall, next to the big metal gate that led to the airlock. "You text your godmother?"

"Yeah. She'll be here in a minute to let me in. They have to do some kind of ID check on me and then they assign me housing and . . . I don't know. Giorgio?"

"Yeah?"

"What're *you* gonna do?"

"There's a youth shelter 'bout a half mile from here . . . There's that job. If I get it."

"What if you run into Limmy's bangers?" She looked away. "You'd better take my gun."

"Nah. If anything goes wrong and you don't get to stay—you'll need it." He looked up, saw a security camera swiveling above them.

A voice spoke from an intercom grid. A man's voice, smooth but no-nonsense, said, *"Identify yourselves! If you are not residents or authorized employees, step away from the gate."*

Felice gave her name, and her sponsor's name.

"You may remain. The other individual must step away from the gate."

"Well . . . I'd better go," Giorgio said.

"Look—come back tomorrow, around one—that'll give me time to see if . . . I don't know, if there's work for you in the dome. Maybe you could get a better job here. My godmother might be able to do something to get you in . . ."

"Really?" He shrugged. But inwardly his heart leapt at the chance to see Felice again. "One o'clock?"

"Yeah." The gate was rolling open; she turned to go.

Then she turned back—and kissed him, very quickly, on the lips, before grabbing her pack and hurrying into the airlock.

• • •

Felice felt painfully self-conscious walking from the airlock corridor into the Welcome Garden. The solar reflectors made the flowering shrubs on either side seem to glow. People in sunglasses and elegant clothing stared at her cut off jeans, her mismatched shoes.

"Marilyn, they're all staring at me."

"Don't worry about them," Marilyn said airily. Felice's godmother was a tall, slender woman, who might've been sixty but looked thirty-five. She had artfully coifed silver-blonde hair, a wide mouth with maroon lipstick, matching tinted sunglasses. She wore a white suit and cream-colored pumps; her sculpted fingernails were the same color as her lipstick and tinted glasses. The glasses, Felice knew, were SmartLookers hooked into a comm-system.

"Now," Marilyn said silkily, "all we have to do is stop in at Genetic ID and . . . ah, here comes our escort."

Two tall, perfectly groomed white men with cold smiles and light gray-and-black uniforms were approaching down the crushed-quartz path. They wore tinted sunglasses—one pair tinted golden yellow, the other powder blue. Streaks in their hair matched their sunglasses. On their hips were guns of a sort Felice didn't recognize.

The air in the dome was almost achingly clean; the light a bit harsh. Beyond the Welcome Garden was a plasglass wall topped with security cameras and beyond that were stacks of shiny multicolored condos, rising high into the air, nearly to the dome interior. Small trams moved along transparent rails between the buildings; robotic birds pretended to flit between imitation trees.

"I feel kinda weird in here," Felice said. She looked at Marilyn. "What'd you say about genetic something?"

Marilyn pursed her lips and spoke to her in a quiet aside as their escorts waited a few paces away. "Felice . . . when your mom was dying, I tried to get her into the dome—and I couldn't get permission. But they are always looking for young people with good genes and . . . well, she got a DNA sample from you, so you'd have a chance. It's taken this long for a spot to open up."

"What's the DNA sample *for?*"

"Breeding, hon, not to put too fine a point on it. You'll be offered a selection of mates—three or four to choose from. We do need the fresh genes. You'll only be required to have a couple of children. Starting next year probably. Ah, here's Officer Danforth and Officer Mercer. Gentlemen, lead on, my little darling is here!"

• • •

Giorgio felt stupid, leaning in the doorway of an old warehouse across the street from the dome, uncomfortable in the early afternoon mugginess. He was probably wasting his time here—there was no way she'd find a spot for him inside.

But—she'd kissed him. He could still feel her lips on his.

It was humid outside, the air thick with impending acid rain, and he was sweating. He was glad he had the acid-repellent slicker they'd given him at the shelter.

He glanced at the clock on his instacell. She was late. Probably not coming at all. The sky was roiling with ugly clouds; an automated garbage truck drove out of an underground garage across the street, around the curve of the dome. As soon as it reached the street it attracted a swarm of enormous bluebottles, a living cloud of flies buzzing after the truck as it trundled away.

Giorgio snorted. He was outside with the trash, and that was probably where he'd stay.

He glanced at his instacell once more. She was an hour late. *Don't be a sucker, hodey.* He shrugged, stepped on to the sidewalk and began walking away from the dome, his heart sinking. He didn't mind not getting a place inside, probably wouldn't fit in any way. But he'd probably never seen Felice again. That bothered him.

He hurried along, wondering if Limmy's bangers ever came to this side of town. Maybe he should go to San Francisco to get clear of them, if he could get a travel permit.

He heard a rumble behind him, the roar of an engine, turned to see a big box truck looming up, a powerful freight carrier—coming right for him. It must be out of control. He looked around for some place to run to, get out of its way . . .

The truck screeched to a stop, right in front of him. He looked up and saw Felice in the driver's seat.

He gaped at her. "Felice! What—?"

"Hi!" she called, grinning, as the window rolled down. "Look—I got a truck! Get in quick, I stole it so we gotta get out of here!"

"You stole it?" But he didn't argue, he ran around to the other side of the truck, climbed up into the cab beside her. She started off before he'd managed to close the door and he almost fell out.

"Damn, Felice!"

"Sorry. You okay?"

He got the door closed. "You gonna tell me what's goin' on?"

"Oh, well—I was trying to figure out what to do, how to get away—didn't seem like they were just gonna let me leave. Then I started watching the autotrucks in the dome. How they come and go and almost nobody's paying much attention. I climbed up into one in the delivery line and I found the manual override! Switch off the computer and you can drive it. I'm a pretty good driver, my dad had a—"

"Felice, whoa, hold on—what do you mean, figure out what to do? What happened in there?"

She sighed. "I don't want to be used for a breeding program. That's how my godmother got me in! I'd have to contract with some random jerk! Have his baby. And I don't want to live with those people anyway! They spend most of their time hooked up in VR playing weird games with each other. They're all obsessed with their weird little lifestyles and they treat the people who work there like robots and . . . no. Not me. But—I needed some way to get us out of town and I saw the truck and . . . I stole it. They hadn't offloaded it yet, they won't get to it till tomorrow! It's full of freeze-dried food, all the stuff they can't raise in the dome! So we can eat some and sell the rest and—"

"But they'll come after us!"

"It's not like they have much security on an autotruck, no

26

one actually wants to leave their plasglass 'paradise.' The unloaders were out to lunch so I got their delivery lists and changed 'em, made it look like this stuff was already unloaded. It'll take them a long time to figure it out. And you know what? If you get far enough away, they don't bother to chase you—it's just too expensive."

"But—where are you *going?*"

Felice chuckled. "Long ways east and a long ways north! This is a hydrogen cell solar hybrid, hotey! It'll go three thousand miles without more fuel! We're going out east—you don't need a travel pass to go into Nevada. Then up north to Montana!"

"*Montana?* You're joking!"

"Naw! I told you about that one place—there's beautiful clean land up there, you just got to know where to go . . ."

Giorgio sat back, stunned. But feeling better with each passing second.

He looked at the rear-view video screen—no one was following. "Wow. You've got some nerve, girl."

"I got something else too. A truck full of food. And my gun, in the backpack behind your seat." She veered the truck around the corner, and glanced at him. "And something else—some*one.*"

It took him a moment to realize she meant him. And he suspected that, creepy people in the dome or not, if it wasn't for him . . . Felice probably wouldn't have taken the chance of stealing the truck. It would have been hard, but she'd probably have accepted a comfortable life in the dome, pay her dues with a couple of babies.

Really, it was more than a suspicion. He could *feel* it, through the hidden ribbon that twined the two of them together.

She sniffed. "Of course—you don't have to go with me." She shrugged as if she didn't care. "Whatever. You don't *have* to."

"Hell, no, I don't *have* to." He grinned and said, "You going to let me drive some of the way, Felice?"

"We'll see. I'll think about it . . ."

They got to the freeway, and headed east, and as she drove Felice started rapping out a thug-jug lyric, one he knew very well. After a moment, he joined in.

The Salt Sea and the Sky

Elizabeth Bear

It was a bright morning, cool and clear, when I realized I was going to break her heart. It was high summer, two weeks before the solstice, and I was up with the birds to watch the dawn. I had skinned out the usual clutter and shut off texting and my new cheapest-model Omni, a seventeenth birthday present from my dad.

So it was just me and the sea and the quiet town and the sunrise. If I ignored the lack of cars, I could imagine I was back in the twentieth century. Of course, the sea would have been lower then, the beach unprotected by the seawalls that now held the ocean back.

I was up because I hadn't slept. I'd been out with Shaun to the cinema and after she went home I hadn't been able to stand the thought of doing the same. The little terraced house I shared with my father and half-sister and my half-sister's son seemed too much like a cage.

It was a little after four in the morning, and the sky was already streaked with peach and silver, the stars washed away by light. It was bright enough that I scuffled down the bluff without undue risk of killing myself. I turned to put the water on my right, the bluffs and the town on my left. Ahead, fingers of gray-and-black basalt, crusted with weeds and barnacles, broke up the stretches of fine sand. Low, slow breakers hissed across the surface of the softly rolling sea.

The tide ebbed as I walked east and then north along Balbriggan Strand. I wasn't dressed for the beach, and still wore last night's skirt and slippery shoes and no sunblock. But the skirt was loose enough that I could climb in it if I kept the hem up. And even a pale-skinned redhead like me wouldn't get sunburn in a half-hour at sunrise.

So I pulled my shoes off and hung them through my belt by the laces. They swung there, bumping my thigh with every wet step through the streams that ran across the beach and down to the ocean.

I'd have to be careful of rocks and shells, especially in the half-light of morning, especially in the rougher sections of rock and weed. The barnacles could slash your feet to ribbons.

But it wouldn't be so bad if I were careful. The sunlight was already starting to creep down the face of the bluff, casting a pall of crimson over its beige surface, shaggy with vegetation. As long as I didn't look directly at the sun and dazzle myself, it was more than enough light by which to pick my way.

Seals played alongside the rock reefs, just dots wriggling through the water as I climbed. A gray heron flew low across the water, its slowly beating wings casting a writhing shadow as the sun peeked over the edge of the world. Out in the Irish Sea, a tall ship cruised under box sails—the ship still in shadow, the sails lit by the sun—and I changed my mind: I could imagine this was the nineteenth century, the age of exploration and sail, and that I was on my way to Dublin to meet the ship that would take me to America, to Asia, to the world.

By the harbor, the fishing boats awaited the tide, their masts bare and the rigging sagging. They went out and came back. With a fair wind, you might make Wales overnight—but none of them ever went that far.

They couldn't call to me as the kite-rigged cargo vessel did. *I can't stay here*, I thought. *I'll die if I stay here*. Reflexively, I thought of calling Shaun—or at least of texting her. Just as reflexively, I stopped myself. I thought I already knew what she'd say. "Don't be ridiculous, Billie. We have each other here; isn't that enough?"

Shouldn't it be?

I turned my back on the ship and the sea and scrambled up the bluff for a better look—eventually. It wasn't until I reached the top that I realized I was crying.

• • •

There are no rocks on the top of the bluff so I sat down in the grasses, careful to avoid any nettles, my back to the land and my face to the sea. The sun stung my eyes, though I turned my head at an angle. Across the water lay England—London—and beyond that the continent. Freedom.

The ship I watched sailed south, toward Dublin, and I wondered what cargo it carried precious enough to be worth the long sea journey. I knew from history that, once upon a time, great cargo vessels—even aircraft!—had burned fossil fuels bringing exotic fruit, liquor, toys, from all the world over. In those days it was actually *less expensive* to make a thing in a foreign land and ship it than it was to live on what could be had locally. "Cheap foreign goods" was a concept I could only just begin to understand—anything that came from far away was luxurious and precious, and not for the likes of me. Not now, likely never.

But it wasn't luxury that drew me to the idea of travel. It was . . .

. . . freedom.

I had finished my mandated schooling the previous month. There was no chance of University with my background and aptitudes, not unless I'd managed much better marks, and no chance of Employment without University. I already knew how I'd spend my life: here in Balbriggan, making do with whatever subsistence payments and goods allotted me. They'd be adequate to keep me alive and housed—but not much more than that. And almost *nobody* could afford travel.

The world needed far fewer workers than it had people. And with economies of scarcity a thing of the past since the Green Sustainability Bills passed in the mid-twenty-first, there was nothing much for those surplus people to do.

And I was one of them.

So was my dad, and so was my sister.

And so was Shaun Mellor. That, at least, had always been comforting. She was as trapped here as I was, even if it chafed her less. We had each other. Always had, always would.

We planned to live together when we turned eighteen and could find housing. If we applied for subsistence as a childless gay couple, we'd get a little bit of additional support—as long as we stayed that way. Not reproducing. Not making more useless mouths to feed.

It was a natural thing, Shaun and me. We'd grown up together in the village—not best friends, but aware of each other—and started being girlfriends at fifteen. She had olive skin and straight dark hair that blew in the wind, and her eyes were so brown you could only see the detail in them when the sun shone across them.

Nobody had ever understood me better. Nobody had ever loved me more. Our families both assumed that we'd settle in together and so did we.

I'd never thought I was going to be the girl who broke Shaun Mellor's heart. But as I watched that ship sail into the sunrise, I knew that was what was going to happen.

Because I was leaving Balbriggan. Leaving her. Some way. Somehow. I'd go to Dublin. My ancestors might have gone to London to seek their fortune—but sailors had to come from somewhere, didn't they? I didn't imagine they'd be University types. And surely, no matter how automated modern shipping was, you needed somebody on board to trim the sails and helm the thing if something went wrong . . .

I reached with one hand to tap my Omni back on. The contact lens for the interface dried my eye, but everybody assured me it would get less annoying with time. I was still looking out through clouds of protein buildup from crying, however.

Just as I thumbed it on, though, I heard Shaun's voice behind me.

"Billie?"

I'd turned off my Omni and she'd tried to text from bed, of course. She'd gotten worried and come to find me, and she'd known exactly where to look. That was how well we knew each other.

And it wasn't as if Balbriggan were a big place, after all.

She said, "Are you okay?"

It was my moment of supreme cowardice. "Fine, love," I said, holding up an arm so she could sit down inside its bend. "Just thinking of you."

She snugged herself into my side and kissed me, long strands of dark hair curving her cheek.

I was the worst person alive.

• • •

My dad was up by the time I came home. He always made a virtue of punctuality and keeping to a schedule, just as if he were Employed. He said it helped lend purpose to the day, and when I compared him to the rest of my friends' moms and dads, spending all day down at the pub or sleeping until afternoon, I thought he had it right.

The clouds had rolled in, tall and tattered, and the wind smelled like coming rain. I watched it twist the leaves of the willow in the front garden as Dad came down the steps to meet me.

"Shaun was looking for you," he said.

"She found me," I said, and kissed him on the cheek. He'd been taking out the composting. I lifted the bag from his hand and carried it over to the bin in the garden corner.

"She's worried about you," he said. "So'm I."

It stopped me, one hand on the composter's solar lid. The lazy whirr of windmills along the terrace filled my hearing. A white-waist-coated magpie hopped up, eyeing the multi-colored kitchen waste inquisitively. I shut the bin in its face.

"There's no call to be worried," I said. "You should right-mind it out."

He sighed. I knew perfectly well that he didn't need remedial rightminding. Dad was one of the most stable people I'd ever met, and he was rigorous about keeping up with his emotional controls. They really worked best after twenty or so—I'd been told often enough that the erratic shifts of adolescent hormones were hard to balance out, no matter what surgery, cognitive measures, or chemical supports were used.

Maybe, I thought, when the rightminding kicked in properly I'd be able to let go of my dream of going to sea.

Except I'd already decided that wasn't going to be what happened. I supposed I had the rightminding, to the extent that it *was* working, to thank for the fact that I could have a conversation with with him rationally. We were taught in school that young adults were once notorious for their emotional lability.

"Now, Billie," he said. "You know I just want to see you contented. Not—"

"Not like Mam?" I asked.

His face paled.

Now that was cruel, I thought. Maybe my rightminding wasn't so good after all.

But he saw through the cruelty, I guess, to my hurt. "You're not your mam, Bill," he said. "I've never thought so. You wouldn't run out on people who love you."

He said it with kindness. He reached out to touch my arm.

Shame filled me up until I wanted to vomit it out. Wasn't that exactly what I was thinking of doing?

• • •

I went upstairs to bed—my half-sister Katy was just getting up, so I didn't have to share the room with her and her fretting infant—and slept for six hours, which still had me up by noon. When I came down again, Dad and Katy were both out. I thought Dad might be at his painting class (he's terrible) and I seemed to remember that Katy's son David had an early

35

rightminding appraisal (he's two). I thought about using some of the water ration to shower and decided to get some work done in the back garden instead. I sat in the parlor and ate two pieces of toast with butter while I was considering the chores and staring at the dusty guitar hung over the old fireplace.

We had a typical Irish terraced house with a typical Irish garden, which was about six meters by five and bounded by gray stone walls too high to see over. There were roses in two corners, scarlet runner beans planted where they'd climb the through the rose branches and up the walls. We had courgettes, culinary herbs, sunflowers for the oil. Two brown hens scratched around the margins. When I went into the garden I first took a few moments to search for their warm brown eggs.

Our house had been built before Greening, but the roof had been retrofitted with a green frame that grew herbs and sweet potatoes and tomatoes and lettuces. We had an apple tree and a solar water reclamation system. The house was well-insulated and snug.

We had everything we needed right here. And what we didn't have we could buy from the shops in the town. Any reasonable, rightminded person would be perfectly happy here.

Except what we didn't have was any purpose beyond subsisting.

The stepladder was in the community shed—none of our neighbors were using it this early, and nobody was signed up to use it until five. Having decided I would work on the roof garden, I pulled out the ladder, rolled it home on its wheeled side, braced its foot pads, and clambered up. The overlay from my Omni helped me identify and pull weeds while avoiding the seedlings of desirable plants. The pink and white valerian would take over everything if you let it. It was pretty, but as far as I was concerned it smelled like a cat. It could stay in the chinks of the stone walls, where it belonged.

As I worked, I tried to calm my mind—but I couldn't help it. Over and over, I wondered again why Mam had left.

Dad's first wife, Katy's mother, had died of a cancer the health service hadn't been able to do anything for. After a while, he met and married my mam but she didn't stick around past my fifth birthday, and she'd never told us where she was going or sent word back that she was a alive.

For a long time, nobody and no amount of rightminding could convince me it wasn't my fault she'd gone. After a while, I'd started to accept it had been something inside her that had driven her away. The realization had come about the same time that same something had begun to rear itself in my own head.

I patted the last marigolds in among the tomatoes—organic pest control—and made my way back down the ladder. I folded it up and took it back to the community shed.

Because I'd been thinking so much about the past, about escaping to it, I imagined what it would be like if we had our own ladder. Not to have to work around everyone else in the community or sign up months in advance to work on the roof.

I imagined every house on my street with its own stepladder. Its own lawnmower. Its own hedge clippers.

It was a little dizzying. *So much stuff.* Where would you *keep* it all?

Wasteful. Like the airplanes and the food from far away and the internal combustion engines that used to race around the streets. You could see it all in old movies, which people used to buy on disks made of polymer, in boxes made of polymer, and just pile up on shelves.

It's better to keep everything in the cloud. I know it is. It's better to use only what you need, when you most need it, then put it back where everybody else can use it too.

But is it really better to spend your whole life in comfortable purposelessness? All those people in those old movies, zipping around in their ocean-raising cars and their storm-causing airplanes.

They're not like me. They all look as if they're going somewhere.

I went inside to shower, thinking I'd earned the use of a water ration now. Besides, if it rained again this afternoon, it'd help fill the roof tank. We'd be in pretty good shape still.

And I couldn't stand the feeling of dirt and grease in my hair.

• • •

Showers are a good place for making life-changing decisions. The hot water seems to unstick the brain cells and if you cry, nobody can tell. Not even you, really. I probably pushed my water ration a little, but I'd make up for it by not being here later.

When I was clean, I made myself a cup of tea—worth importing, even in these times—and skinned out all distractions except the obligatory emergency channel before settling down with my interface to do some serious research.

Career inquiry, I entered into my Omni. *How does one become a long-distance sailor?*

Fifteen minutes later, I knew. There was a school for it—but at least according to the cloud, most people learned to sail by simply sailing. Finding a captain who would take them on as unskilled labor and teach them the ropes—quite literally.

I also knew that it didn't pay significantly better than staying on the dole. And that it was considerably more dangerous.

And that I wanted it more than anything in the world.

I closed up all the research windows floating in my peripheral vision, skinned back into reality, and made myself another cup of tea—chamomile, this time, locally grown—while I figured out the letter I was going to send to Shaun. My dad and Katy were easier: I just told them over the dinner table.

"I'll write," I said. "I'll telepresence. I'll AR you. You'll hardly know I'm gone."

Dad stood up to take my plate. "Who'll do the washing up, then?" he asked, but I knew that was his way of saying he would miss me.

"I'll do it," Katy said. "At least there'll be one less plate."

The sun didn't set that night until almost ten.

• • •

I used the daylight packing. Summers were better than winters—in summer, you never got enough sleep, but in winter it was always going to bed early so you didn't outrun your electricity allotment. Katy was downstairs with David, letting him nap in the shady part of the garden. I imagined they were both skinning out my sounds, not wanting to be reminded.

While I was staring at jumpers spread out on my bed, I heard Dad's step upon the stair.

He paused in the open door to my room. I didn't turn at first, but caught his eyes in the mirror, looking at me. I had his coloring, the same red hair and freckles, though his had gone sandy with the years, but my cheekbones and pointed chin were all Mam's.

He didn't say anything, just stared at me with love and sorrow. I held his gaze in the mirror until I couldn't stand to anymore, and looked down.

I wondered if he also saw Mam in my face just now, or now more than ever.

"I'm sorry, Dad," I said.

He had two glasses of wine that had come by tallship from France. He saved it for special occasions. He handed me one, then went to the bed and pushed one of the jumpers aside to make an edge to sit on. He looked up at me and pursed his lips, and the seriousness and hush in his voice made me strain to hear.

"Don't ever tell Katy this," he said. "But when I was your age, I wanted to go to Dublin and be a musician."

I thought of the dusty guitar in the living room. I knew he could play it, so I must have seen him play, but I couldn't summon up a memory of him with the thing in his hands. Certainly, I'd always wondered why we had one when nobody in the house used it much—a wasted resource, just warehoused like that.

Now I knew.

"I'm sorry," I said.

"Don't be," he said. "I made another choice, and I got you and Katy and David."

I nodded, too tight up for words. Was this what grown-up choices were like, then? This hollow feeling that nothing I could do would be right?

He'd never gotten the regret rightminded away. The brain bleachers could have fixed it for him, made it not hurt anymore. The way they had my mam leaving, for me, when I asked.

"Call every day," he said. "Or if you don't have the

bandwidth, send email." He stood, and got that particularly Irish rising stress in his voice as he said, "And don't you be afraid to ask for help if you need it. Anywhere in the world, we'll get you home."

"I love you, Dad." It was all I could say.

He stood up. He kissed my hair on the way out of the room.

Dearest Shaun,

I don't know how to start this letter, and I hope you won't think I'm an awful person for doing this. In fact, I think I'm an awful person, but I would rather you didn't. Still, I'll understand if you do.

I'm leaving. I'm going to get a job on a ship if I can and see the world.

This isn't because I don't love you. I love you more than anything. But I can't do what my father did.

I know I can't expect you to wait for me when I don't know when I'm coming back. But I will wait for you until you tell me not to, and when I do come back, I'll bring you stones from every port I call in.

I love you,
Billie

I didn't email Shaun the letter until morning, when I was packed and ready to leave for the station. I didn't take much—some trousers, some shirts, a tube of sunblock. My Omni. I was wearing the jumper Dad had pushed out of the way.

I walked up Bridge Street to the train station via the footpath with the River Bracken on my right, locked away down in its stone channel with the valerian and ferns and ivy growing from the gaps in the rock all around. The path leads up a little rise behind the seawall, overhung with flowers and with a wooden rail on the right. I was passing through the narrow stone doorway, the train station on the right, when I heard running feet behind me and a breathless voice call, "Billie Rhodes, you stop right this instant!"

I stopped, because I couldn't do otherwise. Clutching the strap of my backpack with my right hand, I said, "Shaun, you shouldn't have come."

I didn't turn back to look at her. I couldn't. Not until she came pelting up the path toward me, put her hand on my shoulder, and spun me around. Her cheeks were bright with running. She was wearing jeans and a pajama top, and her feet were bare. She minced a little, as if she had bruised the right one on a stone.

"Aw, Shaun," said I.

She put her fists on her hips, the wind raveling her tangled hair across her face. She stood framed in the gray stone door and spat, "What on *earth* were you thinking?"

"Shaun—" There was nothing I could say, really. Nothing that would make it better at all. The air was full of the rank, stuffy smell of valerian and the tang of the sea. It had stopped raining for once, though her hair was damp, and the broken clouds piled up and tossed behind her.

I sighed and said, "I'm sorry."

"I'm sorry. That's all you've got?"

I shrugged. I hated myself for shrugging. I did it anyway.

She tilted her head. She wasn't crying, but that was only because she was too angry. Unshed tears glistened in the corners of her eyes. "Will you at least tell me why?"

What's out there that's more important than me?

"I want to do something that matters," I said.

Something in her face changed. Softened, as if she couldn't

hold on to her anger. She started to say, *And you can't do that here?*—I could see her start to say it. And then she paused, swallowed it, and said instead, "I don't matter?"

"You matter most of all. But you're not something I *do*, love. You're your own thing. Your own person. What am I supposed to do about what I need?"

"Get it rightminded out," she said, so fast I knew she'd been thinking about it.

"But it's *me*."

"But it hurts you. It hurts me." She shook her head, not understanding. "If it hurts you—"

"You could come with me," I replied.

She stepped back.

I nodded. "Exactly. You don't want to. But you could get that changed, too."

She looked down. *Stalemate*. "So you're leaving me."

"I'm not," I said. "I'm leaving Ireland. I'll only leave you if you don't want me anymore. We'll have the cloud, we'll have mail. I'll come home. Maybe while I'm gone you'll find something to be as well."

The light was climbing up the wall behind me. In the distance, I heard the whistle of the solar train. Once they had run every few minutes—but now, if I missed this one, the next wasn't until the afternoon—and the tickets were expensive. It didn't matter. I stepped closer to her and pulled her into my arms. "We've always been trapped together," I said. "We could rely on that. Don't you want to see if we can still rely on each other if we're not trapped?"

She leaned her head on my shoulder. Her back and arms stayed stiff and her weight wasn't behind the caress. "We'd have to . . . *choose* each other."

"And fight for the choice," I agreed.

She drew back. She looked at me with her dark eyes, and I realized that her ancestors—at least some of them—had come to Ireland from some faraway place, bringing that lovely skin and her beautiful straight black hair. She was Armenian on her mother's side, but I'd never thought about what that meant.

My ancestors had come here, too, with their red hair and pale faces, from Denmark, a thousand years before hers. Travelers, explorers still.

"We can do this," I said.

She kissed me.

In the Clearing

KIERA CASS

The light was sharp to my eyes as the blindfold was removed. I shielded myself while trying to survey my surroundings.

"Shit, Dylan, what were you thinking?" someone said. The room was full of people, more people than I could have imagined would be willing to live like this. Part of me whispered that I should be scared, and as I thought it, something icy crawled through my veins.

"She saw me," my captor complained. "I had to take her."

"You've gotta be kidding," a man said. His stance gave him the look of a leader. "They already know we're out here. Taking her just makes us seem dangerous."

My captor—Dylan—shook his head. "I don't know what came over me. I froze. I'm sorry, Jesse."

The others in the room were murmuring. Some gave my kidnapper a look of shame, others a look of pity. One woman—a middle-aged type with a child on her hip—was busy looking at me. She appeared to be trying to comfort me with her kind eyes.

"She looks shaky," said someone toward the back and, as he said it, I realized I was trembling, if only slightly.

"She probably needs to eat," another nameless face suggested.

Jesse nodded. "She won't be able to handle this. Give her something, Dylan."

I looked up to the captor, to Dylan, who reached into his heavy-laden bag and pulled out one of the prepackaged snacks that he'd stolen from my house.

"What's wrong?" I snapped, trying to seem unfazed. "Something wrong with your food?"

These Outsiders were the pain of our society. Everything was so calm now. But every once in a while, you'd hear of something like this—of clothes taken, toothbrushes stolen. Never a person. I didn't understand for the life of me why they'd opt to live in a cabin somewhere, crammed in like rabbits, rather than in the vast, peaceful streets in town.

Dylan smirked. "Trust me, nothing's wrong with our food. Go ahead and eat."

I smacked his hand away, a gesture I hadn't used in years. Everyone seemed shocked. "I don't want anything from you."

Dylan, despite being the greedy crook who'd broken into my house, bent down and spoke softly, kindly. "It's not mine, remember? It's yours. Eat it."

I sighed and ripped into the package. I took a bite and almost instantly felt better. I hadn't even realized I was hungry.

A girl, sounding irritated, asked the group, "You know who you took, right?" Everyone turned to look at her. "That's Mackenzie Shepard. The mayor's daughter."

Nearly everyone in the room shook their head. It was a terrible idea to have someone like me in their midst. I didn't know if it was more dangerous for them or me.

"Well," Jesse said. "Guess we better put her somewhere."

• • •

I prided myself on not making mistakes. A few years ago when some of the other guys and I had begun to sneak into the towns, the older ones weren't thrilled. But they didn't stop us. No one could deny the benefits of our efforts.

Besides, all those pretty houses with their unlocked doors were so very tempting.

But I'd screwed up today. Bad. I was always careful when I snuck into the towns, even more so when I went into the houses. I was an excellent thief. I watched people, looked for routines. She wasn't supposed to be there.

When she walked around the corner, we both eyed each other, motionless. I could see her eyes looking me over. My clothes were like hers but mine were obviously more worn, and my skin was tan, which wasn't so common anymore. I also knew I had the look of someone who hadn't been living in the sterile, dull stream of society. She inhaled, and I was sure she was going to scream. Instead, she passed out and fell into my arms.

I could have left her there, but I didn't. I took her, and I didn't know why. I blindfolded her, slung her over my shoulder, and carried her back here.

The girl had been taken away now to finish eating and everyone else had gone back to work.

"Dylan, what the hell came over you?" Jesse asked, still angry. "Taking anyone at all is bad enough, but the mayor's daughter? They'll come for us now. For sure."

"I thought . . . I thought she could help us," I stammered. It was a lie, but I had to say something.

"Help us? How?"

"She's got access to stuff. I figured once she was out, she'd want to help. She has to know *something*."

Jesse was shaking his head before I was even done. "Look

at her. She's completely glazed. If we don't keep her that way she'll flip out. She can't handle it."

"If we take her down slowly, maybe she could . . ."

Jesse shook his head again, he clearly didn't believe me. Hell, I didn't believe myself. "Listen, Dylan, you're the best raider we have. I need you, and I trust you. Everyone does. But you can't make mistakes like this."

"I know."

"I don't know what the hell to do with her. I'm not sure we'd be able to take her back. Not now anyway. Until we figure it out, she's your responsibility."

I huffed and fidgeted. How the hell was I supposed to be responsible for a girl?

Without a word, I left Jesse's and went down to the west forest. I was on chopping duty. I passed several houses along the way and tried to ignore the looks I was getting.

Our community was nestled away in unpopulated woods where my parents had helped build the houses. That was before they were taken away. We'd avoided being discovered because of one simple geographical aid: the mountain. Jesse was the one who knew about the cave and that it led to a spacious, green circle. From the top of our outposts, we'd seen the Regulars come looking for us, but no one ever found the cave's dark sliver of an opening.

I made my way to the far side of the woods where Gabe and Andrew were chopping tree trunks into more manageable pieces. Without a word I lifted a spare axe and started chopping alongside them.

"Someone's grumpy," Gabe said. Andrew laughed, which was his usual response. He rarely had an original thought.

I huffed.

"I don't know why you're in such a bad mood, man. We're grateful," Gabe continued.

"Yeah," Andrew added.

"About what?" I said between swings. "That I've brought more pressure on us to be careful? That all the food I just gathered for Doc Sara will go to the girl? That our supplies are going to be even more stretched now?" I swung again. "Yeah, everyone should be thanking me."

"She's gorgeous," Andrew spat. It didn't sound like a compliment so much as an assessment. "I'd eat less for a chance with her."

My axe sliced through a chunk of wood. What did he say?

"Yeah," Gabe agreed. "I'm so tired of looking at our girls I could scream. That Mackenzie? She's *nice*."

I turned around and grabbed Gabe by his shirt—between the two of them he was the real threat. "You keep your hands off her. She's not something for you to play with."

Gabe struggled to get out of my grip but didn't bother swinging. He knew I could hurt him if I really wanted to. Realizing I'd done enough stupid things for one day, I turned to leave.

"I think you need a snack, Dylan," Gabe called after me, but I tuned him out.

In a matter of seconds, all the events of the morning became incredibly clear. For years I'd been stealing things for the group, making sure everyone had what they needed. Today, for the first time, I took something for myself. And it was the dumbest thing I'd ever done. There was no way we could actually keep her here for long, and, if we did, girls didn't fall for boys who stole them.

• • •

The woman with the toddler on her hip escorted me to a cabin near another building that was almost exactly the same size. The one ahead of me looked neater though, at least from the outside.

"Where are you taking me?" I asked. The threat of some unnamable thing hung around my periphery but never came into focus.

"Don't worry, honey. No one here means you any harm."

"Is that what you say to everyone you kidnap?" I asked, not quite as angrily as I'd intended.

"We've never taken anyone before. And Dylan's usually smarter than this." She sighed and shook her head. "In the meantime, you might as well get acquainted with the other girls."

"Huh?" I asked.

Without explanation she walked up the wooden steps of the cabin, across the tiny porch, and knocked on the door. The angry girl from before answered the door. "Seriously?"

"Where else would we put her?" my guide said in a warm, pleading voice.

The angry girl begrudgingly opened the door. My guide motioned for me to enter and I followed her into the small house that was really little more than a box.

"This is the girls' place," my guide explained. "This is Monica," she said, motioning to the angry girl, "and that's Alicia and Tanya."

I looked around and noticed two girls smiling at me from their bunk beds. Clearly they didn't mind the company. The woman pointed to where the bathroom was in the back, pulled out some sheets that were obviously stolen and set them on a bed that was intended to be mine.

"Play nice," she said and left. I was alone with the three

girls. I looked around the room and sat on the edge of my bed, not sure what else to do.

"So," Alicia started, "how are you liking it so far?"

Was she serious? Who liked being taken from their home?

"I see clothes haven't changed at all," Tanya added, looking me up and down. It was true. I'd pretty much worn the same dark slacks and loose shirts for as long as I remembered. The girls were wearing similar clothes, stolen from who knows where. But they'd dyed the shirts, stained them with grass or something. On purpose. "I'm not as brave as Monica or Dylan. I could never go out there and see it for myself."

I stood and picked up the sheets and tried to process what they were saying, which was a little difficult. Their words seemed fast. Everyone seemed fast here. Quick hands and sentences wherever I turned, disorienting me more than the fact that I'd been taken.

"Monica's so sly. She never gets caught," Alicia said, her voice full of admiration.

I looked to Monica who was tying knots in a piece of rope and looking very pleased with her admirers. I felt for a moment that if I could see the reverse of myself in a mirror, she would be it: tall, lean and dark, and very focused. I was too soft, too short, too passive to live here.

I shook my head. It felt fuzzy, which happened from time to time. I started putting my bed together. There was no way to fight being here at the moment. In fact, if there was a way to fight at all I wasn't sure how to go about it.

As I worked on tucking in a corner, I found my arm suddenly twisted behind my back. I cried out.

"Monica, what are you doing?" Tanya shouted.

"Listen, zombie," she whispered in my ear. "I'm going to get you out of here. And I plan on being nice about it. But let me make it clear, if you so much as put a hand on Dylan, I'll break your fingers."

She released me as quickly as she'd grabbed me and went back to her space in the corner. There was something tingling down my back that I hadn't felt in years. A rush of cold crept in, almost like what I had felt in the big cabin, but this time it was both worse, and better.

"Don't worry," I said, as the feeling retreated. "I'm not interested in that Neanderthal."

• • •

I hid until dinner. I didn't go back to the guys' bunkhouse or to the Big House to see if I could be helpful. Today was a good day to lie low. I stayed tucked in the outskirts of the woods, trying to align my thoughts.

I took Mackenzie for myself. I was still shocked at the thought.

I'd seen her before when I'd been out watching the houses, and she always seemed a little different. I remember once—before I raided her neighbor's place—watching her pick a wildflower. People in towns didn't do things like that anymore. Another time I saw her stretch and pull her body all the way up on her tiptoes. That was months ago. Apparently, I'd been watching her far more than was essential. The only thing I could attribute it to was affection for her and, now that I understood that, I had to figure out what to do next. I decided I only had two options: throw myself into it full force, or take her home immediately.

The bells rang in the distance—time for dinner. Thankfully I now felt calm and hungry enough to rejoin the others. Still, I waited a few minutes. I wanted to give her time to eat and leave if she wanted to.

The main cabin—the Big House—was a mess at meal times. It was the one place that could hold all sixty-four, well sixty-five, of us at once. By the time I entered, nearly everyone had settled into their usual places: families in groups, couples and singles together in the back, and the kids running around between bites.

I saw that Monica, Tanya, and Alicia had brought Mackenzie. Gabe and Andrew were sitting with them. I planned to grab my food and go. Mackenzie looked so uncomfortable in the middle of that swarm, and I could only make it worse.

I flew down the line grabbing the last few scraps of the meal. It was a meatless night.

"Hey, Dylan!"

I turned to see Monica at the table, smiling and waving me over. Mackenzie looked almost nervous. Impressive.

I walked over and sat across from Monica and next to Tanya. I didn't know what to say, so I just listened to Gabe explain to Mackenzie that we weren't bad people, it's just that we needed soap and shampoo and stuff.

She didn't seem interested. Her eyes were flickering over our trays, and then down to her prepackaged meal in front of her. I could see her begin to question the difference and to look at ours with obvious longing.

Finally, as though she'd given up on being offered any of the cornbread or apple slices on our trays, she picked up a fork and started eating. She had chicken. I was a little jealous.

"So," Monica said to me, ignoring the rest of the table, "when's the next raid? I'm itching to go."

"I think I've done enough damage for a while," I mumbled.

Mackenzie quietly giggled.

Monica shot her a look, and I guessed they weren't going to be best friends. Jesse had told me Mackenzie was my responsibility and I realized the things she would need the most protection from were at this very table.

"But we need new clothes for the little ones, Dylan," Monica whined. "The twins have all but destroyed theirs."

A little slowly, Mackenzie spoke. "You guys have babies here?"

The table slowly looked at her. I guess she thought we weren't capable.

"Yes, cow," Monica started. "We have babies here. We have a doctor and everything."

Mackenzie scowled as she took another spoonful of smoothly whipped potatoes. "I'm not fat," she said quietly, sounding confused instead of angry.

Monica sighed and whispered to me. "Can you imagine living with that?" She stood up and moved to where her parents were sitting. Monica was the only one of us who wasn't an adult but who didn't live with her family. The rest of us didn't have families to go to, so we just made our own groups. But what could I say about Monica? She's just always been independent.

Andrew got up to go get seconds and Tanya followed. With the group so small, I felt even more nervous about being around Mackenzie, but she was very at ease.

She took a few more nibbles at her food, and then looked at me. "Thanks for not killing me," she said almost comically.

I smiled. Maybe trying to win her over wouldn't be so hard. "Any time."

She ate everything on her plate and sat there quietly as

people came and went. Sometimes she closed her eyes and just listened to the sound. I bet things never got this loud around her before.

Then I realized that winning her over like this, with her being the way she was, wasn't exactly fair. My hope fell too quickly to be caught.

• • •

I woke up refreshed, like usual, after sleeping soundly. It took me a moment to realize I wasn't under my purple comforter in my purple room. I looked up at the dark wooden slats of the roof and was suddenly stricken.

"Dad?" I breathed, my heart starting to race. "Dad?"

"Huh?" someone said. I could barely hear it over the sound of my shallow breaths coming in and out of my mouth.

"Oh, no!" someone yelled, coming to my bed. I couldn't place the face. Who was this person? "She needs something! Quick!"

"Monica, go! We'll watch her."

I heard a door slam while two intruders hovered above me. They were going to take me. No! No, wait, I was already taken. Were they going to hurt me? Had they already?

My eyes were swimming, and I called out louder. "DAD!"

"What's going on?" said someone else, a boy this time.

"She woke up like this. Monica's getting her food," a girl answered.

Food? I didn't want any food. I wanted my dad. If I could just stop shaking and get away from these people I could go find him.

Two strong hands grabbed my face and made it still. "Mackenzie, can you hear me?"

I sucked in a jagged breath. Fingers went to my eyes and

wiped away hot tears. I could finally make out the face. It was him. It was Dylan.

"Mackenzie, just nod your head. Do you hear me?"

I nodded.

"Everything's fine. You're scared and you don't know why, right?"

"You kidnapped me! I want my dad!" I screamed.

"I know, I know," he said, trying to calm me. "Shit, she's bad."

"I've got juice! And a muffin!" someone called entering the room.

"Thank God," Dylan said. "Juice first."

There was a moment of fumbling and then liquid splashed on to my face.

"Hold her still," an angry voice instructed.

I tried to fight, but someone was holding my nose so I had to open my mouth. I coughed and gagged and swallowed juice I couldn't taste and then . . . and then . . .

I dropped my hands, which were gripping Dylan's wrists. I hadn't realized I was doing that. My body was still shaking but it slowed and though I'd just woken up I felt exhausted.

I looked around the room, and began to recognize the faces. Tanya and Alicia were standing there, disheveled and anxious. Monica held a plastic-wrapped muffin in her hand, and Gabe stood there doing nothing. And Dylan. Dylan was sitting on my bed, his hands still on my face. Slowly, he released me.

"Sorry," I said. "Did I hurt you?"

He held back a laugh. "No." He looked at Monica. "From now on, juice in the room. Or something. I'll have to get more, soon."

He made it sound as if I were going to be here for an awfully long time. Maybe until I grew old or died. "What about my dad?" I whispered.

Dylan looked at me with sympathy in his eyes. Without a word, he stood and left.

Something deep inside me wanted to cry more, but I couldn't. Instead I just rolled over and went back to sleep.

• • •

I went to the workshop and tried to direct my anger into something productive. The Dodson twins were getting to the point that they needed highchairs, so I was trying to build some. I'd never made anything but tables and benches before, and we all worked on the cabins. I had no instructions, which meant this was bound to be a long project.

It was going to take some serious focusing to get this right, which was just what I needed. Mackenzie looked so lost this morning I could barely stand to look at her. My thoughts kept bouncing between what was right and what was wrong, to the point that I could feel my head aching.

On the one hand, I'd rescued her from the mind-numbing treadmill that life with the Regulars had become. I was convinced she could be happy here. She'd be able to remember what it was like to really feel happy. In that sense, I felt like a hero.

But she'd never asked to be taken from that world. She didn't even realize there was anything wrong with it. She just wanted her dad. So if I was keeping her from the only thing she wanted, how could I think that what I'd done was good?

I kept trying to convince myself it was. If I could just get some time . . . I shook my head, and focused instead on the wood. It would have to be sanded. I began the task, blocking out all other thoughts.

Sometime mid-morning, there was a knock on the workshop door. Without waiting for an answer, Monica walked in.

"You okay?" she asked. "You seemed really tense this morning."

"Obviously," I said, measuring the wood. "We can't have her freaking out like that. She could hurt someone."

"It's not my fault," she snapped.

"Didn't say it was."

Monica grumbled and walked around the room. Dust stirred in the light around her, trying to escape the space she was heading to.

There was something about Monica, no doubt. If I were asked to pick any of the girls here to pair off with, it'd be her. I imagined she felt the same way. We had our reasons to be angry with the world and understood those things in each other. And we were both fast and strong, easily the most daring in the bunch. So, sure, she'd make a good choice.

But, really, was that a choice? If you're in a desert and your options are sand, more sand, and water . . .

"Look, Dylan," she said, sighing, "Doc Sara's used most of what little you were able to bring for the Masens. The homeopathic stuff is slow and she's just trying to keep them comfortable. With the cow needing at least three meals a day, we're going to need more food. Lots more."

I sighed. I really didn't want to go on another raid. I didn't want to leave Mackenzie here alone.

"Unless you want to take her back," Monica suggested.

"No," I answered just a little too quickly. Monica searched my face, and I could tell she was seeing through any trace of cool I thought I had. She saw my worry, my shame, and maybe even my hope.

She pursed her lips in anger, turned and walked toward the door. "We should go today."

The door slammed behind her. I sighed again, and went back to measuring.

• • •

Alicia's fingers in my hair were so soothing. I didn't know how to French-braid on my own and my dad couldn't do it, of course. Her hands dredged up memories of my mother's hands, tickling my scalp.

"I think Gabe likes you," she whispered as she braided. "Don't say anything to Tanya. She kind of has a thing for him."

"Dylan, Gabe. Anyone else I should avoid?" I replied dreamily. "Is Andrew yours or something?"

She laughed out loud at that. "No, Andrew is no one's. I kind of have my eye on this older guy, but he doesn't notice me. But that's okay. I knew it might be like that here."

Like that *here*? Wasn't Alicia born here?

"Anyway, like I said, don't say anything to Tanya."

"Don't worry," I assured her. "I'm not interested in Gabe. I don't really feel that way about anyone."

It seemed like this scenario—this girls-who-liked-boys-who-liked-other-girls thing—was typical here. Back home, I never felt that way. None of my friends seemed to either. In fact, wasn't that one of the new programs being set up? A dating service to help people be more active, a change from all the hard work they were doing . . . So some people were interested in getting out there like that. Not me.

"No one?" she asked skeptically.

I shrugged my shoulders. "I have school and work. I don't have time for a boyfriend."

I did have friends. Just enough though to keep me satisfied. Kimmy probably knew by now that I was gone. I hoped she wasn't too worried. I imagined how far behind I'd be in school by the time I got back. I'd probably have to do the whole year over, I'd have forgotten so much. Thanks a lot, Dylan.

Dylan. I couldn't figure him out. Sometimes I felt as if I should be upset with him, but then it didn't seem worth the effort. What in the world did he think he'd achieve by taking me? I tried to reason it out. He must want money. If they had money, they wouldn't have to steal from people's houses anymore.

"Alicia, you came here on purpose?" I asked, a little surprised at myself for asking.

Her hands froze for a moment, but then continued. "Yes, I did."

"Why? Don't you miss the nice houses and the food and the freedom?"

To my surprise she laughed. "I did miss my freedom. That's why I left."

I scrunched up my forehead in thought, trying to understand. How could you call living in a little room in the middle of the woods freedom?

In the distance, a bell rang.

"Lunch time!" Alicia cried and hastily finished my hair so we could leave.

On the way she pulled my arm as she half-jogged to the dining area, but I was more than content to walk. We were among the first there anyway and lined up to get our food. I was looking forward to at least having some of the strawberries that had been laid out. They looked so bright and delicious.

"Here you go," an older woman said handing one of the pre-wrapped food trays from home to me.

I took it but was confused. "Can't I just have what everyone else is having? I won't eat too much. I promise."

The woman kindly shook her head. "Not today."

Disappointed, I took the tray over to the place we'd sat the day before and waited for the others. Alicia hurried through the line to sit with me; Gabe and Tanya weren't far behind. I peeled back the polymer film on top of the food tray and looked at it sadly. It's not that it tasted bad or anything. It's just that fresh fruit was so tempting and I wished they were willing to share.

"Hey, Mackenzie," Gabe said, sitting down beside me. I took a peek at Tanya, who did actually seem a little disappointed that he'd sat next to me and not her.

Alicia mercifully took the reins of the conversation as Andrew sat down. "Where's Monica? Anyone know?"

"Oh, yeah," Gabe said, popping one of the delicious-looking strawberries into his mouth. "She and Dylan left. Said they won't be back until late. We're supposed to watch her," he said, nodding his head at me.

Dylan was gone? Suddenly, a rush of sensations swept through me. I couldn't quite identify any of them apart from the fact that some were good and some were bad. I knew there was a bit of hope. If he'd left, he must be giving his demands to my dad. That meant I'd leave soon. But then, he was with Monica, and something about that didn't feel right to me.

"You all right?" Tanya asked.

I snapped out of my daze to find the four of them looking at me. "Yes," I said simply. To make my point, I lifted a forkful of rice to my mouth. Seconds later, I didn't even care that Dylan was gone.

• • •

"Dammit, Dylan," Monica whispered.

We were sitting quietly at a bus stop, taking things in. We'd planned on hitting up several houses while people were still at work and school. This was simple. Food only. Food and then home.

The problem was the posters. Mackenzie's face was on the bus-stop shelter, on a bulletin board by the library, posted on nearly every phone pole . . . everywhere. This was the closest I'd ever seen Regulars come to feeling apprehension.

There were no outraged cries or even children rushing faster than normal to get home. But people knew she was gone. As they passed, they looked at her picture and murmured stuff like, "Aww, that's too bad."

"Just stay cool," I told Monica. "No one's going to suspect us as long as we keep our heads down. You go left, I'll go right. We'll meet back in an hour?"

"Sounds good," she said. Before she walked away, she leaned back down and whispered, "Don't pick up anyone else, okay?"

I knew it was meant to be a joke, but it bothered me.

After she was gone, I walked away, too. I stopped only once, to take one of the flyers down and tuck it into my pocket.

We were smart and efficient, and within an hour we had at least two weeks' worth of food. We met back in our secret place, just on the edge of a public garden, where we pretended to admire some flowers until the coast was clear, and when it was, we disappeared into the woods.

We shared the load so it wasn't too much work but we still had to focus on our steps in the dimming light. I figured we'd just stay quiet, until Monica cleared her throat.

Wanting to cut off whatever she was about to say, I spoke first. "You did a great job today. Don't tell anyone, but I think you might be better than me."

Monica smiled. "Of course I'm better than you. No one suspects a helpless girl," she replied, batting her eyelashes.

I smiled back and returned to focusing on the path.

"Do you like her?"

I tried to dodge the question. "Like who?"

"Mackenzie." Her tone made it clear she knew I was playing dumb. "You seem awfully worried about her."

I shrugged. "She's kind of helpless. And Jesse said she was my responsibility."

"Still," she said. "Why did you kidnap her in the first place?"

"I thought she might know something," I said. "She's the mayor's daughter."

"But you didn't know that until I said it."

"Yes, I did," I lied. "I just didn't want to make a big deal out of it. Maybe I was wrong and she doesn't know anything. Didn't want to get people's hopes up."

Monica seemed to be pacified with that, but I was sure she saw through all the little holes in my story.

When we got through the cave and into the clearing it was just before sunset and the field of houses was beginning to slip into the shadows. Monica and I headed over to the Big House to drop off our hauls and ran into Tanya leaving with a tray of the prepackaged food.

"Tanya, those aren't for you," I complained.

"It's not for me, idiot," she shot back. "Mackenzie passed out this afternoon around two and wouldn't wake up for dinner. I'm taking this over for when she finally gets up."

I reached over, took the tray, and flipped it over. "You're going to have to get another one. And tell whoever serves her to read."

Tanya squinted at me.

"Look at the writing on the bottom. This is a lunch portion," I pointed to the tiny printing on the back of the tray and Tanya's face lit up with understanding. "She won't be up for hours."

"Ugh!" Monica whined. "I don't want to be up with her in the middle of the night."

"Fine," I said, dropping the bag of food and grabbing the single tray. I'd had all I could take of Monica's attitude toward Mackenzie.

"Where are you going?" she called after me.

Without stopping, I answered. "If you don't want to stay up with her, I will. I'm taking her to Doc Sara's."

• • •

I dreamed of blue. Blue-green. Like the grass and the sky melted into one. I swam in it, as if it were thick water, and worked every muscle to be able to move. The effort felt good, and the color was so vibrant I feared it wasn't real.

As my eyes started to crack open and I realized my fears had come true, my heart sank. I just wanted something to be real. I looked around the room and discovered I wasn't in my bunk with the other girls, but on a cot in another room. I shifted and saw that Dylan was there, looking out the window.

"I thought you were gone," I mumbled. My voice was raspy from sleeping. I felt so stiff.

Dylan moved quickly to my side. "I'm back. How do you feel?" he asked as he tore off the cover from a tray of food. "Why don't you have something to eat?"

"What time is it?" I asked. It looked sort of pearly-blue outside. Must be close to dinner.

"About five in the morning. You must be hungry."

"Five in the morning? How did that happen? I remember feeling tired . . ." I searched my thoughts, trying to find something more, but that was it. I had been really tired, so I crawled into bed.

"Why don't you just eat?"

"I don't want to. I'm not hungry," I protested.

"Sure you are."

"Just stop for a minute, okay?" There was a small edge to my voice that seemed to make him nervous. "Could I just walk around a little? I feel so achy."

Dylan checked his watch. "Fine, but I'm coming, too. And so is the food."

I rolled my eyes, threw off the blankets, and stood. I didn't bother with shoes, I just pushed open the door. I was a little disoriented. I'd never seen the grounds from this viewpoint. I looked around and saw what would either be considered a small lake or a large pond and walked on to a little floating dock. I went to the edge, not waiting for Dylan, and sat down, sticking my feet in the water.

It wasn't the blue-green water in my dreams. It was the shadow-covered gray of early morning.

"Did you leave a ransom note for my dad?" I asked, aching to know how soon this would all end.

"Ransom? No," he replied, appalled.

"He has money, connections. He'd give you whatever you want," I offered.

"I doubt that," Dylan said quietly. There was a sadness to him just then that didn't fit in with the confident, dangerous, wild person I thought he was. It confused me.

"I don't understand what's going on," I said. My breath hitched, and I realized that I might cry. It was the first time in years that I'd felt so . . . hopeless.

Dylan shook his head, trying to decide something. He looked at his watch again, then the food, and then me.

"Mackenzie, you've felt strange since you've been here, right? Not just because you're in some new place but because you keep feeling normal, and then it starts to slip away and then, suddenly, you get it back, yes?"

I nodded. He'd summed it up better than I could.

"Did you notice that you usually start feeling better after you eat?" he asked.

I tried to remember. I didn't seem to relate it to the food, but I remembered that earlier I'd been bothered that he was gone and then not so much, if at all, once I'd started eating.

"There are opiates in the food," he said slowly. "Drugs."

"What?" I shook my head. "That's ridiculous."

"It sure as hell is ridiculous. It's also true. Thing is, it's getting worse, and I suspect in about half an hour you're going to start screaming again if you don't eat."

I eyed the plate. "I don't believe you. You're just trying to scare me."

"Are you scared? Think about how you felt yesterday when you woke up. How often do you feel that way?"

I almost shouted out the answer: *Never*.

"Think about the world you've been used to, Mackenzie. There's no crime because everyone's too mellowed out to be bothered to try. You don't even lock your doors anymore. And there's enough work for everyone, right?"

I nodded.

"That's because it takes three glazed people to do the work of one. And I bet you've never kissed anyone, never even thought about it."

I looked down and felt the weak and unfamiliar heat of a blush.

"How do you know?"

"You're all too doped up to care about anything."

I considered what he'd said. Maybe that's what the new dating service was for, to encourage us to do what we couldn't do on our own. And the food. I remember my dad telling me one night as we ate soft apples in a cinnamon sauce how he'd grown up near a farm and used to pluck apples right off the trees and eat them on his way home from school. Nothing like that happened now.

We had three meals a day at regular intervals, and sometimes a snack. I'd never seen any fresh food growing anywhere. It was all done somewhere else, somewhere that wouldn't bother us with the noise and smell and equipment. That's what we were told.

"I still think you're lying," I told him and picked up a pastry from my tray and took a bite.

He nodded his head. "I thought as much, but it won't matter," he said, standing.

"What do you mean?"

"Well, Jesse located some friends of his. They'll be here tomorrow," he answered.

"So what?"

"So tomorrow you're going to get a firsthand look at what it's like to get off of that," he said, pointing to my tray.

Dylan walked away, leaving me alone with my food. I tried to be bothered by what he said, but I just couldn't anymore.

• • •

Jesse had been talking about his friend Aaron for years. He always said that Aaron would want out. But when Jesse found his opportunity to disappear—a moment that coincided with my parents being hauled off—he didn't have time to save his friend Aaron, too.

He'd been searching for him ever since. It took a long time, but finally he found him and, even though Jesse avoided leaving the safety of the cabins, he did leave for Aaron. After a few outings, a little research, and one very long road trip, he'd come back, with his friend. Aaron wasn't on his own, though. He had a family. His daughter, who he was supporting as they walked through the clearing toward us, didn't look much older than ten. I was glad I was a guy and closer to his son's age. I didn't want to have to watch a kid go through the withdrawal. Aaron's wife was already shaking.

Andrew and I went over to help carry their things. In the few days between their discovery and now, we'd made them a space in the Donnelleys' cabin. It would have to do until we could build them a new one.

Jesse introduced me as we escorted them in. "This is Dylan, my right-hand man."

I smiled. It made me glad to know that even though I'd screwed up by bringing Mackenzie here, he still felt he could trust me.

"Dylan, we're gonna take them straight to Doc Sara. They've already missed a meal, so we might as well let it play out. I want you with Austin here," he said, motioning to Aaron's son.

I nodded, feeling exhausted already. He wasn't as big as Gabe or me, but he still looked like he could to put up a fight.

"What are you doing to them?"

I turned and found Mackenzie standing there, her face almost alight with concern.

"Don't worry," Jesse said. "These are my friends. They want to be here."

Aaron turned to Jesse. "I don't know how we'll ever repay you. We knew something wasn't right but we could never put our finger on it. Thank you. Thank you so much."

Jesse shook his head. "You can thank me in three days. Come on. Let's get you to Doc Sara."

They moved ahead, and as I watched them walk away I paused to talk to Mackenzie.

"I know you think I'm a liar. I understand why you would, but if you want proof that there's something inside you keeping you in a daze then you should come. I bet they could use someone younger to help with the girl." I looked at her, imploring her to come. I needed her to know that this was real.

She looked as if she was going to leave, but then sighed. "Fine, but only because I know you're wrong." She walked ahead of me, and I felt both relieved and dejected. I wasn't exactly thrilled by what she was about to see.

• • •

It was awful. I'd never seen a person act that way. The little girl, Elaine, stayed in bed and wept as Alicia and I kept her company. She didn't seem to have the energy to do much more. Occasionally, she pulled up and heaved into a bucket. Alicia gave her water, and then she'd fall back asleep. Still, at least I wasn't next door, where in another small room her brother was yelling obscenities. I felt the force of his (or someone else's) body slam into the wall from time to time. Clearly, he wasn't taking this easily.

It didn't take too much to convince me that Dylan was right. I searched for another explanation, and couldn't find one. It had to be the food.

While Elaine slept, I asked Alicia if it were true, if that was what she meant when she'd said she'd wanted her freedom.

"Yes. I knew something was wrong. At one point I got sick and couldn't eat for a few days, and I went through something like this. But then," she paused, shaking her head. "everything became clear. I ate half portions for a few days while I recovered, and I was still aware of things that I hadn't really felt before. Like how much I loved my mom. It wasn't just that I was attached to her, but I really, really loved her.

"Anyway, Tanya and I were neighbors. I explained how I felt one day and she already knew about it. We decided that we'd rather be able to feel than not, and we left. Monica found us in the woods at just about the time we'd decided we were giving up and going back. We were starving."

I considered this. "But if you loved your mom so much, how could you just leave her?"

"At least I can still feel that I love her. And I can miss her. I know that sounds like a poor substitute for actually being with her but you're still in it," she said. "You don't know what you're not feeling."

I tried to focus in on myself. If there had ever been an

opportunity to do that, this was it. It was just before lunchtime, and now that I thought about it, my ability to perceive things did seem easier now, given the time that had passed since breakfast. I tried to dig deep and feel something.

I closed my eyes and tried. I clenched my hands and scrunched my forehead and tried to will myself to feel something more than satisfactory, pleasantness, something beyond the almost warmth of happiness, the diluted weight of sadness.

A knock came at the door. It was Doc Sara.

"Mackenzie, it's time for you to eat. Dylan has your lunch," she said, coming in the room and taking my place. "Two doors down on the left."

Thrown off by the failure of my own heart, I left. I opened the door two down on the left and found Dylan sitting on one of two thin beds in the room, a tray of his own food in his lap and mine waiting across from him.

"What happened?" I gasped. Dylan had a purple bruise on his cheekbone, just by his eye.

He gave me a small shrug. "Austin's a fighter. I'm sure you heard."

"Yes, but still." I walked over and put my fingers lightly on the bruise. It was warm. "You should get Doc Sara to look at that."

"Already did," he said. "Nothing to do but let it run its course." He hesitated for a moment. "But your hand feels nice."

I looked away from the lump and into his eyes. There was something there, something just below the surface. I didn't know what to do, so I just went to sit on the other bed where my food was waiting.

I peeled back the film and was pleased to find it still warm.

They could be eaten at room temperature, but warm was always better. I looked over at what Dylan was having. Soup and another bowl of those vibrant strawberries. He caught me looking at them and debated something in his head. He picked up a strawberry and held it out to me.

"Just one," he said.

I felt a thrill of . . . excitement. That's what it was. And in the moment, I didn't think clearly. I should have used my fingers to take the strawberry from him, but I didn't. I bent over and bit it in from his hand, my lips brushing against his own fingers as I did.

It was a rush of too many things. The taste of something so fresh in my mouth, the knot that unexpectedly knit in my stomach, and the look in Dylan's eyes.

His eyes. I stared into them and recognized them as the same blue-green I'd dreamed about. His eyes flashed down to his fingers, still holding the stem, and then back to me.

It was too much to take. I scooped a mouthful of whatever it was on my plate—something soft I couldn't even taste—and escaped.

● ● ●

It was a long three days but it was worth it. Elaine was running through the fields, alive with joy, and everyone was lifted by the sight. Until then, she'd probably never even had the urge to run. And Austin, it turned out, was actually a nice guy. Every time he caught a glimpse of my eye, he apologized again.

Jesse wasn't quite so tense now that his long-lost friend was back, and everyone was gladdened by the arrival of new faces. Everyone except for maybe Mackenzie. She watched them closely, and we all knew why.

It was obvious that finding out the truth was bothering her, and not just because she had been tricked, but also because she couldn't decide if she wanted to stay how she was. I'd felt it, that day at Doc Sara's. She'd looked at me and she'd felt something and it scared her.

Scared me, too.

I'd been keeping my distance, trying to give her room to decide what to do, but I couldn't stand being away from her any longer. I found her on the dock at our tiny lake, one foot in the water, thinking. She heard me coming and looked back.

"Mind if I join you?" I asked.

She shook her head, and I went to sit beside her.

She was quiet for a long time, but I didn't mind. It was nice to just sit by her again. I thought it was funny that she kept coming back to the dock, dipping her feet in. Most people gave up on feeling anything, including temperature or texture. Even in her haze, she could appreciate it.

"Where are your parents?" she asked.

I didn't like to talk about it but considering everything I'd done, I figured I owed her. "They're in prison. They got caught telling others about the drugs. Told the wrong person, I guess. Jesse told them he'd watch me when the cops came, and two hours later, we were here. My parents actually helped build this place."

"Did you go through what they did? Austin and Elaine, I mean?"

"Not exactly. My parents had a garden, so I only ever ate one of the issued meals a day. I felt sick when I did, but it wasn't as bad. And it was over quicker."

She was quiet again, and traced the patterns in the wood slats with her fingers. Something was up.

"My mom's dead, you know."

"No," I said quietly. "I didn't know. I'm sorry."

"That's the thing," she said. "You feel sorry. You feel sorry for me, for her, probably even for my dad. But I don't feel anything. I can't even miss her. It doesn't seem fair. And I've been away from my dad for what, over a week? Except for that moment in the cabin, I can barely muster up the will to want him back."

Even as she spoke, her voice stayed calm. It was as if there was some disconnect in her somewhere, like wiring gone wrong—knowledge in one place, emotions in another, and they weren't allowed to touch.

"I feel like there's a layer of something over everything," she confessed.

I chuckled. "Like a doughnut. That's one of our names for the Regulars. Doughnuts, cows, zombies."

I smiled at her but she didn't return it. "I want to miss my mom, Dylan."

I took in a deep breath and then let it out. Was she asking for too much? Wasn't this what I was hoping for? But this decision wasn't about me.

So I let her make it.

• • •

I cried a lot, like Elaine did. I tossed and turned on the mattress, blinking in and out of a cloudy delirium. I'd feel tired, and then I'd fidget for an hour. I'd drink water and then throw it back up. The world kept going in and out of focus, as if a magnifying glass were being whipped back and forth in front of my brain.

But every time I'd catch a glimpse of reality, he was there. Dylan pacing the floor, Dylan running his hands though his hair, Dylan staring out the window, Dylan asleep beside the bed.

Those three days were horrible. But at least I could tell that they were.

• • •

I didn't know how many people I'd seen go through that, but watching Mackenzie was the worst. Usually, I got fighters. Mackenzie whimpered a lot, as if she were lost. But when she woke up on the third day, I could tell it was over. She looked around the room and, as boring as it was, she seemed enthralled with every little detail. She looked at her own hands, touched the quilt, inhaled deeply. She looked up at me and smiled.

I'd been waiting for that smile. Since she'd been here, I'd been hoping for a look of recognition with nothing blurring the edges. She hopped out of bed, alive with excitement, and ran into my arms.

"You didn't leave," she breathed into my neck.

"Didn't have any other plans," I joked.

She pulled back and gave me a face, and I was elated just to see that tiny bit of expression. Slowly, the look on her face shifted. I felt something that, in all these years of feeling, I'd never come across before.

The door flew open. "Is the cow done ye—"

We stepped apart, but not fast enough to escape Monica's gaze. She didn't even look at me, she just raked her eyes over Mackenzie and left.

"Huh," Mackenzie said once we were alone again. "I was wondering how long it would be before I wished I couldn't feel something."

• • •

I ran, I touched, I laughed out loud. I squished grass between my toes and missed the comforting arms of my father. I sat in the sunlight and wished for my mother with an ache so big I felt it would crush me. And as awful as it was, I loved it. I loved the feeling of soft air, my own elbows, my new determination. I loved things that, before I even knew what it was to feel, I always suspected I would. Like sisterhood and polished glass and the sensation of really moving.

And then, surprisingly, there were things I loved that I never could have imagined.

I couldn't stop looking at Dylan. I kept wondering what he felt about me. Though it seemed strange to me that I should like him at all, I did. I trusted Dylan. Without me ever knowing I needed it, he rescued me. And since I'd been here—an Outsider myself—his only actions had been to protect me, help me.

Maybe it was because it was the first time I'd really thought about a guy at all, but I couldn't tear myself away from him. These feelings for Dylan, of all the new things I felt, were the most powerful, the most consuming.

I tossed and turned all night wondering if he felt the same way about me.

• • •

I worked myself into exhaustion so I would sleep at night, but it didn't come easily. I would catch myself thinking of Mackenzie's laugh, or the way she played with the little ones, or the sight of her cross-legged on the dock with quiet tears on her cheeks.

I wanted to ask her about everything she was feeling. One thing in particular.

Maybe it was my imagination, but I caught her looking at me a lot. And it seemed in those quick seconds after she turned away, her cheeks would flush pink. I kept hoping there was something there, but I had no real reason to think there was.

I couldn't stand it anymore. I got out of bed and went outside to clear my mind. I guessed I could go to the workshop. I had a ton of projects to complete. I took the long way, just to be outside longer, but stopped dead in my tracks when I saw the tiny silhouette on the dock. Night or day, light or shadow, I'd know Mackenzie anywhere.

She saw me coming and gave me a small wave as I walked out to where she was sitting.

"Can't sleep?" I asked, stating the obvious.

"I've had a lot on my mind."

She sounded sad. "Something wrong?"

"I have this feeling . . . I don't even know what to call it," she said.

"How does it feel?"

"It's two things, conflicting. It's confusing."

"Ambivalence," I said. "Simultaneous conflicting feelings. Ambivalence."

She nodded. "Not a fan of this one."

"What are you so conflicted about?" I asked. "Maybe I can help."

Mackenzie's eyes flashed back and forth in the night and then she held in a small smile. "Okay, well, now I'm feeling nervous, but suppose, just hypothetically, that someone took you away from here and put you in a place that was completely foreign to you."

I chuckled. "Okay."

"And then let's pretend they confused you, told you

everything you'd ever known was a lie, and never exactly explained why they took you in the first place, or told you all these things," she said.

That wasn't nearly as entertaining. "Okay." I stared at the water, afraid to look at her.

"And then . . . suppose you thought the person who did all these things was . . . wonderful."

I didn't dare move. I couldn't believe I was hearing this. There was a smile in my voice when I spoke. "Okay."

"Well, what would happen if you told that person they were wonderful? Anything at all? Or maybe they don't really want you to think they're wonderful . . ."

She'd been afraid I wouldn't want to hear that? I looked over to her, and she had one of her legs pulled up to her chest, both arms wrapped around it. She was hiding her nose behind her knee and clearly didn't want to look at me.

I gazed just past her and confessed. "Maybe the person would tell you that . . . that they noticed you a long time ago." I saw her head perk up at those words. "Maybe they would say they've thought you were wonderful all along, even before they knew why. They might tell you they're sorry they hurt you, and wished they could've seen you this happy without making you go through so much." I took in a breath. "They might tell you that you thinking they're wonderful kind of changes their whole world."

I finally dared to look at Mackenzie. I didn't know if she intended to come across that way, but she looked as if she were pleading with me.

I placed a hand on her cheek and kissed her.

• • •

Suddenly, everything made sense. The moment Dylan kissed me, all the other things I'd felt became even stronger. So many emotions hung on this one. Grief, hope, anger. They all became crystal clear in that second.

I'd never felt such a need before. Not even hunger or thirst came close. It was as if I couldn't get him closer to me, couldn't have his hands on me, I would just wither away. And, amazingly enough, it seemed he felt the same way.

Dylan's hands gripped me, pulling me so close not even a whisper of wind could come between us. His fingers traced the curve of my hip, the arch of my back, the shy spot behind my knee.

Every time his lips moved or his hands went somewhere new, I tried to find a way to describe it to myself, so I could hold on to it. When it got to be all too much, I didn't bother, and was happy to find I didn't need to.

· · ·

It felt as if hours had passed in no time at all. We held each other on the dock while the moon slowly crept across the sky, completely content in each other's arms.

I wracked my brain for a way to prove to her that this was it for me, that no matter how many people came and went or whatever hardships we would face I wasn't ever letting her go. I thought of my dad. He used to bring my mom flowers and give her gifts all the time. I remembered the way her eyes would light up, as if she couldn't believe he'd thought about her, still. My heart suddenly ached, wondering if, wherever they were now, were they still showing each other love? Were they able to?

I shook the thought away. They'd given up their freedom

so I could have mine, and what they would want was for me to be happy. So I took a cue from dear old Dad. I would give something to Mackenzie.

Starting tomorrow, I would build us a cabin. If I did that and worked on the place for Aaron's family at the same time, it would take the better part of a year. Mackenzie would be eighteen by then, and I'd be nineteen. By our standards, no one would say that was too young for us to live together, to consider ourselves a family.

I could even build our place by the lake. She really liked it here. I was so excited thinking about it, I nearly told her right then. But I decided not to. It would be better if I had something to show her, like a foundation or the cornerstone or something.

With a plan in mind, I felt peaceful, and settled into Mackenzie, and then slept like I did when I was a kid, like I did when I knew I was loved.

• • •

Letting Dylan go was almost impossible. I wanted to stay curled up with him until the sun came up. But then everyone would know and for now, I was happy to have a secret. At about four, we said our goodbyes and crept back to our cabins. I watched him walk away until I couldn't see him anymore. He had this mischievous look on his face when we kissed goodbye, and I wondered exactly what he was planning.

I was so lost in thought, I didn't even notice Monica sitting outside our cabin until she spoke.

"Let me tell you why you're making a huge mistake," she said.

I leapt back in surprise. "What are you doing here?"

"You can't stay here forever, you know. Dylan might be too gaga to tell you, but they're looking for you back home."

"What?"

"They're looking for you. Your picture was everywhere, honey. It's only a matter of time before they find us." She was looking at me with fire in her eyes. "You know what will happen then, don't you? It's not like they'll just let us rejoin society. We'll all be in jail. It wouldn't surprise me if Dylan and Jesse got the worst of it, since they'd be considered our leaders."

I shook my head. "No one could possibly find us." Even I had no idea where I was. I knew we were on the other side of a thin, high spike of rock, something like a mountain. I knew that the rocks gave way and led into the clearing. But I had no idea how to get out or how to find my way back to town. This place was incredibly well hidden.

"Oh, they'll figure it out sooner or later," she sighed. "The little ones will be given away to respectable families. Can you imagine if the Dodsons had their twins taken away? What that would do to them?"

Something in my chest split. Mrs. Dodson fretted over her babies. It seemed to be her whole life, chasing them around. She was never upset when they got dirty and she never complained about exhaustion, though I know she had to feel it. She just reveled in the joy of being a mother.

"Monica, that would never happen," I said, gasping in a broken breath as a tear escaped down my cheek.

She stood and walked over to me. "You can't promise that. Your father's the mayor. You think he's giving up on you? It's been a month now. You have to imagine they're getting close."

"I can't just leave," I whispered. "I know you're upset, but I love—"

"You actually think you love him?" she spat. "You've never felt anything at all until a few weeks ago, and now you think you know what love is?"

I knew she could be lying, trying to manipulate me, but I didn't think she was. How could I know for sure this was love? She'd spent years here, and she seemed to know better. And I was sure that, given how powerful my father was, I would be a priority. If Monica was right and they'd been looking all this time, surely they'd be very close to finding us.

"What do you want me to do?" I asked.

A hint of a smile played around her mouth, never truly surfacing. She pulled out a sash of cloth from her back pocket. "Come with me."

• • •

I found out last. I'd skipped breakfast and went straight to the workshop so I could saw boards and missed everything.

Andrew was the one who told me what he'd heard someone say that someone else had said. Apparently, it was all too much for Mackenzie. She couldn't handle everything she was feeling, and the emotions overwhelmed her. It was to the point that she begged Monica to get her out of here in the wee hours of the morning.

Monica was said to be feeling awful about it but that she hadn't known what else to do. Mackenzie was a mess, she said.

So, just like that, it was over. In a matter of hours, I'd lost the only thing that had made this place really, finally feel like home. Andrew left to do his work, and I stared at the planks of wood.

In about half the time it took me to turn the raw materials into beautiful, steady boards I rendered them to kindling.

• • •

"So you're saying you have no clue as to your kidnapper's whereabouts?" the officer asked me again.

"None, I'm afraid." I tried to speak dully, the way they expected me to.

"So your kidnapper was a lone Outsider?" he clarified.

"Yes, he took me and kept me in a tent. I think he was planning on asking for a ransom. He never seemed to get around to it. Then he just brought me back. He didn't seem to be a very good criminal," I said with a light giggle.

The officer smiled. "Apparently. And he didn't harm you at all, you say?"

"No. Like I said, I think he wanted to keep me healthy so he could ransom me. He had stolen a lot of our food and kept me fed and warm. He didn't hurt me at all."

The relief on my father's face was unmistakable. It was clear he'd feared the worst. I just couldn't get over the fact that he feared. When I returned, I'd planned to go and hide in my room until sunup. But Dad had been in the kitchen, looking at pictures of me and crying.

At first, I was shocked. Then I was angry. He'd been spared. He'd been allowed to feel all this time, and he'd kept me in the dark. Over the course of the morning, I recalled a detail that seemed obvious to me now.

Dad and I had separate food. He even went so far as to mark and count his, making sure they never got mixed up. Unless you were above the haze, you'd never think to question it.

The officer flipped his notebook closed. "Well, it looks like this was an isolated attack. Considering what a poor job he did, I don't think he'll be back."

I wanted to cry because I was sure that was true. Dylan wouldn't know why I left, and there'd be no way he'd risk visiting me. And I couldn't find him if I wanted to. I'd never see him again.

"Do you think we could install some locks? I know it's almost unheard of anymore, but perhaps city officials should have some," my father suggested.

"I'll look into it, sir. You certainly have a good reason," the officer replied. "Well, young lady, if you think of anything else, don't hesitate to call."

"Thank you, officer," I said as he left, closing the door behind him.

Once he and my dad were gone, I turned and looked at my tray of food. It was lunchtime, and I was expected to eat. And maybe it would be a good thing. Wouldn't it be nice to stop feeling like this? To numb the throbbing emptiness in my chest?

I picked up a spoonful of the syrupy fruit cocktail. What would it be like to go back to how I'd been? I could let go of Dylan, and it might not even hurt. But it would also mean that I wouldn't think of my mother, wouldn't notice smells and light, wouldn't think clearly.

I considered the food again. Because I could. I could think about what it would mean if I didn't eat it. And that alone was enough to make me push the tray away.

• • •

I basically spent every waking moment wondering one thing: Would being numb be better than feeling this way? Would a hazy feeling for Mackenzie be better than how pointless it felt to live without her?

I took out the poster I'd stolen from town. I stared at it. And I wondered.

• • •

It had to come sooner or later. I had to eat, and I was surprised what I found once I did. The edges of what I felt were softer for sure, but I could still feel. I could only assume that being aware of the opiates changed your perspective, that fighting it actually meant something.

I wanted to tell someone this, but who was there to tell?

I was glad I could hold on to my thoughts because, after thinking it through, I decided I was happy to miss Dylan. The same way I was happy to miss my mom. I let myself ache for him, because the hurt made it real. When I was alone, I let myself cry. I let myself be alive.

But I didn't let my heartbreak consume me. I had work to do. It was lucky we didn't bother with locks anymore. It made it almost too easy to break into my dad's study. There were three massive filing cabinets in the room, not to mention the organized boxes on the shelves, but I knew I'd find something here. It would take weeks, maybe a whole year if I was unlucky. But that didn't matter.

I was awake now. I had to look.

• • •

"Dylan, you've gotta snap out of it, man. You've been moping for weeks." Jesse was, for all intents and purposes, my dad. It was only a matter of time before he gave me this little talk.

"I can't help it," I said, feeling sick again. "I miss her so much, I can barely breathe."

"She wanted to go, Dylan. You have to accept that. Now

you only have two choices, you can get over her or you can go after her, and there's no way you could live out there."

"Why not?" I asked. Didn't he think I was strong enough to find alternate food on my own? Hell, half the food we grew here only happened because my parents taught me how.

"Okay, maybe that's not what I mean."

"Then what do you mean?" I asked, exhausted. I was so worn down I didn't have time for games.

"I mean, I couldn't stand it if you left," Jesse confessed. I looked up at him, and his usually stern eyes were full of sadness. "You know I hate it that you have to live without someone you love, but you don't know how much you mean to me. I don't know if I could survive without you."

I fidgeted in my seat. It was humbling.

"You know you're like a son to me. The way you miss your parents? That's how I'd miss you. And there's more than that. We all need you," he said, motioning to the window. "Those people out there are free because of you. You support us more than anyone."

"You'd manage without me," I objected.

"We'd manage, you're right. But we thrive with you here."

Jesse looked at me so fiercely, and I knew that there was no way I could just walk away from him or this place.

I'd lost the girl I loved but, apparently, I'd had a family all along.

• • •

I found myself thinking of Dylan at the most random times, and that was one of my favorite things. I loved that my mind wandered and held on to him and brought him back to me in the middle of washing my hair or folding a shirt.

I'd smile to myself, fix his face in my mind, and go on to the next task. And right now, the task was one that left me both elated and terrified.

I'd found it. I'd looked in the hardest to reach places first, and in the very back of the highest drawer in the corner of my dad's study was a collection of papers updating this year's quantity of opiate per pound of food. Following it were suggestions for things to keep the masses moving forward. Mandatory after-school events, daily workout schedules, and a stronger push on the new dating program were the most popular among them. Lists of things for the walking dead to do.

I went to the library, where I could use the copier in a back corner of the basement. It was working overtime. I'd made a few hundred copies of the most incriminating page, pausing only for a moment to wonder if I was doing the right thing. But I decided that, if I'd had the choice of knowing or not, I'd choose to know. Monica chose that. Aaron did, Tanya did. It just seemed like knowing at least gave you options.

I knew I was risking jail. If they figured out who leaked this information I'd be in prison, numbed beyond reason. Or worse, I'd be dead. But I'd figured out a solid plan—including distributing the information at night, and suggesting that perhaps my old kidnapper returned—and I figured that between those two things and the classic playing dumb, I'd be safe. I didn't care if I wasn't.

I'd been in love, and I knew it now. Dylan's absence only made me sure of what I'd already known and what Monica didn't believe I'd be able to know. Dylan was it for me. If I couldn't have him, who else would I share my life with? I might as well spend it with inmates.

I couldn't fit all the copies in my backpack and had to

carry an inch-high stack in my arms as I walked home. My mind took me to a time when we'd all gone swimming. I remembered Dylan swimming under the water and grabbing at my ankles, making me squeal. A small smile crept onto my face and stayed with me as I turned the corner to my house. I was so deep in my memories that I didn't notice the guest on my doorstep.

I looked up and saw a boy with blue-green eyes waiting for me. My heart leapt in my chest, and I was sure he could see just how happy I was to see him.

I swallowed and stared at him and, even though it was risky to do outside, I quietly started to cry.

He stood and walked to me. "You can still feel?" he asked, astonished.

I nodded. "Very much."

I took my free hand and slid it into his. The tiny gesture was enough to make my heart beat fast. When I felt him squeeze it back, I knew it wasn't just me.

"I thought you might not even care I was here," he confessed.

"Of course I care," I whispered intensely. "If I was under a pile of drugs, I'd care. Dylan, I didn't want to leave. Monica said that I had to. They were looking for me. And you should go before someone sees you. I couldn't bear them taking you away."

A look of confusion crossed over his face and then faded into absolute clarity. "Monica," he said. "Of course it was Monica."

As he shook his head, it dawned on me just how easily she'd fooled me. And standing in front of me was her motivation. Could I really blame her? If it had been the other way around, wouldn't I have chased her away?

That didn't matter now. If Dylan still wanted me the way I wanted him, then I couldn't let anything come between us.

"I love you," I said. "I'm so sorry I left."

He pushed his lips together, trying to keep his smile from being too big. "And I love you."

That was all I needed. Dylan loved me. I could handle whatever came next.

I sniffed back the tears and shoved the pile of papers into his hands. "That's good. Because I've got a job for you."

Otherwise

Nisi Shawl

"Let's cross it while it's still floating."

Aim was always in a hurry these days. Nearly eighteen, and she didn't figure she had a whole lot of time left before she'd go Otherwise.

"Hold up," I told her, and she listened. I listened, too, and I heard that weird noise again above the soft wind: an engine running. That was what cars sounded like; they used to fill the roads, back when I was only eleven. Some of the older models still worked—the ones built without no chips.

A steady purr, like a big, fat cat—and there, I saw a glint moving far out on the bridge: sun on a hood or windshield. I raised my binoculars and confirmed it: a pickup truck, headed our way, east, coming toward us out of Seattle.

"What, Lo?" Aim asked.

If I could see them, maybe they could see us. "Come on. Bring the rolly. I'll help." We lifted our rolling suitcase together and I led us into the bushes crowding over the road's edge. Leaves and thorns slashed at our trouser legs and sleeves and faces—I beat them away and found a kind of clear area in their middle. Maybe there used to be something, a concrete pad for trash cans or something there. Moss, black and dry from the summer, crunched as we walked over it. We lowered the suit-case, heavy with Aim's tools, and I was about to explain to her why we were hiding but by now that truck was loud and I could tell she heard it, too. All she said was, "What are they gonna think if they see our tracks disappear?"

I had a knife, and I kept it sharp. I pulled it out of the leather sheath I'd made. That was answer enough for Aim. She smiled—a nasty smile, but I loved it the way I loved everything about her: her smell; her long braids; her grimy, stubby nails.

I thought we'd lucked out when the truck barreled by fast—must have been going thirty miles an hour—but then it screeched to a stop. Two doors creaked open. Boot heels clopped on the asphalt. Getting louder. Pausing about even with where I'd ducked us off into the brush.

"Hey!" A dude. "You can come out—we ain't gonna do ya no harm."

Neither one of us moved a hair. Swearing, then thrashing noises, more swearing, louder as Truckdude crashed through the blackberries. He'll never find us, I thought, and I was right. It was his partner who snuck up on our other side, silent as a tick.

"Got 'em, Claude," he yelled, standing up from the weeds with a gun in his hand. He waved it at me and Aim and spoke in a normal tone. "You two can get up if you want. But do it slow."

He raised his voice again. "Chicas. One of 'em's kinda pretty but the other's fat," he told Claude. "You wanna arm wrestle?"

Claude stopped swearing but kept breaking branches and tearing his clothes on the brambles as he whacked his way over to us. I stayed hunkered down so they'd underestimate me, and so my knife wouldn't fall out from where I had it clamped between my thighs. I felt Aim's arm tremble against mine as Claude emerged from the shadows. She'd be fine, though. Exactly like on a salvage run. I leaned against her a second to let her know that.

The dude with the gun looked a little older than us. Not much older, of course, or he'd have already gone Otherwise, found his own pocket universe, like nearly everyone else whose brain had reached "maturity"—at least that's how the rumors went.

Claude looked my age, or a year or two younger: fourteen, fifteen. He and his partner had the same brown hair and squinty eyes; brothers, then. Probably.

I leered up at Guntoter. "You wanna watch me and her do it first?"

He spat on my upturned face. "Freak! You keep quiet till I tell you talk." The spit tickled as it ran down my cheek.

I didn't hate him. Didn't have the time; I was too busy planning my next move.

"Hey, Dwight, what you think they got in here?" Claude had found our suitcase and given me a name for Guntoter.

"Open 'er up and find out, dickhead."

I couldn't turn around to see the rolly without looking away from Dwight, which didn't seem like a good idea. I heard its zipper and the clink of steel on steel: chisels, hammers, wrenches, clamps, banging against each other as they spilled out on the ground.

"Whoa! Looky at these, Claude. You think that ugly one knows how to use this stuff?" Dwight took his eyes off us and lowered the gun like I'd been waiting for him to do. I launched myself at his legs, a two-hundred-twenty-pound dodgeball. Heard a crack as his left knee bent backward. Then a loud shot from his gun—but only one before I had my knife at his throat.

"Eennngh!" he whined. Knee must have hurt, but my blade poking against the underside of his chin kept his mouth shut.

I nodded at Aim and she relieved him of his gun. Claude had run off—I heard him thrashing through the bushes in the direction of the road. "Be right back, Lo." Aim was fine, as I'd predicted, thinking straight and acting cool. She stalked after her prey calm and careful, gun at the ready.

I rocked back on my haunches, easing off Dwight's ribs a bit. That leg had to be fractured. Problema. How was I supposed to deal with him, wounded like this? Maybe I shouldn't have hit him so hard. Not as if I could take him to a hospital. I felt him sucking in his breath, winding up for a scream, and sank my full weight on his chest again.

"Lo! You gotta come here!" Aim yelled from the road.

Come there? What? "Why? You can't handle—You didn't let him get his truck back, did—"

"Just come!" She sounded pissed.

Dwight wasn't going anywhere on his own any time soon, but just in case I tugged off his belt and boots and trousers and took away the rest of his weapons: a razor poking through a piece of wood, a folding knife with half the blade of mine, and a long leather bag filled with something heavier than sand. I only hurt him a little stripping off the jeans.

I got to my feet and looked down a second, wondering if I should shoot the man and get his misery over with. Even after years of leading salvage runs, I didn't have it in me, though.

I loaded dude's junk and Aim's spilled-out tools in the rolly and dragged it along behind me into the bushes. When he saw

I was leaving him he started hollering for help, like it might come. That worried me. I hurried out to Aim. Had Claude somehow armed himself?

Claude was nowhere in sight. Aim stood by the truck—our truck, now. She had the door open, staring inside. The gun—our gun, now—hung loose in one hand and the other stretched inside. "Come on," she said, not to me. "It's okay." She hauled her hand back with a kid attached: white with brown hair, like his brothers. They must have been his brothers—I got closer and saw he had that same squintiness going on. "Look," I said, "leave him here and climb in. If they got any back-up—"

Boom!

Shotguns make a hecka loud noise. Pellets and gravel went pinging off the road. Scared me so much I swung the rolly up into the truck bed by myself. Then I shoved Aim through the door and jumped in after her. Turned the ignition—they had left the key in it—and backed out of there fast as I could rev. Maybe forty feet along, I swung around and switched to second gear. I hit third by the time we made the bridge, jouncing over pits in the asphalt. Some sections were awful low—leaky pontoons. Next storm would sink the whole thing, Aim had said. I told myself if the thing held up on the dudes' ride over here it was gonna be fine for us heading back.

I looked to my right. Aim had pushed the kid ahead of her so he was huddled against the far door. I braked. "Okay, here you go." But he made no move to leave. "What's the matter, you think I'll shoot? Go on, we won't hurt you."

"He's shaking," Aim reported. "Bad. I think he's freaking out."

"Well, that's great. Open the door for him yourself then, and let's go."

"No."

I sighed. Aim had this stubbornness no one would suspect unless they spent a long time with her. "Listen, Aim, it was genius to keep him till I drove out of shooting range, but—"

"We can't just dump him off alone."

"He's not alone; his brothers are right behind us!"

"One of 'em with a broken leg."

"Knee." But I took her point. "So, yeah, they're not gonna be much use for making this little guy feel all better again real soon. C'est la flippin vie." I reached past her to the door handle. She looked at me and I dropped my hand in my lap. "Aw, Aim . . ."

Aim missed her family. I knew all about how they'd gone on vacation to Disney World without her when she insisted she was too old for that stuff. Their flights back got canceled, first one, then the next, and the next, till no one pretended anymore there might be another, and the phone stopped working and the last bus into Pasco unloaded and they weren't on it.

"Hector—" She couldn't say more than his name.

"Aim, he's twelve now. He's fine. Even if your—" Even if her mom and dad had deserted him like so many other parents, leaving our world to live Otherwise, where they had anything, everything, whatever they wanted, same as when they drank the drug, but now for always. Or so the rumors said. Perfect homes. Perfect jobs. Perfect daughters. Perfect sons.

"All right. Kid, you wanna come with us or stay here with— um, Claude and Dwight?"

Nothing.

I tried again. "Kid, we gotta leave. We're meeting a friend in—" In the rearview I saw five dudes on foot racing up the road. One waved a long, thin black thing over his head. That shotgun? I slammed the truck out of neutral and tore off. They dwindled in the dust.

Aim punched my shoulder and grinned at me. "You done good," she said. I looked and she had one arm around the little kid, holding him steady, so I concentrated on finding a path for the truck that included mostly even pavement.

Here came the tunnel under Mercer Island. Scary, and not only because its lights were bound to be out—I turned the truck's on and they made bright spots on the ivy hanging over the tunnel's mouth. That took care of that. Better than if we'd been on foot, even.

But richies . . . more of them had stayed around than went Otherwise. Which made sense; they had their own drugs they used instead of Likewise, and everything already perfect anyways. Or everything used to be perfect for them till too many ordinary people left and they couldn't find no one to scrub their toilets or take out their garbage. Only us.

When things got bad and the governments broke down, richies were the law, all the law around. What they wanted they got, in this world as much as any Otherwise. And what they wanted was slaves. Servants, they called us, but slaves is what it really was; who'd want to spend whatever time they had before they went Otherwise on doing stupid jobs for somebody else? Nobody who wasn't forced to.

We drove through the ivy curtain. I jabbed on the high beams and slowed to watch for nets or other signs of ambush. Which of course there were gonna be none, because hadn't this very truck come through here less than half an hour ago? But.

"Can't be too careful." Aim always knew what I was thinking.

The headlights caught on a heap of something brown and

gray spread over most of the road and I had two sets of choices: A. speed up, or B. slow down more; A. drive right over it, or B. swerve around. I picked A and A: stomped the gas pedal and held the steering wheel tight. Suddenly closer I saw legs, arms, bloated faces, smelled the stink of death. I felt the awful give beneath our tires. It was a roadblock of bodies—broken glass glittered where we would have gone if I'd tried to avoid them, and two fresh corpses splayed on the concrete, blood still wet and red. A trap, but a sprung one. Thanks, Claude. Thanks, Dwight.

The pile of rotting dead people fell behind us mercifully fast. I risked a glance at the kid. He stared straight forward like we were bringing him home from seeing a movie he had put on mental replay. Like there was nothing to see outside the truck and never had been and never would be.

"Maybe this was what freaked him out in the first place?" asked Aim. "You know, before he even got to us?" It was a theory.

We came out into the glorious light again. One more short tunnel as the road entered the city was how I remembered the route. I stopped the truck to think. When my fingers started aching I let go of the wheel.

A bird landed on a loose section of the other bridge that used to run parallel. Fall before last it had been the widest of its kind in the world, according to Aim.

She cared about those kinds of things.

The sun was fairly high yet. We'd left our camp in the mountains early this morning and come twelve mostly downhill miles before meeting up with the kid's brothers. The plan had been to cross the bridge inconspicuously, on foot, hole up in Seward Park with the Rattlers and wait for Rob to show. Well, we'd blown the inconspicuous part.

"Sure you don't wanna go back?" I asked Aim. "They'll be glad to see us. And the truck'll make it a short trip, and it's awesome salvage, too . . ." I trailed off.

"You can if you rather." But she knew the answer. I didn't have to say it. Aim was why I'd stayed in Pasco instead of claiming a place on the res, which even a mix had a right to do. Now I had come with her this far for love. And I'd go further. To the edge of the continent. All the way.

Rob had better be worth it, though. With his red hair and freckles and singing and guitar-playing Aim couldn't shut up about since we got his message. And that secret fire she said was burning inside him like a cigarette, back when they were at their arts camp. He better be worthy of *her*.

"Stop pouting." She puckered her face and crossed her eyes. "Your face will get stuck like that. Let me drive. Chevies are sweet." She handed me the gun, our only distance weapon— and I hadn't even gotten Dwight's cartridges, but too late to think of that—then slid so her warm hip pressed against mine for a moment. "Go on. Get out."

The kid didn't move when I opened the passenger door so I crawled in over him.

Aim drove like there was traffic: careful, using signals. Guess she learned it from watching her folks. The tunnel turned out clear except for a couple of crappy modern RVs no one had bothered torching yet. One still had curtains in its smashed windows, fluttering when we went by. We exited onto the main drag—Rainier Avenue, I recalled. Aim braked at the end of the ramp. "Which way?"

"South." I pointed left.

Rainier had seen some action. Weed-covered concrete rubble lined the road's edges, narrowing it to one lane. A half-burned restaurant sign advertised hotcakes. A sandbag bunker, evidently empty, guarded an intersection filled with a downed walkway. A shred of tattered camo clung to a wrecked lamppost. Must be relics of the early days; soldiers had been some of the first outside jail to head Otherwise, deserting in larger and larger numbers as real life got lousier and lousier.

"Wow. What a mess." Aim eased over a spill of bricks and stayed in low gear to rubberneck. "How're we gonna get off of this and find the park?"

"Uhhh." Would we have to dig ourselves a turnoff? No—"Here!" More sandbags, but some had tumbled down from their makeshift walls, and we only had to shove a few aside to reach a four-lane street straight to the lakeshore. We followed that around to where the first of the Rattlers' lookouts towered up like a giant birdhouse for ostriches with fifty-foot legs. A chica had already sighted us and trained her slingshot on the truck's windshield. Her companion called out and we identified ourselves enough that they let us through to the gate in their chain-link fence. Another building, this one more like the bunker on Rainier, blocked the way inside. Four Rattlers were stationed here, looking like paintball geeks gone to heaven. We satisfied them of our bona fides, too, using the sheet of crypto and half a rubber snake their runner had turned over with Rob's message. They took my knife. I didn't blame 'em. They let us keep our gun, but minus the bullets.

"What's in the back?"

I hadn't even looked after tossing up the rolly. Dumb. When the sentries opened the big metal drums, though, they found nothing but fuel in them, no one hiding till they could bust out and slit our throats.

Four of those, and the rest of the bed was filled with covered five-gallon tubs: white plastic, the high-grade kind you use to ferment beer in. And that's what was in the ten they checked.

"Welcome home," one chica maybe my age said. Grudgingly, but she said it. She walked ahead to guide us into their main camp.

Didn't take her long. A few minutes and I saw firepits, and picnic tables set together in parts of circles, tarps strung between trees over platforms, a handful of big tents. We pulled up next to their playground as the sun was barely beginning to wonder was it time to set. The chica banged on our hood twice, then nodded and scowled at us. Aim nodded too and shut off the ignition.

The kid opened the truck's passenger door. Aim and I looked at each other in silence. Then she grinned. "I guess we're there yet!"

Maybe it was the other littles on the swings and jungle gyms that got through to him. He slid to the ground and walked a few steps toward them, then stopped. I got out too and slammed the door. Didn't faze him. He was focused on the fun and games.

"What have we here?" A long-haired dude wearing a mustache and a skirt came over from watching the littles play.

Aim opened her door and got out, too. "We're a day or so early I guess—Amy Niehauser and Dolores Grant." I always tease Aim about how she ended up with such a non-Hispanic name, and she gives me grief right back about not having something made-up, like "Shaniqua" or "Running Fawn." "We're from Kiona. In Pasco?"

Dude nodded. "Sure. Since Britney was bringing you in I figured that was who you must be. I'm Curtis. We weren't expecting a vehicle, though." He waved a hand at the truck.

Britney had hopped up on the bed again while we talked, lifting the lids off the rest of the plastic tubs. "Likewise!" she shouted. "Look at this!"

Aim and I leaned up over the side to see. Britney was tearing off cover after cover. Sure enough, the five tubs furthest in were all at least three-quarters full of thick, indigo-blue liquid with specks of pale purple foam. I had never seen so much Likewise in one place.

Curtis lost his cool. "What the hell! We told you we don't allow that—that—" He didn't have the vocabulary to call the drug a bad enough name.

"No, it's not ours—we stole this truck and we didn't know—" Aim tried to calm him down. She tugged at the tub nearest the end. "Here, we'll help you pour 'em in the lake."

"You seriously think we wanna pollute our water like that?"

"Look, I'm just saying we'll get rid of it. We didn't know, we just took this truck from some dudes acting like cowboys on the other side of the bridge, the little dude's big brothers, and they had a few friends—"

That got Britney's attention. "They follow you?"

"Not real far," I said, breaking in. "Since when we took this we left 'em on foot." And they hadn't shot at us more than once—the fuel explained why. "They ain't the only trouble you got for neighbors, either—I'd be more worried about Mercer Island if I were you than them bridge dudes—or a load of Likewise we can dump anywhere you want."

"Right." Curtis seemed to quiet down and consider this. "Yeah, we'll dig a hole or something . . ."

No one had proved a connection between Likewise and all the adults talking about living Otherwise, then disappearing. No one had proved anything in a long time that I'd heard of. But the prisons where it first got made were the same ones so many "escaped" from early on, which is the only reason anyone even noticed a bunch of poor people had gone missing, IMO. News reports began about the time it was getting so popular outside, here and in a few more countries.

Some of us still cooked it up. Some of us still drank it. How long did the side-effects last? If you indulged at the age of sixteen would you vanish years later, as soon as your brain was ready? Could you even tell whether you went or not?

The ones who knew were in no position to tell us. They were Otherwise.

Britney went to report us to the committee, she said. A pair of twelve-year-olds came and showed us where to unload the fuel drums. I helped Aim lower the rolly from the bed—how had I got it up there on my own? My arms were gonna hurt bad when the adrenaline wore off—and she handed them the keys. They drove to the bunker with the Likewise for the sentries to watch over.

Aim had to head back to the playground after that. The little dude seemed thoroughly recovered: he'd thrown off his jacket and was running wild and yelling with the other kids like he belonged there.

The Rattlers' committee met with us over dinner in this ridiculous tipi they'd rigged up down by the swimming beach. Buffaloes and lightning painted on the sides. I mean, even I knew tipis were plains technology and had nothing to do with tribes in these parts. But, well, the Rattlers acted proud and solemn bringing us inside, telling us to take off our shoes and which way to circle around the fire, and damn if they didn't actually pass a real, live pipe after feeding us salads plus some beige glop that looked a lot worse than it tasted. And tortillas, which they insisted on calling frybread.

Tina, their eldest, sat on a sofa cushion; she looked maybe Aim's age, but probably she was older. Trying to show the rest of the committee how to run things when she was gone. Otherwise, she asked about folks at Kiona: who had hooked up with who, how many pregnant, any cool salvage we'd come across, any adults we'd noticed still sticking around. Aim answered her.

There were two dudes, one on either side of Tina—husbands, maybe? Rattlers were known for doing that kinda thing—and a couple younger chicas chiming in with compliments about how well we were doing for ourselves. I waited politely for them to raise the subject they wanted to talk about. Which was, as I'd figured, the five tubs of Likewise.

They decided to forgive us and opted to pour the stuff in a hole like Aim suggested.

Tina had brains. "What's interesting is that they were bringing this shipment *out* of Seattle." She stretched her legs straight, pointed her toes up and pushed toward the fire with her wool-socked heels. August, and the evenings were on the verge of chilly.

"Not like the whole city's sworn off," one of the chicas ventured to say.

"Yeah." I had the dude that agreed pegged for a husband because he wore a ring matching the one on Tina's left hand. "That crew up in Gas Works? They could be brewing big old vats of Likewise and how would we know?"

The second dude chimed in. "They sure wouldn't expect us

to barter for any." He wore a ring that matched the one on Tina's right.

The young chica who'd already spoken wondered if it was their responsibility to keep the whole of Seattle clean, suburbs, too. Husband One opined that they'd better think a while about that.

"Next question." That was Tina again. "What are those bridge boys gonna do to get their shipment back?" She looked at me, though it was Aim who started talking.

We hadn't told Claude or Dwight where we were going, or made a map for 'em or anything, so I thought the Rattlers were pretty safe. Plus I had hurt Dwight, broken at least one bone. But the committee decided the truck was a liability even if they painted it, and told us we better take it with us when we departed their territory. Which would have to be soon—

"Tomorrow?" asked Husband Two.

Aim folded her lips between her front teeth a few seconds in that worried way she had. We'd expected more of a welcome, considering her skills. Kinda hoped she'd be able to set up a forge here for at least a week. Were the Rattlers gonna make us miss her date with Rob? But according to the committee's spies he was close, already landed on this side of the Sound and heading south. He'd arrive any minute now. So we could keep our rendezvous.

Dammit.

Then I finally got to find out more on where all those corpses in the tunnel came from.

Richies, as I'd suspected. Didn't seem like the committee wanted to go further into it, though. The dead people were who? People the richies had killed. How? Didn't know. Didn't think it mattered; dead was dead. And why were they stacked up on the road all unhygienic-like instead of properly buried? Have to send a detail to take care of that. And the two fresh ones? Tina said she figured the way I did that they were fallout from Claude and Dwight's trip through the blockade.

So why? Well, that was obvious, too: use the dead ones as bait to catch us, alive, to work for 'em.

It became more obvious when Curtis took us to where we were supposed to sleep: a tree house far up the central hill of the park's peninsula. He climbed the rope ladder ahead of us and showed us the pisspot, the water bucket and dipper, the bell to ring if one of us suddenly took violently ill in the night. Then he wanted to know if we'd seen his little sister's body in the pile.

"Uh, no, we kinda—we had to go fast, didn't see much. Really." Aim could tell a great lie.

"She had nice hair, in ponytails. And big, light-green eyes."

Anybody's eyes that had been open in that pile, they weren't a color you'd recognize anymore. Mostly they were gone. Along with big chunks of face. "No, we, uh, we had to get out of there too fast. Really didn't see. Sorry."

He left us alone at last.

Alone as we were going to get—there were a lot of other tree houses nearby; dusk was settling in fast but we could see people moving up their own ladders, hear 'em talking soft and quiet.

"Lie down." I patted the floor mat. She came into my arms. I had her body, no problema. I did hurt from heaving the rolly around, but that didn't matter much. I stroked her hair back from her pretty face that I knew even in the dark.

"What'd they do with Dwayne?"

"Who?"

"Dwayne, you know, the little dude?"

Right: Claude and Dwight's kid brother. "That what you wanna call him?"

Aim snorted. "It's his *name*. He told Curtis. I heard him."

My fingers wandered down to the arches of her eyebrows, smoothing them flat. "You worried about him? He looked happy on the playground. They must have places for kids to sleep here. We seen plenty of 'em."

"Yeah. You're right." The skin above her nose crinkled. I traced her profile, trying to give her something else to think of. It sort of worked.

"Why don't the committee care more about the Mercer Island richies? That was—horrible. In the tunnel."

I laughed, though it wasn't the littlest bit funny. "Fail. Mega Fail—they were supposed to be protecting these people here and the richies raided 'em. I wouldn't wanna talk about it either."

I felt her forehead relax. "Yeah." She reached up and tugged my scarf free so she could run her hands over my close-clipped scalp. That was more like it. I snuggled my head against the denim of her coat.

That was our last night together as a couple.

She only mentioned Rob once.

• • •

Next morning my arm felt even sorer. And my shoulder had turned stiff. And my wrist. Was getting old like this? No wonder people went Otherwise.

Aim and I woke up at the same time, same as at home and on salvage runs. "Good dreams?" I asked. She nodded and gave me a sheepish half-smile, so I didn't have to ask who she'd dreamed about. It wasn't me.

106

What kind of universe would Aim make if she went Otherwise? It wouldn't be the same as mine.

Curtis had pointed out a latrine on the way to our tree house. We dumped the pisspot there and took care of our other morning needs. It was a nice latrine, with soap and a bowl of water.

Down we went, following the trail to the main camp. Aim held my hand when we could walk side by side. Sweet moments. I knew I better treasure 'em.

I helped set out breakfast, which was berries and bars of what appeared to be last night's beige glop, fossilized. Aim retrieved the rolly from where we'd left it under a supply tarp. She cleaned the gun, which she called Walter, and shined up her tools. Soon enough she attracted a clientele.

First come a dude could have been fourteen or fifteen; he wanted her to help him fix up an underwater trap for turtles and crayfish. Then he had a friend a little older who asked her to help him take apart a motor to power his boat. Actually, he had taken it apart already, and wanted her to put it together again with him.

Aim called a break for herself after a couple hours of this so she could go check out how Dwayne was doing. And she wanted to bring him a plum from the ones I'd collected for snacks. I waited by the tools for her to come back. A shadow cut the warm sun and I looked up from the dropcloth.

"Hey." A dude's voice. All I could see was a silhouette. Like an eclipse—a gold rim around darkness.

"Hey back."

"You're not Amy."

"Nope."

He sat down fast, folding his legs. "Must be Dolores, then? I'm Rob." He held out a hand to shake, so I took it.

Now I could see him, dude was every bit as pretty as Aim had said. Dammit. Hair like new copper, tied back smooth and bright and loose below a wide-brimmed straw fedora. Eyes large, a strange, pale blue. Freckles like cinnamon all over his snub-nosed face and his long arms where they poked out of the black-and-white print shirt he wore. But not on his throat, which was smooth as vanilla ice cream and made me want to—no. This was Aim's crush.

His hand was a little damp around the palm. Fingers long and strong. I let it go. "Aim's around here somewhere; she'll be back in a minute, I think, if you wanna wait."

"Sure." He had a tiny little stick, a twig, in the corner of his mouth. His lips were pink, not real thin for a white boy. Dammit.

"Where's your guitar?" I asked.

"Left it back home, at the bunkers. The Herons'll take care of it for me; too much to travel with. But I packed my penny-whistle." He swapped the stick for something longer, shiny black and silver. He played a sad-sounding song, mostly slow, with some fast parts where one line ended and the next began. Then he speeded up, did a new, sort of jazzy tune. Then another, and I recognized it: "Firework."

Aim recognized it, too. Or him, anyway—she came running up behind me shouting his name: "Rob! Rob!" She hauled him up with a hug. "I'm so glad! So glad!" He hugged her back. They both laughed and leaned away enough to look each other in the eyes.

"Oh, wow—" "Did you—" They started and stopped talking at the same time. Cute.

Dwayne had showed up in Aim's wake. He stood to one side, hands in his front pockets, looking about as awkward as I felt.

Rob and Aim let go of each others' arms. "Who's this?" he asked her, bending his knees to put his face on the kid's level.

"I'm Dwayne. I come all the way from Issaquah." Which was nine times more words than I'd ever heard him use before. Maybe he liked white dudes.

"That's pretty far. But I met somebody came even further."

"Who're you?"

"I'm Rob. I live in Fort Worden, other side of the Sound."

"Issaquah is twenty-two miles from Seattle."

"Well, this chica I'm talking about sailed to Fort Worden over the ocean from Liloan. That's in the Philippines. Six thousand miles."

"She did not!"

"I'm telling you."

Here came Curtis over from the playground. He said hey and dragged Dwayne back with him with the promise of a swim, "—so you can get packed quick."

The Rattlers wanted us gone yesterday. While Rob met with their committee to tell them the news out of Liloan—how the Philippines had been mostly missed by the EMPs and other tech-killers thrown around in the first mass panic—Aim loaded her tools in the rolly, and I went to find the truck. At the fuel shed they directed me up the remains of a service road. The twelve-year-olds had parked at the end of it; they were just through filling in the hole they'd dug, tamping down dirt with a couple of shovels. The empty Likewise tubs lay on their sides in the dead pine needles.

"Thanks," I said. "We were gonna do that."

"'S'all right," the bigger one said. "Didn't take long."

"Yes, it did." Her friend wasn't about to lie. "But we're done, now, and nobody drunk it."

"Have you ever—" The smaller girl smacked the bigger one on her head. "Stop! I was only asking!" She turned to me again. "You ever taken any Likewise yourself?"

Once. A single dose was low risk—I'd heard of adults with the same history as me, twenty-four, twenty-five, and still not Otherwise.

"Tastes like dog slobber," I told her. "Like spit bugs crapped in a bottle of glue."

"Eeuuw!" They made faces and giggled. I thought about the questions they didn't ask as they brought me back down in the truck. About how Likewise felt, what happened when I had it in me.

You could call it a dream. In it, my mom had never hit me and my dad had never got stoned. I was living in a house with Aim. The drug was specific: a yellow house with white trim, a picket fence. We had a dog named Quincy Jones and a parakeet named Sam. The governments were still running everything. We had a kid and jobs we went to. I remember falling asleep and waking up and getting maybe a little bored at work, but basically being happy. So happy.

Seemed like that dream went on for years. I was out for eight hours.

• • •

We could have driven all the way to Fort Worden, only Aim wanted to see the Space Needle. "C'mon, when are we gonna have another chance?"

I rolled my eyes. "You can *see* it from freakin *anywhere*, Aim. Ask *them* if *they* see it." I pointed up at the chicas in the fifty-foot-high lookout.

"Okay. Touch it then. I mean touch it."

Our first fight.

Of course Rob took her side. "Yeah, the truck; tough to let it go, but there's no connections for us in Tacoma. Olympia either; can't say who or what we might run into going south. I told the captain up at Edmonds I'd be back in a week. Maybe he can stow it for us? And even if we're early that's our best bet. North. So the Space Needle's not much of a detour."

Aim looked at me. "*All flippin right!*" I said.

I drove again. Aim took the middle seat, but it wasn't me she pressed up against.

Rattlers had told us where to avoid, and I did my best. From Rainier I had to guess the route, and sometimes I guessed wrong. And sometimes my guesses would have been good if the roads didn't have huge holes in 'em or obstacles too hard to move out of our way. We didn't see anyone else, only signs they'd been around: coiled up wires, stacks of wood—not a surprise, since anyone on a scavenge run would have lookouts. Groups had mainly settled in parks where you could grow crops, and we weren't trying to cross those.

We reached Seattle Center late. No time to find anywhere else to spend the night.

There'd been action here, too. I remembered the news stories, though they hadn't made any sense. Not then, and not now—why would anyone fight over such a place, so far off from any water? But tanks had crawled their way on to the grounds, smashing trees and sculptures, shooting fire and smoke back and forth. They left scars we could still see: burned-out buildings, craters, bullet holes.

The Space Needle stood in the middle of about an acre of blackberries covering torn-up concrete—what used to be a plaza. Old black soot and orange rust marked the Needle's once-white legs. I tooled us under a pair of concrete pillars for the dead Monorail and backed in as close as I could get without slicing open a tire. "There you go," I said. "Touch it." Which was a little mean, I admit.

Rob climbed out the window without opening the door and got up on the truck cab's roof. He stuck his arm in and hauled Aim after him. I heard the two of 'em talking about chopping a path through the thorns if they'd had swords, and how to forge them, and a trick Aim knew called "damascening." Aim recited her facts about how high the thing was, how long it took to erect, et cetera.

Then I didn't hear anything for a while. Then her breath. I turned on the radio, like there'd be something more than static to cover up the sounds they were going to make.

One of them shifted and the metal above my head popped in and out. That gave me courage to hit the horn—a short blast like it was an accident—and open the door. Very, very slowly.

Shin deep in brambles I unhooked from my trousers one by one, I took a blanket from the boxes of supplies the Rattlers sent us off with. Then I couldn't help myself; I looked. They both had all their clothes on and were sitting up. For the moment. Aim waved. Rob pretended to stroke a beard he didn't have and smiled.

"In a minute," I said, meaning I'd come back. Eventually. Give me strength, I thought, and I smiled, too, and waded carefully along the trail the truck had smashed.

She wanted to be with him. I loved her anyhow. To the edge of the continent. All the way.

I would follow her.

But tonight I would sleep alone.

• • •

At least that was the plan. When it came down to it, though, I didn't dare rest my eyes. Dark was falling. The place was too open—bad juju. I had a feeling, once I got out from under my jealousy. So I found a trash barrel, rolled it up a ramp in the side of some place looked like a giant scorched wad of metal gum. I set the barrel upright, climbed and balanced on its rim, and scrabbled from there to lie on my stomach on a low roof—must have been the only flat surface to the whole building, even before the howitzers and grenade-launchers and whatever else attacked it.

Me and Walter settled in to keep watch. The Rattlers had returned his magazine when they gave me back my knife, and there were seven rounds left.

Aim and Rob were maybe fifty feet south. I still heard 'em clear enough to keep me awake till Claude and his friends showed up.

Trying to be smart, the bridge dudes turned off the headlights of whatever vehicle they drove blocks away. The engine's noise was a clue, and its silence was another. Insects went quiet to my east in case I needed a third.

Starlight's not the best to see by. I couldn't really count 'em—four or five dudes it must be, I figured, same as yesterday. They zeroed in on Aim and Rob, who were talking again.

"Hands up!" a dude commanded. How were they gonna tell, I wondered, but one of 'em opened the truck door and the courtesy light came on. There was Aim and Rob, a bit tousled up. Too bad I didn't want to shoot *them*. Couldn't get a line on anyone else.

"Get your sorry asses outta me and Dwight's—outta my truck." That would be Claude.

"Daddy? Where's Daddy?" And that would be that kid Dwayne? His age was all wrong for Dwight to be his dad, but who else was it rising out of from that supply box, pale-faced in the yellow courtesy light?

The kid must have stowed away. He held out his arms and kicked free of something and Claude stepped up to grab and lift him and now I had a great shot. Couldn't have been better. But I didn't take it.

Next minute I wished I had when dudes on either side yanked Aim and Rob out of opposite doors. I heard her yell at them and get slapped.

Someone else was yelling, too—not me, I was busy shimmying off the roof while there was cover for my noise. "No! Don't hit her! No! Put me down!" Little Dwayne was on our side?

Brightness. Someone had switched on the truck's headlights. I ducked down. Aim was crying hard. They shoved her to the pavement. I hadn't heard a peep outta Rob. When they marched him into the light I saw one dude's hand over his mouth and a shiny piece of metal right below his ear. Knife or a gun—didn't matter which. Woulda kept me quiet, too.

Only four of 'em. Plus Dwayne. Seven bullets seemed plenty—if I didn't mind losing Rob.

I didn't. But Aim would.

Bang! Bang! Walter wasn't quite loud as a shotgun. Glass and metal pinged off the pavement, flew away into the sudden dark. Only one round each for the truck's headlamps. I was proud of myself.

Light still came out of the cab from the overhead courtesy. Not much. I couldn't see anybody.

But I could hear 'em shouting to each other to find the

chica, and shooting. Randomly, I hoped. No screams, so Rob had probably got away all right.

I shifted position, which made the next part trickier, but would keep the dudes guessing where to kill me. I went round to one side, with the frame of the open driver's door blocking my vision. Walter stayed steady—I gripped him with both hands and squeezed. Got it in one. I was good. Total night, now. I squirmed off on my belly for a ways to be sure no one had a flashlight, then crawled, then stumbled to my feet and walked. Headed north by the stars, with nothing on me but Walter, my knife, my binoculars. A blanket. Not even a bottle for water.

It was a shame to leave all the provisions the Rattlers had given us. And too bad I had to damage a high-functioning machine like that truck. Aim would cuss me out for it when we caught up with one another at Edmonds.

Aim would be fine. She always was. Rob, too, most likely.

• • •

It took the rest of that night and part of a day to walk there. It was easy: 99 most of the way. The stars were enough to see that by, and the Aurora Bridge was practically intact. I wondered what facts Aim would have told me about it if we were going over it together. All I knew was people used to kill themselves here by jumping off. Kids? Didn't we used to have the highest rates of suicide?

If Aim didn't show up at Edmonds in a few days maybe I'd come back. Or find some Likewise.

I snuck in the dark past where they used to have a zoo, worried I might run into some weird predator. I didn't. When the animals got out they must've headed for the lake on the road's other side.

The sky got lighter and I began to look for pursuit as well as listening for it. Nobody came. The stores and restaurants lining the highway would have been scavenged out long ago. I was alone.

No Aim in sight.

Rain started to fall. I hung the blanket over my head like the Virgin Mary. Because of the clouds it was hard to tell time, but I figured I turned on to 104 a couple of hours after sunrise.

I went down a long slope to the water. Rob had said if we got split up to meet by a statue of sea lions on the beach.

This was my first time to be at the ocean. It was big, but I could see land out in its middle. Looked like I could just swim there.

Route 104 continued right on into the water. The statue was supposed to be to its south. The sand moved, soft and tiresome under my wet chucks. I spotted a clump of kids digging for something further toward the water, five or six of 'em. They didn't try to stop me and I kept on without asking directions. A couple of 'em had slings out, but I must not have seemed too threatening; neither chica pointed 'em my way.

A metal seal humped up some stairs to a patch of green. Was this the place? I climbed up beside it. At the top, a garden. I could tell it was a garden since it wasn't blackberries, though I had no idea what these plants were. But they grew in circles and lines, real patterns. And more metal seal sculptures—okay, sea lions—stuck out from between them.

Definitely. I was here. I curled up in the statue's shelter and the rain stopped. I fell asleep.

A whisper woke me. "Lo!" My heart revved. Aim? Eyes open, all I saw was Rob.

"You can't call me that."

"Sorry. Didn't want you to shoot me."

I sat up straight and realized I had Walter in my hand. Falling asleep hadn't been so stupid after all.

Rob's ice-cream throat had a red, inch-long slice on one side, so it had been a knife the bridge dude held there. He seemed fine besides that. "Is she around?" he asked. "She and you came together?" I shook my head and he folded up his legs and sat down beside me. Too close. I scooted over.

We didn't say anything for a long time. Could have been an hour. I was thirsty. And hungry. I wondered if maybe I ought to eat from the garden.

Rob held out his water bottle for me and I took it and drank. When I gave it back he didn't even wipe the mouth off.

The clouds pulled themselves apart and let this beautiful golden orange light streak through. The sun was going down. I'd slept the whole afternoon.

"Look," said Rob. "Look. I know you and Aim—"

"You can't call her that."

"Yes, I can! Listen. Look. You were with her before me and I don't want to—to mess with that."

As if he hadn't. "And?"

"And—and we were talking."

Among other things.

"And she was saying if we got married—if she got married she would want to marry *both* of us."

I stared at him hard to make sure he was serious. Me and Aim had teased each other about being married ever since we met in gym class. Even before people over eighteen or so began going Otherwise.

Apparently I wasn't the only one it was more than a joke for.

"So would you?"

"Would I what?" But I knew.

"Would you freakin marry me! Would you—"

"But I'm a lesbian! You're a dude!"

"Well, duh."

"And only because you wanna hook up with *my* chica? Unh-unh."

"Well, it's not only that."

"Really?" I stood up. He did too. "What? You're in love with me? I'm fat, I'm a big mouth, a smartass—"

"You're plain old smart! And brave, and Aim thinks you're the closest thing to a goddess who ever walked the earth."

"What if I am?" I wanted to leave. But this was where she would come. I had to be here. I wrapped the blanket around me and tucked my arms tight.

"Yeah. What if you are? What if she's right? I kinda think—" He quit talking a minute and looked over his shoulder at the beach. "I kinda think she is. You are."

If he had tried to touch me then I would have knocked the fool unconscious.

Instead, he turned around and looked at the beach again. "That's him," he said. "Captain Lee." He pointed and I saw a bright yellow triangle sailing toward us out of the west. "Our ride's here ahead of time. I have to go meet him and tell him we need to wait for Aim." He left me alone with my wet blanket.

It was almost dark by the time he came back, carrying a bucket. "Here you go. Supper." I was ready to eat, no doubt. Inside was a hot baked yam and some greens with greasy pink fish mixed in. I washed it all down with more of Rob's water.

We took turns hanging out at the statue. Rob had

connections with the locals, the Hammerheads and this other group, the Twisters. He stayed with them, and I bunked on Lee's boat.

Three days dragged past. I got used to a certain idea. I let him put his arm around me once when we met on the stairs. And another time when he introduced me to a dude he brought to pick some herbs in the garden—they were for medicines, not that nice to eat.

And another time. We were there together, but with my binoculars I saw her first. I shouted and he hugged me. Both arms. I broke away and ran and ran and yes, it was Aim! And Dwayne, which explained a lot when I thought about it afterwards, but I didn't care right then.

"Aim! Aim!" I lifted her in the air and whirled us around and we kissed each other long and hard. I was with her and it was this reality, hers and mine and everybody else's, not one I created just for me. I cried and laughed and yelled at the blue sky, so glad. Oh so freakin glad.

Of course I had known all along she'd make it.

And then Rob caught up with me and he kissed her, too. She held my hand the whole time. So how could I feel jealous and left out?

Well, I could. But that might change, someday. Someday, it might be otherwise.

Now Purple with Love's Wound

CARRIE VAUGHN

Like the dozen other girls taking part in the Claiming, Elspa wore a simple gown of undyed wool, and a hood covering her face. They were all guided into the dusty space outside the fortress wall. The hoods confused some people. Some thought they were to make the girls anonymous—to make the Claiming fair, so that the boys couldn't choose based solely on the color of her hair or the fineness of her face. But they were wrong. The hoods were for the girls, so they would not see who claimed them until exactly the right moment.

A gray-cloaked minister walked with each girl. The ministers supervized the Claiming of the Nymphs from first to last. From identifying Nymphs—girls who have had a monthly bleeding for a full year, and who therefore had a good chance of being fertile—to choosing which boys among the sons of the chieftains deserved to claim a wife. Townships sometimes went to war over Nymphs, who some said were more valuable than oil. Once a year, all the townships under the Warlord's rule gathered in the city, the large collection of shacks surrounding the adobe fortress, to watch the Claiming.

To be a Nymph waiting to be claimed was a very great honor.

When the minister guiding Elspa squeezed her arm, she stopped. She could sense the girl in front of her, and the girl behind, shuffling to a stop as well. The murmuring hum of a crowd passed over them, hundreds, maybe thousands come to watch, sitting in bleachers around the dirt field where the girls now stood.

Elspa's heart raced, and sweat curled down her skin under her straight woolen dress. She trembled, and wondered if the crowd could see it.

The Claiming happened every year, but this year was different. Special. This was the year the Warlord's eldest son would make his choice. No doubt many of the girls hoped he would claim them. Would he claim *her*? Not that it mattered who claimed any of them, it all turned out the same.

The crowd hushed—the silence came abruptly, as if someone had snuffed out a candle. The arena became so quiet Elspa could hear footsteps in the dirt—distant, but coming closer. The line of boys, entering the arena. They would not be wearing hoods.

The boys had already made their choices. From behind shadowed curtains made of gauze, they had watched the girls at a morning feast held in the merchants' hall. They'd already seen all the girls, and their faces. They knew which villages and families they came from, and had received advice from their fathers about which alliances would be beneficial.

The girls told stories about how in some past years a Nymph or three had tried to sneak away, to catch a glimpse of the boys, to get some hint of what was waiting for them on the day of Claiming. The stories never ended well; the girls always came to some horrific end, shot by guards who thought them thieves, or banished from civilization for their arrogance. Elspa had no desire to cause any trouble at all. This was an honor, being named a Nymph, taking part in the Claiming. An honor that felt as if it were an execution. The air inside the hood was hot, and she had a hard time catching her breath. If the hood did not come off soon, she might faint, and then no one would claim her.

It happened quickly, so that she was never sure afterward the exact sequence of events, or how she felt. Footsteps continued, then stopped, and a nervous voice in front of her said, "I claim her."

The minister at her side grabbed her, tilted her head to the side, and jabbed a needle into the base of her neck. She didn't have time to struggle, only to brace her legs to keep from falling over. Her hands flung out to grab at nothing.

The serum entered her, and warmth flowed through her, turning her muscles to butter, her bones to wool. Her nose filled with a sudden smell of lavender and strawberries. Somehow, she stayed upright, but marveled at her own sudden happiness. She had never felt such contentment, such *love*–

The hood came off, the minister stepped away. Everyone stepped away, except for the boy standing in front of her.

She could have stared at him for days. Forever. She studied him: the fall of black hair over his sun-darkened brow, his mahogany-brown eyes that shone with depth, with somber courage. He was taller than she by just an inch, but he seemed to fill the sky. If she could be permitted to touch him, to simply brush her fingertips along the back of his hand, she would die happy, in ecstasy. Her belly clenched thinking of it, and that thick warmth rushed through her again. She could feel her cheeks burning.

The Warlord's son, Thom, had claimed her, and she loved him, so much.

He took her right hand, lifted it, squeezed it, and her breath caught. She was drowning on the air itself, unable to open her lungs. She wanted to fall into his arms. She could hardly think. She clung to his hand, her hot skin against his cool.

He led her forward, away from the line of girls, as one of the other boys said, "I claim her," and another minister injected another girl with the serum that would bind her to her fate forever.

• • •

She could not stop looking at him.

His family—the Warlord's family, she had to remind herself, rulers of all townships within a thousand miles—held a feast for them. Elspa's family was well off—her father had the region's largest flock of sheep and produced the wool that everyone in the fortress wore—but she had never seen so many delicacies, or drunk such fine wine. The Warlord took all the best for himself as the price of maintaining order, everyone knew that. But until now she'd had no idea what that meant.

She was part of that wealth, now. Thom had chosen her not just to bind her prosperous family to his, but because she was an ornament. Draped in red silk and gold jewels, she sat beside him at the high table, sparkling like treasure given as tribute. She was a figurehead to be admired. The finest Nymph in all the land.

But she didn't care about any of that. Matters like statutes and politics were for the men and soldiers to worry about. She only cared about *him*.

He wore a jacket made of the same fabric as her gown, bound with a belt of linked gold plates. Leaning back in his chair, one hand resting on his knee, the other on the table, he had a serious, regal expression, eyes steady, lips frowning. He was a prince surveying his domain.

The feast wasn't for them, it was for the Warlord and his followers, for his feudal servants and the community at large—for everyone to see that continuity would be maintained, that the day's ritual had been successful, that the young heir had chosen well, and that his bride truly loved him. Seeing all that, they grew loud, drunk, rowdy, and eventually passed out.

She didn't care about any of it. She couldn't wait to be alone with Thom. But that would come later. Strictly speaking, they weren't married yet. Bonded, yes—for now and forever. She'd be nurtured and protected, as prized as any jewel in their vault. When they both turned eighteen, in another year, the final ceremony would take place. It seemed a mere formality to her.

No one paid any real attention to Elspa, which was fine with her, because it made her feel as if she and Thom were alone. He continued to behave officially—admirably—as was required by his rank. She would sit by his side as long as necessary, until the last reveler was gone.

She didn't know how much time had passed when he turned to her and spoke. "Why do you keep looking at me like that?"

Immediately, she looked away, looked anywhere but at him, and squeezed shut her eyes against a sudden stinging of tears. The reproach in his voice stabbed through her, but she didn't want to seem weak.

"I don't mean to offend. I'll do whatever you want," she said.

His frown deepened. "Don't say that. Don't talk like that."

"You're not happy," she stated.

"I'm not—" He sighed, shook his head. "I'm not *un*happy."

"Do you want me to leave?" It wasn't what *she* wanted. He wondered if he saw the pleading in her eyes. *Let me stay* . . .

"Maybe that would be best."

"Then I'll go," she said, quickly standing.

"Elspa—"

She'd heard her name a million times before, but now, suddenly, it sounded beautiful. She froze, waiting.

"I'm sorry," he said finally. "It's not your fault."

She stared at him. "What isn't? What's wrong?" If he were ill she could help. She could try to help, or at least comfort him.

His brow furrowed, as if he were surprised that she'd spoken. As if he hadn't expected to see her standing before him at all.

"Never mind," he said, and the smile he donned was sad, his gaze distant. "Go and rest. It's been a very long day. We'll talk more tomorrow."

"I look forward to it," she said.

He frowned at his hands. As a last gesture, in lieu of words she couldn't find, she curtseyed to him, bowing her head low. Then she turned and fled to her room.

• • •

Elspa had never had her own room. Her father was chieftain of a relatively wealthy township—it even had a plumbing system leading from the major well—but even so, their adobe buildings were windswept and battered, needing constant repair. She had shared a room with the other teenage girls who had left their mothers' care and waited to learn their fates while working at endless chores: cleaning, cooking, spinning wool, caring for younger children.

Here, now, she didn't have to do any of that, and she had a wide, sunny room with a soft feather bed all to herself. The space, all hers, felt vast and lonely.

She never had any doubt that things would be all right, eventually. She refused to feel homesick—how much better off was she, with Thom? But it would take time for the new situation to feel normal, no doubt.

She had never thought about what it would feel like to be in love. It felt . . . *strange*. But she liked it. It felt a little like floating, and nothing mattered but what lay right in front of her.

• • •

As he promised he would, he visited her the next day. They sat together on a bench on a shaded porch, sipping glasses of sweet, filtered water flavored with lemon. He remained silent, and seemed to avoid looking at her.

She ventured to speak. "What's wrong, my lord?"

He flinched a little at her voice, and his smile was forced. He seemed as pensive as he had the night before. "Do I tell you? Do I tell you the truth?"

"Oh, please. You can tell me anything, you know you can."

The sadness in his gaze cut her. "You don't really love me, you know."

"How can you say such a thing?"

"It's the drug they give you."

She blinked. "I would love you without the drug. The drug—it doesn't mean anything."

"It's the drug that makes you say that."

"Then nothing I say will convince you."

"That's the joke of it."

She didn't dare ask if he felt anything at all for her. Not that

126

it mattered. She only wanted him to be happy. "Isn't it enough that I love you?" she asked.

"It should be, shouldn't it? I'll never have to wonder."

Not like she did. She hesitated, then decided she really did want to know. "Why don't they use the drug on you? On the boys?"

He blinked, startled. His mouth worked, taking several attempts to reply. "Because you—the girls—are the ones who must be controlled."

"Why?"

"Because you bear children. To control the children, we must control *you*."

The way the men controlled sheep, water, scant oil, and anything else that was rare, valued and traded. It made sense on some level, but it didn't change how she felt.

She said, "I suppose the drug is stronger than chains, in the end? Is that it?"

The smile lit his eyes this time, warming his whole face. He seemed near to laughter, which made her smile in turn.

"Yes," he said. "I suppose it is."

She shrugged. "Still, it hardly seems efficient. When you could just *ask*."

"I don't know that anyone's tried that."

"You could ask me."

His manner turned cold again. "It hardly matters now."

Now she felt angry. He was so sure he was right. "I'd feel the same, with or without the drug." Shaking his head, he looked away. "How can I prove it to you?"

"You can't."

"Give me time, I'll find a way."

"Could you, really?"

"If I put my mind to it."

"But would you want to? You might not like the answer you found."

"Then again, I might. Or *you* might."

"You're very odd," he said, regarding her with as much interest as he'd ever shown her, which was an improvement.

He finished his glass of water and left her alone.

• • •

Only ministers were allowed in the fortress offices, which were temple-like in their isolation and further sanctified with the respect and awe that people showed toward them. Cloaked figures, ministers going about their duties, ensuring the safety of the empire and everyone in it, went back and forth along the corridor behind the tall steel gate that separated their wing from the rest of the fortress.

Elspa borrowed a plain brown cloak from the kitchen maid who brought her breakfast. Wearing it, she was nearly anonymous, and looked like one of the servants. She could linger briefly, studying the goings-on behind the gate—at least as much as she could see.

That was how she learned that the kitchen servants took food and wine to the ministers. At mealtimes the guards unlocked the gate to allow them to file in carrying baskets and pitchers, sometimes in pairs but often alone. They went with their heads bowed, their faces cloaked, to show their humility. No one even looked at them.

She could do this.

The next day, when the kitchen maid brought Elspa her noonday meal of bread and dried apples, Elspa didn't eat it, but carried it to the gates of the ministry and joined the line of servants taking meals to the ministers. She merely acted as if she were one of them.

No one stopped her.

Once inside the ministry halls, she didn't know where to go next. She didn't dare act as if she had no idea—she had to keep moving, to pretend she knew what she was doing, as if she belonged here. She walked purposefully—not too quickly, definitely not dawdling—glancing through open doorways and into rooms, or through the empty windows cut into walls to let in more light.

In one room she saw tables filled with glassware, tubes, braziers heated by candles. A heady scent of perfume drifted out. A laboratory. She went inside.

Other than the long tables filled with equipment, mysterious bottles, and bubbling concoctions, the room had many cupboards. The ministers must keep the drug for the ceremony in one of these. They made the drug—but did they bother with an antidote? Why anyone would want an antidote to love, she couldn't imagine. Perhaps if a girl were claimed, and then her boy died—

Her heart nearly stopped thinking of it. If anything happened to Thom . . . why, she'd rather die with him.

What she felt—no drug could make her feel like this. This was so much stronger than whatever they'd given her. She had no doubt.

Wishing her brown cloak would make her like a shadow, and keep her hidden for the next few moments, she set down the tray of food, crept to the first of the cupboards and tried the door. Locked. So was the next, and the next. Every door had a tiny keyhole under the handle, and every door was locked.

Then she heard footsteps outside the door. Rushing, she

grabbed up the tray and hoped she had time to flee. But a gray-garbed minister was standing in the door, blocking her way. He stared, and she did, and for a moment she thought she might faint.

"Who is that meal for?" the bearded man asked. He might have been the one who injected her on her Claiming, only a few days past now but it felt like a whole life. He might have been all the ministers, standing there, accusing.

Elspa froze, her skin burning. Somehow, her mouth knew what to say. "It is for you, lord." She waited, heart stopped, for an answer.

"Ah, excellent." He smiled. "Put it here."

He pointed at the table, and she gratefully set down the wooden tray. Then she fled.

• • •

The cupboards, one of which might hold the antidote, were locked. She had to steal a key. If she could only figure out how. And from where.

When Thom came to sit with her the next day, he asked her a question. "What have you been doing?"

She blushed, even though she didn't think she had anything to feel guilty about. "What do you mean?"

"You were gone from your chambers for several hours yesterday afternoon. No one knew where you were."

She'd been so careful. "You're spying on me?"

"No—" Now *he* was blushing. And how precious and vulnerable the pink in his cheeks made him look. "No, not really, not like that. I'm just . . . I'm just concerned. About you. Do you feel all right?"

"I feel fine. Wonderful, even. As long as you're here with me."

He gave his head a frustrated shake. "I wish you'd stop saying things like that."

"But it's true."

"Where did you go? When no one could find you?"

She shrugged. "I just went exploring. I want to know all about my new home."

"You're lying," he said. Oddly enough he didn't sound angry—merely curious.

"I would never hurt you," she said. "Do you believe me?"

"Of course I do. You could never hurt me. The drug ensures it."

He kept trying to cut holes into her devotion. But she'd show him.

• • •

The trouble was, after the day of the ceremony, she had no reason to encounter the ministers, and they had no reason to deal with her. They kept to their chambers, conferred with the Warlord and his chieftains, did what they did to manage the running of the empire, and never concerned themselves with women who'd been properly disposed of. She'd never come into contact with them. How, then, could she steal a key to the cabinets? She guessed that they carried keys safely on their person, on some kind of chain around their necks or on their belts. She wasn't above stealing one—except for the fact that she would never, under normal circumstances, get close enough to try.

She would have to open the cabinet without a key. This seemed a much more reasonable scenario. She talked to blacksmiths and ironmongers, charming and wheedling, asking about the function and mysteries of keys, and if she might find one that could be altered to fit a certain lock. She learned of skeleton keys and lockpicks. She traded bits of silk scarves and a few links of the gold chain Thom had given her as a gift—the gift did not mean as much as this quest—for instruments from tinkers and flea markets, keys of every size and shape, picks, tiny wrenches and hammers that the peddlers told her could be used to open any lock.

Finally, she sat in her room, her prizes spread out before her—bits of twisted steel and rusted iron, squares and triangles and needle-thin probes, all meant to open any lock, reveal any secret.

But she hadn't had time to learn what kind of locks the cabinets used. She'd have to bring all of it, try each one by one, and she'd never have time.

Perhaps she could be more direct.

• • •

"You're very strange, you know that?" he said to her when he came to visit, a month after the ceremony. Only eleven months until they could be married. Far too long.

"Not really," she said, studying her hands, laced together in her lap.

"You wander all over the fortress talking to everyone. The other Nymphs stay in their rooms, out of sight. I've always thought that women preferred to keep to themselves, that they were happy out of sight. But not you. What could you possibly be doing?"

She hadn't meant to draw attention to herself, but she wasn't sorry either. She lifted her gaze and scooted closer to him.

"You're going to be Warlord someday."

"I suppose." He didn't seem particularly happy about it, which she thought meant he would be a very good Warlord—he'd see the position as a responsibility, not a privilege. She never had any doubt that he would rule well.

"And I will be your consort."

"Yes—"

"Well, I want to be a good one. I want to know everything about the empire and how it works. I want to be able to help you." It was an excuse, but it was also true. Everything she did was intended to help him. In one way or another. "I talk to people to learn."

"But Elspa, all you really need to do—all any consort needs to do—is be my companion. To have children. Many children—you won't have time for anything else."

She waved him off. "There's plenty of time for that. But wouldn't you like someone to talk to? Someone who knows you and loves you, who you can really trust? Who isn't scheming for some political reason?"

"You're scheming, but I don't know exactly for what."

"I told you. I'm going to prove to you that I really love you."

"Elspa, you don't—"

"Yes, I do. I must, so you don't keep looking at me like I'm . . . a burden."

"You shouldn't keep interrupting me."

"Yes. But I can see by the shine in your eyes that you like it, at least a little."

He smiled at that.

• • •

She was being too subtle, she decided. Too careful, creeping and sneaking about, worrying what others thought. She didn't need to be subtle, she needed to be *quick*. Get into the laboratory, learn what she needed, get out. They would find evidence of what had been done, they might even discover that she'd done it. But in the end, what could they do to *her*, the heir's chosen?

All she brought with her the second time she infiltrated the minister's laboratory were a chisel and a hammer.

She entered as she had before, as a servant with a tray of food, flush with excitement at the trick she was playing and that no one had yet discovered her.

The first time she passed the laboratory room, one of the ministers was there, writing something in a ledger. Elspa kept walking, past the door and down the hallway until it stopped at a closed door. She could only do this—keep walking, pretending that she had a purpose—for a short time before she drew attention. She turned around and continued back the way she'd come. If the laboratory were still occupied, she'd leave and try again tomorrow.

This time the room was unoccupied. She looked up and down the hallway, which was empty, and slipped inside.

The room looked much as it had the last time she'd been there, with all the tables and rows of equipment she couldn't identify. She drew her tools from the pouch hidden under her shirt and started with the first cupboard.

What she needed was in the cupboards in the back, she was sure of it. She drew her tools from the pouch hidden under her shirt and started with the first cupboard.

The lock wasn't strong. She wedged the chisel between the door and frame, and one sharp crack with the hammer ripped the lock from the wood, and the door swung open. Inside, racks of glass tubes held murky brown liquids. She was looking for a potion that smelled of lavender and strawberries. Staying as still as she could, she let the smell of the place fill her nose.

The brown liquid smelled of dried moss.

She shut the cabinet, crammed the lock into place to hide the damage, and moved on to the next.

When she cracked open the third cupboard, the scent of lavender and strawberries pressed at her. The memory rose up, of that amazing day when she saw Thom for the first time, when her life and fate appeared suddenly before her, a paved and shining road. The feelings surged, her heart lurched in her chest. She had to catch her breath.

Three glass flasks sat on the bottom shelf, corked and inert. She picked one up, swirled it once or twice, studying the purplish, syrupy liquid within. So innocuous, yet so hated by Thom. She frowned. He was wrong; this had not decided her fate. Her love was her own—she couldn't *not* love Thom.

She returned the flask to its shelf and quickly studied the rest of the cupboard. The other shelf held just one flask, containing a liquid blue as a twilight sky. It smelled of rainy nights. If she were to concoct an antidote, she would keep it next to the poison. But would the ministers? Was this simply colored water or some deadly mixture?

She drew the flask from the cupboard and held the label to the light. Not that it helped—she couldn't read the symbols. But this had to be the right one.

In the fourth cupboard she found hypodermic needles. She took one and drew it full of the blue serum, re-capped it, then wrapped it in her scarf and tucked it in her pouch. Before she left, she put everything back the way she'd found it.

• • •

At supper, she listened closely for rumors, whether the ministers were looking for a thief, if some criminal disaster had befallen their compound. She heard nothing, then wondered—would they reveal any weakness? Would they ever let on that someone had breached those sacred walls? Perhaps not, if they thought nothing was missing.

She couldn't help but smile at her victory.

• • •

Very early the next morning, Elspa arrived on the porch and sat in her appointed chair to wait for Thom. Too early, giving her mind time to flop and tumble, with all the uncertainties. She'd hardly slept the night before. One way or another, he would know how much she loved him, by the lengths she'd gone to proving it.

"Elspa. How are you this morning?"

She started. She'd been gazing at the sky, lost in her worries. Smiling, she looked at him. "I'm very good. And you?"

"I'm . . . good. It's . . . good to see you." He was picking at the hem of his shirt, as if nervous. But why should he be nervous?

"It's very good to see you," she said.

"Yes. You . . . I've been wanting to tell you, when you go out all day—"

"I hope you're not angry with me—"

"Oh no. I meant to say—the sun on your face. It brings out freckles. I . . . I like the way it makes you look."

Her heart rose at that, her smile doubling. "I've found a way to prove it."

He blinked, confused. "Prove what?"

"Prove that it's real." She unwrapped the needle, which gleamed like a jewel in the sunlight. The blue liquid drew the eye.

"What is that?"

"The antidote. I think."

"You *think*?"

"It was in the same cupboard as the drug, so I assumed—"

"But you don't know?" He reached forward and grabbed her arm.

She brushed him off, pushed up her sleeve. "It doesn't matter. I'll still love you after I take it, so you'll see that it was me all along, and not the drug at all." She stretched out her left arm and placed the needle against the skin at the crook of her elbow.

"Elspa!" He grabbed her hand, stopping her from pressing home the needle. "Don't, Elspa. I—I—"

"How else am I to prove that I love you? That I really love you?"

"But . . . but I—"

She tilted her head, trying to read his confusion, the tense set of his jaw. He kept hold of her wrist, and his arm was trembling. What did he want?

"You're worried," she said, finally recognizing the panic in his eyes. "Are you worried that this will hurt me? Or that I'll stop being in love with you?"

He didn't answer, couldn't. He seemed torn—what would he do? Take his hand away, or take the needle from her?

Staring at one another, gaze to shining gaze, they waited until one of them decided.

Berserker Eyes

MARIA V. SNYDER

They watched us. And we watched each other. Searching for the telltale signs—a raised voice, clenched jaw, fisted hands, muscles as tight as security, and the serk gaze—we watched and waited. Any one of us could be next. Every night before lights out, I stared at my own reflection, seeking the rage that might lurk behind my blue eyes. *Will I be next?*

Blue-colored eyes and blond hair were recessive genes. Would other recessive genes also manifest before my body stopped growing? The question plagued me as, I was sure, it did the others. I imagined a huge black question mark floated above my head.

Today, though, was a rare day in the compound. Molly had been cleared. I'd walked with her to the administration building. Only security and teachers were allowed inside. And the cleared. There they rejoined their families and left the compound for good.

A small crowd of well-wishers had gathered to say good-bye, which was technically against the rules but in this case security overlooked it—however, the guards eyed the new seventeen with suspicion. What was he doing here? He stood apart from the group and from the four guards waiting to escort Molly inside. Molly slowed, gnawing on her lower lip as she glanced at them and then around the compound.

I didn't need to turn my head to see what she saw—squat gray cinder-block buildings interspersed with dirt-covered playing fields and all surrounded by a tall chain-linked fence topped with barbed wire. High security towers anchored the corners of the parameter.

"You're not going to miss this place," I said.

She pulled her brown-eyed gaze to mine. "No, but I'll miss you, Kate."

"For five seconds. Once you're reunited with your family, you'll forget all about me."

She grabbed my arm, stopping me. "Never. You're my best friend."

I smiled to ease the tension. "If I'm cleared, I'll make sure to find you out there." My comment made her tighten her grip. "You'd better. Promise me that you'll do everything you can to leave this place. *Everything*."

"What—"

"Just promise me right now."

"Okay. I promise."

"And stay out of trouble."

Puzzled, I searched her expression. "I always do. Why—"

She glanced at the new seventeen. "He keeps staring at you. Stay away from him. Okay?"

"All right." That won't be hard to do. Security brought him in recently. Usually they arrived with zeros, ones and twos, but he was placed with the seventeens when they escorted him into the compound a couple weeks ago. So far, he'd spent most of his time in detention for multiple escape attempts. I wondered again why he was even here. The few days he'd been free, he'd avoided everyone.

We continued to the admin building. Molly handed me the too-delicate-for-her-backpack wire vase she had made for her older sister. Molly had been a four when she'd arrived and, unlike many of us who had been brought in much younger, she remembered her family. I held the vase while she hugged friends and said goodbye but, impatient to finish their day, security hustled her along and into the building before I could say farewell and return the gift for her sister.

Rushing forward without thought, I slipped inside before the door closed. I paused for a moment to let my eyes adjust from the bright sunshine outside. I looked around in disappointment. The hallway resembled all the hallways in the other buildings. We had elevated this building to superstar status and I'd expected marble floors and extravagant paintings on the walls. Or at least rugs. But, no. The plain linoleum floors were as well worn as the ones in our dorms and the walls as equally scuffed.

Voices to my left woke me from my musings. I turned in time to glimpse the end of the group turning down another corridor. Following the voices, I hurried to catch up but slowed as I drew nearer. Surely they wouldn't punish me for returning Molly's sculpture? And it seemed odd that we had gone down a number of steps. Perhaps I'd followed the wrong group.

I hung back, but when they entered a large room I decided to approach them and get it over with. Stepping across the threshold, I paused. Everyone faced Molly, who stood staring at them with a quizzical expression.

It happened so fast. A movement. A crack. Her forehead shattered. Surprise in her eyes as she flew back onto a plastic sheet.

The shock robbed me of breath and saved my life. Unable to utter a sound, I watched in silence as they wrapped her body in the plastic. A surge of self-preservation finally kicked in and I ducked out, running down one hallway after another. Eventually, I stumbled into a dead end and collapsed on to the floor.

The images of her murder replayed over and over in my mind. She'd been cleared! Why would they kill her? She was no longer a danger to society. Horror and fear boiled in my chest, churning into pure rage. Energy surged through my muscles as all my senses sharpened.

My body demanded action so I jumped to my feet. The desire to kill the guards who had murdered my friend pumped in my heart. My fingers curved into claws and I knew without a doubt I could rip those four men apart with my bare hands. The thought of blood and gore inflamed my need. Four men wouldn't be enough to satisfy me, I would kill them all.

Running fast down the halls, I hunted by scent. When I heard voices, I stopped as a memory tugged from deep within me. It had been very important to follow voices. I glanced at my hands. The vase Molly had painstakingly constructed from thin silvery wire had been crushed beyond recognition in my fist.

But I grasped that one moment of lucidity and hung on to it, pushing the blood lust aside. My first clear thought was the realization that I'd serked. Witnessing Molly's murder had triggered the Berserker gene, which, until now, had lain dormant inside me. I was now a mindless killing machine and would be terminated.

Except, I had snapped out of it. Or had I? Fury still surged through my veins, but I sucked in deep breaths, calming my ragged nerves. I clutched the vase. The wires dug into my palm and I concentrated on settling my emotions. Leaning against the wall, I closed my eyes and forced the need to destroy from my mind. My jumpsuit clung to me as sweat dampened the rough blue fabric.

"Kate, what are you doing in here?" a male voice demanded.

I startled and stared at the guard. His hand rested on the butt of his stun gun. Anger flared, but I kept a firm grip. Instead of lunging for his throat, I held out the ruined wire sculpture. "Molly forgot this," I said, proud my voice didn't shake. "I wanted to give it to her, but . . . got lost."

He peered at me, seeking guilt. I tried to appear scared and frightened about being caught in a forbidden area. It wasn't hard.

"Did you see Molly?" he asked.

"No, sir. I couldn't tell which way they went and then . . ." I gestured helplessly. "I'm sorry, sir." I hung my head. "Can I stop by my room before reporting for detention?" A shudder ripped through me. I'd only been in trouble once in my seventeen years here. Once was more than enough.

How could that new kid stand it? Although in light of what happened to Molly, it was better than being dead. But for how long? Anger and grief mixed dangerously. The need to see the guard's blood on my hands pulsed through my body.

The guard considered. "No need for detention Kate. You're not one of the trouble makers."

The tightness in my throat eased. I followed the guard out into the compound. He gestured to the southeast corner. "Better hurry or you'll miss curfew and your dorm mother will give you detention for sure."

"Thanks," I said, meeting his gaze. Had he been one of the

guards escorting Molly? Rage shot through me. I turned away and ran toward my dorm.

Thanks to the now-active berserker gene, my super-charged leg muscles were threatening to carry me across the compound in a quarter of the time it usually took, alerting everyone. It required concentration and effort to slow down and by the time I reached my room, my jumpsuit was soaked with sweat.

We each had a single bed, a dresser, and a desk in our rooms, along with a washroom. The washrooms were supposedly the only places in the entire compound that didn't have any cameras—hidden or otherwise. It made sense for us not to share a dorm. If one of us serked in the middle of the night, our roommate would be dead before security could arrive.

Keeping control of my conflicting emotions had been exhausting. I curled up on the tile floor of my washroom and let the boiling anger follow waves of grief. At one point I was at the edge of giving in to the rage and becoming a mindless Berserker. I felt a certain satisfaction in the thought of killing as many security guards as I could before they terminated me.

Or did they terminate the serkers? That was what they told us, but they also told us the cleared went home. Liars. Not to be trusted. Was anything they told us true?

According to the history teacher, genetic scientists played around with our genes to create designer babies. At first the changes were minor—hair color, eye color, height and weight—but then everyone wanted their children to have an edge over the others, to be smarter, more attractive. And the military had been keen to produce super soldiers who were faster and stronger than our enemies.

In their haste, mistakes were made, mutations occurred, and evolution's survival of the fittest rule kicked in. The seventh generation born didn't appear to be any different than their ancestors until they reached maturity. Then they went berserk and killed everyone—family, friends, co-workers—everyone. Stronger, faster, and out for blood, they banded together and decimated the population.

Finally the government's emergency agency, Domestic Security, exterminated the Berserkers and the gene slicers, but couldn't eradicate the gene without killing fifty percent of the survivors. In response, DS tested every child born in a hospital for the Berserker gene. Those who had it were sent to compounds to be watched. Which was why a few soon-to-be mothers—like Molly's—avoided hospitals. Most of those kids were found within five years. However the kids who didn't serk by age eighteen were allowed to go home—that was supposed to be the up side, the prize. But now . . .

Another round of all-consuming rage left me gasping. I pressed my cheek to the cool floor as sweat dripped from my forehead.

A knock on the washroom's door pulled me back from a spell of blood lust.

"Kate, are you all right?" my dorm mother asked with concern. "Lights out was an hour ago."

"Stomach bug," I said.

"Oh, dear. Can I come in?"

I scrambled to kneel in front of the toilet. "Sure." Flushing the water, I wiped my mouth on my sleeve as Mother Jean entered.

She fussed over me, taking my temperature, helping me change into my nightgown, fetching me a glass of ginger ale, and tucking me into bed. The whole time I fought the desire to rip her arms off and strangle her with my bare hands.

When she finally left, I was glad I hadn't killed her. She was one of the sweetest dorm mothers—as long as you didn't break any of the rules. If you did, she was one of the most feared. Or so I heard. After two days locked in a two-foot by four-foot dank cell without light, food, or water when I was a seven, I'd vowed never to get into trouble again.

I used the stomach-bug excuse to stay in my room for the next couple days. But I couldn't keep hiding. Eventually, Mother Jean would insist I go to the doctor, then they'd know about me for sure. Deep down I knew I was just delaying my termination. Being cleared or going berserk ended the same way, so why fight it? Yet, I couldn't give in to the blood lust. I had promised Molly. Only now I wondered why she hadn't promised to get cleared. Did she know?

Perhaps I could escape. Except the new kid that tried that kept getting caught. But he didn't grow up in this compound and know every inch of it. A rough plan formed. Could I really break the rules? Just the thought made me queasy. In the end, only my promise to Molly kept me from chickening out.

The next morning I joined my dorm mates at breakfast. My hands shook as I filled my plate, but even though I was beyond starving I didn't take too much. Eating mass quantities of food was another sign of someone on the edge of serking.

I kept tight control over my emotions, letting the conversation flow around me.

". . . they brought zero twin girls in yesterday. Have you seen them? They're adorable!"

"Greg won the sixteen triathlon yesterday . . ."

". . . Missy told me she heard Bethany tell Mother Jean . . ."

"This is the third day in a row that Jayden's been out of detention. Do you think he stopped trying to escape?"

The last comment caught my full attention. I glanced around the dining room. Round tables were filled with noisy seventeens. All familiar to me. All wearing regulation blue jumpsuits. The girls had their hair tied in regulation knots and the boys wore their hair regulation short. To a new person, we probably looked identical.

But not to us. We had grown up together, starting out with close to a hundred of us, we were down to forty-three—even with the older, later additions—mostly due to serking. I swallowed as rage pushed up my throat. Molly had been the fourth person in our class to be cleared. Had the other three been killed as well?

Suppressing murderous thoughts, I turned to Haylee, who sat next to me. "Jayden?" I asked. "Is that the new seventeen's name?"

"Yep." She pointed a fork toward the far corner.

Jayden leaned back in his chair with his arms crossed, scowling at the few people who dared to sit at his table. They ignored him.

"I'm surprised he hasn't serked by now," Haylee said.

Emotional upheaval, like being arrested and sent to an internment camp, was one of the triggers. Or watching your best friend's head shatter. I bit my lip to keep from losing control.

Pulling in a deep breath, I said, "I'm surprised he didn't get caught sooner. Seventeen years without visiting a doctor—"

Haylee leaned close. "His mother's a nurse or something like that, and his family lived in the woods away from civilization. Or so he claims." She stared at him. "He's been trying to convince us to band together and take control of the compound. Have you ever heard anything so ridiculous?" Haylee speared

146

a sausage link with her fork. "At least he's entertaining. We've a bet going on how long he'll stay out of detention this time. Do you want in?"

"No. I lost a bet to Doreen and had to change disgusting diapers for two weeks."

Haylee wrinkled her petite nose. "She had me doing dishes for her. Doreen always wins, I think she cheats."

Since we had no money, the bet winner won the right to exchange her most hated chores to the losers. I realized I would need money if I escaped. What else would I need? I glanced at Jayden. Perhaps I should talk to him.

The bell rang for our first class. It was the longest, most exhausting day of my life. Each instructional class period was followed by a physical activity like dodgeball, capture the flag, kick the can, and various sports. All of which I had to pretend to be normal at. My body wanted to show off my new quick reflexes and speed, but I kept firm control.

I never really questioned all the activities before. But after being knocked out of dodgeball, I stood to the side and contemplated why we spent so much time playing these games, apart from the physical exercise. Perhaps the teachers wanted to provoke us into serking. That happened quite a bit but, then again, kids serked in class, too.

Watching the two teams, I noticed the good team worked together, feeding balls to the kids with accurate aim, using strategy to knock out the better opponents on the opposite team.

"Training," a voice said next to me.

I jerked in surprise and had to press my hands against my thighs to keep them from harming the speaker before I could turn.

Jayden met my gaze. His eyes were a pale blue. "They're training you so you'll be better fighters when you serk."

Before Molly died, I would have scoffed at the notion. Instead, I asked. "So after spending a couple days here, you're suddenly an expert?"

"I've been here fifteen days." His tone was tight.

"The ones in detention don't count."

"I know—"

Furious in an instant, I said, "You know nothing. I've been here seventeen *years.*"

He stared at me calmly. "You're right. I'm unfamiliar with everything in this prison. But I recognize training exercises when I see them."

His quick agreement and the word "prison" snapped me back to sanity. In all my life, I'd never considered this place a prison. We weren't criminals. We were here as a precaution—to keep our families and the remaining population safe. But now I didn't know what to think.

"A couple days ago you disappeared into the administration building and something happened while you were inside, didn't it?" Jayden asked.

I said nothing as the memories of Molly threatened to send me over the edge. And that's how the rest of my day played out. Me finding a way to avoid participating in the games, and Jayden joining me, pointing out the obvious wrongness of my world. Obvious now that I viewed the compound with my Berserker eyes.

"Have you noticed that not many of the seventeens have light-colored eyes?" Jayden asked while we waited to be freed during capture the flag. "It's recessive—"

"I know it's recessive." I snapped at him. Was he

purposefully trying to provoke me into killing him? "So is blond hair. So what?" I glanced at his newly shorn blond hair.

"I'll bet Pete will be the next kid to serk. He has both. Plus he's twitchy."

"I don't bet anymore."

"Really? 'Cause you're betting with your life right now."

Before I could demand an explanation, Haylee ran over and freed us from jail. I took off for home base. If only getting out of here was that easy. And why hadn't I asked Jayden about the outside?

During eighth period, I was running my best obstacle course time ever when David cut me off. I tripped and fell, landing hard on my right elbow. Pure rage flowed. Without thought I went after David with murderous intent.

Someone grabbed my left wrist, jerking me to a stop.

"Is your elbow all right, Kate?" a voice ahead.

I tried to shake the annoyance off, but it wouldn't let go.

"Elbow, Kate?" Louder this time. "Kate?"

Jayden's calm insistence cut through my haze. I blinked at him. Concerned, he peered back at me, but kept his tight grip on my wrist.

"Are you all right?" Mr. Telerico asked me. "Do you need to see the doctor?"

I realized everyone was staring at me. Probably wondering if I'd serked.

"No, sir. I just bumped it."

Mr. Telerico nodded and yelled for us to resume our exercise. "Take a minute Kate and we'll restart your time."

"Thank you, sir," I said.

He returned to his post.

"You can let go now," I said to Jayden.

He didn't. "If you can keep it together for another couple days, you'll make it."

"What are you talking about?" I yanked my arm with more force that I should have, but he held on. His strength quite a surprise.

"It's takes about five to seven days for the serker rage to settle. Once that happens you can control your emotions."

"That's ridiculous. How could you possibly know that?" I tried again to free my wrist. No luck.

"I've been through it."

I scoffed. "No way."

"Then why can't you break my hold?" he asked.

"Jayden, you're up," Mr. Telerico called.

He let go and ran to the starting line. I watched him as he navigated the obstacle course. Jayden's muscular physique matched the bigger boys. He didn't appear to be faster or stronger than they were, but his graceful movements made the activity look effortless.

I realized I should have thanked him for stopping me from killing David.

• • •

Over the next two days I struggled to contain my rage and blood lust. Jayden kept close to me. And I'd focus on him whenever my fury surged.

Of course my friends noticed my strange behavior and long silences.

"Stop moping, Kate," Haylee said the next morning—day six since I'd serked. "You've hardly said anything since Molly left. You'll see her on the outside."

"I've been sick—"

"Come on, it's me. Mother Jean might buy that lame excuse, but I know better."

"I miss her." I admitted.

She squeezed my shoulder. "We all do, but she made it. And you will too, if you stay away from Jayden."

"What do you mean?"

She gave me a "don't-be-stupid" look. Her light-brown eyes matched her hair exactly. "No one buys his recent good boy routine. We all know he's plotting another escape attempt and I don't want you to be caught in the middle. You're going to be an eighteen soon. I know he's hot, but you can't serk now and ruin your chance to go home."

It was an impassioned speech. I opened my mouth to confide in her about the bitter truth when a realization hit me so hard I almost gasped aloud. So focused on myself, I hadn't considered my friends. Heck, the seventeens were my family. And they would all die within a year.

I gripped the edge of my seat to keep my expression neutral. Someone had to stop it. But how? They had hundreds of guards, fences, barbed wire, security cameras, and weapons.

Haylee didn't appear to notice my panic. She took my silence as agreement. "Besides, if Mother Jean or Father Bryan see you're spending too much time with him, you'll be transferred. And I don't want to lose you so soon after Molly."

The last thing Domestic Security wanted was for two people with a recessive berserker gene to become romantically involved. If any of the dorm parents suspected a couple, that couple disappeared—supposedly to different camps far away. Although, now I wondered if any of them made it out of here alive. My fingers punched through the vinyl cover of my seat.

Focus. Breathe. Don't kill anyone.

151

• • •

Eight days after Molly's murder I woke feeling as if a fever had broken. I could think clearly again. The rage had settled into a simmer under my heart. It waited for me instead of rushing through my body, demanding action at every little thing.

Since Haylee's comments, I'd been avoiding Jayden. However, today I sought him out. I managed to talk to him while waiting for our turns during a co-ed relay race.

"You made it through," he said. "Not many who serk do."

Questions over his comment boiled up my throat, but I didn't have much time. "Does anyone leave these compounds alive?"

"Yes."

"Who?"

"The serkers. They're encouraged to give into the blood lust and then become DS soldiers for special army units."

"That's crazy. No one can control them."

Jayden gave me a tight smile. "They've learned a lot from these prisons. They don't want to waste mindless killing machines after all." The bitterness in his voice said more than his words.

"If that's the case, then we need to stop them."

Jayden laughed. "Good luck with that. I just want out of here."

"But you can't just stand by—"

He stepped close to me. His expression didn't change but he growled in a low voice. "Don't you dare presume what I can and can't do. Safe and secure here in your precious camp all these years, you've no idea what I've been through."

Stunned, I needed a moment to collect my thoughts. "But Haylee said you were trying to get everyone to revolt?"

"To provide me with a distraction. But you've all been brainwashed and are useless. No one will believe me about the truth of this place."

"What's the truth, Jayden?" I asked.

"This place is a serker factory. It's sole purpose is to produce serkers for the army."

• • •

Later, I couldn't recall what my response to Jayden had been. The next day passed in a blur as my mind replayed our conversation over and over. A few inconsistencies churned out. Like why was Jayden here? They would have tested him when they had found him and discovered he had serked. He could be working for DS.

I decided it would be best to avoid him altogether. Except that he wouldn't get the hint and leave me alone.

"I helped you. Are you going to help me?" he asked after third period.

"No," I said.

"You're living on borrowed time. Sooner or later they'll find out about you," he said after fourth period. "You can come with me."

"I'm not leaving my friends," I said.

"Then you'll die." His confidence was unnerving.

"So will you." I shot back.

"All the more reason for us to leave."

"You act like it'll be so easy."

"I've a plan, but it needs both of us."

I waited.

"We'll need to get inside the administration building. It's the only way out."

"No." I walked away.

After seventh period, he intercepted me. "You can't do anything to help the others while you're in here, Kate. There are people on the outside who've been trying for years to overthrow Domestic Security and return us to our democratic roots."

"Years? Seriously?"

"Yes, why?"

"Will they succeed?" I asked.

His voice deepened. "Not without more serkers working for us." He glanced around. Most of the others headed toward the sports field. "You're the only one who's seen the truth of this place, Kate, and I need you."

His words *truth of this place* haunted me that night. The desire to help all the children living in the compound warred with my promise to Molly. In all the years I'd lived here, no one had tried to rescue us. If we didn't reunite with our families, then what were our families told when we were taken from them?

After a sleepless night, I decided that I needed more information. Unfortunately that meant spending time with Jayden, which would alert the guards or our dorm parents. I stared at the small red light shining from the ceiling. When it was dark, they used heat sensors to make sure we remained in our rooms. There had to be places other than the washrooms that weren't under surveillance. There was only one person I could ask. Doreen.

• • •

"So Miss Goody-Goody wants to know the sweet spots," Doreen said at breakfast the next morning.

Her mocking tone failed to provoke a reaction from me. If

it had been a few days ago, I probably would have gone after her. And just knowing that I had the power to tear her to pieces gave me a boost of confidence. "What's it going to cost?"

"How do I know you won't run to Mother Jean and squeal?"

"Cut the act, Doreen. You know I won't tell."

She studied me as she chewed on a fingernail. "True, you're not a squealer, but then again you disappear as soon as there's a hint of trouble. This is new. Why are you so interested all of a sudden?"

I glanced at Jayden sitting across the dining room.

She followed my gaze and snorted. "Wow, Kate. When you decide to break the rules you go all out. You know you'll eventually get caught. Right? Couples don't last long in here."

"I'm aware of the risks. How much?"

"Depends. Do you want a few trysting spots or all the locations?"

"All of them."

"It won't help him escape. He'll need more than that." That was the reason Doreen won the bets about people—she was scarily perceptive. She leaned forward. "What's really going on?"

Jayden's words, *you're the only one who's seen the truth of this place,* echoed in my mind. The seventeens didn't trust him, but they trusted me. The bell rang and I made a quick, and hopefully not fatal, decision.

Surrounded by the clatter and scraps of chairs, I told Doreen about Molly.

She grabbed my arm. "You serious?"

"Yeah."

"Berserking nuts! I figured something wasn't right. If you start thinking about it, there are all kinds of clues. Like how we never get letters or anything from our families. But to murder us!"

"Easy, Doreen," I said, hoping to calm her. "Just breathe."

She drew in deep breaths as we walked together to our first class. Doreen didn't say another word until we reached the classroom. "Never thought serking would be the preferred choice."

"I'm going to stop it."

She laughed, but it had a shaky, almost hysterical edge. "How?"

"I'm working on it. How much for those locations?"

Doreen peered at me as if she'd never seen me before. "I'll have a map for you by the end of sixth period."

As promised, Doreen slipped me a paper with information and a diagram of the compound on it. The locations hidden from the cameras were marked in red. "Memorize it and flush it. You *don't* want to be caught with this."

"Thanks."

She paused. "Just don't leave without us. Okay?"

"That's the plan."

. . .

Half way through the eighth-period races, I managed to get close to Jayden. He'd been ignoring me all day.

"If you want my help, meet me during free time." I explained where.

His stance didn't change and his gaze remained fixed on the races. A nod was the only indication he'd heard me.

"Can you get there without alerting anyone?"

Annoyed, he looked at me. "Of course. Can you?"

"I think—"

"Don't over think it, Kate. Just act like you belong there. No nervous glances or any hesitation. Understand?"

"Yeah."

According to Doreen's information, no seventeens occupied the top floor of our dorm so the cameras had been turned off to save power. Producing energy had been the biggest hurdle after the Berserkers destroyed all the electrical power plants.

The dorm's stairwells were watched, but during free time the activity inside them increased. Plus security concentrated on the common areas at that time. If Jayden and I could reach the third floor without alerting security, we should be safe. Key word: *should.*

I followed Jayden's advice and climbed the steps as if I did it every day. Sunlight filtered in through the windows located at the two ends of the hallway, but a murky semi-darkness filled the middle. At least no red lights shone from the ceiling.

No sign of Jayden. Worry and impatience mounted as I waited. Finally the door on the far end opened. He met me in the middle. After scanning the ceiling, he pointed to dorm on the left. We entered the room, disturbing a layer of musty-smelling dust. No red light greeted us, but Jayden led me into the washroom anyway.

He leaned on the sink and crossed his arms over his chest. "Does this mean you'll help me?"

"Sort of."

Jayden waited.

"I need some answers first," I said.

He motioned for me to continue.

"Why didn't they know you've serked when they captured you?"

Pain flashed across his face but he closed his eyes for a

moment, wiping away all expression. "Our unit had been betrayed and the DS sent a force that surprised and overpowered us. My mother ordered me to act normal so they wouldn't . . ." Every muscle in his body strained against the fabric of his jumpsuit. He swallowed. ". . . slaughter me with the others."

I pressed my hands tight together. "Everyone?"

"Except those carrying the berserker gene. They were sent to breeding compounds."

It took a moment for the words, *breeding compound* to sink in. "You mean—"

"Yep. Without the gene slicers, Domestic Security is forced to create more serkers the old-fashioned way."

Horror threatened to overwhelm me. I focused on the one positive. "At least your mother wasn't killed."

Digging his fingers into his forearms, Jayden said, "She was past her childbearing years. My father lacked the gene and my two older brothers were killed trying to protect us. I'm the only one left. I would have taken out as many of those bastards as I could have, except my mother made me promise to find a way to escape."

This wasn't going the way I had imagined at all. I scrambled to find a safer, or rather, kinder topic. "So the doctors didn't test you?"

"They scanned me for the gene, but since I wasn't serking all over them, they figured I'd either serk in the compound or be cleared and go to the breeders."

Molly's shocked face filled my vision. "Then why did they kill Molly?"

"Is that what triggered you?"

I nodded.

He considered. "Either she was unable to have children, or they planned for you to witness the murder. Or both."

"But—"

"They need serkers more than breeders right now. Obviously you were a prime candidate for serking." He leaned forward. "What woke you from the blood lust?"

I explained about Molly's wire vase.

"That's amazing."

"Why? You made it through, too."

He huffed. "Because my brothers sat on me for five days." His rueful smile faded. "Are you going to help me?"

My mind swirled with everything he had told me. Could I even believe him? "One more question."

"Make it quick, free time is almost over."

"Why haven't any of your people tried to rescue us? Wouldn't they want to shut down these serker factories?"

"How do you know we haven't?" He shot back.

I waited.

He sighed. "They're too well defended. And large explosions tend to be indiscriminate. We didn't want to harm the kids."

A lame excuse. I might not know all about what's going on beyond the fence, but if I were rebelling against DS, neutralizing the serker armies would be my priority, not freeing a bunch of kids. I let it go for now. "Okay, I'll help."

Jayden peered at me with suspicion. "Just like that?"

"I won't guarantee success. What's your plan?"

He quickly detailed his idea for us to get inside the administration building and fight our way out. "They don't have cameras in there and with two of us, combined with the element of surprise, we'd be out of there before they could form ranks."

Voices kept me from telling him that his plan sucked. Jayden held a finger to his lips as he eased the washroom's door open a crack.

"... nowhere else."

"... his last confirmed location was in dorm seventeen, stairwell two."

"... check the right, we'll take left."

Oh no. The guards were searching for us.

Jayden pulled me away from the door. "They're looking for me. Stay here until it's quiet."

I grabbed his arm before he could leave. "What are you doing? You'll be caught and thrown into detention."

"Better me than you."

"But—"

"You need to maintain your . . ." A genuine smile sparked. ". . . innocence. Just don't do anything rash while I'm gone. Okay?"

I must have nodded because he headed out. After a couple seconds, the sounds of a scuffle and harsh shouts vibrated through me. Curling into a ball to keep from rushing to help him, I waited. In those awful minutes, I understood just a fraction of how it must have felt for Jayden to not fight while his family died around him. A deep respect for him nestled inside me.

• • •

While Jayden was in detention, I had entirely too much time to fret and watch the compound to *not* come up with a fantastic escape plan. Unfortunately, I had plenty of ones that sucked.

I also considered my other problem—the rest of the kids. Would the seventeens be willing to stage a revolt? Some might serk from the stress alone. Then what would we do? Was there a way to determine who would serk and keep them out of the plans? Approximately fifty of my classmates had serked. I spent my free time writing down all the triggers I could remember. The list was impressive—basically anything at any time could trigger someone. No help at all.

So back to Jayden. While there were places hidden from the cameras, there were still guards and teachers all around the compound. Jayden was right. In order to escape, we needed to get into the admin building, but security was always tight. My ability to get in unnoticed before seemed unlikely the more I studied the shift changes. Which made his comment about the guards wanting me to see her murder sounded less ridiculous each day.

And the thought that they'd killed her just to make me serk sent dangerous spikes of rage through me.

Focus. Breathe. Don't kill anyone.

I needed to confirm if Molly could have children or not. The information would be in the doctor's office. Time to use my good girl charm, but first I needed to talk to Doreen.

• • •

"Breeders?" Doreen wrapped her muscular arms around her waist. "I think that's worse than dying."

"Maybe you'll serk instead," I said. It was sixth period and we were taking a break between games of dodgeball.

"Not funny." She studied me. "How's the plan coming?"

"Terrible."

"No surprise. This place is sealed tight."

"And I need more information. You up for a little deception?"

"Always. What do you want?"

I outlined my plan.

"You're going to have to be quick. There won't be a lot of time."

"I know."

"When?"

"Eighth period."

"Ah, the obstacle course. Good choice."

Nervous energy wasn't good for a serker. I fidgeted through seventh as my emotions rolled from calm to panicked and back again. Finally eighth period started. Keeping close to Doreen, I ran a few courses to burn off my anxiety.

Once my nerves settled, I started the ropes course. Half way through, I tripped and fell hard. I clutched my right ankle, yelling as if in pain and caused a scene until Mr. Telerico arrived.

"Twisted or broken?" he asked.

"Don't know," I panted.

"Can you put weight on it?"

I tried to stand, yowled, and flopped back on the ground.

Mr. Telerico spotted Doreen hovering nearby. "Doreen, help her to the infirmary."

"Yes, sir," she said. She hauled me to my good foot, wrapped my arm around her shoulders, and escorted me to the doctor's office.

As expected a couple guards trailed after us.

"Do you think they'll follow us inside?" Doreen whispered.

I let my "injured" foot touch the ground and shrieked, insuring they would. Pain was one of the serker triggers.

"Next time warn me about the noise, will ya?" Doreen grumbled.

We entered the infirmary. A nurse led us to an

examination room. As she brought up my records on the computer, Doreen dumped me on the table and retreated to the hallway. One of the guards hovered in the doorway until the seventeens' doctor entered and shooed him back, shutting the door. No cameras were allowed in the exam rooms.

He smiled at me. "What happened?"

I recited my tale and he *tsk*ed over my ankle.

"It doesn't look—"

". . . watching us all the time!" Doreen's aggravated tone grew louder. "She's injured not serking you idiot!" Ominous thumps sounded. "Stop it. Stop watching us!"

The doctor and nurse exchanged a worried glance. He pulled a syringe from his pocket and dashed for the door with the nurse on his heels.

As soon as they left, I slid off the table and raced to the computer. My fingers raced over the keyboard. Finally a good use of my serker skills. Pulling up Molly's chart, I scanned it, and then switched back to read through mine. I hopped back on to the table just as the doctor returned.

"Is she all right?" I asked.

"Yes. Just a bit of heat exertion. She's resting. Now let's see about that ankle."

I played injured. The doctor concluded it was a bad sprain. He wrapped my ankle and gave me a couple pain pills. I limped to my dorm, hoping Doreen wouldn't get into too much trouble.

Only when I reached my washroom did I allow the information I'd found to sink in. Staring at my reflection, I focused on the blue in my eyes. Little flecks of gray dotted the irises. Funny how I hadn't noticed them before.

My chart claimed I was too even-tempered to serk. Molly's reported she was in the peak of health. Mine said drastic measures would have to be used in order to trigger me. Molly's said she would become troublesome once she learned the truth.

In other words, they murdered her to trigger me. I closed my eyes as fury rushed. When I could think again, I had a plan—the only one with a slight chance of working and which depended on whether they'd try to make me serk again. I hoped Jayden was right about the DS needing serkers more than breeders. He didn't know it yet, but he was about to risk his life on it.

• • •

Doreen returned after a couple days of detention for attacking a security guard.

"Almost lost it," she said, joining me between classes. For the first time since ever, Doreen looked scared. "Yeah, I almost serked." But then she shook it off and smiled. "I can't be next. I've bets with five seventeens and four sixteens that Pete will be next. I can't ruin my winning streak."

Her comment about Pete stopped me. Jayden had said the same thing. "Why him?"

"Red-headed, attached earlobes, and he gets upset about cheaters."

"Attached earlobes? Seriously?"

"Yep. They're recessive, along with—"

"I know. Has anyone bet on me?" I asked.

She kept a straight face, but humor sparked in her hazel eyes. "No one."

"But I have—"

"You have the calmest temper in the entire compound. It's a losing bet."

Ha. I could prove her very wrong, except I'd be stunned and carted off to Berserker boot camp. Doreen's comments about Pete gave me a few things to think about. Did DS know people could "survive" serking?

• • •

Jayden was released from detention after ten days. The longest time for a detention. Ever. Healing bruises and cuts marked his face and he walked with stiff legs, heading straight for the dorm. Students stared after him with mouths open in amazement or nodding with respect.

I suppressed the desire to chase after him, planning to let a few days pass before I approached. But the next morning, he sat in the corner with elbows propped on the table and his head in his hands, appearing miserable. I hoped it was an act for the guards.

When the bell rang for first period, Jayden didn't move. As everyone filed out, I crouched next to him.

"Go away, Kate," he said without glancing at me.

"If you're late—"

"I won't go back to detention. They'll have to kill me first." Now he lifted his head and gazed at me in utter defeat. "I've thought about my plan. It sucks. There's no way out of this place. When they come for me this time, I'm not going to pretend to be weak."

"No, you're going to first period." I grabbed his wrist and jerked him to his feet. Towing him from the dining room, I headed toward the science building.

He stayed a step behind me not resisting, but not quite cooperating either.

I talked to him as we crossed the compound. "You can't give up, now. You made a promise to your mother, and I made a promise to my friend. If we break them, they'll haunt us forever, or so I've heard." I took his snort as a positive sign. "Besides, I have an idea on how to get us both into the administration building."

He jerked me to a halt. "How?"

"You might not like—"

"I'll do *anything* to get out of here."

But could I?

"Tell me."

I did.

He stared at me as the information sank in. When he drew breath to speak, I stopped him. "Think about it. You'll be in the most danger."

"When do we start?"

So much for thinking it through. As we continued to our class, I explained. "It has to be subtle. Little gestures at first, then more . . . reckless."

"Okay, I'll follow your lead."

I asked him if Domestic Security knew people could survive serking.

"Yes, but they don't want it to happen. Mindless soldiers don't argue or worry about things like morals and basic human decency."

Before we entered the building, Jayden paused. "Does this mean you've given up on rescuing everyone?"

"No."

He waited.

I sighed. "One problem at a time."

• • •

And so Jayden and I started sitting together at meals. Haylee didn't waste time warning me again.

"They'll send you away," she said.

"We'll be careful," I replied. A queasy feeling in the pit of my stomach roiled as I lied to her.

Doreen watched us with suspicion and challenged me during sixth period. "What are you doing? You're supposed to be working on a way out of here, not falling for the new guy."

And snap. The answer to my other problem popped into my head along with ten reasons why it wouldn't work. Plus Jayden wouldn't agree. Too bad.

I kept my expression neutral as I said in an even tone, "There's no way out. We're stuck here and might as well make the best of it."

"You're a lousy liar, Kate." She stormed off.

• • •

Jayden and I continued our . . . what to call it? Courtship sounded ancient. Our fake affair? Occasionally ducking into a hidden spot, we would emerge after a few minutes. My regulation knot would be askew and he'd have a goofy smile on his face. Each time we took bigger and bigger risks.

One night during free time, Doreen surprised us soon after we slipped into the blind spot behind the math building.

Ready for a fight, she didn't hesitate in confronting us. "You're planning to escape without helping the rest of us. Aren't you?"

"Yes. It's impossible to save everyone, so we're saving ourselves."

Confused, Jayden glanced at me.

Doreen sucked in a breath.

"You're not worth saving, Doreen," I said. "You're just a big bully. All talk. No action. I mean, really. You were depending on *me* to be a savior? I avoid trouble. You're as stupid as you are ugly."

Jayden hissed at me. "Are you insane—"

"You're dead!" Doreen wrapped her hands around my neck with amazing speed as she serked. Digging her fingers in to my throat, she snarled as the blood lust filled her eyes.

Pain and panic froze me for a moment. I needed air. Then my own serker instincts kicked in and, with Jayden's help, we pinned Doreen to the wall.

He called her name over and over in that calm tone he'd used on me. She stopped fighting, but still hadn't come to her senses.

"I'll bet you can't control your emotions, Doreen," I said, matching his even tone. "I'll bet you'll let the blood lust rule you, Doreen. I'll bet you a month's worth of chores that you can't overpower your genetics like I have, Doreen."

"You are insane," Jayden said.

With a visible effort Doreen focused on me. "You're going to lose, Kate."

"I hope so."

Jayden rounded on me. "You wanted her to serk! What if she didn't wake? You could have ruined everything."

"This was the only way I could help my friends and keep my promise."

"And I didn't merit being informed about this little diversion." Anger spiked each word.

"I didn't know if it would work."

He bit off a furious reply as Doreen responded to the emotion, straining against our hold.

"Just keep it together," I soothed. "Ride it out like a muscle cramp. Eventually it will pass. You can do this."

When she stabilized, Jayden released her. "She's yours now, Kate. Good luck with your pet project. I'm done." He left.

· · ·

I kept Doreen focused and centered over the next five days just as Jayden had done for me. He stayed away and everyone believed we had broken up. Funny, it felt as if we had. We hadn't done anything but talk during those pretend trysts, but I missed them.

Once her serker rage settled, Doreen didn't waste time targeting the next person. "I'm going to play cards with Pete and cheat. He'll serk."

She did, and I helped to wake him. But keeping close to him proved more difficult. During fourth period, Pete lost his temper playing basketball, drawing the guards close.

Doreen and I couldn't intervene without causing suspicion. If he gave in to the rage, I'd have to stay longer. But that was a problem since my eighteenth birthday was only a week away. I couldn't leave Doreen alone. There had to be at least two serkers left behind or we had no chance of taking over the compound. Anxiety swirled.

Just when it appeared as if Pete wouldn't recover, Jayden stepped close to him and talked Pete through it. Relieved, I studied Jayden and wondered if he'd talk to me again.

· · ·

"So that's your plan?" Jayden tilted his head toward Pete. Our group was running the obstacle course. "Trigger all the seventeens so you have your own personal serker army?" His voice held a hard edge.

"Yes, except it will be Doreen's serker army. I've my cleared appointment with the doctor in five days." I noticed his alarm. "Don't worry, I plan to serk before then. Put on a show and take out a few of them before they stun me."

"Not a very good plan."

"No, but I screwed up the original one so . . ." I scuffed my shoe in the dirt, working up the nerve. "I'm sorry I didn't tell you about Doreen, but I knew you'd—"

"Refuse to help?"

"Yeah."

"You're right. I'd have refused, but how was I to know you could trigger her?"

"That's the other part. I didn't. I knew she'd had a couple of close calls and I know her sensitive spots." I gave him a wry smile. "Being the good girl is hard work. In order to avoid getting into trouble, I kept on everyone's good side. Which means I know quite a bit about all my fellow seventeens. When I thought about all my classmates who'd serked—I mean really considered the causes—I eventually recognized a pattern."

"Why didn't you tell me all this?"

"It was just a theory."

"Well, it worked." He considered. "Let's hope your other plan goes as well."

"Are you sure? We only have a few days."

"Then let's not dawdle." He grabbed my hand for a second, squeezed, and let go. Jayden returned to his place in line with more energy than I'd seen from him in a while.

It didn't take long to start the seventeens buzzing over our reconciliation.

Haylee blocked me on the stairs as we headed down to

supper. "You are two days away from being cleared! Are you insane? What are you thinking?"

I leaned close and whispered, "Talk to Doreen. She'll explain everything to you."

· · ·

"Are you ready?" Jayden asked me.

Yes. No. Yes. My stomach churned. Unable to trust my voice, I nodded. We sat close together in the dining room in plain view of all the seventeens.

Jayden stood and pitched his voice so it could be heard over the general din. "I don't care who sees us." He pulled me to my feet and kissed me, wrapping his arms around my back.

A collective gasp followed instant silence. No turning back now. Jayden deepened the kiss and I forgot to be worried as strange tingles flowed through me. It was a long kiss. Why not? No sense wasting what could be our last chance at . . . well, everything.

Rough hands yanked us apart. The four guards *tsk*ed and scolded us as they marched us into the administration building. I kept a firm hold on my emotions. Would they try to make me serk again?

Yep. They led us down to the room decorated with plastic. The place where they had murdered Molly. Three guards pulled their stun guns, aiming toward me. But this time, when the remaining guard grabbed his revolver, Jayden moved to stop him.

My guards turned to the commotion, and then I moved. So lovely to use my full abilities without worry. I could have easily killed all three—their actions were so slow compared to mine. I dodged the stun gun prongs, knocked weapons from

171

their hands, and rendered them senseless with strong kicks to their temples.

"Fun, isn't it?" Jayden stood over the man who would have shattered his forehead.

"Lots."

"Ready to get out of here?" He threw me a stun gun, keeping one.

"Oh, yes."

He grabbed my hand and we raced through the hallways. There really wasn't much more to the plan beyond getting inside. We encountered a few guards, knocked them out, and then kidnapped an office worker. Jayden forced him to lead us outside. We dashed into the woods.

I knew the ease of our escape was not the real battle. The real battle would entail convincing the rebels to return with us to help Doreen's serker army free the others.

But like I said before. One problem at a time.

For now, I let the pure joy of running full serker speed with Jayden take control.

Arose from Poetry

STEVE BERMAN

Allard huddled in the cramped, hot van. Resting his chin on the scuffed knees of his trousers, he watched a spider hiding in a crevice beneath the door latch. Only a bit of daylight slipped through the scattered bullet holes that pockmarked the opposite panel. The spider's body—fat and spiked, legs like crooked needles—trembled as the van drove over rough roads, which meant they had left the capital far behind. Allard's instructors had mentioned that spiders spin many different kinds of webbing, some stronger than steel, some so gossamer light that infant spiders use it to fly away.

He wished he could fly away. A metal manacle encircled his left wrist, chafing it raw. Attached to the manacle was an unbreakable plastic cord no more than two feet long, which bound him to the side of the van. It was so short it prevented him from touching the door. A steady ache already inhabited his shoulder—he'd been in the van at least two hours. He worried it might be more.

His captors played the State music stream from the speakers, loud enough for him to hear in the back of the van. A chorus of schoolchildren sang what had once been a tired anthem, but now sounded to Allard like something of a taunt.

No one will grant us deliverance,
Not god, nor tsar, nor hero.
We will win our liberation,
With our very own hands.

He had been within sight of the station when they took him. The van had swerved, nearly running him down. They had laughed when he'd told them he was a Citizen. They did not care that he carried ID. They should never have taken him. Allard's parents worked for the Party. His father was a high-level clerk in the Ministry of Agriculture and Food. His mother posted the most popular, if insipid, poetry extolling the State on NationWeb.

The van reeked of old sweat. Allard imagined it crammed full with doleful men and boys taken from the street. They would sit pressed together, their eyes closed. Some might even resort to prayer, hoping the State was wrong, that an abstract deity high above would comfort them and keep them safe when they reached the Front Line.

The van's brakes screeched as it came to a sudden stop, jerking Allard, tugging his left arm and sending fresh pain through his side. Drops of sweat beaded on his forehead, in his armpits, ran down his back and made his dress shirt stick like a layer of skin, not cotton. He'd lost one shoe when they took him.

The harsh voices of his captors, a press gang that chuckled and sneered around words spoken with an accent that suggested they did not belong to a world of villas and clerks, perhaps not even crowded cities, eclipsed the sickening patriotic hymns. Had they reached their destination? Allard had no grasp what the Front Line was—an actual boundary, a barrier?

What or who was on the other side? No vid or instructor would offer information, suggest any clue. No official would tell. When asked, his father had gone silent and his mother had muttered, "The enemy of the State," and asked him to read her latest verses, concerned they sounded too metallic.

Why did he let his hormones cloud his judgment last night? Why did lying to his parents about studies after dinner, slipping out of the villa, boarding the speed rail into the city, making his way to the Workers' district and breaking curfew to see Kyet, merit this fate? He should be waking up in his soft bed. His stomach grumbled. His father's position ensured three good meals a day. Breakfast was the best, with fresh fruit, a hecto of meat, and even pure honey on light bread.

He hoped that whatever militsiya in charge at the Front Line would be reasonable. They would check his ID, permit a vid-call home and all would be well. Yes, there would be punishment, but Allard would gladly endure it to avoid whatever else might be awaiting him when they released him from the van.

Footsteps sounded just outside the van's rear doors. The spider paused, and then crawled back to its hiding space a moment before the doors opened.

Allard blinked at the daylight. Behind the men, he glimpsed an empty landscape surrounding a cracked ribbon of asphalt that stretched all the way to the distant horizon. Nothing but barren land crowded the road. No farmland, no vegetation. Just loose dirt caught in the breeze.

Two of the three men carried an injured boy in their arms. They tossed him into the van, near Allard's feet, as if they were throwing in a bag of garbage.

"I don't belong here," Allard shouted at them.

The nearest man slapped him hard across the face but the sting faded when they unlocked the manacle from the wall of the van. A brief burst of hope rose in Allard—they were going to set him free, even if it were in some forsaken wilderness—until the second man, who had a thick unkempt mustache, lifted the fallen boy's right arm and snapped the manacle around the wrist.

"Here's some dead weight for you," he told Allard. His breath stank of the spices the State's commissary used to hide the cheapest cuts of dog meat. At least, that was what Allard's mother would say.

But she was a liar. He had proof in his pocket.

The boy at his feet wasn't dead—Allard could see his chest rise and fall beneath the grimy overalls that marked him as a Worker. Not that Allard was biased; Kyet might never become a Citizen, but he could steal your breath with his looks. This boy also had a handsome, dark-skinned face, though it was marred by the dripping gore from the bloody cut at his temple.

Maybe Allard preferred boys who would never read poetry. Perhaps that was betraying the State. His parents would rather he pursue engineers at the university.

He nudged the boy with his foot. The boy stirred.

· · ·

Tetch woke to nausea layered over a massive headache, worse than any hangover he'd ever had—when had he swallowed a live rat and how could it be scratching at the inside of his skull? He tried to press a couple of fingers against his throbbing temples and felt a drag, a constraint on his right arm. He pulled harder and heard someone yell in the surrounding darkness.

"Don't do that."

"Do what?" Tetch spat as he sat up. It was either that or retch, which felt tempting, but he doubted it would help soothe his head. Hot metal lay beneath him. Moving metal, based on the vibration. He had trouble opening his eyes. Blood that had seeped down his scalp glued them shut. He was in a vehicle. How?

"We're shackled together."

Tetch opened his eyes and looked up at the boy sitting inches away. Young. Privileged. Clothes a bit dirty. They both must have been picked up by the militsiya for breaking curfew. Though the boy wasn't bad looking, Tetch thought he was too soft—he even wore glasses, a social affectation since the State promised every Citizen good eyes for life.

Tetch lifted up his left hand and saw the manacle tight around his right wrist. *That* had not happened the last time he was picked up. Had they decided to add some new cruelty to their punishment for a petty offense?

"What's your name?" the boy asked him.

"Don't you mean 'What does the State call me?'" He closed his eyes and tried to remember what had happened. He had been walking home from an illegal second shift, cleaning gears in the Ministry of Timekeeping until the late hour of 13:00 . . .

"I know you're not a Citizen. But you have a name."

Tetch groaned. He felt around for something to lean against, found the metal ledge the annoying boy sat on, and pulled himself up. He made sure to tug hard at the cord binding them, to test just how heavy and strong the boy might be. He almost toppled. Tetch smiled.

"If the State cared about its people—all its people, not just the ones with good homes—neither of us would be sitting here." Tetch blew his nose clear. He caught a whiff of cologne. "You may not be street, but you still stink."

The boy stiffened on the ledge. "I don't stink."

"Oh, yes you do. Not like garbage or piss. Lemme guess. What's all the perfume the Party debutantes wear these days? *Loyalty No. 4*?" Tetch leaned close to the boy and breathed in deep. "No, I think it's *Nepotism*." He laughed, which left him wincing from the way it hurt his head.

"It's not perfume. It's cologne. And it's not even mine—"

"Well, you reek of it. So either you're finally lying like a good Party boy or you've been sweating the sheets with some—"

"Sweating the sheets?"

"Sure. Never heard that one?"

"No." A moment later, the boy chuckled. "But it's not a bad one."

"No, it's not."

They sat there in silence a while.

"This isn't for breaking curfew."

"No."

"Shit. What are they blaming me for?"

"I don't know. I don't think anything. They're a press gang."

Press gangs. He had grown up with his older sister telling nightmare stories of such men stealing children if a window were ever opened for fresh air. And all Workers would refer to someone who angered the State enough to "disappear" as being "pressed" into service.

He was going to disappear.

Tetch vomited then, throwing up the meager food he'd spent his wages on to take the edge off his hunger after he'd worked so long, so often. It didn't look like much splattered on the van's floor, but the stench helped cover up the other boy's cologne.

"They're bringing us to the Front Lines," Tetch said as he wiped his lips.

"I think so. I tried reasoning with them. They can't just take a Citizen off the streets—I mean . . ."

Tetch stared at him, seeing the embarrassment on his face color it red.

"Sorry. Look. Just because you're a Worker and I'm not, doesn't mean we have to hate each other. I like Workers—"

"I'm so happy to hear that. Makes everything all right, knowing I have a Worker Sympathizer shackled to me."

The boy blinked. Then he turned away. Just as well. Tetch closed his eyes and pretended to sleep. Maybe his heartbeat would calm down. The Front Line. Shit.

• • •

The van began to slow down. Allard looked at the Worker youth, who had opened his eyes.

Then came the sound of an explosion. Tires bursting. The van shook, tilted and toppled.

Allard found himself atop the other boy. He was very aware of how sweaty and hot the Worker's skin was against his own. The Worker had hazel eyes.

"You okay?" asked Allard.

"Once you roll off me. What happened?"

They listened. Screams began. The men of the press gang shouted foreign words in terror. Gunshots. The sound paralyzed Allard. He pressed tighter and closer against the Worker. Instinct, he told himself, the instinct to find comfort in holding another when you're scared. The Worker struggled to push him off and rise but Allard whispered in his ear not to move. He didn't know for sure that was the wisest decision, but he couldn't imagine it would be wise to bring attention to themselves in the back of the van. He didn't know what was outside but as long as it didn't know they were *inside*, they'd be safe. Or, at least, safer.

The screams stopped. Not tapered off. Just stopped.

What is it? mouthed the Worker.

He didn't know, all his years of instruction rendered useless. Allard just looked into the Worker's pretty hazel eyes. Kyet had nice eyes, but not hazel eyes. Good hazel eyes that the State had probably never touched but were perfect based on genetics alone.

What?

Heavy footsteps. Many. As if a mob walked around the van. No, not a mob, because there was a pattern to the falling feet, as if it were the marching sound of a military parade. The notion, so ridiculous but somehow so apt, made Allard smile, which must have perplexed the Worker, who looked lost.

"A parade of thousands," whispered Allard.

Then, whoever was outside began to beat on the walls of the van. It drowned out the streaming music—in fact, the speakers in the van died—as if they sought to turn the van into a metal drum and signal their violence to the entire State. Allard bit his lip. There was a rhythm, a definite meter, one that tantalized his memory with familiarity. Where had he heard it before?

The pounding did not last long. Again came the sound of countless feet in unison stamping the hard earth. But they moved away until all was silent.

His sweat dripped from his forehead on to the other boy's

chin, right where a scattering of early whiskers was beginning to grow. He dwelt a while on the motion of the Worker's chest beneath him. Up and down. He realized that, only hours ago, he would have given anything to be in a similar position with Kyet. He had been spurned, laughed at, but now found himself atop someone even more alluring.

He had the urge to lower his head a bit and kiss the Worker. He had never kissed anyone before. He had watched vids of it being done and wanted to know the sensation. Would it occupy his entire mouth? He suspected his entire body would know it was being kissed, despite just lips touching one another.

The smell of sweat and the intimate smell of the Worker filled his lungs. Not a terrible smell. Not bad at all. He focused on that, not whatever lurked outside, not on Kyet, and breathed deeply.

"I think they're gone," the Worker whispered.

"Uh-huh."

The Worker moved beneath him, then stopped. "You're enjoying this."

Allard realized he had an erection that was pressing against the Worker's leg.

"Sorry."

But the Worker now wore a smirk, one that both embarrassed and consoled Allard, who stood up. The Worker followed, of course, thanks to the cord linking their wrists. But while he peered out through one of the bullet holes in the van wall, Allard stared at him.

• • •

Tetch did not know if he should tell Citizen-boy what he saw through the holes. He wasn't really sure himself. Perhaps he was wrong. There are no such things as metal spiders. He must have seen a piece of debris dropping from the van.

"It looks . . . clear enough."

He turned back to Citizen-boy, whose interest had subsided enough not to be so noticeable, though he still looked flushed and embarrassed. Tetch could not help but give him a smile—there were Worker sympathizers and then *Worker sympathizers*. Plus, well, it was kind of flattering to know that being kidnapped did not detract from his appeal.

"Your family know you like boys in overalls?" Tetch asked. He made a show of pulling at the edges of the hook-and-loop fastener at his collar. Now some of his chest was exposed. Citizen-boy's eyes widened.

"Uhh . . . no."

He took a step closer to Citizen-boy and, with his unshackled hand, lifted up the slack on the cord connecting them. "I think you're starting to like this." Nothing wrong with ensuring that the guy did exactly what Tetch needed. Or wanted. It had to be a long way back to the capital.

"I–I . . ." Citizen-boy swallowed. "Maybe."

"Let's get out of here," Tetch said.

The doors were still locked. Together, they kicked at the latch until it broke.

Tetch blinked at the light and enjoyed the sensation of the cooler air greeting his skin.

They moved around to the side of the van. Whatever had happened to the front end had left it twisted and broken. Slashed tires were hanging in tendrils of black rubber and metal wire. The windows were shattered, leaving the ground glittering with broken safety glass. The driver-side door had been torn off and thrown twenty feet away. But thrown by what?

Tetch saw blood on the ground. He should go check—not to see if they were dead, he didn't doubt that—but the press gang might have a v-comm or something useful.

Something skittered near Tetch's foot. Citizen-boy yelped at what looked like a cross between a human hand and a spider, with legs tipped in gleaming metal and trailing a segmented cord as it crawled over the roof of the van.

"What was that thing?!"

"I don't know."

Moments after he slowly began moving back toward the open van doors, he realized he had taken hold of Citizen-boy's hand. He looked down at their fingers, sweaty in the heat, glanced back up at Citizen-boy's face, which still wore an expression of fear, and realized the guy hadn't yet noticed the gesture. So he squeezed the boy's hand. Not hard. Fondly.

"Stay behind me."

"That was my plan."

He saw a shadow—and stiffened, raising a fist ready for a fight—before he saw the figure itself. Then he saw the face and took two steps back, nearly tripping over Citizen-boy. That face would not remain still, the robotic eyes rotating to and fro, the slack mouth full of tiny feelers, or maybe antennae, motioning like pistons in and out to test the air. It wore a red-and-black State military uniform and one of its arms lacked a hand. Only for a moment, because the crazy spider-like thing they had just seen was now crawling up the figure and then finally attached itself to the arm's metal stump.

"Shit," muttered Citizen-boy behind Tetch.

The figure's head turned with a jerking motion. It spoke, or rather, a speaker inside the chest sounded:

How many times these low feet staggered—
Only the soldered mouth can tell—
Try—can you stir the awful rivet—
Try—can you lift the husps of steel!

"No. It can't be. I know that," said Citizen-boy. He sounded as if he'd been elbowed in the gut.

• • •

Allard wondered if he were dreaming. Although the figure standing in the hot sun before them belonged in nightmares, what it recited made the moment difficult to believe. Words, lines of poetry with the same meter that had been pounded out on the metal walls of the van earlier. Lines of poetry that belonged to his mother's most recent, most widely read post on NationWeb.

His unshackled hand went to his trouser pocket and clenched the library stick he had found by his mother's terminal early last night. Library sticks were contraband; the only texts permitted by the State were on NationWeb. His instructors had showed Allard such sticks and warned him they usually contained sordid reading material written prior to the Founding Citizens. He had not understood why his mother would possess one until he took it back to his room and slipped it into his terminal.

The stick contained poetry. Page after page of poetry. He had searched and found every line that his mother had ever posted, every one of which she claimed had come to her in seizures of creative and patriotic fervor. Allard did not know what to call her. Not a traitor, but there had to be some black word worse than liar. A thief maybe.

Or worse. A troubling thought—his mother could have

discovered the missing stick while he'd been in the capital. In a rage, she could have been so horrible as to take his father's v-comm and demand someone in the Party have a press gang pick up her son. Or maybe he was paranoid. Press gangs could have been stalking stations. Maybe it was just a coincidence. But why then had they refused to let him prove he was a Citizen, why did they laugh when he promised that his parents would pay any reward or ransom?

A person could be betrayed by more than the State.

We are the Front Line, the figure recited. It repeated the verses again.

"Do you understand what it's saying?" Worker-boy asked Allard softly.

Allard nodded. He whispered into the Worker boy's ear, "Now we know what they do to pressed people. Turn them into some machine soldier. Only, they've gone past their programming. The poem . . . I think, inspired them to revolt."

"Fuck the State," Worker-boy muttered.

"More like the State is fucked." It was the first time in his life that Allard had ever said such a thing. It felt as liberating as a kiss. Or so he imagined.

"So the reason we're still alive is because it remembers that it was once like us?"

"I hope. It would explain why the press gang is smeared." Allard held out the library stick.

"What is that?" the Worker asked.

"A key. Maybe. Or a conscience. Or it might be nothing at all. But they deserve it more than we do."

He held the library stick out to the Front Line, which picked it up by growing fingernails that grasped the stick and brought it up to its strange mouth where it clicked and connected.

The Front Line extended one arm and, with one smooth and swift gesture between them, severed the manacles' cord. It turned and began following the tire tracks of the van.

"Wait," shouted the Worker. "What's out there?" He gestured toward the horizon.

The Front Line's head twisted around to face them even as it kept walking. *Others. Like you.*

"Huh." Allard kicked off his remaining shoe. He almost fell and had to grab hold of the other boy's arm to keep steady.

"Others like me." The Worker shook Allard's hand. "Tetch."

Allard smiled. "Others like us. Allard."

"Us. That sounds like an invitation for a kiss," Tetch said as he grabbed both of Allard's hands.

"Or to recite some poetry."

"No."

And the kiss, such a marvelous kiss, was just the beginning.

Red

Amanda Downum

In the dream I'm in a garden. In the dream I'm not alone. A girl stands beside me, a girl with eyes red as poison apples. She takes my hand, and her skin is cold.

"We have to go north."

I wake with the taste of storms in my mouth and screams echoing down the hall. Slow and dream-sticky and for a second I don't know where I am, but I'm on my feet with my gun in my hand before my eyes are all the way open.

A second later I sigh, rubbing crust out of my eyelashes left-handed: it's only Amber and her nightmares. I was dreaming too, but it's already crumbling like sandcastles. Even familiar screams shouldn't be ignored, though, so I ease the door open and glance both ways before I slip down the hall.

Amber's awake when I get there, sobbing and gasping while Kayla pats her back and murmurs soothing nonsense. Kay gives me a nod and I lower the gun. The metal is cool and heavy against my thigh.

"You okay?" I ask, still foggy from sleep.

Amber nods, scrubbing away tears. Her hair stands in tousled cockatiel-spikes, the bright red of salvaged Kool-Aid faded now to dirty pink. "Yeah, sorry. It's just—" She waves a

187

hand at the barred and shuttered window, at the hissing rain beyond.

"Yeah."

"Everyone okay?" Dave calls from down the hall. He's shy about the girls' rooms.

"All clear," I yell back.

Kayla lights a candle and I squint at Amber's creepy Kit Kat clock—nearly eleven in the morning. Early for me, but I doubt I'll get back to sleep, or find the dream again if I do.

"Get some more rest," I tell Amber. "I'll do your detail today."

Kayla gives me a smile, probably thinking of my good karma. She doesn't call herself Wiccan anymore—*an it harm none,* didn't last long after the end of the world—but old habits linger.

I wash and dress in my room—I miss running water most of all, I think. A pint of cold water and a washcloth don't measure up to a real shower. Kayla makes us oil scrubs and baking soda shampoo and all kinds of hippie stuff, but it's not the same.

The rain slackens, sighing against the window. The storm is almost gone. I glance at my door, double-check the flimsy hook. Just a quick look . . .

I ease the shutters open, wincing at every tiny squeak. The others would never let me live this down. It's stupid and dangerous and puts the whole house at risk. But I have to see.

Crooked bars behind the shutter, glass cracked and streaked behind them. Beyond that, the storm.

The sky is the color of the space behind my eyes, red-black and shot through with distant lightning. The end of the world is alizarin and crimson, ruby and garnet, tangled streaks of scarlet on my windowpane. The end of the world is beautiful.

The smell leaks through the chinks—copper and iron, bitter and salty and cloyingly sweet. Not exactly blood, but close enough. I remember the taste of it and swallow hard.

Distant thunder growls and its voice is the voice of my dream. *North*, it says. I shudder as images surface: a garden blooming with poison-red flowers, unfurling their creepers in the twilight; a girl with eyes the same poppy red. *North*.

My hands shake as I close the window tight. We forgive each other all manner of quirks to live as we do, but the others won't forgive this. My secret, the taste of red rain on my lips. I tasted the rain and I'm still alive—still human, still sane—but I feel the storms coming now, and the monsters that sprout like mushrooms in their wake. Kayla thinks I'm psychic, and I let her. They'd kill me or turn me out if they knew.

I've lost two families already to the apocalypse rain. I can't bring myself to give up this one.

• • •

Amber was on clean-up crew today, so I help Seb sweep and do dishes. There's extra scrubbing—tomorrow we're hosting a gang-meet. We check in with each other whenever we can, but every three months one gang hosts the others for a formal get-together. I get a quiet nagging fear before every meet, and I know the others do, too: What if this time someone doesn't come?

Seb is probably disappointed about the schedule switch, but he doesn't say anything. Seb doesn't say anything ever, as far as I can tell. He's certainly never said he has a crush on Amber, but my intuition still works, even if the water and electricity don't. He's the youngest of us, still just a kid when the first storm came—now he's callused and hard-eyed, the fastest of all us on the draw. You'd never know he's only fifteen.

Not even two years younger than me, but some days I feel a hundred years old.

Kayla comes down by the time we're finished. I make coffee and we sit in the gloomy kitchen waiting for the red storm to blow out and the next to blow in. It always rains after, a real rain. We don't know why—new weather patterns, or maybe the world is trying to clean out the contagion. We don't know much of anything, except to adapt or die.

After a long quiet, Kayla nudges my foot under the table. I look up, realizing I've been staring into the dregs of my coffee. "What's up, kiddo?"

"I had the dream again," I say, though I didn't mean to.

"North?"

I nod and swallow cold coffee to keep my mouth busy. I've told her about the thunder, but not the garden. And not the red-eyed girl—that part is new.

"It comes with every storm, doesn't it?"

If Kayla weren't smart and perceptive, she never would have held the Orphans together this long. Still, sometimes I wish she were a little less smart. "Pretty much, yeah."

"What do you think it means?"

"I don't know. But it feels important. It wants me to answer." I give her a crooked grin. "That's probably a bad idea, though."

It's Kayla's turn to frown at her mug. A familiar clatter and bang drifts in from outside—Nick and Geoff setting up the catchment. The clean rain is here.

"Probably. We'll talk about it later. After the meeting."

After the rain stops and the boys give the all-clear on the

weather, I suit up and do the rounds. It's been quiet lately, and it's starting to bug me. Not the itch in my blood that means something's really wrong, but a vague distrust. Nothing moves outside, but my hand stays near my gun as I circle the grounds.

Home is a castle. A little castle on a hill in the middle of downtown Austin. A military school back in the 1800s. I don't know what happened to it after that—it was closed and boarded up when we moved in. It's not as defensible as Las Calaveras' headquarters, or as gorgeous as the Spooks', but it's got a great view.

The last rain clouds snag and tatter against the skyscrapers. Glass spires and ziggurats fade into the haze, their grimy windows reflecting the light in streaks and flashes, crackle-finished. Below them, a young forest grows. Nature moves fast now that the world's fallen apart.

Too fast, sometimes. The trees are pressing against the fence again and we had pruned only a week ago. Lately the plants have started to change, too, strange new flowers and fungi sprouting in the shade. Kayla doesn't like the look of them. She keeps a close eye on the greenhouse since we saw the first one, but so far we haven't been menaced by bloodthirsty tomatoes or zucchini.

Ivy twines through the fence, leaves and spiraling tendrils softening the harsh lines of the wire. I rip it away with gloved hands, trying not to think about the garden in my dreams. The original fence couldn't have kept out a lazy dog, let alone zombies, so we put up chain link and razorwire. Geoff and Dave talk about building a real bricks-and-mortar wall, but I like being able to see what's lurking on the other side.

Halfway through my circuit I get a shiver, the nasty kind, but it fades too quickly to figure out where it came from. I can't see anything moving in the brush, except a couple of squirrels that don't seem any more vicious than usual. The gates are all locked, the tripwires unsprung. I'm less scared of shamblers than of other people, really. We have a sturdy truce with the Spooks and Las Calaveras, but you never know. Things were ugliest during the gang wars, when you couldn't trust anything that moved, living or dead. It calmed down after the Kings and Hammers got slaughtered, but I worry. We're still human, and even a good apocalypse can't cure humans of stupidity. And I won't feel humans coming.

I check in with Dave after my rounds. He's the last of the Hammers, the only one who didn't go down to monsters or to other gangs. He's really not so bad, now that he doesn't call himself Thor. It took a while, but losing enough fights with Geoff finally knocked the racist bullshit out of his head. We don't even flinch at his swastika tattoo anymore—it's just another scar. We're all orphans here.

• • •

After lunch I take my knitting and sketchpad up to the tower. I'm halfway through a scarf that I think will be Amber's birthday present, if I finish it in time. My grandmother taught me to knit, another world ago—other than my middle name, it's all I have left of her. And twelve inches of pointy steel are nice to have around. The sketching is just for me, the last part of me from before the rain, when I was a daughter and a granddaughter, a sister and a girlfriend, a student and an artist. All the things I lost when I became a survivor, an Orphan.

Underneath the chilly gray November sky, I can almost make believe the world is still alive. Except for the silence. No more traffic, no more humming wires, no more distant voices.

Not even screams and gunshots lately. Just the wind and the last of the rain dripping from the gutters, the soft scrape of my pencil on scavenged cold-press paper.

The shiver comes back, a prickling below my skin. I glance up from my drawing and scan the yard, one hand drifting toward my gun. Nothing inside the perimeter, or on the road . . . There. On the slope below the house, amid crumbling cement terraces and rusting rebar, the bones of stillborn condos, something moves.

A girl.

She stands there, watching me through the fence. Her stance hits me first—not the dazed sway or wary crouch of the shamblers. She stands hip-shot, one thumb tucked into a pocket of her tattered jeans. Like a living person. I raise my hand, lips parting to call, when the rest sinks in: her sickly gray pallor, the ugly wound stretching across her right shoulder, blood streaking her face. My hand falls.

She cocks her head and waves back.

I stand there for a minute, gaping. I swear she grins at me. I've never seen a zombie move like that, and it's too bright out for the nastier things. But the rain evolves. All we can do is try to keep up.

Footsteps rattle the stairs and before I can second-guess myself I shake my head at her, make a shooing gesture. I don't trust Seb or Dave not to shoot first and think later. But it's only Nick. By the time he climbs up, the girl is gone.

I have a new secret.

Nick isn't even wearing his gun and I should bitch at him, but I'm too busy trying not to look nervous. It must not work because he says, "Sorry, did I scare you?"

"It's the quiet. It gets to me after a while."

He nods. "Do you mind?" he asks, pausing with one foot still on the stairs.

"No, come on up." I pull my yarn bag out of his way, sneaking a glance at the hill to make sure the girl is still gone.

Nick is a year older than me—he would have started college this year. Tall and skinny and beaky-nosed, with dark hair that's always flopping in his face. He liked gaming once, and movies and computers and rock climbing. The sort of boy I would have been friends with. The sort of boy I might have dated. It hurts to hang out with him sometimes, a sharp thorny feeling in my chest. We all get that pain; it's called *before*.

We stand in silence, leaning against the crenellations and watching the clouds tatter and drift away, and I wait for the awkward moment to come. Nick's been trying, in his quiet way, to ask me out. Not that there's any *out* left. Don't get me wrong—he's cute, and I'm tempted. A lot tempted. I can't even remember my last kiss. But so much could go wrong, besides any of the usual relationship messes.

Michelle was six months pregnant when she got caught in a storm. She died slow and screaming for five days before Kayla finally shot her. Nobody talks about it, but we can't forget. And even if a baby didn't kill me from the inside out, who knows what the lingering traces of rain in my blood would do?

I swallow sour spit and turn to collect my sketchpad. My drawing stares up at me—a forest, rough and smudged, thick graphite shadows between the trees and flowering vines dangling from the branches like spiders.

I flip the sketchbook closed and gather my stuff.

"Audra—" Nick looks so sad, and I know we can't put the conversation off any longer. "Did I do something? You keep avoiding me . . ." His hair falls over his long-lashed dark eyes and I want to tuck it back.

"I'm sorry. You haven't done anything. It's not you—" Nick snorts, and I can't finish the sentence. Some lines don't get any less lame even after the world ends. "It's everything." That's still horrible, but it's true.

"Yeah." He smiles, wry and understanding, and I wonder if maybe I'm being an idiot. "It's not like either of us could move out if we had a bad breakup."

"I'm sorry." I lean in to kiss his cheek, my bag held between us like a shield. The smell of his hair nearly undoes my very limited virtue.

"It's okay." He touches my arm awkwardly. "I'll see you around, anyway."

We laugh, but it's strained. My eyes are blurring by the time I get back inside. I blame hormones.

• • •

I'm restless all day, picking up a dozen projects and setting them down again. Finally I put my leathers on and take another walk around the perimeter. What I'd really like is to walk outside, down Castle Hill and through the broken streets, a different view to clear my head. But outside is too dangerous alone.

I feel a shiver at the northeast corner. To the north lies an overgrown driveway and the broken remnants of a house nearly consumed by trees and brambles. East faces downtown, and slabs of broken, weed-choked cement below the fence. I can't see anything but a few birds moving in the trees and the leaves sighing in the breeze. I glance back, but I'm alone in the yard; the turret is empty.

Leaves crunch, a single deliberate footstep. I spin, hand dropping to my gun.

The girl. She stands at the bottom of the terraced wall, watching me through the fence. When I flinch, she shows me her empty hands, slowly and carefully as if I were the one who might bite.

She's my age. Was my age. Dressed in dirty jeans and a tank top, thick black hair pulled back in a braid. Her skin must have been a warm golden-brown once, a shade or two darker than mine. Now it's cold and gray. The wound I saw this morning is still there, a nasty gash on her shoulder, skin flapping to expose raw flesh. No blood or infection, just dark red meat and pale marbled fat. Her eyes are wide and shadowed under thick, arching brows.

Her eyes are red. Not zombie eyes, bloodshot and clouded, but clear and bright, carmine and carnelian.

My breath catches. "I saw you—"

She raises her eyebrows, living movement on a dead face. "This morning, yeah." Her voice is soft and raspy, but human. She draws breath to speak; she wasn't breathing before.

"No. I saw you in a dream."

She smiles, flashing white teeth. "That's romantic, but we're taking things a little fast, don't you think? I don't even know your name."

My face goes hot. Zombies don't smile like that. They don't tease. Even the other things, the ones that prowl outside camps at night, crying and wailing like lost children—even they don't *flirt*.

"You're different," I whisper, mostly to myself.

Her smile widens; her eyeteeth are thick and sharp. "And you haven't shot me yet, so maybe you're different too."

"What are you?" I flush again, hotter this time. I've shot dozens of monsters, but that was just rude. "I'm sorry. I mean—"

The dead girl laughs at me. "I'm Natalie." She presses one palm against the fence.

"Audra." I squat down so we're closer, but don't touch her hand. I may be going crazy, but I'm not stupid. "What are you doing out there?"

"The same thing you're doing in there: surviving."

"Are you . . . hungry?"

"All the time." Her smile twists and falls away. "But I don't eat what you eat anymore."

I was afraid she'd say that. "You're hurt." Which sounds stupid, considering she's dead, but that cut makes my skin crawl to look at.

"This?" She pokes at the skin flap and I cringe. "It doesn't hurt, really. Sort of itches. I have to keep the bugs out, though." She grimaces, which is terrifying.

"I should go," I say, my mouth dry. "Don't—Don't talk to any of the others. They might not—"

"Care that I'm different?"

"I'm sorry."

She shrugs. "Not your fault. Thanks for not shooting me."

"I—You're welcome." This isn't the strangest conversation I've had since the world ended, but it's close. "What are you going to do?"

Natalie takes a step back. "I'm going north." My mouth falls open, and she pauses. "You dreamed of that, too, didn't you?"

Before I can answer someone calls my name. I turn to see Geoff halfway across the yard. When I look back Natalie is gone.

"What is it?" Geoff asks as I hurry to meet him. Trying not to act like I'm hurrying.

"A cat. He looked healthy, but he ran away."

Geoff frowns sympathetically. His shirt is soaked, and stray soapsuds cling in the black cloud of his hair. "Sorry, Aud. You know we can't have pets."

"I know. I just miss my old cat."

He pats my shoulder. "Yeah. Get your laundry, kiddo. We don't want to stink for our guests."

I don't look back as we go inside. I don't open my window. But when I dream that night, I dream of red eyes.

• • •

The others arrive before noon the next day. I stand on the turret with Nick and Amber to watch them ride in, waving the blue flag that means all clear.

It's hard to look tough riding bicycles, but Las Calaveras manage in their chains and painted jackets. The Spooks pedal up the hill behind them, dressed all in black, as usual. We laugh about the colors sometimes, but I have to admit they look pretty impressive.

Las Calaveras sent six people this time, the Spooks five, putting the temporary population of the castle at eighteen. Nearly ten percent of the city's current population. Math didn't use to depress me this much.

Gang-meet means presents. Our guests bring cookies, tortillas still warm in an insulated bag, two bottles of wine, a bag of yarn, two ten-packs of AA batteries, and a fancy set of knives. We give them fresh vegetables, a leather jacket, a fountain pen with an extra nib and a bottle of ink, a pair of blankets that Kayla and I knitted, and a zombie teddy bear still in the original box. Maybe that shouldn't be funny, but I think it's pretty cute. Cat, the head Spook, coos at it like it was a baby and hugs Kayla. We've run out of so many things, but Cat never seems to run out of eyeliner or hair dye. There's lots of hugging and "You look good!" and manly handshakes between the guys.

Usually we draw straws to see who attends the meeting and who keeps watch, but today is different. Marisela, the leader of Las Calaveras, asks all the girls to join them, and the guys to wait outside. Geoff frowns and Nick raises his eyebrows, but no one argues with her—she makes the tortillas. I sit in the back next to Amber, trying not to feel like I have "Fraternized with the enemy" written across my forehead.

"Lupe had her baby," Marisela tells us, after we've settled in the kitchen and coffee and cookies have been shared. "A boy. She named him Carlos, after his father." Carlos Senior died six months ago, so the congratulations are a little sad. Marisela accepts them like a proud grandmother. She's not even forty, but her brown face is seamed, her hair already gray.

"That brings us to my main concern," she continues. "I've discussed it a little with Cat, but it affects everyone. We need children, or we'll never rebuild."

I shiver, despite the body heat filling the kitchen. Beside me, Amber does too. The idea makes my stomach sour. She wouldn't say that if she'd seen Michelle. Or maybe she would. Marisela's seen her share of terrible things. She had a daughter, *before*. I don't know what happened and, besides, the thing is, she's right.

"We'd need more resources for children," Kayla says. "Better security."

Marisela nods. "My people are already working on it, for

Carlos. Children will make these things happen. It's too easy to put it off, to say *maybe next year*. And then a dozen next years have passed and half of us are dead. If we want to survive here, to build, it has to happen."

Kayla doesn't answer for a minute, and her shoulders sag. "I've tried. Me and Geoff, I mean. For the past six months. I know that's not very long, but . . . I have tried."

I lean back at the news, frowning. Amber startles. Nice to know I'm not the only Orphan with secrets.

Marisela nods, her dark eyes creasing with sympathy. "Give it time. It's not only your burden." She looks around the room, and I try not to duck when her gaze touches me.

"It shouldn't be anyone's burden," Kayla says, catching that glance. "I want a baby. Amber doesn't, and Audra is too young."

Amber's never talked about children one way or another, but I know what Kayla really means. The nightmares, the panic attacks, the way Amber shuts down when the storms get bad—she's the most fragile of all of us that way, and I doubt a baby would help. Especially after Michelle.

"I don't want a baby either," Cat says, picking at her nail polish. "Never did. But Mari's right—we have to do it, or Austin will be empty in twenty years." She nods to one of her companions, a skinny girl not much older than I am. "Angel is willing to try."

Marisela looks back to me, and I want to crawl through the wall. "How old are you, Audra?"

I swallow a stray cookie crumb scraping down my throat. "Seventeen next month."

Marisela frowns and nods. "Young, but not too young to consider it."

Kayla scowls. "You can't make—"

"Of course not. But I can ask. And you can think about it. Which leads me to my other idea. We should consider an exchange of members. One or two people, for a few months a time. So we could learn new skills, make new friends."

Meet new people we might want to have babies with. My stomach is sick with the weight of sugar and caffeine. I have a dozen excuses to say no. I'm too young. There's no one I like that much. I'm terrified of the idea. But I can never share the real reason—the red seed inside me.

"We'll think about it," Kayla says, her lips pinched. "Any other news?"

Cat sits up straight. "We've seen a couple of scavengers creeping around downtown. The human kind. We've tried talking, but they run. I don't know if they're crazy or dangerous or just scared, but keep your eyes open."

"I have a question," I say, before the meeting ends and turns into socializing and dinner. All eyes turn to me and my cheeks scald. "I—Some of you know that I . . . feel things, right?" The last word comes out a squeak. I may be effectively proving that I'm too young for anything. Marisela and Cat nod. Kayla frowns, but gestures for me to go on. I take a deep breath, forcing the rest out in a rush.

"I've been having dreams lately. The same dream. I hear a voice telling me to go north. And I wondered if anyone else has had that dream."

Silence fills the kitchen, broken by the scuff of shoes and rasp of cloth.

"Tia Soledad has dreams like that," Marisela says at last. Soledad is the Calaveras matriarch; a curandera, they say. I've only met her once, but I'm willing to believe she's a witch. "She says she dreams of a garden, a place of death." She crosses herself, though she's a Catholic the way Kayla used to be a Wiccan. "It makes her afraid. And even if it didn't—" she catches my eye for an instant "—'north' is too vague to go looking."

Others nod, and I can't argue. I can't argue that in my dream, the garden isn't a place of death, only of different life. A place of change. The way I'm changed. Maybe the way Natalie is, too. I can't say any of that, though, so I shut up and help clean up for dinner.

• • •

The Spooks and Las Calaveras spend the night, which is weird but nice. Weird to have strangers in the castle, people we don't know and trust like our own skin. Nice to hear laughter and new voices, to see a dozen people camped out downstairs as if it were a grade-school sleepover. Cat brought hot chocolate. The miniature marshmallows are fossilized, but no one complains.

The warm fuzzies last until Marisela finds me in the kitchen, rinsing out the cups. Her company should be reassuring—she's strong and smart, with a brusque competence that reminds me of my mother. But after today's meeting, I would rather face a zombie.

"I scared you today. I'm sorry."

"It's not you." The line doesn't sound any better than when I said it to Nick. I set the last cup in the draining board and start wiping down the silverware.

Marisela snorts. She's had twenty extra years to hear lame excuses. "I'd like you to come back with me. Not to get knocked up," she adds as I fumble a handful of forks. "Just to visit for a while. Tia Soledad would like to hear about your dreams."

And I want to know about hers. If I dream of the garden because I'm tainted, does that mean Soledad is too? Or is there another cause? I don't know how I'd ask her without giving up my secret, but I'm almost willing to try.

"I don't know," I say. "I'd have to ask Kayla."

"I talked to Kayla already." I duck my head so she can't see my grimace—of course she did. "She says it's your decision. I'd send someone to replace you, of course, so the Orphans wouldn't suffer."

The Orphans are the smallest group, barely enough of us to keep ourselves safe and fed after Michelle died, and Jamie before her. But we like it here, like being together. Marisela's exchange-student program is a good idea, but I'm afraid it will lead to the Orphans finding new families.

"Thank you for the invitation," I say, risking a glance at her face. If she has any ulterior motives, I can't read them in her eyes. "Let me think about it."

"Of course."

• • •

Dawn is a peach-and-periwinkle glow behind the jagged lines of downtown when I leave my room. Dreams ache in the pit of my stomach—not the thunder dreams, but nightmares about Nick and Michelle and red-eyed babies. I shove my first-aid kit under my jacket, guilt like a hot hand on the back of my neck.

Kayla has the morning watch, which is good and bad. She doesn't need explanations when I tell her I want to go for a walk alone.

"You've been restless for a while, haven't you?" she says. That's the bad part. "Before yesterday."

I hadn't thought about it, but she's right. The answer is obvious: ever since the dreams started.

"You want to go north."

I shrug, shoulders hunched to hide the bulge under my jacket. "I know it's stupid, but yeah. What if this is real? What if it's important?"

"I don't know. I guess you have to decide what's most important to you."

"Marisela thinks that Tia Soledad could help me understand the dreams."

"Maybe she can. Do you want to go with her?"

"No," I say, as honest as it gets. "But if you want me to . . ."

"I don't want. But it might be a good idea. It would make Marisela happy, and you'd learn things. I don't want things to get bad between the gangs again."

No one would survive another war.

"Let me think about it. And let me go for a walk. Outside. I'll be careful."

Her forehead creases. "All right. But don't go far, okay?"

"I won't."

Natalie is waiting for me in the same spot, crouching below the wall where no one in the castle could see.

"Hi," she says. In the soft dawn light, her smile looks like a living girl's.

I try to smile back, but it feels crooked and wrong. "If I come out of the fence, are you going to eat me?"

"No eating. I promise." She traces an X over her left breast. "Cross my heart and hope to be pecked apart by buzzards."

"Are you alone?"

Her smile fades. "Completely." Loneliness on a dead girl's face is the saddest thing I've ever seen.

I unlock the padlocked lesser gate, holding the chain carefully so the links don't rattle. My skin crawls at the sudden vulnerability, but I don't feel anything but the familiar itch of Natalie.

She keeps her distance as I creep down the slope, trying not to scare me. Or maybe she's scared, too.

I duck low to keep out of sight of the castle, crossing the wide expanse of graffiti-scarred cement till we're behind a broken wall.

"I'm leaving soon," she says, jamming her hands into her pockets.

North? I nearly ask, but I already know the answer. "Alone?" I say instead.

She shrugs. "I don't have anyone else."

"You could stay—" I know how stupid it sounds before I finish the sentence.

She lifts her eyebrows. "And wait to get shot? Besides, I heard your friend—you can't keep pets." I wince, and Natalie ducks her head. "Sorry," she mutters. "That wasn't fair."

I swallow a dozen replies that wouldn't help anything. "Sit down," I tell her instead, pointing to a chunk of concrete. "I'm going to fix your shoulder."

"What?"

"It's driving me crazy. You're not afraid of needles, are you?"

That makes her laugh, and she sits. She laughs again when I rinse the cut with hydrogen peroxide, but I remember what she'd said about bugs. Nothing's hiding in the wound now, thank god.

The guilt is back, stronger than ever. I wouldn't feel bad about giving her food, but these are medical supplies we might never replace.

"Tell me about the dreams," I say as I thread the needle. Her skin is the same temperature as the air, dry and firm. She doesn't smell dead, which is a nice surprise. A little like dry leaves, but mostly like nothing at all.

"They started in the spring." I hear the pop as the needle pierces skin. She sits very still, watching thread slide through meat.

"Does that hurt?"

"It feels weird. Like popping an earring through a closed hole." Her hands twitch in her lap, as if she wants to gesture when she talks. "They come with the storms. The dreams, I mean. I was finally getting used to . . . you know. Then they started. First the thunder told me to go north. Then I saw the garden."

"Did you—" I concentrate very carefully on holding torn skin closed. "Did you see me?"

"Not at first. Not until I got close. I came from San Marcos."

"On foot?"

Her shoulder shakes with her laugh, and I wait till she stops to keep sewing. "A zombie riding a bike would be a little ridiculous, don't you think? And besides, I don't get tired anymore. Only—"

Hungry. I'm glad she doesn't say it, though. Her face is only inches from mine, inches from my throat and other soft bits. Adrenaline stings my cheeks, and my hands tingle on the needle. Natalie turns her head away, and I appreciate that too.

I tug the last stitch through and tie off the thread. They're not quite even, but it's a lot nicer than looking at raw meat.

Natalie stretches, testing the thread. "That feels better. Thanks." Her red eyes meet mine and she leans in.

I freeze. My life doesn't flash before my eyes, but I do have a long second to think *ohgodnostupididiotnottheface.* Then she kisses me.

Her lips are cool and dry. She tastes like storms. Her fingers brush my cheek, soft as a moth's wing.

My pulse beats hard in my mouth when she pulls away; my stomach is floaty and too small.

She raises a hand, lowers it again. The sun clears the broken towers, rinsing her face with pale gold. Her eyes, at least, are alive; wide black pupils contract at the touch of light. "I didn't mean to do that," she whispers.

"I—" I lick my lips. I'm not sorry, and that probably means I'm crazy. "It's all right."

We stare at each other in the rising dawn. I don't know what to say, and for a moment it doesn't matter. Then Natalie's nostrils flare and her eyes move, tracking behind me, and the moment is gone. Footsteps crunch broken stone.

I spin, clumsy and slow. The air is thick and sticky as honey, dragging at my limbs. I wait for the thunder of a gun, but it doesn't come.

Nick stands on the terraced hill, one hand on his gun, the other sagging under the weight of a pack. It's my pack, and that confuses me more than anything else. Then it clicks: he brought my bag because he knew I was leaving. Kayla and Marisela must have thought I'd made up my mind.

Natalie hisses, sharp teeth flashing. Nick's gun clears his hip.

"No!" I twist in front of Natalie. It's not the stupidest thing I've done today. "Don't. Nick, please. She's different."

"Audra?" His voice is tiny and confused, but he doesn't shoot.

"It's all right. I'm not—" Not infected. But that's not true. "She didn't hurt me," I say instead. "She won't hurt you."

"What's going on? Kayla said you might be leaving."

"She was right." I have made up my mind now, and the rush of knowing dizzies me. "But I'm not going with Las Calaveras." Behind me, Natalie makes a small surprised sound. I can't go back to the Orphans now. Nick might keep my secret, but I won't ask him to. I can't stay with the Orphans, and I can't go with Marisela.

"Where?" he asks. He lowers the gun, but doesn't put it away.

I glance at Natalie. She nods, her hand brushing mine.

"North. Tell Kayla I went north. I need to know what's there. I—I'll come back if I can."

Even if I do, how could the Orphans ever take me in again? I see the thought mirrored in Nick's eyes. He nods, his face slack and sad. My bag drops to the ground with a thump. He twitches as I get close.

"Thank you." Kissing him goodbye seems like a bad idea.

"They'll come looking soon," he says, taking a step backward.

I shoulder my pack. Natalie's hand is cool and dry in mine as we start down the hill.

Foundlings

Diana Peterfreund

The secret to accomplishing anything is to break down the process into a series of manageable steps. I'd tried explaining this to Emily before, but she always thinks with her heart, not her head. My attempts to be rational were always deemed boring, until she got the positive. Then the fact that I could make a plan of action was suddenly the most fascinating thing in the universe. More interesting even than Robbie, who promptly (and like the cowardly loser I always told her he was) vanished off the face of the earth.

The first step was tricking the P-sweepers, of course. This is where most girls get tripped up. The stalls at school notice if you don't buzz in to go to the bathroom for nine months, and though everyone knows how to get clean urine for a drug screen, it's ridiculously expensive if you want a long-term supply.

We were covered there, though, because of me. Once you get used to peeing in an old peanut butter jar and saving it—mine to give to Emily, Emily's to hide in her purse and then empty out into the garden every night—it's not as gross as you think.

We were lucky Emily didn't get too sick, because my Step

Two strategy for reading up on how bulimics handle vomit-concealment was not my finest moment.

Step Three was packing on the pounds. Emily's weight gain would be far less noticeable if I matched hers with mine. It's funny—we used to do whatever we could *not* to look identical. Now, we fought to look the same.

It was the subsequent steps where things started to get a bit hazy. Neither of us knew what else to expect when she was expecting, and it wasn't easy to do a search without setting off WOMB alerts. We couldn't even pretend it was school research. After all, they couldn't argue that we were incapable of handling it if they taught us how to handle it, could they?

Emily got all hormonal and freaked out about the future from time to time, but whenever it happened I just reminded her to focus on the steps, not the future. The future would take care of itself if we followed all the steps. Don't worry about what happens at the end of nine months. Think about tomorrow. Think about how to get enough folic acid in every meal (Step Four) and what to wear that will best hide your belly (Step Five). Let me sit and wonder if the people from the Foundlings (Step Six) were really WOMB agents in disguise, or if Robbie would rat her out. I could handle it. I was the sensible one. I believed in the steps. We just had to follow them.

Seven months into the program, it all went to hell.

• • •

WOMB believed in steps too. They didn't get here overnight, with their maternity centers and their P-sweeps and their school monitors in their trim red-and-gray uniforms. Our mom once told us that when she was a girl it was just a bunch of concerned mothers. There'd been a rash of murders—crazy women so desperate for a child of their own that they would kill pregnant moms and steal the fetus. Some would break into hospitals, dressed as nurses, and take newborns right out of the mothers' rooms. Others would stalk neighborhoods, looking for mailboxes with pastel balloons and "It's a Boy/Girl" announcements. The Women's Organization for Mothers and Babies was founded to protect newborns and their mothers from those who'd harm them.

From there it just became a question of what constituted *harm.*

• • •

Emily had a bad day on Thursday. She sat out in P.E. for the third time in a month, which meant she was sent to the nurse's office. And that meant she lingered by the doorway of my advanced calculus class long enough for me to notice and ask for a hall pass. We've done the old switcheroo before, of course, swapping shirts in the bathroom. Unless you're a twin, you probably don't realize how little people actually notice about you—even your closest friends. Most of the school thought I was the utilitarian, practical twin with her hair up and she was the pretty, girlish twin with her hair down. Emily might have been one of the most popular girls in school, but the truth was, fooling people took little more than a ponytail.

I noticed in the bathroom that she was flushed and had dark circles under her eyes, but that had been the norm for the past month. There'd been plenty of tossing and turning from her side of our bedroom every night, though I wasn't sure if the cause was physical or psychological. After all, I hadn't been sleeping great, either.

211

But I wasn't the problem. You had to watch out for girls like Emily. Girls who went out and got themselves pregnant . . . well, there was a reason the government put them in WOMB.

"Sakasaka, Em?" I asked. By mutual agreement, we'd kept the twin-talk to a minimum since hitting high school, but sometimes no other words would do.

She curled her index finger over her temple. "Sakasaka. A couple of cramps, but they're the fake kind." Scott, our Foundlings contact, had explained to us that we'd know the fake ones from the real ones if they stopped when she changed position. "I'm just tired."

"Well, don't fall asleep in class." I said. "Like last time." I'd made her serve my detention. Fair's fair.

"I'd be more scared there's a pop quiz." Math is not Emily's strong suit.

At the nurse's office, I played it off as a headache, though, naturally, the nurse couldn't see anything wrong with me. The WOMB monitor was there, and she gave me a once-over and even flipped through Emily's chart on her tablet.

"You've been putting on weight, Emily," she said. Our WOMB monitor's name was Stricter. How's that for irony? She looked the part, too, with steely hair scraped back into a bun so tight it was like a bargain-basement facelift. She was bony more than skinny, and her mouth twisted into a permanent, puckered frown. I always looked her in the eyes. Lack of eye contact was a red flag—it's how I nailed Emily to start with.

I shrugged as I straightened my shirt over my jelly belly. "I probably should have gone out for track this year."

"Is everything all right with you?" she asked. "You know, my position here at the school is one of counsel for young women."

"Young *pregnant* women," I clarified.

It's impossible to smile and pucker at the same time. Monitor Stricter failed miserably at her attempt. "Any young woman," she said. "It's important that you girls understand I'm only here to help."

"I absolutely do." *Understand what you are here to do.* They think we don't keep track of the girls who vanish. It's usually something as simple as a P-sweep that catches them. Or if not that, a rumor, or a friend rats them out, or the boyfriend turns them in when they go to him for help. Or maybe the girls turn themselves in, the way we're taught to.

Not my Emily. She didn't need WOMB to take care of her. She had me. "You don't need to worry about me," I said. "My sister and I are abstinent."

Was that too much? Maybe I shouldn't have mentioned myself. If they did a simultaneous test, we'd both be toast.

"Emily," the nurse said. "Seventh period's almost up."

I hopped down from the table, conscious that Stricter's eyes were still focused on my belly. I pretended to hike up my pants so she could see the roll of flab I'd so carefully cultivated hanging over the edge of my jeans. *Fat, not baby, Stricter.* She made a note in her tablet and I breathed a sigh of relief.

Like so many things, it was premature.

• • •

You'd be surprised how quickly you can win any argument about safety with five simple words: Is it worth the risk? Is it worth the risk of killing your baby to have a ham sandwich, even though the doctors tell you that lunchmeat might give you food poisoning? Is it worth the risk of having a mentally retarded baby to drink a beer?

I used to take this tack with Emily. Was it worth the risk of getting pregnant in order to have sex with slimy-ass Robbie? Was it worth the risk of having your heart broken by him? The answer seemed obvious to me, but not to her. She never thinks, just follows her heart.

The answers are clear-cut to everyone when it comes to babies, though, whether they're thinking with their hearts or their heads. No one is going to get very far saying babies should have *less* protection. And, after a while, it wasn't enough for WOMB to just protect mothers and babies from nutjobs with knives and nurse uniforms. First there was the WOMB consumer advocacy board. They went after child products, and pregnancy wear, and formula, and vaccines.

It wasn't long before they started going after the moms. There were just too many things out there that had the potential to hurt mothers or babies. It wasn't worth the risk. Thanks to the tireless efforts of WOMB lobbyists, it soon became illegal for a pregnant woman to drink alcohol, to smoke or take painkillers, or drink coffee, or order sushi or soft cheese or buy house paint—even if she swore it wasn't for her. Was it worth the risk, all those bartenders and pharmacists and sushi-peddlers of the world? They didn't install P-sweeps at the door of every coffee shop, but the army of WOMB agents was there to remind people of the law.

And what happened if you broke the law? At first, there were warnings and fines put in place. For repeat offenders, the government agreed with WOMB—it wasn't worth the risk.

• • •

The biggest risk we'd taken so far was hooking up with Foundlings, though it's not like we had much of a choice. I made a chart for Emily, delineating each of her options.

Option 1: A freak with a clothes hanger. The con of that one (apart from the obvious) was that if she got sick or if the dude was undercover, the penalty for even *attempting* to terminate is, at best, life without parole.

Option 2: Ditch the baby on a hospital doorstep and hope they don't catch you. The con of that one was that neither of us had the slightest clue how to deliver a baby or cover up the fact that we'd delivered one.

Option 3: The Foundlings.

Option 4: Turn herself over to WOMB, to be placed in one of their facilities. I kept that one as a last resort.

The name of the game, I told her, was risk management. Option 1 would end the need for concealment, but the stakes were the highest, and the penalty could very well be death. Option 2, the "safe harbor" strategy, could also backfire, especially if something went wrong with Emily's delivery. Option 3, The Foundlings, was the best choice because, if rumors could be believed, they provided medical care for their girls. But contacting them was dangerous. You never knew if you were dealing with a WOMB agent in disguise.

Scott says the Foundlings have the same fear every time they meet with a new girl—that she's a plant. Emily didn't like Scott. She didn't trust him.

I thought it was a bit late for her to start becoming suspicious of men.

. . .

Today was not one of our bi-weekly appointments with Scott, but I saw his beat up old Prius in the school parking lot as we left the grounds. Since I'd met Emily at our locker after the nurse's station, we hadn't bothered switching back, but it didn't make a difference. Scott always knows who's who with us. I figured it's because he spent so much time dealing with pregnant women. Though if that was the case, wouldn't Stricter have sniffed Emily out months ago?

Scott was standing by the car door, all lanky and nerdy-looking with his faded jeans and his plaid shirt and his square glasses. He could have been a student teacher, or someone's big brother, visiting home from college. He could have been someone's boyfriend.

"Get in," he said as we approached.

"What's going on?" I asked warily, looking back at the school. Even from across the parking lot, I could see Stricter in her crimson uniform standing in front of the doors, surveying the crowd of dispersing students. And then, as if from nowhere, there were two more women in red. And then five.

"*Now.*"

"Did someone turn us in?" I asked as Scott opened the back door and hustled Emily inside. We'd been so careful. We'd followed all the steps. Not a soul knew of Emily's condition, except Robbie, and she swore up, down, and backward that he'd never tell anyone, that he was too fearful of the paternity fine. Even so, I had my doubts about how well he'd hold up under interrogation.

I hurried around to the passenger side, my mind racing. Was it me? Had I tipped off Stricter? Had Emily had a spill in the toilet that set off the P-sweeps? Had we somehow tripped over one of our steps?

Three doors closed and the child safety locks automatically engaged (mandatory on all models built after 2015, thanks to WOMB). He drove us away in silence. I looked in the rearview. The monitors were wandering through the crowd. They were looking for someone. They were looking for Emily.

Scott didn't speak to us until he'd passed the first checkpoint on the highway. "You guys didn't slip up," he grumbled, his eyes on the road. "We did."

• • •

We always knew that it would only take a single break in the chain for things to fall apart. Emily forgetting her peanut butter jar. Me wearing a shirt that didn't fit her when we switched. A bout of morning sickness. A rat inside the Foundlings.

Likewise, things could have gone differently with WOMB, back in the twenty-teens. Maybe if there hadn't been that fertility scare in 2016. Maybe if they hadn't overturned Roe vs. Wade or outlawed sexual education in school. Maybe if the Opposition hadn't lost that election to the Party. So many variables that led up to the Juvenile Protection Act.

There were so many things we couldn't control, which made it all the more important that we held fast to what we could. I kept that in mind—I controlled my emotions, I controlled my sexual urges. Emily didn't—or couldn't. And now I needed to be the one to control the consequences.

Scott guessed we had about forty-five minutes until our face hit the casts. Then he, too, would be a fugitive, thanks to Amber laws. All of a sudden, there was a whole series of extra steps I had to add to the plan. I had to plot a route that avoided the checkpoints. I had to find a place to sleep at night. I had to explain to my sister that this wasn't going to be over in another month like we'd hoped. That like it or not, we'd been caught.

"Where are you taking the other girls?" Emily asked him after we got off the highway. It was too dangerous to stay on government roads, what with the checkpoints. Twins were far too conspicuous. "Is there a safe house?"

Scott said nothing. I checked out Emily's reflection in the rearview and curled my finger over my temple in reassurance. She was looking at me, scared, but not nearly as scared as she should have been. After all, I was there, wasn't I? The girl with the plan. The girl with the answers. And as usual, she hadn't done the math.

Scott had no plan. There wasn't any safe house. There were no other girls. He was on his own, and so were we.

• • •

WOMB eventually decided that the biggest danger of all to unborn babies was a mother's irresponsibility. And who is the most irresponsible mother of all? The drug addict? Sure, but everyone's on board with that one. Sock 'em into WOMB, dry 'em out. The woman in failing health who gets pregnant anyway? Even *she* thinks she needs round-the-clock care. But what about the pregnant teenager? So irresponsible she got pregnant by accident. So irresponsible the government hasn't even classified her as an adult yet. So irresponsible she can't vote, or hold office, or join the Party, or drive. Way too irresponsible to be tasked with growing a human life. She needs to be monitored, cared for. She certainly shouldn't be allowed to choose who gets to keep the baby.

And her family isn't up for the job, either. After all, they weren't responsible enough to keep her from getting pregnant. My mother failed. I failed. But there was no way in hell I would let Emily down now.

• • •

One of the reasons I liked Scott so much was that he could keep his head, even when his whole world was crashing down around him. Like how he took time out of his busy schedule of being on the run to make sure that he stocked his car with tents and sleeping bags and food supplies so we could hide out in the woods. We'd turned off all our tablets, for fear they'd remote-activate the embedded locators.

It was well past dark by the time we had our campsite set up. Emily was no help. When she wasn't hysterically crying, she was near comatose. This was to be expected, what with her hormones and all—another reason WOMB says you can't trust pregnant teens to make the right choices for their babies. Once the tents were up, I put her in ours, curled up with her and rubbed her back until the hiccups stopped.

"What are we going to do?" she sobbed.

"Shh," I said and stroked her hair. "Sakasaka. It'll be okay." But it wouldn't. Right now, right this minute, Emily was being classified as a criminal. Fetal endangerment and violation of the Juvenile Protection Act. I snuggled closer and put my hand on Emily's belly. I could feel it kicking. It didn't seem like it was in danger, here, in the cozy, safe confines of our tent.

"What about Mom? They're probably taking her in for questioning right now."

"Yes." I said. "That's why we made sure that she had nothing to hide or lie about. In case this happened." Of course, there was no guarantee that the government would believe her. Poor Mom. "Don't worry about her. Just try to relax. The stress isn't good for the baby."

"And what about his parents?" Emily asked. She insisted

the baby was a boy, though we had no way of knowing. Are they in trouble, too . . . for going through the black market?"

"I don't know," I replied. The Foundlings had let Emily choose which of their applicants would receive her baby. She'd picked the Bruckners, who, unlike most of the other waiting parents were not members of the Opposition. (Unless you're in the Party, it's almost impossible to be approved for adoption through the normal channels.) This appealed to my sister, who figured a baby's life was hard enough without making it some kind of political statement. It was the most rational thing I'd ever heard her say.

I wondered where the Bruckners were now. If they, too, were being questioned. If they would even be able to take the baby. There was too much I didn't know.

I stroked Emily's hair, pushing it back behind her ear and she caught my finger with her own. She curled her finger over her temple, our little salute, but it did nothing to ease my nerves. Finally her breathing softened and I knew she'd gone to sleep. That's Emily. She can sleep through everything. Because she's got me.

"Sakasaka," I whispered into her hair. But it wasn't.

As soon as I was sure she was out I left the tent. Scott was stirring up the fire. "Everything okay?" he asked.

I shrugged. "Did you set up a latrine or anything?"

He gestured south. "Over there. There's a red flag—can't miss it."

I grabbed a flashlight and took off into the woods, but I bypassed the latrine. Thirty paces, fifty, seventy-five . . . This was far enough. I shoved my fist in my mouth and screamed. I kicked at the fallen leaves. I grabbed a fallen stick and beat the hell out of a tree trunk.

We were so close. So, so close. And now it was all ruined. All those months, all those lies. The disgusting stench of the peanut butter jars, the way none of my clothes fit anymore, the pop quizzes Emily had failed on my behalf, the sleepless nights, the constant stress. The sound of Emily weeping in the darkness on her side of the bedroom. I'd done everything I could to save her, and it wasn't enough.

The stick broke, so I let it fall to the ground and started in on the trunk with my hands. The bark scraped my knuckles and the wood bruised the heels of my palms but I didn't care. Nothing mattered anymore. Nothing.

Two hands grabbed me from behind, trapping my arms to my sides. I screamed again, but this time in terror.

"Shush," said Scott in my ear.

I wriggled out of his grasp and whirled away in a rush of leaves and whimpers. "What's the point?" I cried. "What was the point of all this?"

His voice remained infuriatingly calm. "To keep your sister out of WOMB, I thought."

And fail, anyway. "Maybe they're right. Maybe it's where she belongs. We wouldn't be freezing in a tent in the woods right now if we'd just followed the rules."

"That's what they want you to think," he said. "They were the ones that forced us into this. That took away all your other options. WOMB says Emily can't take care of herself—but they don't even give her a chance. If Emily had been able to, she would have gotten health care. She wouldn't have been sneaking around."

"Why not? Emily did plenty of sneaking around before she got pregnant." I shoved my hands in my pockets so I wouldn't punch anything else. So I wouldn't punch *him.* "I gave up everything. My grades, my body, my freaking *pee*. I didn't do anything wrong, and I'm the one on the run now! All because she couldn't manage to keep her zipper up."

I heard him shuffle toward me through the leaves. "I know. You've made a huge sacrifice . . ."

"Do you know that Emily hardly spoke to me for the four months she was dating Robbie?" I said, as if Scott would care. "It's like I didn't even exist to her anymore." Tears spilled over my cheeks, but even then I didn't stop. "I didn't even matter. And then, the second he vanished, all of a sudden she loved me again. Because I was the only one who could help her. So selfish. So, so selfish." And so unlike her, which was what hurt the most. "I hate her," I hissed. "She belongs in WOMB." The second the words escaped my lips, I wished for them back.

"No," Scott said firmly. "You don't. You love her. You love her so much that—" he got real quiet. "My sister went to WOMB." He paused again, as if even now he wasn't sure he wanted to tell me. "Eight years ago. Gwen was fifteen, I was ten. My folks thought they were doing the right thing, just like the announcements say. Just like the law says. She went in at three months, when they caught her. But she never came out."

That was what I was afraid of. That's what you heard about the WOMB girls. I never knew anyone who had been in WOMB. No one did. Where did they go after the babies were born? Why didn't they come home?

I reached for him, but I couldn't find him in the darkness. There was no light pollution from screenglow here, no buzz from the casting towers. Nothing but the wind, and our voices, and the terrible words we could finally say.

"My parents tried for ages to find out what had happened to her, and they got so many different stories. She'd been transferred to a facility across the country. She'd decided to become a WOMB agent and changed her name to hide her shame. She had applied for and been granted emancipation and didn't want to have anything to do with my parents, who'd not raised her well enough to teach her the importance of abstinence. She'd run away from the facility and was on the lam. She had . . . died in childbirth. They hired detectives, they hired lawyers, but they couldn't get a straight answer. They never found out what happened to the baby, either."

That's why I couldn't let Emily go to WOMB. I couldn't risk losing her. Not again.

"That's how they hooked up with the Foundlings. We've been working for them ever since." Scott was close now. So close I could hear his breath, could feel his heat. "We don't know what happened to Gwen. But we can try to make sure it doesn't happen to Emily."

"Yeah, but now what?" I whispered. I turned toward what I knew was his face in the blackness. "You're crazy to be helping us. You had advanced warning. You could have run away."

"No, I couldn't."

"Yes, you could," I insisted. "I don't even know your last name. If WOMB picked us up, even if we ratted, they never would have found you."

"No," he repeated. "*I couldn't.*"

The forest itself went silent for a moment, his words sweeping away everything—the wind, the rustle of the leaves, the sound of our breath and the rush of blood in my veins. My hands found his in the darkness, and it didn't matter that neither of us could see a thing, because I knew that Scott had never needed his eyes to see me anyway. I could be packing twenty extra pounds, I could be dressed just like my sister—our own mother sometimes couldn't tell us apart—but Scott always knew who was who.

"I didn't come for Emily today," he said, bending his head close to mine. "I came for you."

• • •

Even if you follow all the steps perfectly, you might be surprised where they end up leading you. I could tell you about every step of the next month. I could tell you about that first night, sitting in front of the fire, with Scott's hand, so warm and reassuring, wrapped around mine. I could tell you how I didn't sleep that night—not from worry over whether or not the police would find us (which I should have)—but because my heart was beating too hard in my chest to relax. I could tell you about days spent trying to find a safe house, or keep Emily healthy, or stay one step ahead of the police. I could tell you how careful I was to stay focused on the tasks at hand, how I never lost my head, how Scott kept Emily calm, how he kept us moving forward, how we both said that the other was the one holding it all together.

Instead I'll tell you how we were both wrong.

Scott was late returning from a scouting trip. We'd been squatting for a week at a lakeside vacation cabin. It was winter and the family who owned the place would never come back just to take in the mud flats and the mist. I thought Emily was napping and I was sitting by the window near the driveway, letting tea go cold in my hands as I waited for Scott to return.

But then I saw Emily, trudging up the road, her pregnant waddle unmistakable even at this distance. She looked ready to burst out of her too-small coat. There was no way we could have hidden it now. Even if I gained more weight, I couldn't make myself look like her.

I met her at the door, fuming. "What are you doing out there!" I cried. "Were you down by the main road? What if someone saw you?"

"Relax, sis." Emily was puffing a little. She was almost always out of breath these days. "We can just switch again. I'll hide if anyone comes up to the house. One fat chick's as good as the next in this weather."

"Our face is all over the casts these days," I said. "It's too dangerous for us to go out."

"Exactly," said Emily. She brushed past me and inside, where she started to undo her scarf and coat. "We didn't do all this to hide and we can't keep running."

"Who says?" I replied.

"The baby says." She turned to me. "I'm not going to be pregnant forever."

"We'll figure it out."

"I did figure it out," she said. "I contacted the Bruckners. They still want the baby."

"You *what?*" I slammed the door, as if that could somehow keep us safe. "You contacted them? What if they're cooperating with WOMB? You put us all in danger!"

"We're in danger already," she replied. She sounded so *calm*. "We are, and what's more, the baby is." She cradled her stomach again. "I've thought this through. We've been running for weeks. If I'm going to get caught, I'd rather not hand my baby over to WOMB, and if I'm going to have to remain on the run, I'd rather my baby not grow up like that, either. Taking a chance on the Bruckners is our only option."

I opened my mouth to complain, to scold, to disagree, but I couldn't make myself speak. Emily had a point. While Scott and I were trying to figure out how to cover our own asses, she'd been thinking about the one member of our party who couldn't yet speak for himself.

"How do you know you can trust them?" I asked instead.

"I don't." She looked away out the window, and was quiet for a moment before going on. "Not about WOMB or us, I mean. But I know I can trust them about the baby. They want this baby. They want it for themselves." She turned to me. "And I want it for them, too."

I looked at her, at the face I knew better than any other in the world. The person I'd loved best since before I was born. Everything I'd been taught to believe was that Emily couldn't take care of herself, that she didn't know what was right, that she couldn't be trusted, as she'd failed at the single thing it was paramount for a young woman to do—guard her body.

But what if none of that was true? I'd always thought I was doing the right thing, but I'd never felt so right as I have since I started breaking the rules to keep Emily safe. And now, even though all that rational, practical instinct I've always prided myself on said that Emily's plan was dangerous, there was something greater, something stronger, that said that Emily's plan was *good*.

I heard the crunch of gravel outside. Scott was coming back. Emily was still looking at me, waiting for my verdict. As if she needed it. After all, wasn't this always about letting her do what she wanted with her body, with this baby?

I opened my mouth to reassure her as Scott came through the door.

"There's a new cast," he said without preamble. "You aren't going to believe it."

• • •

Monitor Stricter was almost unrecognizable. Her hair was down and had been styled into a cascade of waves on her shoulders. Bright red lipstick had been dabbed across her wrinkled pucker of a mouth. She looked ten years younger. And she was crying.

"I should have known something was wrong," she said, dabbing at her eyes with a hanky. "She's not usually like that."

The interviewer wore a concerned expression and shook her head in sympathy. "How do you mean?"

"Well," said Stricter. "I hate to say it, but Emily has always been so . . . charming. Charismatic, really. She could get anyone to believe her. She's one of the most well-liked girls in her class. Her sister is . . . not. Naturally, this would make it easy for Emily to manipulate her twin. The poor girl."

The three of us stared at the screen in frank disbelief. For a moment, I wondered if there were something wrong with Scott's tablet. Like his Prius, it was several generations old.

"Who knows how long they'd been forcing her to help them?"

"Forcing?" I spluttered. "Forcing *me*?"

The screen switched to a shot of my mother in a taped interview. "She's always been such a good girl. Always followed the rules." The cast proceeded to show evidence to back up that statement—evidence that included my detention record versus Emily's. Ironically, the one detention I did have on my record had been Emily's fault.

"I just wish she'd felt safe talking to me," Stricter was saying now, her eyes still watering with crocodile tears. "She was dropping hints the last time I saw her, telling me about her sister—about herself, I now realize. If only I'd picked up on it."

"They can't be serious, can they?" I asked.

Scott snorted. "No, there's an angle. Wait for it . . ."

"My poor girl," they showed my mother saying. "Dragged into this. If only she'd just call me. It's not too late to save all three of them."

"They're not talking about me, are they?" asked Scott.

"No," Emily said. "They're talking about the baby."

I watched for a few more minutes as the programmers delineated their version of events. It was as elaborate a plot as any I could dream up . . . except they didn't think I'd dreamt it up. No, they believed my charismatic, manipulative sister was either convincing or coercing the staid, rule-following *me* into doing her dirty work. It cast Scott as a cruel seducer, as Emily's boyfriend, as the father of the baby.

Emily laughed out loud at that part, but I was fuming.

"Come on," she said. "You've got to see the humor in that!" She rolled her eyes. "I mean . . . Scott?"

"Hey!" Scott said. "I'm right here, you know." He played it off like a joke, but his ears had gone a bit red, and he wouldn't meet my eyes.

And I wasn't laughing.

Emily sobered. "Look, sis, what is it that's got you so angry? That they aren't giving you credit for your dastardly plan or that they think you're the weak link and most likely to rat?"

"Both," I grumbled. Was WOMB right? Was I helping Emily for the right reasons, or was it only because she was manipulating me into it?

"None of it is real." Scott patted me awkwardly on the shoulder, then pulled his hand away. I almost reached out then, almost caught his hand and put it back. I wasn't Emily. I didn't find the idea of being with him laughable. Sure, I'd been playing it cool this last week, but it was a necessity. I didn't have time for romance in high school, and I certainly didn't have time for it while on the run from WOMB. "It's just what they think will get the best response."

"So they think I'm a meek little sheep?" I snapped.

"Or they hope you'll get angry at being called that and make a mistake." Scott shrugged. "And if it doesn't work, next week they can come up with a different story."

"I wonder if they'd keep their word?" Emily's head was tilted to the side as she studied the tablet. "I wonder if you could use the casts to make them keep their word?"

"What do you mean?" I asked.

"Well," she said, "they're basically saying you're not in trouble, right? If their public story is that you've been kidnapped by me and Scott—that you've been forced to do all these things to help us—well, if you went back, you wouldn't be punished."

"I'm not going back!"

"But if you *did*." She sounded thoughtful. "You *could*."

I looked from her to the screen and then back again. I looked at Scott, who was acting like he wasn't even in the room.

Yes, I suppose I could. But now, knowing what I know, I couldn't imagine wanting to.

• • •

Looking back, I suppose I could see each step along the path. I started analyzing the WOMB casts I saw at night. When I knew how they'd twisted our story, it was easy to see the stitching on all the other stories. Those smiling WOMB facility girls weren't real, they were actresses. I recognized one in a toothpaste commercial, another on a store screen at the mall. I also began to notice the scared expressions on the faces of pregnant women on the street whenever a WOMB official would pass. I saw how they'd wear big Party buttons and flash their wedding rings and smile nervously at everyone as if to scream, *I'm harmless. Please don't take my baby.*

I couldn't believe I'd never noticed this before. Scott had pulled the scales from my eyes. So although my entire, perfect, organized plan lay in ruins . . . I was okay. My plan had been designed to sneak around *inside* the system. The system that told me to hate my sister for making a mistake. The system that told me that WOMB had a right to our bodies and the fate of our babies. The system that told us it wasn't possible for us to take care of ourselves or make hard choices or sacrifices for the ones we loved.

It was all wrong.

Of course, there were plenty of areas where I wasn't prepared to help Emily. Labor, for example. I could squeeze her hand, of course, or whisper words of encouragement in her ear. I could even cut the cord between her and the baby boy she delivered after what seemed like an endless labor.

(Yes, it was a boy. Emily was right again.)

But all I could really do was put my trust in people who could actually help us. Scott, who found us a Foundlings-friendly midwife. The Bruckners, who truly wanted nothing more than a baby. They could have made serious money and scored brownie points with the Party for ratting us out, but they might not have been rewarded with their baby. They chose him.

And so it was that on a cold and sleety Saturday, eight months after Emily told me about the positive, my twin sister had a baby. After it was all over, I sat in the room with Emily while she cradled her son for the first and last time. I marveled at how tiny he was—so tiny, and so alone. Emily and I had been born wrapped around each other. Mom told us we used to suck each other's thumbs in our bassinet. But this little guy was on his own. He'd never know what it would be to like to be us. Tears filled my eyes and I looked away, embarrassed.

Emily wasn't crying. She was perfectly calm, beatific even, like one of those old religious paintings of mother and child. She nuzzled him and kissed him and stared into his dark, blue, alien eyes.

"Sakasaka, little one," she said, and I didn't even mind. It seemed right for her to use our language with him. "Farewell." The baby's eyelids fluttered for a moment, and he lifted his tiny hand and curled his index finger over his temple. I gasped.

When it came time for his parents to take him away, Emily squeezed my hands so hard she left bloody half-moons all over my skin. She held me harder now than she had during labor and delivery. This time she was really letting him go.

"What are you going to name him?" she asked Mrs. Bruckner, with a hitch in her voice.

The woman reddened. She was pretty, though fair and tall. Her husband was the same. They looked nothing like us. I imagined her on some playground, explaining away his dark hair and fuller build. *Aren't genetics a funny thing? Oh, he looks like my grandfather on my mother's side . . .*

"We were thinking of naming him Emmett, after you," she said. "Would you mind?"

Emily forced a smile. Probably no one else but me would know how hard it was for her to do so in that moment. "That's beautiful," she said. "Thank you."

And then he was gone. One minute, he was there, this little

squished tomato thing with impossibly tiny fingers that wrapped around yours by instinct, and then the next minute, he was gone forever, and it was just the two of us again. Even Scott left us alone. We lay on the bed, holding one another. For three days, we remained there. Emily took the meds they gave her, the ones that would mask her post-partum symptoms, and Scott came by every few hours with food. We watched old movies, napped a lot, and talked very little.

And on day four, Emily woke up, turned to me and said: "What now?"

I'd been the girl with the plan. But now that we'd achieved its goals, I had no idea.

• • •

Sometimes plans are the result of long periods of study and strategizing, and sometimes they're the work of an instant. Did we get sloppy? Did we have an extra-observant neighbor? Did someone notice that there were two girls—not one—renting that motel room? After all, twins stand out. We stood out as specimens on the WOMB cast they kept rerunning, and we stood out whenever we were together. People might not be able to tell us apart, but when you see double, you remember it.

However it happened, it was sudden. I was standing by the window, as usual, waiting for Scott to get back from a shopping trip. Emily was watching the local casts, which she preferred to letting me rant and rave over the latest WOMB cast lies. I heard her sharp intake of breath just as Scott's Prius slammed up the drive in a cloud of dust and gravel.

"They're coming," he cried out as soon as he came in. "We have to go, now!"

"Grab your coat," I called to Emily and shoved my feet into my shoes. "What can they do now?" I asked Scott. "Emily's not pregnant anymore. They can't force us into WOMB."

"They can detain us for questioning," he said. He grabbed a bag and started shoving our belongings into it. "They can try to track down the baby. They can try to use me to force my parents out of hiding."

Emily hadn't moved. Her eyes remained fixed on the screen. "The locals are showing this," she whispered. "Look, they're going to arrest us on livecast." She pointed the screen at me and I caught sight of WOMB officials in their silver vans driving down familiar roads. They were heading straight for us. They were probably ten minutes away.

"Em, come on!" I tugged on her arm. "We have to go now."

She shook her head and pulled away. "No. They'll find us."

Scott zipped up the duffel. "They'll surely find us if we stay! Think of Emmett."

"I am," said Emily. She looked at me. "They're livecasting this. And no one knows exactly how pregnant I was when I left. No one knows Emmett's already born."

"So?" I asked.

"So," said Emily. "Remember the WOMB cast? Remember how they said they just wanted you to come home? What if you did? What if you turned yourself in on the local livecast? They'd have to stand by their word. They couldn't punish you."

"Why in the world would I do that?" I said. "I don't want to go back."

"You wouldn't be going back," Emily said. "*I* would."

Scott and I stared at her in shock. Scott found his voice first. "This is stupid," he said. "We have to run."

"And you need someone to throw them off your trail," Emily argued. "I'll tell them that Emily and Scott ran away and left me. I'll tell them Emily's still pregnant. And then I'll tell them all the wrong places to look."

"You'll be me?" I asked, stupidly. "For good?"

"This won't work." Scott's voice had grown frantic. "They'll never believe what you say. You'll be imprisoned. You'll be interrogated—especially if they believe they can still get their hands on the baby."

"She'll be livecast by the locals, though," I said. "WOMB made a mistake—they've made too big of a deal about giving me amnesty. They have to stand by their word, or risk alienating other accomplices who might turn themselves in." I turned to her. "But why you, Emily? I can be the one to stay."

She looked at me. "No, you can't. You've already given up too much for me. I don't want you to give him up, too."

Scott cleared his throat and looked away. I sputtered.

"Come on," she said. "I might not be as smart as you, but I'm not an idiot. You love him, and he loves you."

"Emily—"

"We don't really, um, have time for all this right now," said Scott, bouncing on his feet.

Emily grabbed my hands. "I know you think you're being careful, that if you never let yourself fall in love, you'll never get hurt. But Scott's not Robbie. He's good. He's good for you."

And then I realized. She'd been making fun of WOMB's story of her having been impregnated by him for weeks, but not because she found the idea of dating him laughable. It was because she found the idea of him being irresponsible—the way she and Robbie had been—impossible.

234

"Trust your sister," Emily said. "Trust me, the way I should have trusted you."

I looked at her, my mirror, even now after everything, and nodded. "Sakasaka."

. . .

Sometimes—especially when a few months go by without any girls showing up with messages from Emily coded in our language—Scott worries that WOMB has gotten to her and she's turned on us. But I know Emily's stronger than that. It's weird to see her on the casts now, in that crimson and gray uniform, her hair tamed back into a bun. She does look like me. I always said it took little more to fool people than a well-placed ponytail. It's funny; it took her becoming me and me becoming Emily for either of us to be ourselves.

Emily spouts the Party's lines well enough on the casts. She's a regular poster child these days, as charismatic as ever. But the truth is plain as day if you're us. Every time, right at the end, she looks into the camera, and curls her index finger around her temple.

Everything's sakasaka. We just have to be patient, and follow the steps.

Seekers in the City

JEANNE DUPRAU

One gray, blustery February day, Miranda Williams received a letter that would change her life. Her mother handed it to her when she got home from school. Miranda read the return address: *Department of Municipal Investigation, Government Building 51Dn22, 19442 Grand Blvd. E, Area 31, Monument Segment, Berg 12, TK 602857.*

"Look where this is from," she said. "How can it be for me?"

"I don't know," said her mother. "Why not open it?" She was feeding the twins; their faces were splotched with orange baby food. On the TV, cartoon characters shrieked and zoomed. One of Miranda's sisters was talking on the phone, and her grandmother sat at the kitchen table muttering softly as she cut coupons out of magazines.

Miranda opened the envelope and read the letter out loud:

To Ms. Miranda Williams:
Your activities in connection with Section VIa12 of Municipal Code 98 have come to our attention. Pertaining to this matter, you are required to appear at the address above on Wednesday, February

*17, at 2:20 p.m. Failure to appear will result in penalties that may
include fees of up to $25,000.
Signed: Ferris Slocum, Director*

"What?" cried Miranda. "What *is* this?"

Miranda's mother set down the jar of baby food, took the letter, and frowned at it. "It must be a mistake," she said. "Just call and tell them."

But there was no phone number on the letter, and no email address.

"You'll have to go," Miranda's mother said.

"What if they put me in jail?"

"Don't be silly," said Miranda's mother, but not in a very confident voice. In this city, people were arrested for breaking laws they'd never heard of. They got parking tickets that cost a month's salary and spent years fighting through mazes of paperwork and paying endless fees to prove themselves innocent of ridiculous charges. Everyone knew that the best plan for dealing with the city government was to stay out of its way.

So on February 17, Miranda put on a drab brown outfit. She wanted to look unimportant, like someone who would never cause trouble. But when she looked in the mirror, she could hardly stand the sight of herself. All that brown. Her eyes were brown, and her brown hair was tied back with a brown rubber band. She looked as if she'd been rolled in dust. So she wrapped her flame-colored scarf around her neck. She would take it off before she arrived.

She went down the elevator, out the door of her apartment building, and on to the sidewalk, where she joined the rushing throngs of people. There was hardly a moment in Miranda's life when she wasn't surrounded by people: at school in a five-hundred seat auditorium, watching a teacher on a huge screen; on the streaming streets of the city or in the packed subways; at home, with two frantically busy parents, five brothers and sisters, an ailing grandmother, and the cousin of her father's friend's brother, who had come to the city from some disintegrating country far away and was staying with them for a while. It was odd, she often thought, how with so many people around you could still be lonely.

Outside, a mean wind blew grit along the sidewalk. Miranda wrapped her scarf more closely around her neck and started walking. Between her home in Building 3423, 990 Granite Avenue, Area 51, Gravelyard Segment 4, and the building she was headed for in Area 31 lay the vastness of the city—the grids and loops of streets, the freeways cutting through in long arcs, the subway tunnels and elevated trains, the skyscrapers checkered with dark and lighted windows that never opened, the traffic grinding along in the deep canyons between the walls of concrete. And everywhere, people: breathing, talking, eating, coming and going, tunneling out spaces for their lives in the vastness of the city as if they were earthworms in the earth. You had to make an effort to remember, in this teeming place, that your own life, or anyone's, was important at all.

Miranda went down a stairway to a wide underground hall filled with ticket machines, where she lined up behind a tall young man in a black pea coat. He was carrying some sort of cage, holding it with a finger hooked through a ring at the top. It was dome-shaped and covered with a dark green cloth. She had only just noticed this when somebody bumped into her and she stumbled forward against the cage, which on its swing back struck hard against her knee.

"Ouch," she said, and when the person holding the cage turned and looked at her she said, "I'm sorry. Someone pushed me."

His hair was chestnut-brown and he was not much older than she was.

"Are you hurt?" he said.

"No," said Miranda. She pointed to the cage. "It just bumped me." Then, for too many seconds, she couldn't take her eyes from his, because his gaze shot into her and struck a vital spot right at her center. She stared at him for four seconds, or five, or six, which is a long time to look into the eyes of a stranger in the subway ticket-machine line.

The boy blinked and spoke again. "It's a canary," he said, "for my sister." He pulled aside a flap of the cover, and Miranda saw a yellow bird inside. The moment the light struck it, the bird raised its head and released a long stream of notes, like golden bubbles of sound. Even in the roar of the station—the clanging of the gates, the squeal of brakes, the clamor of voices—the notes sounded high and clear.

A rough voice called, "You're up, kid," and the boy turned back to buy his ticket. Miranda bought hers quickly afterward, and as she pulled it from the slot, she looked to her left and saw him walking toward Train 93, in the opposite direction from her train, which was 17. For half a second, she had the urge to run after him and ask about the canary, or ask his name or where he was going, but the crowd engulfed him, and she knew she hadn't the nerve to do it. She was too shy. She hated her shyness! She turned right and moved with the swarm of people down the tunnel that led to her train.

She didn't see the boy stop and look over his shoulder. She

was quite a distance away by then, telling herself that what had just happened was nothing and that she was being stupid to think about it one more second.

• • •

Building 51Dn22 was gray concrete, unlabeled except for the number on its heavy double door. Miranda removed her red scarf and put it in her purse. She went up in an elevator and found Mr. Ferris Slocum in Office 27a.

"Please have a seat," he said, looking not at her but at the papers on his desk.

Miranda did.

"You are Miranda Williams," he said, "forty-four years old, single, resident of Building 29, Ironwood Street, Area 78–"

"No," said Miranda politely, but Mr. Slocum read on without stopping.

"–Leadwall Segment 14. Suspected of involvement in practicing a trade without a license, specifically–"

"Excuse me," said Miranda, more loudly this time.

Mr. Slocum looked up.

"That isn't me," she said. "It must be someone else with my name."

He raised his eyebrows skeptically and pursed his mouth. "I will need documentation," he said, "including birth certificate in triplicate and proof of address–"

"But sir," said Miranda. "It can't be me you want, because look," she stood up, "I'm sixteen."

He frowned at her, narrowing his eyes. "Hmm," he said. He checked his papers again, running a finger down the edge of the page. He looked up at her. "It's true," he said, "that if you are forty-four, you are very young-looking for your age." He

240

smiled, a small smile, but not an unkind one. "Administrative error. Our apologies. Have a pleasant day."

Back in the hall, Miranda took in a deep breath of stale office air. She put her red scarf back on. All the way to the subway station, she felt light and floaty and hopeful about everything. She wasn't in trouble after all! She was *grateful* that she'd been called in by Ferris Slocum, because otherwise she'd never have been at station 47 and never would have seen the boy with the bird. Maybe somehow she'd see that boy again. She could search for him. Why not? It could be a sort of quest, like the ones she'd read about in old stories, where a seeker embarks on a difficult journey to find a treasure. True love, in this case. She smiled. It was so silly—a boy she'd seen once, for a few seconds, a perfect stranger. She didn't care. She made up her mind to look for him.

How to begin? She pondered that on the long ride home. She had two clues: he rode the 93 train through station 47, and he'd bought a canary. What could she do with those two clues? Keep riding the 93 train until she saw him again? Go to all the places in this city that might have sold him a bird?

Yes, she thought. I could do those things.

• • •

The boy's name was Owen Marks. He was a good-looking boy, but not movie-star handsome; his ears stuck out a little, and he was a bit too thin for his height. He wasn't used to having girls look at him the way the girl at the subway station had.

He boarded his train and put the birdcage between his feet. All the way home, he thought about that girl. She had brown, wide-set eyes, and he had stared into them for much longer than he'd meant to, probably longer than he should have.

He'd had the feeling you do when you're walking on something you think is solid and which suddenly gives way and you fall. He had fallen like that into her gaze.

The train's lights flickered, as they often did and the train screeched as it went around a curve. Owen thought, I wish I could see that girl again. She must live somewhere near station 47. He never ordinarily went to that station, which was where he'd needed to transfer on his way home from buying the canary. How lucky that he'd made the trip today! Otherwise, he'd never have seen the girl.

At the Station 49 stop, so many people got on that Owen had to put the birdcage on his lap and wrap his arms around it. He could hear a soft, whispery rustle of feathers from within. Strange, he thought, how that one look and those few words had jolted him. He *would* like to see that girl again. Why shouldn't he look for her? He could think of it as a quest. He would never find her, of course. It would be like looking for one particular grain of sand in a swirling sandstorm. But that's what a quest was—a difficult search for something nearly impossible to find. Why not? he thought again. I'll do it.

· · ·

Daylight was almost gone by the time Owen got home. His sister Emma lay curled on the couch, staring at a soccer game on TV. Emma had an illness that made her so weak that she couldn't walk much farther than down the hall and back. Owen carried a permanent ache in his heart for her.

"Emma," Owen said. "Where's Mom?"

"She went out to buy cigarettes."

"And left you alone again."

"Yes."

Some months ago, Owen's father had left home. He had to get out of the city or die, he said. He would find another, better place, and he would send for them to come and join him. But no word had come, and Owen's mother had begun to fall apart. She couldn't sleep, she didn't comb her hair, she'd forget to shop for groceries until there was nothing in the house but an old jar of pickle relish. She sometimes left Emma alone for hours.

So Owen had to take on responsibilities. He couldn't make Emma well. No one, so far, had succeeded in that. But he could make her happy, or at least happier. That was the reason for the bird. She needed something alive, something beautiful, something other than the TV.

He opened the curtains to let some light into the room and then went over to her. "Look," he said, taking the cover off the cage.

Emma raised herself on one elbow. She peered into the cage. The bird awoke, hopped sideways on its perch, looked up at the light, cocked its head and sang.

Emma smiled. "It's beautiful! I love it," she said. "Thank you, big O."

So Owen was happy, and being happy made him bold. That afternoon, he took the first step in his quest. He applied for a job at a company called Twisto Snax, which sold pretzels at subway stations. He requested Station 47.

"You will need to submit your request in writing," said the person on the phone. "Download Form Y33 from our website and send it in with the five dollar fee. Processing applications usually takes two to three months."

"Two to three *months*!"

"That is correct. Unless you wish to expedite your application by paying a thirty-five dollar fee."

Owen sighed. He was fairly sure the extra thirty dollars would go straight into someone's pocket. But he felt an urgency about his quest, so he sent in the form and the money, and only a week later, he received an email telling him he had the job. His hours would be 6 a.m. to 12 p.m. five days a week. He would have to skip his morning classes, but that didn't matter. No one noticed, in those huge, chaotic classrooms, if any particular student were there or not.

So the first step was accomplished. That was a good sign. I'm an idiot, Owen said to himself, but he couldn't ignore the stirring of excitement at the thought of seeing the girl again.

• • •

His partner at his new job was a man named Clement, a tall, soft spoken man with faded red hair. Clement, who was new to the city, never stopped moving. When customers came, his long pale fingers danced over the cart, working fast, and when there were no customers, he wiped down the cart, organized the cash drawer, or just paced back and forth, arms crossed over his chest, drumming his fingers against his elbows.

Owen, at first, did his job badly. He kept his eyes on the passing crowd, looking for the girl, and so he often gave a customer the wrong kind of pretzel or incorrect change.

"Something is the matter?" Clement asked at the end of the first week. "You seem not paying attention. Please. I can't have problems. If you go I go and I need this job."

Owen tried to do better. He could see that Clement was poor—he wore the same black trousers and shabby jacket every day. So Owen made an effort to keep his mind on the job. Still, between customers, he watched the crowd, looking out for girls wearing red-orange scarves. But he saw no one with a red-orange scarf. At least no one who looked like the girl. Of course, he reminded himself, she might have other scarves. She wouldn't wear the same scarf every day and he'd need to look instead for a young, brown-haired, medium-tall girl. Unfortunately, there were millions of them.

One day, a man in a long overcoat approached the Twisto Snax stand. "Ronald Ripley, government inspector," he said. "Present your permit, please."

"Right there," said Clement, pointing to the side of the cart where the permit was taped.

The man in the coat leaned over and peered at it. "As I thought," he said. "You owe a fee. Fifty dollars."

Clement's eyes widened in fear. "But I was never told—"

"Mister Ripley," said Owen. "We would like to see your government identification. We have a right to know if you are who you say you are."

Ripley put a hand in his coat pocket and came out with a card encased in scratched and grimy plastic. One glance at it was enough for Owen. "I'll just make a phone call to confirm your ID," he said, and he took his phone from his pocket and punched in a number.

Ripley pounded a fist on the pretzel cart, making the condiments jump. "One week!" he said. He pointed a finger at Clement. "I'll give you one more week to make your payment. I'll be back." He scuttled away.

Clement was so shaken he couldn't speak above a whisper. "You made things so much worse!" he said. "Now I'll be in trouble for not paying, and in trouble for speaking disrespectful, and—"

Owen put a hand on Clement's arm to calm him. He explained that no government "official" would bother to come

245

down here to collect fees. "He won't be back," Owen said. "He'll find some other new person to prey on. He's gone for good."

Clement was grateful, Owen worked more conscientiously, and things went well between them. But days passed without any sign of the girl in the red scarf. It grew difficult for Owen to keep believing in his quest. After all, there were other girls. Millions of them. He wasn't even sure if he'd like the girl in the red scarf once he got to know her. And yet—whenever he thought of the look that passed between them, he felt a sort of earthquake in his heart.

• • •

Miranda had by that time made a list of all the pet stores in the city—there were 643. Even if she went to one every day, it would take her almost two years to visit them all, and she couldn't possibly go to one every day. But twenty-two of the stores were easy to reach from the station where they'd met. And he'd been heading toward the 93 train. There had to be a link. First, she began by going to the pet stores via station 47. And after school, at around two o'clock, she'd ride the 93 along its route, and back. It was a hard task for a shy person; she had to gather her courage every time she went into a store, where she would tell the clerk the same thing: "I'm looking for a boy who bought a canary. He's tall and slender and about my age."

And the clerks would say more or less the same thing every time: "You think I remember all my customers? You must be out of your mind."

Even so, Miranda would write down her first name and her phone number and ask if they'd please call her if they saw that boy again.

. . .

A month passed, and in the throngs of people that surged by Twisto Snax at station 47, Owen had not seen the girl with the red scarf. But one day, after work, he stopped at station 79 to buy some groceries, and when he went back down to the subway, he passed a train standing at the platform, its passengers already loaded on, its doors closed. In one of its windows, he glimpsed a bit of red and even through the grime on the window he could see that the red was a scarf, and it was around the neck of a girl, and the girl was looking at him, and she was *the* girl.

He stopped; he stared. Their eyes met. Both opened their mouths as if to speak, and the girl pressed the palm of her hand against the window. But the train began to move. Owen put a finger to the glass and, loping sideways to keep up with the train, he wrote in a few fast strokes: O M A R K S. The tail of the S trailed away as the train pulled forward. He stood watching with his hand still raised, as if he were waving goodbye.

When the train was gone, he realized how stupid he'd been. Why hadn't he written his phone number instead of his name? How was his name going to help her find him? There must be millions of people named Marks in this city, and thousands named O. Marks—Oliver, Otis, Orville, Orlando, Oscar . . .

Stupid, stupid! He'd had a one-in-a-million chance and messed it up! But at the same time, he thought: She saw me! She looked at me that same way! He was not making up the connection between them. Whatever it was, it was real.

. . .

Miranda had taken a break from her pet store visits the afternoon she saw the boy. She'd had no luck, and was feeling discouraged. So to cheer herself up, she'd put on her red scarf and taken the 82 train to the huge shopping mall at the west end of the city, where she was determined to buy some small nice thing.

It was when the train stopped at station 79 that she saw the boy through the window. His face was suddenly there, looking up. A shock went through her. She leaned close to the window; she pressed her hand against the glass. Her eyes met his, and the look shot between them again. She opened her mouth to call out to him—but what to say? No words came. The train began to move. He leapt up and wrote on the window, but the train pulled away from his hand and left him behind.

What had he written? Ƨ Я Я A M O, the letters said, and she reversed them and got O M A R K S. It must be his name, or part of his name. But what was it? It seemed to be Omar. K could be the first letter of his last name. But what was the S, then? Omar K. S. Maybe K was his middle initial. But she could never find him just by his first name. He must have thought he had time to write both first and last.

The train rocketed forward, and she studied the letters on the glass as if they were the key to her life. Maybe he *had* written his last name. Omarks. Or O'Marks. That one gave her an idea, that Marks was a last name. Maybe he was O. Marks. But there must be thousands of people named O. Marks in the city. Whatever he'd written, it wasn't very helpful.

Still, she was elated. He had seen her. He had given her his name and it hadn't been her imagination. He wanted to be found.

• • •

Now that Owen had seen the girl again, his thoughts tortured him. Had he made a mistake by taking the job at station 47?

Did she go more often to station 79? Should he be riding that train, looking for her? He just didn't know.

"Owen," Emma said to him one evening. "My bird doesn't sing any more."

"Not at all?"

"No."

He hadn't even noticed. What a bad brother he'd been, mooning over a girl he didn't even know and neglecting his sister! He felt terrible. He would get another bird, he decided, to keep the first one company. Then they'd both sing. But money was a problem. It had taken him nearly six months to save the money for the first bird and he didn't want to wait that long to get the second. He would need another job. Not a different job—an additional job.

Clement provided the answer. Ever since Owen had got rid of the fake official (who had never come back), Clement had been almost embarrassingly grateful. He leapt at the chance to do Owen a return favor. "I will ask around," he said. By then he had met many others like himself, people who had come from other places and who met to keep each other company and exchange useful information. Very soon, he greeted Owen with an eager smile and said, "I know a job!"

He knew the guy who swept the platform at station 178, he said. This guy had a friend who was a sweeper at station 179, and he knew that the sweeper at station 212 had quit due to a bad case of pneumonia.

Owen got the job. He gave up school for the time being. His life became all work: he sold pretzels at station 47 from six in the morning until noon, then he rode the 89 train to station 212 and swept platforms from three to seven every evening. He lived in the dark, under the surface, like a mole. But it wouldn't be this way for long. He'd have the money for the bird in a month or two, if all went well. And if all went *very* well, he'd see that girl again.

• • •

Several weeks later and Miranda had visited nineteen pet stores. So far, no one had remembered the boy who'd bought the canary. Her quest was going nowhere, but her knowledge of pet stores was growing fast. She didn't always like what she saw.

The Stop'N'Pet store on Rockland Boulevard, for instance. At the back of this huge store were wire cages where puppies with runny eyes slept in heaps. The water in their bowls was scummy and their cages stank. Miranda complained to the clerk. "Those puppies aren't being cared for," she said. "They're not well."

"So you're some kind of expert, I guess," said the clerk.

"I can see," said Miranda. "And smell."

"Good for you," the clerk said. "Leave the rest of it to us."

At other stores, she saw more of the same: a white rabbit crouched in the corner of a pellet-littered cage; kittens with bare patches in their fur; an aviary full of fluttering finches that looked all right until she noticed two of them lying dead on the cage floor.

When she pointed these things out to the salespeople, they either said hurriedly, Oh, yes, yes, they would take care of it right away, or they told her she was wrong and that everything was fine. So Miranda had an idea—she would give Ferris Slocum a chance to bring down the law on something that deserved it. She started keeping a list of stores where animals were mistreated, with notes about what she saw.

As time went by, it was less and less likely that anyone

would remember the boy who'd bought the canary, and it was more and more upsetting to see the poor animals trapped in awful places. They would never be free, never be loved. Miranda started feeling that way about herself. She decided to go to three more stores. And after that she'd stop.

At the twentieth store, the man behind the counter said brusquely that he didn't sell canaries.

At the twenty-first store, a dirty white dog lay in a cage in the window, scratching at patches of raw skin. Inside, Miranda found two women cleaning hamster cages. One of them, a skinny red-haired woman, held a wriggling hamster in her hand. The other woman was short and stout and wore a stained and dirty apron. Miranda asked them her question. The woman with the hamster simply laughed at her, rolled her eyes, and said, "Unbelievable!" The short stout woman stared at her from under heavily drawn black eyebrows.

Miranda felt her face get hot and her heart speed up, but she kept her voice calm. "And I'd also like to tell you something," she said. "The dog in your front window isn't well. It needs to see a vet."

"Don't you tell us our business," said the red-haired woman.

This is a horrible place, thought Miranda but, even so, she wrote down her name and number before she left.

At the final store, a tidy shop called Zoo for You, a red-and-white striped awning shaded the front window. Everything inside was colorful and shiny. The neat blonde woman behind the counter listened to Miranda's question and shook her head. "Nope," she said. "I don't remember. So many people buy canaries, you know. To sort of cheer things up."

Miranda left her name and number, and the search of the pet stores came to an end. I will never see that boy again, she thought. I have to forget him. She got on the 93 train and headed home to write up her list of bad pet stores to send off to Ferris Slocum.

• • •

Owen's new job at Station 212 kept him busy because the platform was always scattered with things to be swept up—candy wrappers, paper cups, cigarette butts, bits of popcorn and pretzels, and the grime and dust left by millions of shoes. He swept the floors and swabbed the walls as people passed on all sides of him as if he were a stone in a river.

He had been there two months now, but he hadn't been able to save money as fast as he'd hoped. His mother was too disorganized by sadness to manage the household finances. Owen had to step in. He paid the electricity bill when his mother forgot to. He paid for her cigarettes when she said she would die without them. He paid for extra books and pencils for Emma, because his mother never thought of buying them herself. By the end of the month, he had less than half of what he needed to buy another bird.

He was tired of working two jobs and thought he should probably quit his job at Twisto Snax. He'd given up hope of seeing the girl at station 47 but he liked selling pretzels better than pushing brooms. And he liked Clement. Maybe he should quit his sweeping job and double his hours at the pretzel stand. Yes, that's what he would do. He decided this on a Thursday afternoon, at the beginning of the rush hour. When his sweeping shift was over, he'd go to the supervisor and say he was leaving.

At the very moment he'd made this decision, he heard a shout above the general clamor. Then many shouts, loud and urgent. "Help! Quick! Man on the tracks!"

Owen broke through the crowd to the edge of the platform and saw him, five feet straight down—a gray-haired man in a business suit, lying on his back with one leg bent under him, his arms flailing, his face twisted in terror, trying to get himself up. People on the platform stood gaping and shouting, but the train was due in seconds, and no one had jumped down to help.

It was easy for Owen. He lowered his long-handled broom and yelled, "Grab on!" The man took hold of the broom handle, Owen pulled with all his strength, and the man rose and stood on one leg. The other hung useless. "Get him, someone! Hurry up!" Owen yelled. He had to yell it twice, scream it, before a couple of beefy guys stepped forward. They stretched out on their stomachs, reached down, and grabbed the man's free hand. They pulled, Owen pulled, and the gray-haired man was hoisted up out of the trench and dragged onto the concrete platform, groaning and gasping.

The train arrived twelve seconds later.

The rescued man looked up at Owen and tried to speak. "Saved my life," he managed to say. "Tha-tha-tha-"

"You're welcome," said Owen.

As Owen learned later, the man's name was Ernest Bonovik, and he was a vice president of the Long-Term Pavement Company. He insisted on giving Owen a generous reward, far more than enough to buy the bird for Emma.

• • •

Though she had given up on pet stores, Miranda wasn't quite ready to give up her quest. All she could think of to do was keep going to station 47 where she'd seen the boy the first time. She began to sit on a bench near the ticket machines but even though she didn't see him, she liked sitting there, doing nothing but watching swarms of people and being quiet in her mind in the midst of the rushing throngs. It was a relief not to have to talk or listen to anyone—not her harried parents, not her rambunctious brothers and sisters, not the ever-blasting TV or radio, not her grandmother's cracked, sad voice, and not her uncle's friend's cousin Clement, who was still staying at their house until he could make enough at his job selling pretzels to afford his own place. Here at station 47, she had a little bit of time and space she could call her own.

• • •

Sometimes a girl with spiky blond hair bought a pretzel from Twisto Snax. She had a sweet smile and red-painted finger-nails, and she always said a few words to Owen as she made her purchase. He could get to know her. He could ask her out. She could make him forget about his quest.

But as he was riding the subway to work, or in the moments before he went to sleep at night, it was the girl in the red scarf he thought about. He wondered if she were looking for him.

With his reward money, he finally went to get the second bird for his sister. He took the 93 train, just as he had when he saw the girl in the red scarf for the first time. Of course he wouldn't see her again, he told himself.

And he was right. Everything else was the same as the first time: the big store, the chubby clerk, the cage of yellow birds to pick from. He transferred to the 93 train at station 47, standing in line for the ticket machine. But this time an old man in a knit hat stood behind him. "What's in the cage?" the old man asked.

Owen was angry at the man for not being the girl. But he kept his voice steady. "A canary," he said. "It's for my sister."

His heart felt gray. He bought his ticket and headed home.

• • •

A little after five on a March evening, Miranda's phone buzzed. She was eating dinner at the time. The baby was crawling around her ankles, and her brothers were dueling with plastic swords. Miranda answered her phone and heard an unfamiliar woman's voice, low and slightly husky.

"Is this Miranda?"

"Yes." A flicker of unease. Was the city government after her again?

The woman spoke in a soft, confiding way, very fast. "It's Nan from the pet store, sweetheart, you might recall me, I was there when you asked about the boy buying the canary, you spoke to Patty. She was holding a hamster. Remember? I'm short and round?"

"Oh!" Miranda pressed the phone closer to her ear. She jumped from the table and went to the hall, where it was quieter. "Yes!" she said.

"I remembered that boy, dear," Nan's voice said. "The canary for his sister. I remembered him because of that and because he was a nice boy, and good-looking as well. And I liked you, too, so sweet and determined. And the way you stood up to Patty about that sick dog, which we did take to the vet, by the way. So I kept your phone number just in case."

She said this so fast, with the words all run together, that Miranda could hardly take it in. "Oh!" she said again. "You mean—"

"I know it's a little bit outside the rules, but this is a story of hopeless romance, isn't it? I can't resist romance. So I wanted you to know."

Miranda's heart thumped. "To know what?"

"But I have to ask a question first, dear." The voice on the

255

phone got even quicker and quieter. "Does he want you to find him?"

An image of the boy's face sprang into Miranda's mind. She remembered the look he'd given her. She saw his desperate eagerness as he scrawled letters on the train window. Her heart flipped. "He *does*," Miranda said. "I'm *sure* he does. So you mean—have you seen him?"

"Yes, I have," said Nan, and Miranda could hear a chuckling satisfaction in her voice. "I have indeed, sweetheart. He was just here, buying another bird. He said it was for his sister. Maybe the first one died, I hope not, because—"

Miranda interrupted. "Is he still there?"

"No, no. He left."

"How long ago?"

"Just now. A minute ago. I said to him, 'It's cold out, do you have a long ride home?' And he said yes he did, all the way to Clay Street in Area 19, so I said I'd give him a heavier cover for the cage, and that's all I could find out."

"Oh, thank you!" said Miranda. "You're so kind, I'm so grateful. I have to go now, but really, thank you, thank you."

"You're so welcome, sweetheart," said the soft quick voice on the phone. "Good luck."

To her mother, Miranda said she had to meet a friend, and her mother, wiping congealed milk from the baby's highchair, asked no questions.

Miranda snatched her coat from the hook by the front door, dashed down the hall, hopped from foot to foot while the elevator took its time making its way up to the 38th floor, then making its way down. She ran full speed to the stairs to the subway. She bought her ticket and ran for the right platform and waited again, hot in her heavy coat, boiling with impatience. When the train came at last, she rode standing up, right next to the door, so she could jump out at the Clay Street stop.

She was the first one off the train when they arrived. She dodged the ingoing and outgoing passengers, stretching up as tall as she could, looking for the dark hair and slender shape of the boy named O. The crowds were thick. She couldn't see in any direction, blocked by backs in thick coats, bent heads in caps or hoods. Why couldn't they all *move*? She squeezed between them, she peered past them, and looked for the boy who had probably forgotten all about her.

But she saw no sign of him. Trains came and went, the streams of people gushed out and swirled around her. More people were sucked in and swept away. She saw no one she had ever seen before, much less the one she wanted to see. He was too far ahead—he must be gone already, out into the streets. She knew that if she couldn't find him here, she had no hope of finding him out there, in the midst of the millions.

She stopped fighting the crowd. Her excitement drained away. It was time to go home and forget this quest, once and for all. She sat down on a bench, feeling hollow inside. The quest was over. It had been a waste of time. At least no one had known about it—that was one good thing. There was no one to laugh at her and tell her how stupid she'd been.

The train came. People surged toward it, and that was when Miranda heard a flight of warbling notes, a trill that could come only from a yellow canary.

She spun toward the sound. The crowds were dense; the faces of a thousand strangers pressed toward her. She forgot her shyness—some new person inside her took command. She jumped up on the bench she'd been sitting on, and in a voice louder than any voice she'd known she had, she sang out: "Omar!" She tried all his possible names. "Omar! Omark! O Marks with the bird! Where are you? Where *are* you?"

People stared at her, but she heard the bird again, and she hopped down and ran toward the sound. Hands reached out but she knocked them away, and seeing that it must be some kind of emergency, people made a path for her. Ahead, the boy stood facing her, the birdcage in his right hand half uncovered, a look of astonishment on his face. "Here!" he cried. "I'm here, right here!"

You would think the spell would be broken then, as these two people who had barely ever spoken to each other came together in such a rush. But no. They were strangers who didn't feel like strangers, having been alive in each other's minds for so long. They stood facing each other with the crowds parting around them. He smiled a smile of wonder with his mouth half open. "It's Owen," he said when she was standing in front of him. "My name is Owen Marks. I didn't have time to write all of it on the window."

Miranda was breathing too hard to speak, but she smiled, too. Tears rose into her eyes, but she brushed them away. "Miranda," she said. She took a breath. "That's my name. I heard the bird."

"I was checking to see if it was all right," he said. "When it saw the light, it sang."

"It's so beautiful," she said.

"Shall we go out of here?" he said, and she nodded. He covered the cage again, and they walked up the stairway and into the street, where the afternoon light glinted on the cars. They stopped beneath the awning of a store.

"This bird is a mate for the other one," Owen said.

Miranda just nodded and smiled. For the moment, she had no words.

"It's sad that they have to live in a cage," said Owen. "But at least now they'll have each other."

• • •

A week before Miranda had found Owen, Clement had left his job at the pretzel stand. He'd saved enough money to move to an apartment, and he got a new and better job at a bakery. He kept in touch with Miranda's family, though—he was grateful to them—and one evening when he was visiting Miranda came in with a new friend.

"Owen!" Clement cried.

"Clement!" cried Owen.

Over the course of the evening, with many questions and exclamations from the family, Owen and Miranda told the complicated story of their quests. "If only I knew who you looked for!" said Clement. "I could have saved so much trouble!" He wrinkled his pale forehead and waved his hands around in great distress. "If only I knew! You could be meeting much sooner, much, much easier! It would have been greatly better!"

Owen and Miranda thought back over all that had happened—the obstacles, the longing, the brief moments of hope, the chance good deeds, their stubborn perseverance.

"Don't worry," Owen said to Clement. "A quest is supposed to be hard."

"Yes," Miranda agreed. "It was fine, just the way it was."

The Up

Nina Kiriki Hoffman

I was hiding behind a flowstone curtain near Plantlands, peeking between fingers of stone fringe at Piller, the man I was supposed to mate with on my fifteenth birthday, not far enough in the future for me. Two of the other girls my age in Na Below thought he was handsome. He was tall and strong and had all the right parts to make a good father, and he still had lots of thick dark hair, even though he was over thirty. I might have liked him better if he smiled.

Piller leaned on his walking stick, overseeing a team of four middlers ladling recycled waste into the fertilizer channels along the rows of crops. Light banks hung from the ceiling of the Plantlands cavern, the bright, broad-spectrum light falling hard and white on everything below. Shadows had sharp edges under the lights. Not like the fuzzy shadows thrown by the soft orange glows we used in the home cavern.

The field near the flowstone curtain was planted with rows of corn this season. Raggedy green stalks thrust up from the pale dirt. The waste stained the cool air with the smell of shit.

Fingal, my best friend, tripped, and some of his waste spilled onto the path between rows. Before Fingal could even straighten, Piller grabbed the bucket and ladle out of Fingal's hands, set them aside, and struck Fingal on the back with his walking stick. Three thunks of plast against pulpcloth and flesh, and Fingal sprawled on the ground, his face in the dust, his belly on the fallen waste mixture, his extra-long fingers twitching.

I gripped one hand in the other, wanting to run to my friend and help, afraid to be discovered so far from my own job, in a place where I didn't belong. I pressed my cheek against the cool, waxy curtain of stone.

Arn, Fin's good friend and silent partner, wavered, his waste bucket swaying. Piller turned to glare at him, and Arn put his head down and went back to ladling, shoulders hunched.

The lights flickered.

"Sky take it," Piller cursed, glaring up at the light banks.

Maybe the lights listened. They didn't flicker again.

Piller looked at his other two crewmembers, girls I didn't much like, both of them also scheduled to mate with him when they turned fifteen. Piller's hand tightened and loosened on the shaft of his walking stick. The corners of his mouth curved down. His thick, dark brows lowered, leaving his eyes in caves of shadow. Both the girls stayed bent over, faces toward the ground, working in rhythm along the rows, their backs to Piller, their feet carrying them farther away.

Piller frowned, then turned and poked Fingal with his stick. "Get up. Get back to work."

Fingal pushed up, uncurling from the ground. He was a freak, with extra bones in his spine, extra joints in his fingers and toes, extra long, skinny arms and legs. When he stood up straight, he was taller than Piller, so he never stood up straight when he worked in Plantlands. He faced away from Piller as he picked up bucket and ladle and returned to where he had left off. The front of his green bodysuit was smeared with waste.

I couldn't bear to watch any more. I rose and padded on sock feet along the flowstone to the gap I could fit through. I peeked out to make sure Piller was looking the other way, then slipped out on to the path back to the living cavern and my own job.

• • •

I spent most of my time with Noel, at fifty-three the oldest person alive in Na Below. He was in charge of the puters we had left after more than two hundred years of underground living, and I was his best apprentice. I spent some time training with Revi, our doctor, too. All the middlers did, and all the middlers worked with Noel, and tried to teach what we learned to the littlers. We were afraid of another accident like the one that had killed Noel's puter trainer before she had taught him everything she knew about puters. We lost a lot of knowledge when the falling rock killed her. After that, Bufo, Na Below's leader, decreed that all of us should study with any elders who had useful knowledge, then choose specializations that would best take Na into the future.

There were only forty-two of us left in Na Below, seven men, seven women, thirteen middlers, and fifteen littlers. More than five hundred used to live here, when folk first fled from Weatherdeath to the underground. Our prophet, Silas Smith, had used his earthly aboveground fortune to outfit the caverns for his chosen people while there were still cities and industries and supplies in the Up. The first couple of generations in Na Below built and expanded and scavenged after the big disasters that had killed most everybody in the Up. When the plagues swept through the remaining folk alive in the Up, Silas's grandson, prophet Jacob Smith, shut the cavern entrances, and we hadn't opened the doors since.

We had started out with plenty in Na Below to live on—stockpiles of goods and food and medicine, and machines that could recycle what we shed. Pulp-forming machines took most of our worn-outs and made new: dishes, clothes, blocks of ply we could carve into furniture and other things we couldn't make from the soft limestone of our cave walls. Echo River flowed through our cavern, pushing power into our generators, watering the Plantlands, filling our cisterns. Prophet Silas had left us rules to live by that kept us alive.

Some of us, anyway. For a while.

I pulled my bodysuit collar tighter to warm my neck. In the open living cavern, the temperature stayed a constant fifty-four degrees. The puter room would be warmer.

There weren't any other people on the path, but I kept watching anyway. I wasn't where I was supposed to be; I didn't want anyone spotting and reporting me. I'd had enough shame standing this week.

Everybody else was probably where they belonged. Lunch chime wouldn't sound for another hour, and everyone had work to do.

I snuck past the community hall—a tall, round structure built of carved stone in the center of the cavern—crossed Echo River on the stone bridge, and made it to the puter room, one of many smaller caves carved into the wall of the living cavern, without running into anyone. I was happy to open the door into warmth and light, and the sharp smell of electricity. The puter room was my safe haven.

Noel nodded as I joined him in front of the consoles of the

three puters he kept up and running. He had four backups that worked, and the corpses of six others that had died but could be dissected for replacement parts. The storage cave next to the puter room was full of equipment that didn't work anymore. We had paper schematics for some of it, and sometimes we tried to repair things.

We still had some working comm units, and Noel had three cameras. Sometimes he let me use one of them, but he always supervized. One of his previous apprentices had broken a lens and killed an earlier camera, so he was hyper-scared about the few that were left. We had a whole cupboard full of nonworking cameras, all sorts, tiny and big ones.

Maryam, one of the littlers, was sitting at the third console, poking at keys and studying the screen. She was one of my trainees. All four of us middler puter girls had our own littler trainees. I'd shown Maryam all kinds of things at the console, but she couldn't seem to get the hang of the reading part. She could play the games where she moved colored things around and made explosions, but she couldn't read yet, and she was already seven.

All the littlers had trouble reading.

Of the middlers, I could read, and Fingal, and the other puter girls could, too. Arn couldn't think hard enough to get a letter in his head, let alone a number. Two of the other girls around my age could say the names of letters but couldn't seem to get them when they were put together into words, and one of the boys besides Arn was basically hopeless, but he was really good with machines, so it didn't matter.

"Where'd you go, Daina?" Maryam asked me.

"Waste pit," I said.

She pinched her lips, poked a key combination, and made a

big analog clock face show up on her screen. She touched the three, then dragged her fingertip along the lower curve of the clock to the nine, where the big hand rested now. "That's a long loop of time for the waste pit," she said.

Noel said, "Maryam, that's wonderful! When did you learn to see time on a clock?"

She smiled at him, eyes bright with the screen's reflection. "I watched during the drills."

Noel often set his students to timed drills, bringing up the clock face on one screen while he challenged us to type a piece of text at the other two consoles within a certain period of time. Our littlers watched us drill sometimes.

"Good watching, Maryam! That loop of time is called 'half an hour.'"

"I know that one! That's what the carers tell us at the crêche when we ask for a story before sleep. Half an hour of story!"

"What about this loop?" Noel leaned forward and traced the arc of the clock from nine over the top to three.

Maryam frowned at the screen.

Happy that Noel had successfully distracted her, I sat down at my usual console and brought up the spreadsheet for crops planted thirty days earlier. The corn had been in the ground that long. Piller was supposed to give us measurements every ten days so we could see if things were growing as well as they had last time and the time before and the time before. The data fields for height were empty. Piller had been getting more and more irritated by Noel's requests for information. He told Noel: "I'll tell you if it doesn't grow. If it does, who cares how tall it is?"

He had been angry at Noel's request for an accurate count on the crops harvested, too. Maybe because he didn't want to admit the vines and stalks were growing slower, bearing less, their fruits and seeds smaller.

I switched to the Na Below mating map. There were four fertile women left in the colony, and all eight of us middler girls, presumed fertile until proven not. Each of us middler girls was matched first with whoever was farthest kin. We were supposed to work on getting babies as soon as we turned fifteen. Once we had our first babies, and them grown a year, the next decision would be made about who our second mates would be. If the first babies were normal, we'd be matched back to their fathers. If they came out twisty, we'd be matched with others.

Noel was my father. Leader Bufo was my uncle. Piller was a distant cousin, farther than the other men genetically from me.

I liked Matt, chief baker, of the other adult men, but he was my uncle, too. Taboo forbade me from going with him, at least for my first baby.

Taboo was going to take a beating soon, we were so few.

Of the five boys, Fingal and Arn had been sterilized early in life. Revi the doctor had known Fingal was different, a mutant, of course, from the minute he was born. Anyone could tell by looking at him. Anyone who deviated from human normal was sterilized early, by order of Prophet Silas.

That was a stupid rule. Fingal was better at a lot of things than the other boys and men. His mutations were positive ones. He was smarter than the other boy middlers, too. No trouble reading or working numbers. We'd be lucky to have more like him. We learned that too late.

Arn had taken longer to diagnose. He was slow to learn. The council had made the decision to keep him from fathering.

One of the other boys was Noel's get, my biological brother; the other two were Bufo's get, close cousins.

Piller. My mate. My fate.

I had seen the backs of women who had borne his children: striped with strikes from his walking stick.

Noel gripped my shoulder. I hit a key to hide the mating map, but I knew he'd already seen it.

"Time to contact Geordie," Noel said.

"Yay!" Maryam jumped up from her console and danced in a tight circle behind me. "Yay!"

I glanced at the clock in the upper right corner of my screen. Noel was right: half an hour until lunch chime.

We moved to the radio corner of the puter room, and Noel let me switch on and tune in.

Following Weatherdeath, we used to get signals from six other Below groups. Everybody had agreed to contact each other once a week as long as possible. My mother had told me about how, when she was a little girl, everybody would gather in the community hall to listen to the broadcasts from other people beyond our cavern walls. When Ma was little, we had still been in touch with three other settlements, but we lost touch with Chi Below and Sa Below. Only Yup Below kept our radio dates any longer.

Geordie was our contact at Yup Below. He gave us all the news. I felt as though I knew them at Yup Below, and of everybody I knew in the world, the one I most wanted to meet and maybe mate with was Geordie. He had a soft, deep voice, and an accent no one in Na Below had. He sounded blurry but kind.

"Testing, you Na-folk, testing," his voice said as I tuned. I cranked the tuning knob back so his voice was true instead of thin and strained through the speaker.

I pressed the transmit button. "We hear you, Geordie. Hello!"

"There's my Daina-lassie," he said. "To whom else am I talking this fine underground day?"

"Noel's here, and Maryam," I said.

"Greetings, Na-folk! What news?"

"Nobody's pregnant," I said. "One of the generators is coughing. Lights are flickering in Plantlands. What's happening in Yup?"

"Alas to that generator situation! Hope you can fix it! Dearie me on the lights. I hope it's not dire. We have a new life in Yup Below," Geordie said. "Sergeant Flynn had a baby boy. She named him Jupiter."

"Congratulations!" we all yelled.

"Ouch, my ears! Well, she heard that up in the hospital, I have no doubt." Geordie laughed. I loved his laugh. "How's supplies holding out, eh?"

"Still living off new crops and storing reserves. Did any of your wheat sprout?"

"Had a bit of success there, with the seeds we treated. Private Gina's nursing them along. My son wants to eat the little sprouts, that juicy they look! I would like to eat them myself if I didn't know how much we need them grown. His mum got hold of an old pacifier from somewhere—can you picture that? We thought they'd all rotted. Any road, it did the job and stopped him nibbling on the greenery."

Noel leaned in and pressed the transmit button. "What did you treat your seeds with?"

"Touch of potash! Willy-lad went spelunking about in the unexplored tunnels off our hydroponics cave, and what should he stumble across but an old campsite. Not mapped, that, but someone had sealed the exit to the Up at some point. Still, he found some old campfire rings, and packed the charcoal back. Major Lewis had a survival book with a bit in it about how to leach ashes, and we tried it. Worked a treat."

"Thanks for that," Noel said.

"Sure enough," said Geordie. "Put my dearie back on. Daina-love, when are you dropping by for a visit?"

I wished there was a way I could tunnel to where Geordie's caverns were. Sometimes I got heartsick with longing to see him. I felt all hollow and sad and didn't even want to eat.

Maryam pressed the button. "Never mind Daina," she said. "I'll come visit you, Captain Geordie! Will you give me tea?"

"Mary-me-lass, of course I will, and biscuits too. Drop by anytime."

"I will. I'll come tomorrow."

Lunch chime sounded.

"Geordie, time for us to sign off. Stay well, will you?" Noel said.

"Aye-aye, sir," Geordie said. "Give all your folks our best."

"To you as well." Noel shut down the radio.

Maryam shoved out of the room ahead of us. Noel touched my arm before I could follow. I stood in the doorway to the puter room, watching Maryam dash through the dimness of the living cavern toward the lighted community hall. I waited for Noel to speak.

He came up behind me, a warmth and a breathing presence, taller than I was, with a scent of soap and sweat. "Where did you go this time?" he murmured when Maryam was beyond earshot.

"To Plantlands. To look at Piller," I whispered. I didn't get to sneak away often during work hours. Usually the other puter girls were there. They tattled on me if I misbehaved. Noel never betrayed me, but I wasn't sure whether Maryam would keep quiet.

He touched my shoulder. "The act itself can be over quickly You won't have to endure it for long."

"It's not just the act. I've heard the women talk." Two of the crêche carers had children by Piller, and another had lain with him when I was ten. Day after day she had come to work stiff and sore, with marks and bruises on her back and arms. The other women had salved her wounds and taken over her work. Finally, Revi had pronounced her barren. The crêche carers had celebrated with tiny tots of forbidden drink and stolen strawberries for each of us littlers.

Noel said nothing.

Revi had invited me to attend a birthing three years earlier. Mother and child had died. Before she died, the mother had screamed and sobbed and muttered about Piller. She had strike scars on her shoulders from his walking stick. She had not wanted to live. "If my child is a boy, he is cursed. I don't want to see him become a man like his father. If my child is a girl, she is cursed to live as I have. If my child is lucky, she will die before she's born," she had whispered after hours of labor.

Revi had tried to send me away, but I wouldn't leave. The woman had been one of my favorite teachers in the crêche, and I had wanted to help her. I washed sweat off her face, and tried to soothe her when she screamed and all the veins stood out in her forehead and neck. I gave her water between her pains, when she would let me. I held her hand. She gripped me so tightly a bone broke in my hand. Revi set it. It healed, but my memory was scarred.

Blood had gushed from my teacher. She had died before the

baby made it out, and Revi cut into her, trying to save the baby, but it died, too. By the time it was over we were all stained red and smelled of metal and death.

I never, ever, ever wanted to give birth.

It was a woman's most important job. We had to keep our kind alive. What kind of world would it be if we all died out, our memories and monuments ground to dust and covered over? Thousands of years of human history wiped out by weather. It must not happen. So we'd been taught from birth.

• • •

Fingal sat beside me at lunch, with Arn on his other side. Granny Tordis brought around a pot of porridge and ladled it into people's bowls.

The community hall had been built to hold hundreds. It was too big to heat, so everyone wore cloaks or jackets over their bodysuits during meals. The tables were shaped in arcs. When we fitted them together, they made a circle where all our diminished numbers could sit, facing each other. The circle was close to the kitchen doors so the servers didn't have far to go. Around us in every other direction stretched silent, dark space, its far edges cluttered with furniture we didn't need and anything else useful left from the times of more. Each time we lost someone, someone would go to their home cave and clear out their belongings to add to the store here.

When I was a littler, sometimes the crèche carers brought us here to rummage through things stacked in the dark. We built our own caves with blankets spread over old tables and chairs. Sometimes we found treasures. Other times we found old, worn things to feed to the pulpers and be made into new things.

I glanced toward the shadows. Even back then I had been

looking for places to hide, but Piller had grown up here, too, and explored, and he knew all the hiding places.

"Are you all right?" I asked Fingal when I had eaten half my porridge.

"What do you mean?"

"I saw him strike you," I whispered. I touched his leg, then looked over my shoulder. My biological mother sat next to me. She had been one of my carers, though I hadn't known we were such close kin when I was a littler. We lived together now.

She was talking to Noel. Good.

"What were you doing in Plantlands?" Fingal muttered.

"Spying." He should have known. I was always spying.

"Daina. If anyone catches you, they'll put you down the well."

"I know. I can't help it." The well was cold and dank, the walls slick with moisture, unclimbable. I had been there many times. You waited in utter darkness for someone to let you out, learning each time that you were totally dependent on the others in the community. They always said, "We have nothing but each other, we are nothing without each other," when they came to let me out, and I had to say it back to them before they'd lower the ladder.

I had taught myself to tell stories in the darkness. It no longer froze me with fear.

Leader Bufo stood up and rang the attention chime. All conversation stopped. "Noel. Any news from Yup Below today?"

"Another life has been added to their community," Noel said, "a boy named Jupiter."

Some people cheered. Other people muttered. We'd had no live births in four years. My teacher's death, with her baby, had killed our hope. No other grownup woman had gotten pregnant since, though not from lack of trying, if the whispers were true. The men muttered about that, and the women muttered about the men.

Three of us middler girls would be turning into grownups in the next month, and Piller had first chance at us all. His children were strong and healthy. One of the middler boys would be old enough to father, but he'd try first with a grownup woman.

"Captain Geordie said they'd quickened some wheat seed using potash," Noel said.

A discussion broke out about that. Our wheat had been sickly lately.

After a time, Piller rose, lifting his hand. Leader Bufo sounded the attention chime again.

"Three of our grow lights have gone out," Piller said into the silence, "and we have no more replacement bulbs."

Everyone burst into speech.

Arn leaned in front of Fingal, toward me. "He hit us."

"He hit you, too, Arn?" I asked. Arn almost never spoke aloud. Most of the middlers mocked him when he did, because he slurred. Today he spoke clearly, though.

"Aum. When the light went out. He knocked me down, and Fin too, and then the girls. He made us spill."

"If we have no light," Piller called over our anxious voices, "it won't matter if we know some stupid trick with ash."

The grownups opted to spend the afternoon discussing the situation. The rest of us went back to work.

• • •

After lunch, all the middlers went on energy shift. We went to Plantlands, where one field had been set aside with stationary bikes we could pedal to store energy in batteries. Plantlight shone on us for two hours while we cycled. Prophet Silas had decreed that everybody needed two hours of plantlight a day. We had to work for it, except the babies and the crèche carers, who sat near the cycles as we pedaled and shared the light we produced.

One of the lights had died over the cycles. I sat on one in the shadow spot, with harsh light shining down on the others around me.

"You'll get sick," one of the other girls told me. There were plenty of bicycles in the light.

"This one actually works," I said. Some of the bikes weren't connected to batteries anymore. People usually picked those because they were easier to pedal.

She shrugged. The start chime sounded, and one of the carers beat spoons on a pot in rhythm to keep us pedaling fast enough.

Fingal had picked a bike near mine. I didn't like talking on the bikes because the others were too close to us, and several of them liked tattling, as though it made them safer from shame-standing and the well if they put somebody else there.

Fingal had to hunch to fit into the bike's saddle. His knees stuck up almost to his shoulders when he reached the top of his pedaling cycle. People had laughed the first time he got on a bike, until someone noticed his energy monitor, which showed he had stored more than any of the rest of us.

I was so angry that Revi had sterilized him. He was as distant a cousin as Piller was. If I were going to have to have a baby, I would prefer—

Of course, that didn't matter. All Fingal's future selves were gone.

Geordie. Somewhere out there, beyond the Up . . .

• • •

At supper, Leader Bufo announced the grownups had decided someone needed to go to the Up and find out whether it had settled down enough that we could use sunlight for farming.

"It's a risky task," Bufo said. "We haven't opened the doors in a hundred years, and we don't know if the plagues are still there, whether animals lie in wait, or even feral people. None of us have combat training. We all know what happened when Chi and Sa and Oss and Con went to the Up. Or rather, we don't know—we never heard from them again.

"Without explorers," he continued, "we may not survive. Will anyone volunteer to go?"

Fingal stood immediately, with Arn just after. "I would be glad to go," said Fingal. Arn nodded.

My heartbeat speeded.

"Thank you, Fingal. Your willingness is appreciated," said Bufo.

"A grownup must go, too," Ma said.

Discussion broke out. I sat back, my hands gripping my thighs, as people discussed the risks. Arn and Fingal would never get children. They did jobs valuable to the community, but others knew their work as well as they did. Any grownups with genes to donate should be exempt from a trip to the Up. We needed to hoard all the genes we could if we wanted our kind to have a future.

Fingal. Of course he would volunteer. Maybe I had known that.

"I'll go," said Granny Tordis. She had been barren a long time. My mother was her last child. Granny ran our food preparation, but she had apprentices who could fill in.

"We accept your sacrifice," Bufo said before anybody even discussed it.

"I'll go, too," I said. A tiny knot of heat was burning in my chest, a hard, hot spot of hope and fear and wonder, wrapped in satisfaction because finally, finally, my small collection of sneaky secrets had nudged a possibility into being.

"Daina," Bufo said, "you can't go. We need your mothering. We need your potential and skills. We can't risk your loss."

"Who's going to keep communication open with the Up if I don't go?" I asked. I had trained with the comm units, and none of the other middlers had. "What's the point in going to the Up if we can't tell you what we find there? You have seven other middler mothers." I pointed to the other girls around my age. "I'll go."

"We'll sleep on it," Bufo said. "More talk at breakfast."

• • •

After the meeting, we skipped the evening music. Ma and I went to our cave.

When Rose was caring for me and the others in the crêche, I hadn't known she was my bio mother, but I had liked her best of all the carers, and she had whispered to me that I was her favorite, too, even when I got in trouble for wanting more than my due, or reading too long, or stealing, or breaking something because I wanted to find out how it worked. When I turned twelve and could have picked a cave of my own, I moved in with Ma Rose instead.

Ma had a lot of hidden thoughts, and when we went to our cave for the night, she sometimes told me what they were.

She tapped one light on, a soft yellow glow, making

landscapes of the mounded pillows and thrown-aside covers in our sleep nests. Her clothes rod held four soft-green pulp coveralls. Mine held two, one light blue, and the other pink. I wore my third, which was yellow. They would be recycled when they were worn out, but I couldn't get any more until I'd worn through these, because I was still growing.

I headed for my nest of green and blue and pale yellow pillows, and the pale spinner-silk sheets bunched at the end. Some of my pillows had embroidered pictures on them. I hugged the pillow with the picture of pets on it that Fingal had made for me during story time. We used to spend some of our puter-learn time looking at images of olden days. We saw long-ago people with strange animals snuggled against them. Fur. Textures I had never touched. Fingal had made me a pillow with a dog and a cat on it. The floss he had used was soft. Touching his gift, I almost touched him.

Ma stood in the cave entrance and stared toward the bubbles of downtown buildings, where some glows stayed lit when most people slept. Most of us were on the same sleep-wake cycle. The cavern was vast with darkness, big with moving air and the rush of the river. It was always like that when we stopped making noise for the day. I liked the feel of the soft cool air, the sound of nearby moving water, the clean scent of stone. Comfort. Home. My feet knew the paths. My skin knew air. I didn't want to leave what I knew and trusted. I couldn't stay, because the future promised to be different.

There was a sealed room at one end of the cavern with a glass rod that went all the way to the Up, and we watched the light that came down it to scc when day was. The settlement calendar and clock was set by the rod. Only three grownups worked during sleep, preparing supplies for the day-users.

After Ma closed the door for the night, I asked, "Why did you want a grownup to go to the Up with Fingal and Arn?" I always wanted to know what Ma's hidden thoughts were. She thought wider than anybody else in our Below, including Noel and Bufo.

Ma fluffed the covers on her bed nest. The colors of her pillows and sheets were darker than mine: blues called midnight and purples called indigo. "Brush your teeth," she said.

I went to the wash-and-waste alcove, scrubbed my teeth with reclaimed salt, rinsed my mouth, then spat into the recycle bowl. I returned to my sleep nest, fluffed my covers, and settled. "Why not let them go by themselves?" I asked again. Sometimes Ma wouldn't tell me her thoughts, but sometimes, if I kept after her, she would.

"We have not treated Fingal and Arn well," she said. "I don't know why they'd tell us what they find once they get to the Up. If I were Fingal, I'd go to the Up and keep moving. If I were Arn, I'd follow Fingal wherever he went. We would be worse off than we are now if we lose those two. Someone has to watch them and keep them to task and bring them home after. Granny can do it. She taught them at school. They're used to obeying her . . . Daina, you must not go to the Up."

"My reasons make sense," I said.

"Yes, they do." Ma sat silent, then reached over to tap the light off, leaving us in utter darkness, with only the sound of our breathing to keep us company. "That is not enough," she said. "You should wait until they come back and report. Make sure we can breathe naked Up air and not sicken from Up microbes or be attacked by Up creatures. You do not need to be in the disposable first mission."

"I want to see everything before anyone else spoils it with

telling it wrong," I said. "I want to tell Geordie what I see! I wonder if Yup Below has the same things above. Maybe not! I want to know, Ma, you know I do. Plus, I can use a camera, and the others can't." My words dropped into the darkness. With Noel supervizing, I had taken pictures of everyone at work, and some of people at rest, when the music and stories came out. My pictures were in our records, documenting our days. Noel said I had a good eye.

Ma sighed and didn't say anything else.

She watched everything. She had deep thoughts. Maybe she knew what my real reasons were.

• • •

In the morning, we all met for breakfast in the community hall. Everyone was there, even the littlest littlers, sitting on crêche-carer laps. Granny Tordis had made the porridge special, with diced bits of dried strawberry, and faint traces of cinnamon. I thought we had run out of that spice two years earlier. It was like a farewell breakfast, I thought, but didn't say.

Leader Bufo let us eat for a little while, then rose. He didn't need to use the attention chime; everybody had been waiting for him to speak. "I have considered, and I approve Daina going with Fingal, Arn, and Tordis on this voyage to the Up."

The small hot knot in my chest that had been burning since the night before burst, and warmth flowed through me.

"I've printed out a map of what used to be Up before Weatherdeath," Noel said. He laid out a big piece of paper on the table in front of Bufo. Fingal, Arn, Granny Tordis, and I went to look at it. Noel said, "Probably all this is different now, but maybe some is the same. Daina, you've studied map reading."

279

"Yes." The map showed our cavern's entrance, and the land laid out around it. Brown lines on green background, with two blue river lines running through. Mountainy things, if the brown lines were outlining stuff. I saw hearts and hands in some of the lines where they ran close to each other, and I tried to make it into a picture of ground, but I couldn't quite force it into an image. We had ups and downs in our caverns, open spaces and narrow, twisty paths between walls that wanted to squeeze you, and lots and lots of stalactites reaching down and stalagmites reaching up. We had flowstone draperies and beds of cave pearls. We had a river that rushed in from one side of the cavern and out through another, and we had our own structures and caves in the walls and paths and railings. I had never seen a map of that. But I had looked at maps of the Up. Not to say I had ever understood what I was seeing.

"I packed us survival kits," Granny Tordis said. "Food, water, matches, knives, tarps and lines and tape. A blanket in each, and a jacket, too. Extra socks. Flashlights. Soap, lotion, tooth salt and brush, medical supplies." She handed out stuffed backpacks, and we buckled ourselves into them.

"Daina. Here's a comm unit and one of the cameras, and some charged batteries." Noel gave me a padded black bag with compartments in it that held my devices snug. He buckled a watch around my wrist, then showed me he had a watch around his own, and a matching comm unit. "Check in with me every hour on the hour, all right? At least to start. Let us know what's going on. I'll have my unit on all the time until we know you're somewhat safe. Tell us everything you can."

"Thanks, Noel." I kissed his cheek.

Ma handed us each a headlamp. I hadn't used one since explorer class when I was thirteen. I flipped the switch. A strong light beam shone back toward the community hall. I turned it off.

We all put the headlamps on.

Everyone followed us to the big, bolted-shut door. There were many other blocked off tunnels around the edges of our living spaces, shafts we'd been taught to avoid, tunnels we might have gotten lost in, distances we didn't need. This door was taller than three people standing on each other's shoulders, and wider than four people standing side by side with their arms stretched out. Three large bolts held big padlocks that kept the door shut. We oiled these locks and the door hinges every week, but I'd never seen them open.

Bufo pulled three keys from a pocket and unlocked each one. They rasped loudly. The big door had gaps all around it and air flowed through. "We know the air is good; it's what we breathe," he said. "We don't know what other things you'll find. If it looks too dangerous, come straight back. Piller will guard the door. I'm going to lock it after you, but only one lock."

"All right," said Granny Tordis. She held a walking stick, thinner than Piller's. I wished I had one.

Bufo pulled the locks from the bolts. Piller helped him open the big door. Beyond it was a black tunnel. Cold air rushed over us, a wind stronger than any I had felt before. My hair blew back. Everyone's did. I smelled new things. I didn't know what they were, but some of them made my stomach growl, even though I'd just eaten.

Joy kicked alive. I felt as if I could float.

Ma kissed my cheek. "Good fortune go with you," she said, and then she kissed Fingal and Arn, too. "Take care of them, Ma," she said to Granny.

"I will."

We all switched our headlamps on and stepped into the tunnel. The walls were worked stone, with some sheets of new, glistening calcite buildup blanketing them here and there. The floor was dense with dust. Our feet stirred it up. The wind rushed toward us, until Bufo closed the door, muffling a cascade of good wishes from the others.

We stood in the dark, only our four light lances cutting into it, and I took a big breath.

"Let's go," Fingal said. "Let's go." He took my hand and Arn's and headed up the tunnel.

"Not too fast," Granny said, stick-walking in our wake.

But we couldn't slow. We rushed ahead, up, up, always up, around several crooks in the tunnel, and then we saw light, bright and blinding, stronger than plantlights, so bright it hurt my eyes to look, and we heard birdsong, birdsong! Something I'd only heard on puters before.

I switched off my headlamp. Arn and Fingal switched off theirs. We stood with our faces toward the Up, our eyes shut against the brightest light we had ever seen, and felt the first brush of warmth that came from something other than heaters. So many scents! The air was almost muddy with them! The sound of wind moving through leaves—I had heard that in the few vids we were allowed to watch, seen leaves moving and flickering. I wanted to see them for real.

Granny's stick tapped up behind us, and we all moved forward. I opened my eyes into slits. Already the light seemed softer, but such white in the sky above! I had never seen such a glowing ceiling!

We reached the outer chamber and looked out into the Up. There was so much open I got dizzy and felt like I would fall.

Colors glared at me—greens, browns, grays, brighter than I'd ever seen, and a rippling surface of water that stretched away and away without bumping into anything. The sky had changed from white to blue. All the angry light glared from one hot point low in the sky. It pressed warmth into my face. I swayed, and Fingal caught me. He wrapped his arms around me from behind and bent his head down so his mouth was near my ear.

"Was it worth it?" he whispered. "Sabotaging the lights and sanding the generator?"

I wanted to drop the black bag my father had given me that tied us to the others, still, with untouchable threads of radio and words. I wanted to shed the watch he had buckled on my wrist, its time synched to his. I wanted to tear off the bodysuit, still full of the scent and dust of Na Below.

It was too soon for any of those things, but I already knew I would do them. "Oh, yes," I breathed, my hands over Fingal's on my stomach.

The Dream Eater

CARRIE RYAN

The Cruce knows everything.

I should be in bed. Better yet, I should be asleep. I fist my hands in the pockets of my trousers, feeling the fuzzy slide of paper across my knuckles. The stupid note. Hunching my shoulders against the darkness I use my elbow to push open the thick wooden door to the tower. The hinges creak too loudly, the noise escaping into the night. I stop and listen.

I'm not supposed to be here. I'm not the type of person who breaks rules and sneaks out, slipping into forbidden places. Going to see the Cruce without permission.

Your emotions are not your own. She has taken them from you.

The note had been wedged into a small crevice in the wall behind the door. I thought I'd been the only one who knew about the hiding spot. And maybe that was still true since the note was written with my crooked lefty handwriting.

I shake my head. I don't remember writing the note. I don't remember sliding it into the wall. I don't even know what the words mean and I'm pretty sure I should just turn around and go back to my dreams.

Except that the note said something about the failure. *You failed the Cruce.*

I don't know what that means. I don't know why I would have felt the need to tell this to myself in such a mysterious way.

Because if there's one thing I know for sure it's that I've never failed at anything. I'm not that kind of person.

I creep through the main floor of the tower, dirty straw rustling under my feet. Two at a time I take the narrow winding stairs down to the basement. There are divots in the stone steps from so many feet following this path before me. I think about my first time a few years ago: I was thirteen and thinking I'd be participating in some kind of grand initiation.

I snort in the darkness and trail my fingers along the crooked walls to keep my balance. Already my heart's beating faster because this time I know what I'm about to see. I'm prepared for it. Almost.

I have friends who've come down here since the Initiation—out of some sense of duty or morbid curiosity I guess. Not me. I had enough the first time around. I saw her, understood the bargain she'd made, and have been just fine forgetting about her ever since.

The smell comes first, though you don't really realize it because it's faint in the beginning. Just a sort of heavy stench of rot that trickles in with the damp cellar air. It's not until you hear it—the keening—that you realize how much everything around you has changed. How tightly you're breathing, how hard it is to keep your eyes from watering.

The sound grows as you reach the basement floor and there's still the hallway to travel down—the door's at the far end, a guard sitting in a chair, hunched over with his head in his hands.

In a city where there's no such thing as misery, I wonder if his job is the closest anyone comes to being miserable. Alone here in the dark, listening to the Cruce and being surrounded by her stench.

It's at this point, staring at my destination, that I want to stop, just tear up the note and turn around and escape. But I don't. Because that's not the kind of person I am. I'm not someone who gives up easily. I'm not someone who fails.

I push myself down the hallway, ducking my head under the shallow ceiling until I'm standing only a few paces from the end. The bottom of the door is made up of ill-fitted slats of wood with haphazard metal bars along the top.

The guard glances up at me. I tell him I just want to take a look and he shrugs. He doesn't care that I'm there at all, only cares if I try to touch the girl. And as far as I know, no one's ever tried to reach out to her—not that I've ever learned about at least.

I step past the guard and involuntarily close my eyes. I wish I could close off everything else. It really really stinks and the noise is nearly unbearable. It's what I'd imagine a cat would sound like if you slowly squeezed the life out of it while simultaneously shredding the flesh from its body.

But I have to see her. I have to know what this note means. Because it doesn't make sense. I don't understand why I would write a note to myself. Why I would hide it in a place where only I could find it.

Why I can't remember ever doing either of these things.

I lower my head to my chest and try to take a deep breath. And then I lean toward the gaps in the door and look into the room beyond. I look at the Cruce, a girl whose name I think I used to know. A girl I think I grew up with.

There's very little light—none in the room itself, only what ekes through from the hallway where I'm standing. I see her toes first, nails long and yellow, cracked around the edges. Grime is caked into every crevice of her skin, streaking her with dirt. The room's tiny, narrower than the hallway and barely long enough for her to lie straight so she's forced to curl around herself, no furniture anywhere.

A nightgown so filthy it's falling apart along the seams sags from her body and her eyes are closed, fluttering under matted hair that falls over most of her face. Her skin's wrapped so tight around her bones that she appears almost corpse-like.

She wails, low and raw as she rocks against the earthen floor, her fingers clenching and unclenching at the ground. This is the Cruce, the holder of all misery.

I shudder but I can't stop staring at the creature. I wait for the sear of bile in the back of my throat, for my stomach to heave and my throat to close like it did the first time I saw her.

That this thing in the room had once been a child—a girl, a human being—is unfathomable. She's wretched and gross and ugly and wrong. She reeks of her own stench, of breathing the same air and lying in the same muck for year after year with no reprieve.

This is what my happiness is built on—what all our happiness is built on. This girl in this room in this tower. I watch her sleep, watch her body jolt and cry out as she prepares to enter people's dreams and pull their misery away, take it into herself.

Night after night, this is her duty: dispel misery, keep all evils at bay, ensure prosperity.

For a fraction of a moment I wonder what she's seen in my dreams. I never remember anything in the morning—that's the whole point.

I watch her twitch, trying to recall her as a child. I had to have known her because she's my age. I had to have once chased her in a game of tag or pinched her or been partnered with her in some class or something. Anything.

But all those memories are gone. Just like every other painful memory I've ever had. Eaten by the Cruce while I slept.

Your emotions are not your own. She has taken them from you. You failed the Cruce.

I could call out to her. I could stretch my fingers into the darkness to offer her some small comfort. Some idea that she's not alone.

I could ask her what the note means. What she knows about my failure because as far as I know, I've never failed. Just the idea of it causes the muscles along my shoulders and back to bunch.

But that would undo the bargain. It would cause everything to crash down around me and, like I said, I'm not the type of person who does what's wrong. I'm the type of person who follows the rules and the rules are clear when it comes to the Cruce: leave her alone.

I turn away from the door and feel a little out of place standing next to the guard, as if I should say something. "Anyone else been down here recently?" I ask, nothing else I could say coming to mind. He shrugs again and yawns. I wonder if when he sleeps the misery of his job is pulled away from his dreams—if when he tries to find memories of his past days they fall behind him blank and circumscribed.

I stand there a moment longer, feeling awkward as the Cruce's wailing drifts between us. "Good night, then," I finally mumble and as I start up the stairs I hear him call out, "Sweet dreams," with a touch of sarcasm to his voice.

In the darkness of the twisty corridor I pull the slip of paper from my pocket again. I don't need light to know the words written there. The too girly loop of my "y" and the terrible slant of my "t" and "k." The note doesn't make sense. Why would I remind myself of the Cruce? Everyone over the age of thirteen knows of her, it's part of our duty as Alinians, it's how we accept the Bargain of the sacrifice of one, for the happiness of all.

The imperfection of the moment is tight, squeezing at my lungs and making me uncomfortable. I'm not used to it, don't know how to shuffle free of the new emotions. I feel stupid waiting here in the dark as if I can learn something from silence. As if the tiny room with its pitiable creature below me in the basement holds some secret I was unaware of until now. But it's not true. The Cruce is as she's always been: miserable and wretched. And I am as I've always been: happy, and without failure, no matter what a slip of paper insinuates.

To prove my point I shred the note, the tearing sound echoing in the cavernous vault of the tower. I let the balmy night air take the fragments of paper from my hand and scatter it across the straw-covered floor. I've had enough of notes for one evening. It's time for me to go to bed, to let the Cruce take over.

For a moment I wonder if this is one of the memories she'll take away from me: standing here in the dark, the walls of the tower disappearing into blackness above and the sound of doves roosting in old cracks between the stones.

I close my eyes, trying to imprint this moment. Just as an experiment. I even think of gathering back the scraps of paper and stuffing them into the tiny hiding place where I'd found them. I almost laugh as I think about what tomorrow-me would think finding them there.

And maybe that's why I put the note there in the first place. Next time I shouldn't be so cryptic.

I slip out of the tower and through the empty streets toward home. Around me most of the houses are dark and silent though behind some curtained windows I see dancing and hear laughter. It's the sound of Alini, the essence of joy, so familiar to me.

At home I strip to my boxers and burrow under the covers, twisting them around my body and throwing a foot off the end of the bed. I close my eyes, fall asleep, and wait for the Cruce, to do as she might.

. . .

The quilt is heavy. Unbearably heavy. Crushingly heavy. I want to scream. I want to fight. I want to move but I can't. I struggle. I gurgle. I put every ounce of effort into opening my eyes and waking up but nothing happens. I heave the breath from my lungs to shout but there's no sound.

She comes from the darkness bathed in white. Her arms are by her sides, fingers curled slightly. She looks nothing like she does in her filthy room. She's strong as she strides to me, her eyes almost compassionate in their rage. Her toes are pink and clean.

The guard from the tower stands by the doorway, casually leaning against the wall as if he's seen this a hundred times and perhaps tonight he already has. Who knows where I fall on the list of her duties?

I want to beg for help. For mercy. But the guard will do nothing to aid me. Everyone in Alini has struggled at some point and has been subdued. Everyone must face the Cruce, whether voluntarily or not.

She comes for me in the black night as I struggle to shuffle free of sleep and stand before her. Some part of me knows what's next. Has lived through this every night, some lost corner of my mind. The part that's howling at me in a terror so pure it's deafening.

I want to fight her off. I want to raise my arms and beat against her chest. I've never felt the urge to hit a woman before. I've never felt the deep need for violence against anyone.

Yes, you have she whispers as she comes closer.

I'm not like that, I want to tell her. I'm not brutal.

Yes, you are she says.

My eyes flick to the guard, wondering if he judges me as she does. He's expressionless, almost bored.

She's just in front of me now and I'm embarrassed to notice how the tips of her breasts press ever so slightly against my chest. The scratchy feel of her nightgown shifting over my stomach. The fabric is a halo around her, almost translucent from a light source I can't understand.

I want to slide my hand along her waist, let my fingers trail against her back down and down and down. Self-loathing explodes inside me, fresh hot waves unlike anything I've felt before.

She smiles. Her lips are a glistening pink. Dark. A hollow of blackness peeping between them, the flick of her tongue.

Mercy, I want to beg. Please have mercy.

There's no such thing she says as she leans forward. As she presses those lips against mine and my body goes rigid.

The pain is so exquisite and intense that I can't breathe. I can't think. I can barely exist.

Through my mind it all comes: the marching of horrors. Of every evil act I've contemplated or done, every petty desire, every loathsome thought or deed. The Cruce is breathing into me, her breath a sickly sour taste of dry revulsion.

I can't knock her away, her hands are tightly fisted in my hair, holding my mouth to hers as she exhales and exhales and exhales. First are the memories: my cat dying when I was twelve, my grandmother's passing when I was nine, the ashy pallor of her face as she wheezed her last breath.

I remember every nightmare, the stench of sickness, the desire to hurt and maim.

I remember failing. Day after day trying the same tasks and getting them wrong: trying to write with my left hand cramped around the paper, my fists clutching a rope as I tried to climb it, the notes to a flute that sounded wheezy and dry. I remember girls turning their faces from me, boys mocking me.

I remember failed tests and my parents' scorn.

And still the Cruce breathes it all into me and the taste of her mouth is nothing in the face of every other dark emotion coursing through me. Misery. Terror. As if everyone I loved has died a grotesque death and returned to revisit the experience upon each cell of my body.

When the memories are done it is time for the emotions: desire, failure, depression, need, desolation, defeat, rejection, taunting, embarrassment. The feelings are so new, so sharp that I don't know how to corral them.

It's too much. The sum of my failures and injuries and defeats. I'm drowning under it all.

Her lips curve against mine like a smile. She pushes her body close. Closer. For a moment I sense her desire to hesitate, a simple infinitesimal pause. As if she's waiting for something, but I don't know what it is and so I stand there, captured in the thrall of the pain she's vested on me, waiting.

The tip of her tongue touches the bottom of my lip. I'd have never realized it were it not for how dry my mouth tastes at the time, for how desperate I am for any comfort at all. My breath catches, a heat exploding inside me.

"Will you remember this time?" Her voice aches.

Images flood through me, of us together and how I feel. My eyes open wide, my chest seizing. The strength of it is almost too much.

"I could never forget," I whisper against her.

And then she inhales, pulling all of this from me. Stripping the misery from the molecules of my body. Last, I see her taking today: the confusion of finding the note in my own handwriting, the worry that it might be true, that I might be a failure, the awkwardness of standing beside the guard, the uneasiness of watching the Cruce—*her*—in her room, the confusion of leaving and tearing up the note.

She takes it all from me: every dark emotion, all worrisome thoughts. Anything negative that would spike against my enjoyment of life.

Finally she steps away from me. I feel a peaceful glow, a joy in existence. *Who am I?* she asks.

The Cruce, I tell her, a sticky revulsion welling up from my stomach like bile.

Her eyes water. I wonder if she was expecting a different answer. I've never gotten an answer wrong in my life. It's not who I am.

• • •

"You were talking to yourself." Lit's standing in the doorway, her dull brown hair pulled back in a tangled ponytail. Immediately I feel my cheeks heat up and I turn away, back to a table full of empty red-clay pots waiting to be filled with moist soil. My fingernails are already black with dirt.

"I wasn't," I say.

Lit comes into the greenhouse. I sense the way she moves, the way the air shifts around her.

"I heard you."

It's already scorching in here, I should have raised the vents an hour ago but I've been trying to sweat out the confusion. I shift one of the pots on top of the note I'd found that morning tucked beneath a loose brick under a stack of planters.

"I was talking to the plants. They grow better when you talk to them," I offer, feeling lame. It's a new sensation, this grasping for words. I'm not used to it, as though suddenly this morning my tongue is too large for my mouth.

She walks down the cramped row of tables, peering at all the pots. "They're empty," she points out. "There's nothing to talk to." She stops next to me. "Besides, it's not like we have any trouble growing things here."

I hunch farther over the workbench, fisting my hands in the soil and scowl. "What do you want, Lit?" There's an edge to my voice. I take a deep breath, try to relax my shoulders. I shouldn't be rude to her, it's not her fault she stumbled upon me at the wrong time.

She huffs out a sigh, shoving a frizz of hair from her face and I notice that the skin around her eyes looks dull. "I just thought . . ." Her voice trails off. She reaches a finger toward the glass wall and as she begins to trace through the condensation a bead of water bends toward her wrist.

"What?" I cross my arms over my chest and lean back, pressing against the table. I'm being rude and I know it. It's unnatural for me to be so terse and I almost apologize but instead I press my tongue against the back of my teeth, trapping the words.

Her lips pinch tight together, making the scar that cuts across the left side of her upper lip glow white. "I didn't sleep last night. I saw you going to the tower. I was just wondering why."

I inhale sharply and everything inside me stills. I have no idea what she's talking about. "I never left the house last night," I tell her evenly. "I didn't have any reason to." I think about the tiny scraps of paper I found on the floor of my room this morning, how some of them clearly had my handwriting on them though I couldn't puzzle out the words.

None of it had been there when I'd gone to bed. Not that I could remember, at least.

I think about the note I've hidden under the flowerpot behind me on the table. Every part of my body focuses on it. I want to turn around. I want to flip the pot over, to see the familiar writing. Instead I tighten my arms around my chest, the dirt on my hands rough against my skin.

"I saw you," she says, leaning toward me. She hesitates before adding. "I've seen you do it before. Every evening to the Cruce."

I force myself to inhale deep, letting the anger seep into the air before pushing it from my lungs. "You're imagining things, Lit." I try to sound nonchalant rather than angry but I'm pretty sure I don't pull it off. I've never lied before and I know I'm not good at it. I've never had a reason to lie before—a need to cover anything up.

But I'm not lying, I remind myself, a tingle spreading down my arms.

She looks at me as if I've bruised her and for a moment I see the exhaustion on her face, the weight of her body as she stands facing me.

"You look exhausted," I tell her, returning to my planting. "Maybe you hallucinated it."

She looks at me and I raise my chin as if in a challenge. My systems are flooded with the desire to strike out, to protect myself, to run away. It's a confusing mess and there's no way Lit can't see it all.

Her gaze flickers away first, trailing down toward the empty pots sitting in front of me and up along the vines wrapping the window pulls. "Do you remember who she was before? When we were little?"

I snort. Her question needs no elaboration and my answer comes easy. "The Cruce is no one."

She seems to wince and I almost want to ask her about it but my mind wanders to the note buried under the pot and I press my lips tighter.

"And you think it's fair?" she finally asks. "We get to be happy and she gets to be miserable?"

I look at her until she meets my eyes again. Before either of us was Initiated we would lean from windows and push our bodies out across the narrow gap between our houses and spend the evenings laughing and trading stories. Today I miss those moments and wonder if I've missed them before and just don't remember because the Cruce took the misery from me.

"She volunteered to take it on herself," I remind her.

Lit raises one shoulder. "That's what they tell us."

A sudden jolt of unease hollows against my heart. "It's what we *know*," I tell her.

Her smile is faint but when she grabs my hand her grip is insistent. "It's what they let us remember."

• • •

I should be in bed. Or I should at the very least be home or somewhere with friends—anywhere but striding through the tower and hovering by the stairs leading down to the dungeon. Even though I haven't been here since the Initiation my skin prickles with awareness of what waits below.

The horrible stench of the Cruce. The dark claustrophobic air.

I wouldn't be here except for the note I found in the greenhouse this morning and Lit's strange questions that have left unease running through my veins.

I tore the note up and dunked the shreds in water, watching the fibers of the paper drift apart. For most of the day I tried to forget the words: *You know the Cruce. You can love the Cruce.*

But still they won't go away. I could wait until the night, wait for her to come to me and take the uncertainty from me but my legs won't still, my mind won't stop worrying over what the note meant.

How anyone could love such a wretched creature is beyond me. She's disgusting, horrible and cruel. It's the one bad memory the citizens of Alini are allowed to hold as their own: Initiation and the first introduction to the Cruce.

* * *

It was a beautiful sunny day, a perfect day, when the Architect led me and the other Initiates into the tower. We walked downstairs in a single line and I remember how those before me began to wail as they each approached the doors.

We were unprepared for what waited for us.

Lit stood in front of me, which meant she could already see into the room when I couldn't. I remember the way her eyes grew wide, her face white. The scar on her lip became a brutal red slice as her mouth opened and she started to scream and scream and scream.

I knew at that moment that I didn't want to see what lay beyond that door. That I wouldn't see it. I tried to refuse but the Initiates behind drove me forward, no hesitation in their steps.

I'd wanted to be brave—honorable—when I first saw the Cruce. She was the source of all our prosperity, the reason my life had unfolded so idyllically. I'd wanted to somehow acknowledge her sacrifice and understand it.

But when I saw her I understood. She was the most horrible creature I could have imagined. It's been several years since I saw her for the first—and last—time but I remember how wretched and gross and wrong she was.

I remember Lit falling to her knees beside me, her arms wrapped around her body and her mouth open in a silent scream. In front of her a puddle of vomit spread over the ground, seeping between cracks in the stones. Her eyes were screwed shut but I couldn't stop staring at the Cruce.

What I couldn't believe was that this was what our life was built on. That this miserable creature was the root of my happiness. That everyone else in Alini had seen this girl and accepted her.

I remember one thought: everyone else in my life had met the Cruce, had seen what I saw, and accepted it. This was the way of Alini, and it would become my way as well.

That night was the first time she came to my room, her white gown flowing around her. We'd been instructed about the procedure: to stand still and never raise a hand against her in love or anger. To allow her to take our ills upon herself. The guard was there to ensure we complied though if I've ever struggled, I'll never know. She'd take that memory away as well.

There's one other thing I remember clearly about Initiation. Before that day I have an unending stretch of memories of Lit and I together, growing up next door to one another, and spending long evenings leaning from our windows across the gap between the houses, telling stories and playing games. Since that Initiation day, I've kept my window closed. The Cruce may have taken away any ill feelings between us, but she could never take away the moment when Lit saw the way I stared at the Cruce for the first time—the horror and failure I felt in that moment before I could compose myself. The Cruce has never taken away the embarrassment of my own weakness, or that someone else had seen it.

• • •

When I approach the Cruce's doorway now, the guard doesn't seem to care that I'm here. Anyone's technically allowed to view the Cruce, to understand the sacrifice she makes for the betterment of the rest of us, but still I assume the guard's job is a lonely one.

And for some reason this thought sparks a question and before I can think better of it, I ask him if anyone else ever comes down here.

He shrugs. "None today."

"Do you get to remember?" I ask, wondering if he, like the rest of us, must submit to the Cruce each night after escorting her through Alini.

"No," he smiles broadly, "Thankfully not."

I nod my head and glance at the creature past the door, wondering if anything's changed about her since the last time

I came down here so many years ago. Her gown is torn, her skin filthy and mats tangle her hair so thoroughly it could never be combed free.

My note told me I could love the Cruce but how, I have no idea.

· · ·

When Lit's fingers tap on my window after dusk I lie on my bed and listen. There once was a time I'd fly to answer her but memories of the Cruce are too tight inside me. I wait for her to come to me and take these feelings away. I can't stand to own them anymore. There's not enough room in me for this much misery and I refuse to wonder how the Cruce has such capacity to take it all on herself.

· · ·

My heart beats too heavy as I wait for the Cruce. I sit on the edge of my bed fully dressed, feet tapping against the floor in an approximation of rhythm. When she comes she is nothing like she was in the tower. Now she is enveloped in white, every part of her crisp and clean.

The guard waits in the hall outside my room as she approaches, arms extended to rest on my shoulders. I shudder at her touch, remembering the smell of her from before. Knowing full well her wretchedness.

When she presses her lips to mine I cringe and then she's exhaling and memories flood into me, vivid and dark. All of my spite and rage accumulated over days and years—my failures and insecurities. My ineptitude.

For this moment I loathe myself. I am worse than the Cruce because at least the Cruce serves a purpose in this village. At least she is the keeper of misery so that the rest of us can know only brightness.

I am nothing like that. She is a vessel of worthiness and I am incapable of usefulness, in any shape of the term.

Tears blur my eyes from the pain and then her breath stops and I tremble, begging her to inhale and take it all from me. But she doesn't. Not right away, and my body vibrates with the need for release.

Then, in that infinite pause, a memory floats up bright and clear, damming the misery flowing through me.

It's of her lips pressed to my ear whispering about herself. Night after night, she pauses after pouring back into me my own desolation and then she speaks to me as if I'm a friend.

I realize, then, that I am a friend. That through the impossibility of these moments I've fallen in love with her.

"You," I gasp out. Her eyes shine, her lips spread wide in a smile. Over her shoulder the guard hovers in the hallway, ignoring what happens in this room between us. He has tried to stop us in the past, I know about this now, and she has stopped him. Stripped him of memory and desire to stand between us.

With trembling fingers I twine her hair in my hand, pull the Cruce against me, and kiss her. I let desire sweep over us both, pressing my body so tight to hers that no such thing as misery exists.

In this moment she is nothing but beauty and light. She is no longer the Cruce but the girl I knew growing up. The girl who rounded out the trio with Lit and me.

"You let me remember," I finally say, my lips still pressed against hers. "The note. You let me write the note and hide it for myself."

Her cheeks blush and she nods. "You begged."

Of course I did. "Because I can't stand forgetting this. Forgetting you. Please, can't you just leave me one? A small memory."

She tucks her bottom lip between her teeth and sucks, thinking, and the gesture is so familiar it burns against my sternum. She's tempted. "It would break the Bargain."

"Please," I press, almost panicked by the pending forgetfulness.

She tilts her head to the side, considering me. "You'd trade their misery for our happiness?" Her question echoes Lit's from earlier and I want to immediately revolt against its implications.

"I want you happy," I tell her. "You deserve the right to be happy."

She steps forward and wraps her arms around my neck, her mouth to my ear as she breathes. "I am happy."

When she pulls back she giggles. "Now write your note and hide it. Quick."

I scribble quickly, right hand cupped around my left so that she doesn't see. When it's hidden in the wall I face her again and wait for her kiss.

As she inhales I feel it all leaving me, the last memory to go is the despair at memory's departure.

• • •

The Cruce deserves to be happy. At first I think that's all the note says but as I run my fingers over the incomprehensible words I feel the imprinted traces of another message on a sheet that's since been torn away. I'm standing in the greenhouse when I realize this, and I drag my finger through the dirt of a barren pot and rub it into the crevices until more words appear: *Rescue her.*

I snort out a laugh at the absurdity. The Cruce is a wretched monster, the vessel of misery created to keep our village

302

prosperous. It's because of her that crops grow without blight, that the sun shines without burning, that music always sounds in harmony.

Behind me the door opens, letting in a puff of dry air that slides over my humidity-dampened skin. I glance up, blood pausing in its course through my body at the implication of being caught, as if I've been doing something wrong.

"You reading poetry to the plants this time?" Lit asks, eyeing the paper still clutched in my hands. I barely resist the urge to crumple it in my fingers and shove it from view out of fear it would only draw her attention more sharply.

"You should get more sleep," I say to deflect her interest, nodding my head at her sleep-starved eyes and dull hair. The flush on her cheeks from being outside drains away slightly and she pauses on her way down the aisle between planting tables. She crosses her arms, invisible sparks of anger skittering around her. "The Cruce seemed to spend more time than usual in your room last night," she trades a barb for a barb. "Perhaps you had more to atone for than usual?"

It's my turn to scowl. "It's not polite to spy." I want desperately to glance at the paper again as if somehow I can convince myself that the writing doesn't belong to me—*Rescue her*—outlined in dirt in my own sloppy cursive. Instead I stride down the narrow aisle, pushing past Lit, but she grabs my arm and stops me.

"We used to be friends." Her voice is almost desperate, and I think to myself that it's too early in the morning to be filling the vessel of misery for the Cruce to empty. "Did I say something?" Lit asks. "Do something to change that?"

I think of Initiation, the last time I ever remember seeing the Cruce. I remember my humiliation and how Lit saw it all.

303

She's the only person in this entire village who retains any memory of my weaknesses. When I look at Lit I see the worst of what I can be without the Cruce's intervention.

But I don't tell her this. Instead I say, "If you did, the Cruce hasn't let me remember."

She's quiet for a moment but her grip on my arm doesn't loosen. I don't feel like pulling away. As if doing so would create some sort of irrevocable break between us.

I wonder, sometimes, if the Cruce can take our mental memories but not the physical ones. If I hit Lit, struggled against her, would our bodies remember? Would she wince against me when I saw her tomorrow?

"Do you ever wonder who the Cruce is?" If anything her tone is more melancholy than before. I want to please her—it's who I am. I search my brain as if the answer left an imprint before being taken away one night.

My fist tightens around the note in my pocket as I answer. "Why would I care about the Cruce?"

• • •

I should be in bed. Though the sun hasn't finished dropping past the horizon the weariness of the day rests fully on my shoulders and I want nothing more than to sleep, meet the Cruce, and be done with the memory of this note. It sits like a stone in my pocket, the paper damp from my clutching it for so many hours.

In desperation I go to the Tower, as if seeing the Cruce in person could erase the meaning of the words I'd written to myself. There are some in my village who have spent their whole life avoiding the Tower, as if, like a giant sundial, its shadow didn't stretch to the tips of Alini during the course of the day. There are others who go back once or twice after Initiation, as if they must somehow see her to understand and pay homage to her sacrifice.

I'm a member of the former group, never having had the desire to return to the scene of my Initiation as if I could somehow bury my shame of that moment. And even though it's been years since my first and only descent down the steps to the dungeon, the smells seem almost familiar, as if they somehow burned themselves so indelibly into my brain that I can never escape.

A guard sits by the door, head tilted back against the wall as if in boredom. I stammer something about just wanting to see her and he raises a shoulder. "No touching," as if anyone would want to reach through the narrow bars and touch the horrid creature beyond.

Before I even see her my skin tightens with revulsion. The air is cold, filled with the putrid scent of despair and neglect. Light from the hallway casts itself into her cell, illuminating dirt-stained and wasted skin wrapped tightly around bird-thin bones.

My stomach revolts and I turn away. "Has anyone ever tried to touch her?"

His eyes narrow as if I've issued a threat rather than innocent inquiry.

"It would break the Bargain," he says, but he must realize that's not an answer.

"But has anyone tried? Has anyone ever tried to take her away?" I swallow, nervous, yet needing to know.

His body tenses, ready to leap at me as if I could ever force myself close enough to the horrid creature to press a finger against her, much less follow the orders of the note in my pocket and rescue her.

"She volunteered for the role," the guard tells me. "We honor her sacrifice for our happiness and prosperity. To break the Bargain would be to profane what she's given up." The words roll from his tongue, so familiar to me that I finish the statement in my own head. But then he says something else. "Besides, she's been like that for so long she's probably insane. Even if you did wake her, what would be left of her to enjoy it?"

I stare at the way her thick yellow nails curl over her sickly and broken toes. I find relief in his words, an easing along the muscles along my back as my fist unclenches around the note. He's right. Why would I ever rescue her if there's nothing left to be saved?

• • •

As the Cruce fills me with my own wicked memories I want to pull away but I don't because it's against the rules and I've always been someone who does what he is told. Instead I stand and take it all in me, let it grate along the inside of my skin as if looking for a way to slice free.

Just when I think I will be overtaken by the ugliness of myself, of who I've been, a pure bright thought begins to surface like a bubble that pops open in my chest and reminds me of love and warmth and desire for the Cruce. It eclipses every other emotion.

"Let me take you away from here." I press my words against her lips as we kiss as if I can somehow force them inside her and make her accept it as truth. "Just let me remember and I'll rescue you tomorrow. Please."

I feel her smile, her mouth curving around mine and I groan.

• • •

When I arrive at the greenhouse in the morning Lit's already there, standing in my familiar place, back turned to me and fists shoved into pots empty of everything but dirt. I let the door swing closed as I call out to her cheerily, "Good morning, Lit."

She barely moves her head and I only catch a glimpse of her cheek but what I see makes me hesitate. Red skin, puffed eyes, glistening trails of tears. I glance over my shoulder, realizing I've come too far inside to turn around and leave and so I push myself forward, uneasy in my stomach.

"Lit?" I ask.

She pulls her hands from the soil and for a moment my breath catches, expecting to see slips of paper dripping from her fingers as though she'd dug for my secrets in the dirt.

But she holds nothing but air and then she turns to me and before I can say another word she presses her palms against my cheeks and pulls my face to hers and kisses me hard and deep. She tastes like the earth, like dew-damp mornings and the first unfurled flower of spring.

I start to pull back but she holds me to her, moist soil sliding from her fingers along my skin as she presses her body to mine, shoving me back against the bench.

She's smaller than I am, weaker. I could easily push her away but I don't because I like the taste of her and the clean scent of her and the way she makes my body hum along with every living thing surrounding us.

When she finally pulls away I'm panting, sweat beading my forehead, and she asks, "Could you love me?"

And I want to tell her *yes* but I remember how she looked at me when we first saw the Cruce and the tight pain of embarrassment clenches around my chest again. She is the only one in the world who knows about my weakness. How could she ever want me?

When I say nothing she turns half away and stares down at the dirt smeared over her wrists.

I force myself to ask her, "Do you remember Initiation?"

Her eyes flare wide for a moment but she won't look up at me and my stomach tightens. I could stop now, just walk out of the greenhouse and go about my day as if this conversation had never existed. And then tonight the Cruce could take the memory of uneasy feelings from my mind and all will be right again.

But if the Cruce can take away the misery of this moment, I might as well ask the question I really want the answer to. "Do you remember what I said? What I looked like?"

She lifts her eyes, focusing on the distance, and when she moves her gaze to me she looks everywhere but directly at me. "Is that what stops you from loving me?"

I lift a shoulder.

She raises a dirty finger and trails it from my forehead down over my nose and across my lips. The taste of rich soil reminds me of her kiss. "No," she finally answers. "I only remember the Cruce. Nothing more."

This time I'm the one to pull her toward me. I'm the one to seal my mouth to hers, a heat so deep inside it sets fire to my veins.

• • •

That night, the moment I remember how much I love the Cruce I feel a desperate twist in my stomach and fall to my knees. "Oh no," I moan, shoving my fingers through my hair as I remember kissing Lit over and over again through the afternoon.

I wrap my arms around the Cruce's waist, bury my head against her abdomen and beg her to forgive me. "Take it away from me," I plead. "Make me forget it ever happened. Her, too. Make us both forget. You can take the memory from us. Please."

She caresses my face with her fingertips and I flinch against the touch. "It doesn't work that way, Went. I can only remove the misery, never the joy."

I look up at her, feeling dry and empty. "Then let me leave a note for myself. Please. Let me just know that I can't be with her."

For a moment she ponders my request and I don't wait for her answer before crawling to the table in the corner and scribbling the message.

You do not love Lit. You love the Cruce.

• • •

My days become ones of discovery: of Lit's body, of her dreams. Each secret she shares with me I tuck away with the others, packing them together in my heart that grows with every kiss and stolen moment.

I never knew such a love and longing could exist together.

This morning I whistle as I wander into the greenhouse and I find her bent over the row of pots arranged against the far windows. "Anything new?" I call out to her because we've been trying to get something to grow in that dirt for weeks. The fact that they're still barren is odd for Alini.

Lit's shoulders stiffen and a small slice of unease wavers inside. I approach her hesitantly, noticing that even the air seems off and indifferent. As I draw near I see beyond her that the pots are tipped over, and soil spilled over the table and floor. Spread among the debris are dirt-smeared scraps of paper that she's diligently piecing together.

There must be dozens of the shredded puzzles, most of them already completed.

My eyes narrow as I recognize the handwriting as my own before I can read what the letters spell out. "Lit?" I ask because I feel unbalanced, the tension radiating from her wavering in the air.

I read the first note I come to: *You don't love Lit. You love the Cruce.*

I read the next note and the one after: *You don't love Lit. You love the Cruce.* Over and over again the same words. The same lazy tilt to the letters in my cramped penmanship.

You don't love Lit. You love the Cruce.
You don't love Lit. You love the Cruce.
You don't love Lit. You love the Cruce.
You don't love Lit. You love the Cruce.
You don't love Lit. You love the Cruce.
You don't love Lit. You love the Cruce.

I dash my hand through them, pulling the notes apart at the seams where they'd clearly been ripped once before. "What is all this?" I cry out in a rage, hoping that anger can keep the truth from being known.

I wait for her to turn and look at me, expecting the same despair on her face that I feel in my own heart. But she just keeps arranging the scraps of paper over and over again, lining up the words of my own betrayal.

"I don't understand," I tell her, pulling her fingers from the dirt and clutching them in my own. "I love you, Lit. *You.*"

When her eyes meet mine there's no misery. No rage. Just a bland sense of obligation. "Ask her, then. The Cruce knows everything."

Tugging Lit behind me, I stalk from the greenhouse and through the village to the tower. She doesn't protest and no one thinks anything of the two of us walking hand in hand. If they notice the tension in my face, in my every movement, no one comments as they nod hello and remark on the continued good weather.

In the distance I hear the call of bells signaling the start of a festival, the cheer of crowds watching horses race and the call of gulls banking lazily over the smooth stretched lake dotted with pristine white triangular sails. Alini unfolding perfectly just as it does on every other day.

"Have you been back since Initiation?" I ask as I hold the heavy wooden tower door open, the darkness beyond cut through by slices of sunlight from slits of windows set high in the stone walls.

She shakes her head. "You?" she asks and I tell her the truth. "Never."

The air is cooler in the shadows, becoming almost physical as we take the stairs down to the dungeon. Acrid smells assault me—dirt, decay, and the Cruce's unwashed body. I want to hide my nose in the sleeve of my shirt but I refuse to let Lit see such weakness and so I just push myself faster, hoping to get this over with.

The guard nods at our approach but I stalk past him and bang my fists against the door barring the Cruce. "Explain the notes to me!" I shout at her and the guard wraps his hand around my arm, tugging me back.

"She's not to be touched," he explains.

I glance at him, disgust roiling through me at the smell and sight of the wretched girl sprawled on the other side of the door. "Who would ever touch such a creature?" I ask him and to prove my point I spit at her.

She doesn't move, doesn't react, just curls tighter around herself, the ragged hem of her nightgown trailing over her dirt-encrusted legs.

When I turn to Lit I find her standing still in the middle of the hallway, her face pale and fingers trembling. "It's okay, my love," I whisper against her temple as I pull her toward me. "I'm here. I'm yours."

• • •

"Why do you do this to me?" I ask the Cruce that night after she's filled me with my memories and allowed me to trail my lips along the edge of her shoulder. "Why do you allow me to remember my betrayal and do nothing to fix it? Please,"—I'm on my knees, my fingers wrapped in the brilliant soft white of her nightgown, tugging at the hem,—"let me take you away from the village. Let me remember how much I love you every morning when I wake up. Let me make you happy."

She caresses her fingers across my forehead, down my nose and over my lips and I remember when Lit did this the first time we kissed and my stomach twists.

"You agreed to this Bargain like everyone else," she says, voice noncommital.

"I didn't know," I tell her. "I didn't understand what it would mean."

"You'd make them all miserable?"

"I'd let them determine their own happiness—just to allow you the chance to find your own."

She slips to her knees in front of me until we're nose to nose. She smells like the dizzying, drowning downpour of summer rain. "You'd do that to Lit?"

And here my words catch large in my throat.

"You love her," the Cruce urges.

"Only when you make me forget about you."

The corners of her lips raise. "I never make you forget about me. You are always aware that I exist. You come and visit me every afternoon—but you always find me despicable then."

I grasp her hands in mine. "You take away my ability to remember that I love you."

She looks past me, out the window and I follow her gaze. A short distance away Lit sits in her room, her face turned to the night. Starlight gleams from where tears slip from her eyes.

"She watches us every night, you know," the Cruce tells me. "When I go to her she screams and fights against me. Tells me how wretched you are to betray her. She asks me to take away any memory that she ever cared for you."

My lips feel bloodless. "Why don't you?"

She smiles. "I can only take the misery," she reminds me.

"But you take all of this," I cup her cheek in my hand, run my thumb along the lashes of her eye. "You take my love."

She presses herself against me. "It's a miserable kind of love."

"Then why do you give it back to me? Every night you let me remember. Why not just keep it all?"

For a long moment she examines me, tracing every part of me. "Is that what you'd want?"

No, I think to myself. "Yes," I tell her. It is the most painful word I've ever uttered.

There's silence between us and then she pulls back, going to stand at the window and gaze at Lit only a few feet away.

I stare at her back, wondering at what I'm giving up. How I could be so weak? I should be taking her away from Alini and up into the mountains. My love should be pure enough to rescue us both.

But I'm too scared.

And I can't do that to Lit.

The Cruce traces something over the fog on the glass and I turn away to grab a pencil from the table and scribble out a note, shoving it into a crack in the wall before I stand and go over to her.

The Cruce knows everything. Your emotions are not your own. She has taken them from you. You failed the Cruce.

Maybe someday I'll come across the note and I'll go to see the Cruce and I'll demand an explanation. Maybe I'll be better in the future. Maybe I'll be stronger and wiser and I'll figure out a way to put this puzzle together in a different order to form a new picture where everyone wins and no one loses.

"I love you," I whisper against the Cruce's neck.

She turns in my arms. "You always have," she says, her eyes cloudy with tears.

"Why are you letting me forget?"

As she presses her lips to mine she smiles, "Because I love you." And then she inhales, taking it all from me.

357

Jesse Karp

On the three hundred fifty-seventh floor there was no nighttime. The diseased light that lit the stained, cracking concrete corridors often went into mad seizures of prolonged flickering, a false promise to finally succumb. But in the end, the grim, bruise-colored illumination beat down like an eternal punishment. The bulbs were behind a clear shield that no amount of hammering could shatter. Even in private rooms, where you could switch off your own lights, the alien glare crept in like a fungus under the door. Darkness, which could render the ruin and desperation of everyday life invisible, was at a premium here.

Akil had a knack for darkness. As an orphan, he was seen as a resource drain and thus spurned. Show kindness once and the damned thing could grab hold of you and your family, suddenly swallowing up entire shares of rations and supplies. Better to keep orphans away to begin with. Shout at them when they came too near, kick them if they didn't go. So Akil, an orphan since he was eight, had cause to find places away from the others and was willing to penetrate and explore where others wouldn't— small, hidden places that the light, sometimes, didn't reach. Darkness within abandoned quarters, filled with must and filth and sometimes not really abandoned at all, but home to one of the silent, viper-cruel forgotten tenants. Or the darkness of the old shunned hallway.

Through the twists and turns of the central quarters, on the outskirts of the maintenance and machinery zone, on the outside edge of 357, the shunned hallway curved around a bend that few had ever seen the far side of. The lights here flickered constantly, the walls lined with a multitude of fissures and cracks like wrinkles on the face of an ancient man. Moisture filled those cracks, dripped from the ceiling into foggy gray puddles on the floor.

They said that, years ago, on 358, the filtration and waste systems had undergone catastrophic failure and the halls of that level had slowly filled with fluid. Hundreds of bloated bodies, dissolving in poisonous water and their own excrement, floated above. They said one day the ceiling of the shunned corridor would crack open and disgorge this torrent, meting out the same inevitable fate to the tenants of 357: drowning in shit.

The truth was, no one knew. No one knew what happened on the floor above or even if there *was* a floor above at all. No one knew for a fact that they were on the three hundred fifty-seventh floor. Only that the number 357 was stenciled in fading blue ink on every concrete corner of this place. If they *were* on floor 357, with 356 floors below them, then there may just as well be more floors above.

Akil had, one day when he was twelve and being pursued by three boys who had accused him of stealing some scrap metal, ventured down the shunned hallway, where the dim light became little more than a glimmer on the concrete walls that moldered and festered like open wounds from the constant exposure to moisture. Finally, pushing back toward a dead end of concrete, he found that the lights had failed completely, leaving a patch of immaculate darkness.

Today, Akil had come here because, once again, he had been watching Jendayi—her hair cut nearly to her scalp, her large eyes shining, her delicate hands flickering and buzzing about excitedly like the flickering lights. She, like Akil, had finished her lesson years at fifteen. She was due shortly for apprenticeship to a machinist or hydroponist.

Today was her time. All the others had done it already, you could tell by the gaze-scars splayed across their faces. Jendayi made a show of resistance but allowed herself to be taken, giggling.

Struck cold inside, Akil followed from far back. He could watch from around corners, down the long hallway where he was part of the distance itself.

They took her down the cracking expanses, their chattering echoes springing back to him.

"Don't," he whispered after her. "Don't."

They moved through the pounding hum of the hallways with the temperature equipment, which made the floor vibrate and the air hot and dry, and they came to the outer wall. The window.

The window used to be closed in by a steel shutter that would be opened once a day to let in the light. It was a light unlike any from a bulb; a pure yellow that burned tears of beauty from people's eyes. For four minutes a day, that light would hit the grill on the far wall and charged all of the machines that kept 357 alive. Then the light would shift and dim and the shutter would slide closed until the next day.

Sometimes people would be so taken by the beauty they'd arrange to be lifted into the light. They'd bask, and smiles of sacred enlightenment would take them. Others would gather around them, follow them for the rest of the day and listen to them talk about the quintessence of light. Then, after two or three days, the flesh on the faces of those who had stood in the light would begin to flake and then peel off in hot, bloody pieces, leaving seeping fissures that looked like the dripping cracks in the concrete walls.

They did this for years, such was the draw of the light. Until too many died and the survival of all on 357 was threatened. Standing in the light was then forbidden.

Akil's mother had told him all this. Told him about sickness that could come from an invisible thing called radiation, which traveled in the light. She was a leader—brilliant, but hated for her brilliance. That was what Akil remembered about her, mostly: her knowledge, all the things she told him.

He could hear her voice sometimes, saying those words, those things about the machines, about people, about numbers. "Repeat it back," she would say, again and again. So many things that Akil didn't understand, but could recite. Slowly, over the years, he would understand one of the things suddenly, when confronted with a door no one else could open or a machine no one else could operate. His mother's legacy.

He remembered that about her. That and the feel of her hand on his face. Maybe only once. A soft, cool touch on a fevered cheek. No comforting word. No loving look. Just the touch of the hand on the cheek.

She had forbidden people from the light and they found that unacceptable. So some came together and ripped the steel shutter from its place, exposing the window for everyone, at all times, so when the light was *not* shining in, you could still look.

People did. They looked when the light was not burning in

and they looked and looked and looked again. Slowly, over months, sometimes years, they would acquire gaze-scars, peeling cracks that spread from the eyes and across the cheeks and scalp, but didn't kill. Not immediately. Not so quickly you could prove the link. But adults, some of them parents, some of their faces a riot of gaze-scars, forbade the children from going to look too often. But often enough, the children would sneak to the room, to steal a look out the window. For many, it was a rite of passage.

Akil had never looked. One of the things he had promised his mother before he was old enough to know what he was promising.

"It's like a tunnel," Risa was saying to Jendayi. "The concrete is so thick between us and there. But at the end, there's a . . . a living gray. It *moves*, like the smoke that comes from machines sometimes. It *breathes*."

Voices rose in agreement and awe.

"Come on," Risa continued, always closest to Jendayi, always the first to offer her hand. "I'll boost you."

Jendayi held her spot, looked up at the window, at Risa.

"Come *on*," Risa said, smiling.

Jendayi came forward.

Risa knelt, offered her clasped hands as a foothold. Jendayi stepped in, hoisted herself up. Her face rose toward the window.

"Don't!" Akil shouted.

The uncertain tower faltered, Jendayi landed hard on her feet.

"There," Risa shouted, pointing. They moved as one, surging toward Akil.

But he was already gone, careening down the hallways,

sometimes on the floor, sometimes skittering, ricocheting from the walls themselves, using metal extrusions, pipes, crevices as hand- and footholds to increase his momentum.

They weren't fast enough to catch him at first but Risa and Swayne, the fastest of them, could keep him in sight and as long as he was in sight, they would catch him eventually because 357 was finite and there was only so far you could run.

So he headed as far as he could, as far as 357 could take him. To the other end, the shunned hallway.

He threw himself off one corner, sprang around the other, shot beneath the brown, trickling water, through the mad flickering light, around the curve.

Their voices echoed to him as they pounded to the T-branch.

"He went this way," Swayne's voice coughed out between ragged breaths.

"No," Risa's voice was harsh and husky. "He went down the hallway. He would go down here."

Akil retreated further, past the spattering of water into murky puddles, toward the spot where even the flickering faltered and into the beckoning darkness. They would never dare follow.

"You'd better stay in there," Risa's voice echoed at him.

"Yes, stay there," Jendayi's voice now. "Don't ever, *ever* come out!"

Jendayi, unaware though she may have been, had been his connection, his hope. Without her, he was set adrift without direction or purpose. He laid himself down in the shunned hallway, fetal in the black and blind to the heart pain, not even sure whether his eyes were opened or closed.

Akil's prostrate body was pressed against that dead-end

wall, alone and trembling with grief when, for the second time in less than an hour, his world changed forever.

A razor of light suddenly cut a square shape ahead of him, as if the space behind one concrete slab of wall had illuminated.

Then, with a grinding sound, the slab of concrete recessed slowly into the space behind it and then slid to the side. Then the light burned out, scouring the filthy hallway ten feet away from Akil. It was the same rough, filthy concrete as everywhere else. On the wall opposite the sliding slab, the bright heat lit the numerals, the same three numerals stamped on every corner, at every turn: 357.

He scrabbled backward, pressing harder into the dead-end wall, into the shadows that still clung scantly to him in the corner. His eyes goggled from his face. Fascination, his mother's fascination, slowly bent his body forward. *Yes*, the part of him that was her said, *there would have to be something here. Why build a curving passageway that ends in nothing?*

Abruptly, he was jolted back again. Shadows sheered out of the light, heralding figures. Three gray men stepped out from the wall.

"Do you have her?" a flat, low voice came from one of them.

"I have Persephone at 29 North, 32 West," said another.

"Locked?"

"Locked."

The first of them moved, heading away through 357's corridors and with his back to Akil, who had remained hidden. The other two followed, their hard, clipped steps falling into a rhythm with the leader. Akil saw them in profile, briefly. They didn't seem to have eyes, but something silvery and flat, with a sheen that caught the light as they turned.

As they disappeared ahead, turning into the far curve, Akil was jolted again as the grinding sound filled the hall. The light became an outline again, and grinding cut off sharply, leaving a void of ringing silence behind and the illumination gone.

It took Akil only an instant to decide. He rose and followed.

He stuck to the corners, let the gray men stay well ahead. They walked in their synchronized, assured march as though they knew the exact route to their destination and what would be waiting for them around every curve and corner.

But Akil had never seen them before. No one had. The tenants of 357 were the descendents of those who were on 357 before. Despite years spent attempting to contact tenants below them and above them, no one foreign to 357 had ever been seen, no one who had not been born here and would not die here.

The gray men reached the central zone, where there were other people. A pair of machinists stopped dead in their tracks, and watched these apparitions approach. One machinist nearly leapt out of the way as the gray men, silent and inscrutable, swept by without a glance.

The one who said he had Persephone "locked" stopped in front of a doorway that led into a machine space, one of the hot, sweating compartments where instrumentation throbbed and hummed. When other tenants of 357 came down the passages they too stopped frozen at the sight of these men. Akil kept to his corner, his dark, intense eyes testing every detail, burning every moment of them into his brain.

Two of the gray men went into the machine chamber. The third man remained where he was, standing with his back to the door and his face toward the hallway.

Someone pushed their way through the gaping crowd:

Karkul, the old Punisher. He came through, his face set as it would be when he came to break up fights or carry someone away for an infraction. He advanced until he was five feet from the gray man.

"Who are you?" Karkul said in a hard voice. "Where did you come from?"

The gray man surveyed him. From his corner, Akil could see something flashing silver in the dull light of the hall instead of eyes. There was no answer.

"What are you doing here?" Karkul pressed.

"It looks like . . . " a woman behind Karkul was craning her neck, angling to see what was going on beyond the doorway. "There's . . . there's another compartment within the chamber. A door I've never seen. It leads into . . . I can't tell."

"Let me by," Karkul said and took a step forward. The gray man didn't move. When Karkul spoke again, his voice fell like a hammer striking an anvil. "Let. Me. By!"

The gray man shifted almost imperceptibly so that he was facing Karkul, whose body appeared full of tension. But no immediate motion between them followed. Karkul had no more words. It was a standoff.

Then a ripple pulsed through the crowd as the other two gray men reappeared through the door. They were carrying an oblong load between them, a box as long and wide as a person. They maneuvered it into the hallway with some small difficulty and continued along, back the way they had come, toward Akil.

"What is that?" Karkul said in a low, crackling voice to the figure blocking his way.

In response, the gray man turned and fell in behind the others, offering only his back in answer.

Akil whipped back around the corner, hurried ahead to the next corner, pressed his back to the wall. Without peering back around, he listened, heard the sharp, rhythmic steps. He darted away from his spot, and followed them covertly all the way back to the shunned hallway, between the puddles, silent on the softly worn pads of his shoes.

He found the darkness again, pressed himself into it. They continued with their burden, and paused. There was movement at the wall opposite to the one they had come through. Then the grinding sounded again. Akil felt it vibrate through the wall with his fingertips. And, again, the unfamiliar light poured from the opening, illuminating the numerals stamped on to the concrete opposite. The gray men moved back into the opening with the box and what it held—"she"—"Persephone."

The last gray man went through into the light, the grinding returned, the light became slim, winked out, and the sanctuary of darkness returned. As inexplicably as they had arrived, they were gone.

With a girl.

• • •

Akil waited until the tenants of 357 had retreated to their quarters and the corridor outside the machine chamber was empty. He entered the small room, felt the heat and the thrum off the rusting old hulk. There were many machines in the walls of 357 and the tenants only knew what a few of them actually did.

One of the grimy concrete slabs that made up the wall of the machine chamber had come open like a door and behind it was another chamber. Akil went to the threshold.

Karkul was still within the small inner space, picking about for a clue as to what, exactly, it was. When Akil appeared, the old man's hard eyes swung up at him.

"What do you want here, boy?" Scars and deep age-lines dueled on Karkul's face. His old wounds were not gaze-scars— the marks had been earned at the hands of men and women who had resisted him at one time with their nails, their tools, their homemade weapons.

"I just want to see." Akil's voice sounded strange to him sometimes. He didn't have occasion to speak very often.

The hidden chamber was small, and thick with the smell of old oil and lubricants. The floor was littered with junk.

"Why do you want to see?" Karkul demanded.

"I saw the gray men come and—"

"What are they to you?"

"They're nothing to me. I just saw them."

"Where did they come from?"

"I don't know. I just saw them in the halls."

Karkul glared at him

"You just saw them," Karkul said, his rough voice dropping low. "Your mother kept secrets, too. She was a stubborn, hateful woman." His hard eyes, sharp like little diamonds, drilled into Akil. "But she . . ." he stopped himself, his face tightened and his scars went pale from the stress. "Fine, then. See." He stepped aside and revealed the expanse of the small room.

Dim light filtered in from the outer chamber, illuminating detail in a stingy, selfish glow. A shape that Akil judged to be the size of the oblong box the gray men had carried away made an empty silhouette on the floor, but everywhere else was a scatter of machine parts, bunches of wire, panels of rusting metal. But there were rotting things here, too, things that had once been alive. Vermin, even hydroponic edibles . . .

many nibbled down to their cores. Someone had been here. Persephone. Akil could picture her, hunkered down, on her own, surviving on what she could scavenge. Small enough and young enough to be able to crawl through the spaces between the walls. Perhaps Akil's age or a little older. She could have been one of the forgotten tenants. Akil imagined that she had always run from the gray men, fought a war with them in the spaces the other tenants of 357 couldn't see, in the hidden spaces behind the walls, all alone.

"Where do the gray men come from?" Akil asked, aloud. "Where did they go?"

Silence, then: "They say there are floors above us and below us," Karkul nearly whispered. "And they say there is a floor below everything, below all the others, deeper than the bottom. Your mother spoke of it sometimes, before the fire burned her away. That the lords of this place live down there beneath the bottom. Maybe that's who these gray men are."

Akil's eyes were riveted to Karkul's face.

"Where they go," Karkul shrugged, "no one knows." His own eyes were hard and hot with accusation. "*Do* they?"

• • •

Some had fashioned flashlights for themselves, rough, shoddy things. But Akil, who had embraced the dark, had never needed one. So he returned to the shunned hallway swathed in darkness. He went to the dead end and then, his fingers brushing the rough concrete of the walls, he stepped slowly to the spot where he believed the gray men had come through. His fingers probed, felt the seams between slabs, the dampness that ate into their surfaces. Here. Was this one warmer than the others?

He took the small hammer from his belt, a tool he had fashioned himself long ago from a piece of a pipe and a dense chunk of metal. He had a small supply of similar tools that he had made and deposited in various hidden places throughout 357, though he seldom found use for any of them.

But now he did, and drove the head of the hammer as hard as he could against the concrete he judged to have the telltale signs of heat. The space rang with the sound of the impact, the force of which strained his arms immediately. The tiniest pebbles of shrapnel backfired into his face. He squeezed his eyes shut in the darkness and saw Persephone, alone and trapped by the gray men, their hands clamping over her thin, expressive lips so she couldn't scream. Coiling rough cord tightly around her arms so she couldn't struggle as they packed her into the box and took her away. The image drove strength through his own arms—thus the hammer into the wall, harder and louder, so loud that the ringing of it must have carried along the shunned hallway and down lengths of passage back to the other tenants.

The wall did not yield. But neither did Akil's strength, fueled as it was by his image of Persephone, his heart pounding under both the stress of his effort and the stress of his need to see her. What did yield, finally, was the hammer. The head flew away from the handle, tumbled into Akil's shoulder and knocked him backward on to the floor.

In a heap, his heart and his shoulder pounding, his breath coming in gasps, he glared at the concrete wall in perfect darkness. In the darkness, Persephone reached out for him. He thought, at first, it was a plea for his help, but in truth she was merely reaching out to touch his cheek, fevered with effort and obsession, to touch it with her cool hand. The fingers neared him, her eyes a dark, shining liquid beyond the fingers, and in the darkness of her eyes a spark, a glimmer of life.

The numerals.

Akil rose and spun around to the opposite wall. There had been numerals on this wall, Akil had seen them illuminated by the light that had come from within the other wall. These numerals had not been faded, however, as all the other ones were. These were solid, dense, and they struck something in his head, like a tuning fork. The sound an echo of his mother's voice.

Find the numerals.

His hands searched the wall and his fingers found heat, 357 embedded into the surface.

His mother's voice directed him to touch the numbers, feel their surface, trace their values. Years ago, in the months after her death, he had spent weeks of his life finding every fading numeral throughout 357, tracing them with his small fingers. Nothing had happened, nothing had come of it—just another one of her dozens of futile, memorized directives.

Until now. It was one of those mysterious legacies that had seemed worthless at first, until he found himself in just the right place, at just the right moment.

He found the first form: 3.

Tracing the next numeral: 5.

The last: 7.

The wall behind Akil began to grind and then spilled out light. Akil scooped up the heavy lump of metal that had served as his hammer once and, holding it, stepped into the light, into another world.

He was in a metal box, tall enough to stand in, large enough to fit, maybe, five men. The entire ceiling was a sizzling, white light that poured down, reflecting from the walls. On one of them, buttons: numerals from zero to nine.

Akil's hand flashed up, struck buttons without thought: five, eight, two, seven, seven, one—

A slim screen above the buttons lit up with green numbers: five, eight, two. The slab began to grind closed.

The slab shut.

And the box moved.

Akil scrambled against a wall. It felt as if he were falling . . . but *not* falling. Falling . . . *up*. That was what his stomach told him. He looked again at the numbers: 582.

The sense of movement gathered, rushed through him—his stomach and his ears and his skull—then petered out, came to a stop. The door again ground open, spilling light.

He was back in the shunned hallway. Except here, the numerals on the opposite wall read 582.

Akil strained to poke only his head out, prepared to see this other world but not willing to commit to it. But, then, he already knew what he was going to see. Up the hallway, around the curve, he could see the spastically flickering bulbs, hear the dripping water, smell the rust and grime.

582 had a shunned hallway. *Every* floor had one, his mother nudged in his head. *Because,* she said, *the lords don't want anyone to know where they are, how they move around.*

Persephone must have realized that, too. Others wouldn't have believed her, of course. She would have gone forward on her own, through the darkness, through the fear, found the other floors, hunted by gray men the entire time. Until they finally caught up with her on 357. So close to Akil, so close he could nearly see her face, look into her eyes, feel her hand.

Together, with enough time, the two of them could go from

floor to floor, gather the tenants, show them what was here. Together. But Persephone was below.

Below.

Akil faced the buttons again.

Zero, he pressed. Zero, again and again and again and again and again.

He kept pressing until the screen gathered five zeroes and the door ground shut and the sensation of movement—falling down now—clutched at his insides and he hunkered down in a corner, waiting, feeling the speed in his chest. He clutched the metal of the hammerhead with sweat-soaked hands.

The slowing came eventually, full minutes later, then a thunk and a shudder through the box. At the jarring, Akil sprawled himself across the floor, pressing himself flat. It happened again and again, five times all told. Then—no grinding—but a metallic rasp. Akil looked up.

The box opened into a lighted hallway, made not of concrete but of metal, rusted along some edges, but showing a dull gleam of the light from above. Akil rose, darted out of the box and, pressed against the opposite wall, looked both ways. The hall stretched in front and he saw a second sliding panel before him, a second moving box, he presumed. The light here was of a different quality. Not bruised or sickly, but sterile.

Sounds—footsteps, voices—came from one end of the hall-way. Akil quickly moved the other way.

He flashed by doorways, twisted through turns and branches, trusting that his instinct would record the route. Everything here was different than what was above, but also the same: all metal, better looked after, better maintained, marginally cleaner. The structure was the same: doorways the same size, evenly spaced, the ceiling the same height.

"Stop!" someone shouted at him. He didn't even look, just rebounded off a wall, took flight down another branch.

It took him to a space that was different to what he'd seen before: wider, with a single doorway at the end that was the size of two normal doorways.

He paused, uncertain, until he caught a hint of movement in his peripheral vision. He shot toward the door. It parted before him in the middle and he careened through, faltered and stumbled. Sheer awe drove him to his knees.

Gray men stood throughout the room, interacting with machines, if that's what the things were—gleaming without rust, glowing in parts, slick, they looked like no other machines Akil had ever seen but for their shape and the way the men were using them. Above, filling out the vastness of this room, was a domed ceiling that reached up many times 357's full height. Across that domed ceiling, an image, of dream or nightmare.

Was it a window? No, they were beneath everything, were they not? Where the lords lived: 00000.

Not a window—a screen.

Surrounding Akil, filling his vision and battling with his mind, was—must have been—the rumored area beyond the walls of 357 and 582 and all the other levels of this place. It was the place on the other side of the window that fed the grill in 357's outer hall.

The outside.

The floor was not made of concrete, but was brown and black, cracked and burned. Where it left off, filling the rest of the space above, roiling gray, puffs of . . . what? Something like smoke, but dense and moving, shifting—as one of Jendayi's friends said—*breathing*. From behind these things, light. Just snatches of it, winking through intermittent spaces, scorching down like a vast, limitless weapon.

Occupying this landscape, growing from the cracked ground and clawing up at the gray sky, not just a tower that might conceivably hold six hundred floors of tenants, but *towers*. Dozens of them, hundreds, spaced various distances apart from each other, growing in every direction and all formed of concrete, blackened and fissured where the light sliced it.

Not merely thousands of trapped, fearful tenants, but millions, *billions*, a number *beyond* numbers.

Akil's eyes were streaming tears. His stomach muscles tightened and fluttered uncontrollably. This was what Persephone must have seen, why she had run from the lords who controlled it all. He felt a physical *need* to see her now, clenching his body like a vice. They were the only two who had broken beyond the walls. They were bound by it more inextricably than they would have been if they'd made a family, than by a lifetime together. Their bond was truth that only they knew and could never be forgotten.

He spun around to retreat but the gray men stood behind him, blocking the doorway. A weapon rose. At the tip was a sharp blue light, pulsing slowly. It strobed and like razor blades it sliced his eyes. His skull flashed with needles of this light. His jaw went loose and slack, his chest, arms, legs seemed to fill with liquid concrete and drew him to the floor. His brain was swallowed by flaming blue light.

• • •

He awoke under the illumination from a different light. The section of ceiling directly above him and the floor directly below him were between them projecting a harsh white glow as though the sections themselves were large, square bulbs. Where he felt that glow on his body, a buzzing current of electricity seemed to pass through him. He was able to look around, and realized he was trapped within a small, drab metallic room. A gray man stood just beyond the glow, his flat eyes reflecting the white of the light as though his insides were filled with it and couldn't contain it.

Akil was sitting on something, his body puddled into it. He wasn't bound but, even though he could make his arms and legs move, they felt hollow and empty, as if they'd fallen asleep, and the simple act of flexing his fingers sent waves of electricity through his entire body. A small table stood at the gray man's side. Resting on it were the misshapen metal of Akil's hammerhead and the few other possessions he had been carrying: a length of cord, a small bunch of wires, a set of dull pliers. They were practically within his reach, if only he could summon the strength to grab one.

"How did you find the elevator?" The gray man's voice buzzed through Akil's ears like an angry electric arc, the sound warped by what the light was doing in his head.

"Don't . . . know that word," Akil's voice slurred like a viscous liquid from his crackling jaw.

"The moving compartment that brought you here is an elevator. How did you find it?"

"I was in . . . the hallway when you . . . when your people came. I saw it . . . open."

"You were *in* the hallway?" The gray man's expression was flat, like a machine. His tone was hard to distinguish, but he seemed surprised by Akil's claim.

"Yes . . . the hallway."

"How often do people on your floor go down that hallway?"

"Never. Just me."

The gray man stood and shifted his head as though he were looking at a mechanism that was far more complex once its surface had been penetrated.

"How did you operate it?" he asked.

"Buttons. Numbers."

The gray man cut the answer with an impatient slash of his hand.

"Yes, yes. How did you *know* how to operate it?"

Akil hunted through his sparking brain for an answer that would satisfy. He hadn't *known*, exactly. It was just that . . . what else could you do?

"Just . . . just did."

The gray man's flat silver eyes flashed as he lowered his chin, tallying these unexpected equations.

"Why?" he said when he finally looked up. "Why did you come down here? Weren't you afraid?"

"Yes. Afraid."

"So? Why?"

"For . . . the girl."

"Girl? What girl?"

Through the electricity, a surge of anger burst through Akil. Was the gray man going to deny that she even existed? Deny the most important thing Akil had ever felt?

"Persephone," Akil tried to shout back, but the buzzing in his head made the word sluggish and heavy. "Persephone."

The gray man took a step back, as if Akil had suddenly become dangerous. He was struck into silence for a time.

"Persephone," the gray man said at length, "isn't a girl. It's a machine."

"Don't lie to me," Akil pushed, suddenly feeling, through

his lethargy, that he was in charge of this conversation. "I heard them . . . talking about her. Saw them . . . carry her away in the box. I saw . . . where she lived. And the same . . . truth that she saw." His body was laboring under the effort of getting all these words out. Sweat slicked his forehead, his chest. "We're connected by it . . . forever."

The gray man was shaking his head in slow disbelief.

"Persephone is PERcentage Surviving Electron PHaser ONE," he said, delivering a deathblow with cool detachment. "It's an engine component crucial to a machine that . . . that essentially cleans the air, decontaminates it. Do you understand? We've been looking for it for a long, long time. It was hidden by the people who built it long ago, when their enemies were trying to destroy them."

"The men who . . . came up before . . . called it . . . 'she.'"

"We sometimes refer to machinery as though it were female," the gray man said. "A superstition of sorts, I suppose, a way to make the machines more like us."

Akil struggled to force his drooping eyes onto the gray man's glowing planes of light. The intensity singed his retina, and tears began to flood his eyes.

"I know Persephone is alive. I can . . . *feel* her. Where is she? Tell me . . . where she is."

"*It*," the gray man said. "*It* is below us, deep in the foundations. They're fitting her—" he caught himself. "They're fitting it into place now. It's one of the last components of the machine. If it works—" something like awe passed into the gray man's voice, "if it works, we might actually have a chance of surviving beyond another generation or two."

Below, Akil thought. *There was still more below* this? And Persephone was trapped down there.

"Please," Akil said, the last ergs of his energy ebbing out of him. "Please just let me . . . see her once. Let me speak to her."

The gray man shook his head again, slowly.

"I'm sorry, boy, I really am." He let the glow of his eyes reflect on to Akil a moment longer, then turned away and went to a section of the wall that slid open for him and closed behind him as he left, turning the room back into a prison once more.

The instant he was alone, Akil tried to pull himself forward. His leaden torso rose fractionally, the electric needles buzzing through him, and he slumped back. He couldn't even shift his weight so that he could topple off the chair and possibly out of the light. He fought his eyes, to keep them from closing. Every part of him felt so heavy.

He moved his fingers, stretched them out, trying to get them to lead the hand, the arm toward the small table with the head of the hammer on it. The arm slid forward an inch, two, then the needles became too much, felt like they were eating into his bones.

But what must they be doing to Persephone now, down below? Connecting her to a machine, was that what the gray man said?

Akil flung his foot up, managed to hit the edge of the table holding his belongings. It rattled and teetered, the things atop it sliding to the edges, and then it found its balance again and stilled.

He threw his leg up again, needles firing up his whole body. He would have screamed if he'd had the strength for it. His foot caught the table again, rattled it. The pliers fell to the floor. The head of metal jumped slightly, skittered to the nearest edge.

He had nothing left. His body was alive and burning up with hot needles.

Just to have Persephone's cool hand touch his hot cheek.

He kicked up again, but lost his strength in the midst of it. His foot glanced off one of the table legs. The hammerhead vibrated, tipped, fell.

A heavy crunch sounded from the floor where it had landed and the light from below flickered. Akil struggled. The electricity buzzed through him still, but not quite so deeply now. He could feel the muscles in his arms and legs popping with new strength. Strength enough to grip the edges of the seat, hoist himself out so that he tumbled forward and fell on to the cold metal floor, away from the glow of the light.

He gasped for air as prickles intensified and then slowly retreated from his limbs, his fingers, his toes. Inches away from his face, the misshapen chunk of metal rested on the floor, a crack splaying from beneath it, covering nearly the entire surface of the single plate that cast the light. The plate itself was glass or plastic and it flickered now, brighter and dimmer, much like the bulbs in the halls of 357.

Akil got on his knees and breathed in deeply many times to let the stale air clear the sluggishness from his body. He reached his hand back into the light and quickly pulled out the hammerhead.

He scooped up his pliers, his cord and wires, and stood up. He walked over to the part of the wall that had opened for the gray man, but which remained closed for him.

He pressed himself against the wall adjacent so that if the door opened and someone entered they wouldn't immediately see him. He looked around the room, but it offered nothing he hadn't noticed before. They would come back for him eventually and maybe they would send him down, hook him into a machine. Maybe they would even put him near Persephone. If they did, and if she were the last thing he saw as they bled his life out into a machine then he would take the sight of her into death with him. He could accept that. But maybe they would just take him back to 357 and fix it so that he couldn't get back into the "elevator." He'd be up there, alone forever. And, worse, Persephone would have become a part of the foundation of this place, giving her precious life to—

The door hissed open and Akil swung the hammerhead overhand at the gray man. Akil felt the impact up his arm and through his whole body and the gray man stumbled crazily to the side and fell to the floor, heavy and senseless.

Akil turned to run out of the room, but standing in the doorway now was another gray man, bringing his weapon to bear. Akil shut his eyes tight, so tight that he clenched his jaw in the effort. He slapped his free hand over his eyes and then tried to whip his body away.

He heard the flash of the strobe, felt a brief heat on his body, then opened his eyes and spun backward, hurling the chunk of metal as soon as he had sight of his target.

It struck the gray man in the chest, slamming him against the back wall and causing him to cough sharply. Akil fought his instinct to run, heard his mother whispering in his ears for calm, for a plan that would *work*.

He leapt on the gray man, snatched up the metal and was poised to bring it down on the gray man's skull. But the man remained still beneath him. Akil looked quickly up and down the corridor then wrestled the gray man's body into the room. The door whispered shut behind him and there was an instant of panic. What if he were trapped once again?

But the sound of his mother's voice calmed him and he searched the fallen men. Their belts were packed with things so unrecognizable that Akil could only wildly guess what they were, or what they were used for. He removed one of their belts and, because he was too small to wear it at his waist, he strapped it across his chest as if it were one of the tool bandoliers used by 357's machinists.

At this point the door opened for him, and he ran from corridor to corridor—careening past branches where gray men went by, either oblivious to him or too slow-moving to impede his immediate progress—until he found a place that he knew, near the giant room with the vast screens. He let his instincts find the route again, back to the elevators.

As he turned a corner, two gray men walked ahead, their backs to him. He shot up against the wall behind them, ricocheted and landed in front of them and sped away before they could utter a single sound.

Then he was before the elevators again. There was the one he had come down in and there was the other as well, and if the one he had used led back up . . .

Mounted on the wall by each door was a plate. Akil prodded it and heard a chirp from something on the gray man's belt. The plate lit up and the door slid open.

Footsteps, many of them, were rising hurriedly from around a near corner. He threw himself into the compartment, looked at the buttons and the screen. This was 00000 and above were standard numerals: 1, 2, 3 . . . all the way through 357 and up.

So what is below us, Mother?

Footsteps crashed down the hallway outside. He pressed the buttons: 00001.

The doors closed and the elevator moved.

Down.

It went for a long time, longer than the distance Akil would have judged between any two floors, any ten floors even. But below were the foundations, the gray man had said, whatever that meant. Maybe there was as much below as there was above. Maybe the foundations went down forever.

The elevator stopped and the doors opened. Light from the elevator poured out on to a metal grating with a rail to prevent a fall into the space beyond, which sprawled into a deep, endless black.

He stepped out, on to the grating and felt a hot wind pouring up as if from a raging furnace deep below. The door shut behind him, cutting off the light. Now he could see, over the rail and down, pinpricks of light through the black: red, white, flickering, flashing, glinting from long corners and pointed tips. The lights extended as far as Akil could see, and even farther still. They were giant machines, the size of the unimaginably massive structures Akil had seen on the screen earlier, machines that kept all the floors above working, perhaps all the towers in that impossible landscape working, and did other things that only the machines themselves knew or understood anymore.

Somewhere below, in this world of machines, was Persephone. Her quiet greeting, her welcoming gaze, the relief of her cool hand on his fevered cheek.

So Akil chose a direction and ran, looking for his love, in darkness.

Eric and Pan

William Sleator

All the teachers are cops.

I've seen on TV that kids our age used to do things in class like pass notes and spit little balls of paper at each other. Incredible. Pass a note these days and you get tazed—painfully.

The kids even got into fights, talked back to teachers, and "cut" class in those old shows. Their punishment? Detentions and suspensions. No way now. Break a major rule and you get sent straight to the work camps for a while. Screw up enough and you're there permanently. Or worse. My mom says it's all necessary, that schools have to be "safe environments." That's why teachers became cops, so they could enforce the rules and "protect" the students.

So I can't communicate with Supan—or Pan, his nickname, which he prefers—at all in the two classes a day we have together. The truth is, even if I *could* pass notes or talk to him, I still wouldn't be able to communicate during the boring hours of our classes. My grades are much better than his, and we are assigned seating by grade-point average. That puts me in the front of the first row on the left and he's near the back of the last row, on the right. He's way smarter than me, but the teachers don't know it because he's from Thailand. He has a

341

slight accent, but his English speech is nearly perfect. He just has problems reading English. So he doesn't do well in school. If school weren't so rigid, he'd shine. But these teachers/cops don't care how smart he is. Everything is based on tests and grades—including their jobs and the whole school's budget.

There's only one teacher who's nice to Pan. He tells me about her, when we meet secretly after school. The nice teacher is Ms. Van Houten, who teaches ELL—English Language Learning. She's familiar with foreign kids, so she knows how smart Pan is. She's also nice to me when I go to meet Pan after her class—it's his last one of the day. She doesn't seem to see anything wrong with two boys being together. All the other teachers would turn us in if they knew. Since the Breakdown and the New Constitution—which happened before I was born—it's against the law here.

The place where we go to be together is the Truth or Consequences Motel. It has no cop cameras in the rooms, and that's why it's expensive and takes all my spending money. But there's nothing else I want to spend money on than having a place to be close to Pan. I just worry all the time that our parents might find out. They'd set the real cops on us in a flash. The laws are very strict. Family members are always turning in their relatives and spouses and children.

I've already rented a room at Truth or Consequences for this afternoon because I know that wrestling practice after school has been cancelled today. The coach is out sick. I just made the reservation on my phone. It's lunch break. I went outside to hide behind a big dead tree—dead like all the trees in the city—so the security cops constantly patrolling the school building wouldn't see me. Of course, even that was risky. Phones are not allowed on the school grounds. Pan and I have different lunch periods so he doesn't know about this yet. I can hardly wait till school's over so I can tell him.

Back in the cafeteria I know there's little hope of finding anything I can stand to eat. The line for the food has diminished by now—most kids were hungry and also don't mind this crap—so I breeze past what's on offer at the steam tables behind the invisible electric food protector. Messages scroll by above the offerings: "Have-some-fried-NuFish-with-cream-sauce." "Have-some-sautéed-SoyJoy." "Have-some-synthetic-apple-pie." I pass, and go to one of the vending machines. The chocolate bars cost fifteen credits and I've already used up a lot of credits on the motel. I'm incredibly lucky that my parents don't automatically track what I spend, like a lot of parents do. The motel debits my card as "cash," but the amounts are large enough to raise questions.

Behind me I hear some kids who used to be my friends whispering, "That fruit Eric and his *boyfriend* should go live in the woods across the border in that ungodly state, with the rest of the freaks."

I've heard other whispers about this place before. It's just across the state line. I've been wondering about it. I mean, there are states that don't have laws like ours. That's partially what the Breakdown was all about.

I skip lunch and leave the cafeteria. I don't mind going hungry. Being with Pan is more important than food and, if I'm lucky, Pan's dad will offer me some *good* food when I drop him off at his house. Pan's father makes Thai food and has connections on the black market. Though poor, he can get actual vegetables and occasionally even chicken or pork or fresh fish. It was at Pan's place that I learned about real food. What my mother presents us for dinner microwaved from the freezer isn't nearly as good.

Besides, going hungry helps save my credits for an hour or so at the motel with Pan. I'm not quite eighteen, not old enough to legally rent a motel room—Pan's only sixteen—but for enough credit, the Truth or Consequences ignores that—they ignore a lot, like the fact that we're two boys who are renting the room for a few hours only. They don't ask questions. Sure, they *look* at our IDs, but they don't swipe them, they just take my card number over the phone and debit the credits.

Unfortunately, although the place is expensive—they have to pay off the cops and who knows who else to get away with all these infractions—it's also filthy. The toilets don't flush with adequate conviction, and when they do they often overflow, so the bathrooms are to be avoided at all costs. The beds are also dirty. We've seen insects in them. And there's dust and grime all over the place. So we use the toilets at school before we leave—which aren't very good either, but better than the ones at Truth or Consequences—and we take showers when we get home. We always strip as soon as we get into the motel room—not because getting naked is *all* we are there for. In fact, sometimes we don't do anything more than just hold each other and talk. But removing our clothes keeps them reasonably clean. We don't want our parents to notice anything unusual on our clothes and wonder where it came from.

I stop by Ms. Van Houten's room when I finally get out of my last class. Pan is still in the room, as usual. We don't want to meet in the hall and leave the school together, because then the other kids would see us and report us. All the other kids have already rushed from the classrooms by now, and if we wait a few minutes—using up precious time—they'll all be gone and we can sneak out without being seen. We trust Ms. Van

Houten; we know she won't turn us in. She's the only teacher who doesn't wear a cop badge.

But the cameras and microphones are everywhere.

We trust her so much that I sit in the desk next to Pan and touch his shoulder, casually, as if I'm just getting his attention. He turns and meets my gaze with his dark eyes in his dark face, serious and unblinking. We're opposites. I'm blond with light skin and blue eyes. I look at him just as seriously.

And then I place three fingers, spread apart, on the desk—like an "M"—our secret code: *Motel today*. His whole face lights up.

Pan is a sophomore. He and his father came to America only a year and a half ago. Pan learned to speak his English very quickly. But, like I said, reading is another matter. The Thai language has a completely different alphabet.

Ms. Van Houten smiles warmly at us, then turns around to look at the digital clock display in the top middle of the wallscreen. She turns back. "I think you boys should go now. All the other students have gone. You know, some of the them have been asking me questions about your . . . friendship." She sounds concerned. "I know you just want to help Pan with his reading, Eric, but others, well . . . they talk about things. They might report you and you'd have to go through interrogation. I've heard it's very unpleasant. You have to give them the answers they want, and if you can't prove they're true . . ." She lets the sentence hang, unfinished. Ms. Van Houten *knows*, of course. But she has to be careful too.

"Sure, Ms. Van Houten. I understand." I smile. "I didn't realize it was so late." I got up and left the room. I heard Pan ask if she had any more work for him. No way could we be seen leaving at the same time.

It would have been best for us to take different routes and meet at the motel, but Pan is too poor to have a motorbike, and the Truth or Consequences Motel isn't close. He knows where to meet me—my bike's across the street from the church at the top of Heartbreak Hill.

• • •

The high school has freshman, sophomore, junior, and senior classes. Pan came to the school at the beginning of last year. We met because we both kept looking at each other whenever we happened to pass in the crowded hallways. Last year we had the same lunch period, and Pan always sat alone. The teachers make sure that always happens to new kids. They don't trust anyone new. Especially if they are foreign.

"Hey, where're you goin'?" Jumbo asked me last year when I started toward Pan's table after we'd left the cafeteria line. Jumbo was somebody I talked to back then. "You know we're always supposed to eat at table 33C."

"I . . . thought I'd be nice and sit with the new kid."

"Huh? He's weird and foreign," Luther said. "What kind of sucker are you, anyway? And what if the teachers catch you at the wrong table? You'll get the tazer for sure."

Krawl narrowed his eyes. "What's your *real* interest in that kid, Eric?" he asked me. "Are you some kind of pervo or something?"

"Oh, shut up!" I snapped. "You know I'm going with Dezbah. I just don't like the way everybody ignores that kid because he's foreign. I'll only eat with him once. I just want to find out where he's from and stuff like that. If you had half a brain you'd know it can be cool to find out about other countries." I turned and walked away, not wanting to see their expressions as they stared after me. Being different in any way is just about the worst and most dangerous thing there is.

Yeah, even just sitting with him once—where all the other kids could see—I was taking a big risk. But I couldn't stop myself. I did it because of the way he looked at me in the hallways. It might have been just my imagination, but I felt I could see longing in his eyes. And that was the way I felt when I looked at him, too. I knew there was something wrong with me for being physically attracted to another boy. It was pervo, like Krawl had said. But at the same time—it felt so *right*. I didn't want to admit it to myself, but my feelings for the new kid were much more powerful than my feelings for Dezbah, one of the hottest girls in the class. I didn't care about her much.

The foreign kid looked up at me. He seemed surprised that I was approaching his table.

It was unreal to expect that anything like what I was imagining might really happen between us. Even a lonely foreign kid wouldn't dare put himself in that kind of danger. I swore to myself that I would keep the conversation neutral, not say anything suggestive, just ask him where he was from and stuff like that. And I'd never sit with him again. Or talk to him again in my life. I couldn't allow myself to slide downhill like this. But I had to talk with him just once. I couldn't resist.

I put my tray down across from his and sat down stiffly on the stool. "Er . . . hi," I said.

His eyes were wide, his mouth half open in surprise. His teeth looked very white against his dark skin. He didn't say anything.

"Uh, what's your name?" I asked him as I picked up my plastic fork, even though there was hardly anything on my tray I could stand to eat. "I'm Eric."

"I know," he said softly.

"How do you know my name?" It was awful how much I liked it that he had found out my name.

"Oh, everybody know you because you on wrestling team."

"You speak English really well," I couldn't keep from saying. He smiled, and on him it seemed a beautiful, warm expression. "But you didn't tell me your name."

"Supan," he said shyly. "But back home everybody call me Pan."

"Where is home?" I asked him.

He was holding a spoon. He actually seemed to have been eating with a *spoon*! "Thailand," he said. "A small village way out in country."

"Geography's not my best subject," I said. "I know Thailand's in Asia, but where exactly?"

"Southeast Asia. Thailand is south of Laos, east of Burma, north of Malaysia, and west of Cambodia."

I grinned with embarrassment. "That doesn't help me much. But now I can find it on a map, maybe." I leaned forward. "But how did you get into this state? The military hardly ever lets foreign people come here."

"My father have cousin been living here all their life. Their parent come over long time ago, before this government. They sponsor us to come here after the bad hurricane we have at home. Even they sponsor us, still very scary to go through immigration." He shrugged. "I only want to stay at home, but my father not let me."

I didn't know what to say then and after a few moments' silence it seemed as if the conversation had died. I looked down at my tray. Boiled octopus with some kind of thick, slimy, smelly black sauce on it. Then, I heard Pan say, "I watch you wrestling in the gym one day. You . . . very strong."

I looked back at his face. It seemed so beautiful to me now. And it sounded like he thought I was hot, too! "Do you play any sports?" I asked him.

"Football—here they call soccer. All village at home have team. And I row a lot there, when I go out on the lake with my father, help him get fish from his nets. And I climb tree a lot, to get coconut and other fruit—fruit they do not have here." He paused. "I see you in locker room one time. Your body good, like men who work in my village at home."

I tried to push my lips shut, but I had to smile. I was sure his body was "good" too.

Now he was beaming at me, not shy or embarrassed. "I wish we could—" he looked around the cafeteria "—go some other place, where no people around."

That sealed it. I knew we were on the same wavelength. Nothing like this had ever happened to me before. "Me, too," I said. "Since you helped your father on a lake, you must be a good swimmer." He nodded, still beaming. "There's a swimming pool, way downtown, in a place called the YMCA. The pool's inside, so you can swim all winter. Swimming's good exercise to keep in shape for wrestling. My membership allows me to bring a guest. Would you like to go sometime?"

He nodded again. I had never seen such an intense expression of joy on anybody's face.

So every weekend we went to the YMCA pool, far away from anybody we knew. Nobody from our school went there, even the other kids on the wrestling squad. I looked forward to those weekends more than anything. He was small, but his body was perfectly proportioned, every muscle defined. We became close friends. I was amazed he understood so much about people's lives—and could say it in English. But it was so frustrating that all we could do was change clothes in the locker room, swim laps, and then shower together with other people around watching us. We were hungry for more.

Then I found out about the Truth or Consequences Motel, and everything changed. I knew it was wrong. I knew it was dangerous. And I knew that nothing so wonderful had ever happened to me before.

• • •

Today, after leaving Ms. Van Houten's classroom, I went to my locker to get the helmets, then walked alone up the hill to the church. I left my motorcycle across the street from it this morning—any church is as dangerous as the school, but this one is always closed in the afternoon, and I know nobody will be around. Since I'd planned to go to the motel today, I'd parked here, far away from the school. I wait behind another lifeless tree.

Five minutes later Pan runs up the hill toward me. We don't have to talk—we've done this many times before. We both put on our helmets—it's illegal to ride without them. But it's also an advantage to be wearing them, just in case somebody from school might see us. They only sell one model of bike now and, with our helmets on, it will be difficult for people to recognize us. I sit on the bike and rev up the engine. Pan climbs on to the back of the seat. He can't put his arms around me, which is the safest way for a passenger to ride on a motorbike, because the cops would stop us when they saw that. He has to hold onto the metal bar behind him. I rev up the engine again and pull out to the street.

The roads are pretty clear up here, and quiet. I know the engine will cover up what we are saying. I scream back at him, "We're so lucky you have Van Houten!"

"Yes! She only teacher who understand!"

Down on the main streets into the city the cars are almost motionless—one more thing that shrinks our time alone together. The highway would have been a little faster but motorcycles are not allowed on it. So we can't go fast, which both of us love. And even if there wasn't much traffic, so we *could* go fast, the cops would stop us immediately and soak me with a huge fine. Still, it's better to be on a motorbike than in a car, because the bike can weave around the cars stuck at red lights and get to the front of the intersection—which is always full of motorcycles, spewing poisonous exhaust into our faces. Still, the motorbike is fun. And it's getting to be spring now— not that anything is getting green or blooming. There are no living trees or shrubs or flowers to indicate spring. In the city, you can only tell the seasons by the temperature and weather.

Pan has told me that it's not like that in the village where he lived in Thailand. There's a lot of empty land, even a jungle, and rivers, and lakes, and all the people are farmers, or fishermen like his father was. But his father insisted on coming here when he had the chance, thinking he would make more money here, and that Pan would get a better education.

Finally, the motel. It has a garage divided up into separate cubicles, each one with a heavy plastic curtain over the entrance that can be chained shut. This is to prevent anybody passing by—or spying—to see the makes of cars or the license plates. We're not the only people who come here in secret to be alone together.

I park, we quickly leave the garage, Pan hurries inside the

front door of the motel and I close and lock the curtain, then follow him into the lobby.

The brown carpet, the color of mud, is worn through and unraveled in patches. Bare cement walls are plastered with photographs of young women wearing tiny bikinis, and muscular men squeezed into tight swimsuits way too small for them. Also illegal, also expensive to pay off the cops. But the hotel management seems to feel that pictures like this will attract paying guests, and get them into the right mood.

The various people who work alone at the front desk from day to day all recognize us now. Today it's the bald fat man with the big, white, tobacco-stained mustache that hangs over his upper lip. An evil smelling cigar smolders in his mouth. I hate the stink of it, but I like being in a place where almost every law can be broken.

The bald fat man turns reluctantly away from the TV on the wall. It's showing a news report about a crowd of people going to work this morning who were mashed together in an elevator that crashed from the 93rd floor of the building all the way to the basement. You can hardly tell one body from another—it's just a bloody mass of arms and legs and faces.

"Hey, boys," the man says around his cigar, bored. "You can have 398." He holds out his hand for my credit card.

"I already made a reservation on the phone, and paid," I tell him. "Doesn't it say that?"

He peers more closely at his computer. "Oh, yeah, yeah, it says that." He had been too lazy, and too involved in the TV, to take a good look at the reservations screen. "Here you go." He hands me a small dirty envelope with a plastic card in it and turns immediately back to the TV to see the last images of the people crushed in the elevator.

Room 398 is on the third floor. Neither of us really feels like going in an elevator after seeing that news clip, but there are no stairs in this place. Most people never use stairs anyway, so the owners of the motel saved money by not building stairs. I've heard there used to be laws about how you built things. But not here, not for a long time anyway. It's a fire hazard not to have stairs, because elevators always zip automatically to the floor where the fire is. Guests trapped in their rooms in a fire don't even have the suicidal option of jumping out of windows because the windows are too small, and can't be opened.

The elevator is just big enough for three people, and we're the only ones in it. As soon as the doors close we are in each others' arms, squeezing tightly together. Our fear of elevators has vanished.

The room has the same moldy brown carpet as the lobby. The bathroom is, as usual, so filthy that it's unusable. The stink of it is pervasive. The bed's also dirty, like all the beds we've seen in this motel. There's one bare florescent strip in the middle of the ceiling. We shed our clothes and drape them over the back of the single chair, which seems to be the only place in the room that doesn't have dust and dirt on it. We fall on to the bed.

Even in this disgusting place, it's wonderful. With Pan it's always wonderful.

Afterwards, even though we need to leave soon, we lie there talking. My head is cradled by Pan's smooth chest.

"Make me nervous, what Ms. Van Houten say about kids asking questions. I do not like it," Pan says. This year he's learned to use plurals and sometimes even pronounce the final "s." He hasn't got the tenses right yet though—he has told me they don't have tenses in the Thai language, and they're hard for even somebody as smart as Pan to get used to.

"I don't like what she said either," I say. "The guys I know have been suspicious ever since I sat with you at lunch last year. And Dezbah!" I shook my head and sighed. "She may think something's going on between us, too."

I feel the muscles tighten in Pan's arm around my shoulders as he clenches his fists. "I do not know why they cannot just leave us alone!" he says vehemently. "Who we hurting? Who we make problem for? Not like this in my country. There, men go with men and women go with women if they want. And nobody care, nobody make problem in their life. Nobody say not normal. I wish I never come here!"

That stings. "But what . . . what about me?"

He squeezes me. "You are wonderful, Eric. Best thing ever happen to me. Only, if we in my village, we have freedom. Do not have to worry what other people think, because they do not think anything about it. Do not have to worry about getting caught by cops. But here . . ."

It isn't necessary for him to finish. "But we will still win. I'm *determined* that we will win! Oh. Do you understand 'determined'?"

He shakes his head sadly.

"It means I will not let anybody or anything stop me from being with you. I will do it no matter what. I hope you're the same."

"I feel same way. But different for me," he says. "I from another country. You American. Your parents rich, my father poor. I get in bigger trouble than you here. Yeah, you have trouble too. But maybe cops let you go. Not me. Punish me. Lock me up. Not fair here."

And then it's just as if his words have been heard by the cruel higher being we're forced to pretend to believe in. The powerful supernatural being who enforces all the laws made by the state. (Pan has told me many times that our God is nothing like the Buddha, who is kind and understanding. Not that he can let people know he's Buddhist. He goes to church and pretends he's Christian.) As unreal as we know the American God is, the approaching wail of sirens is not unreal at all. We rush to the small window.

In a moment two cop cars pull up in front of the motel. Cops squeeze out of the cars and move into the lobby. We're trapped. The lobby is the only way out.

We don't say anything. We rush to pull our clothes on. Whatever is going to happen will be worse if we're naked.

And we continue not to talk—if there are no voices coming from this room the cops might think nobody's in here. Anyway, there's no need to talk. I can tell by the way Pan has his eyes fearfully on the door that he has no idea what to do.

Neither do I.

There's a loud knock on the door, and then a click as the plastic key opens the lock. The man at the desk must have told the cops what room we are in, and given them the key.

There are three cops, as many as will fit in the elevator. At first they just glare at us, one hand squeezing each nose against the stink from the bathroom. It's a good thing we both got dressed really fast. With the hand not on their noses, they all pull out their guns. Their uniforms are tight, clinging to their fat bellies. It's hard to picture all three of them in the tiny elevator.

"IDs," one of them says.

We get them out quickly. One cop pulls mine out of my hand, another grabs Pan's. They study them. "Same names that teacher—Van Houten—gave us," one of the cops says. "She got the motel right, too." They pocket them, their guns still pointed at us.

Van Houten turned us in? But we trusted her! And our IDs . . . we can't do anything without them. I turn and look briefly at Pan. He doesn't look back, apparently calm and impassive, his eyes fixed on nothing, his face a mask.

"Wait a minute," I dare to say, panicking. "You've got to give us our IDs back. What are you going to do with them?"

"We'll show them to the sergeant when he books you for indecent behavior. After that you won't need them."

Does that mean they're going to lock us up? I look over at Pan again. His face remains completely blank. Unlike me, he shows no emotion at all. Maybe he learned to be like this when he and his father were questioned at Immigration.

I'm beside myself. I take another big risk. "Can we . . . can we call our parents?"

The cops look at each other. The one who does the talking pushes back his cap, thinking. He turns back to me with an ugly smile. He takes his hand from his nose and flicks his wrist in an effeminate gesture. "Of course—the homo is a mommy's boy," he says in falsetto. The other cops laugh. His voice sinks back to its normal register. "No way, pansy. We'll call your parents from the station. Come on, let's get out of this dump. I can't stand the smell another minute."

One of them grabs Pan's arm, the other grabs mine. They pull us out of the room toward the elevator. At least they're not putting handcuffs on us. They don't need to. They're bigger than we are, they have guns, and I know there are more of them down in the lobby. I saw at least six of them getting out of the cop cars. We're way outnumbered.

As we approach the elevator, terrified as I am, I wonder how five people, three of them fat, are going to fit in an elevator designed to hold three people, max. I think of the elevator on the news, all the mangled bodies crushed together. I'm even more terrified now, my heart racing. Maybe one will ride down with us, and the other two will stay up here until the elevator returns to this floor.

Nope. All three of them squeeze into the elevator with us. The elevator creaks from the weight. When the door slams shut, the whole thing shudders uneasily. I squeeze my eyes closed as we start to descend, my stomach cramping, waiting every second for the sensation of falling, for the crash on the bottom floor. The elevator wheezes.

We don't crash. We edge out into the lobby. The elevator door shuts immediately and I hear it going up.

I'm surprised that there are no other cops in the lobby. Where did they go?

"Keys." The bald fat man at the desk holds out his hand blandly, as if this nightmare were a daily occurrence for him to watch and gloat. Maybe it is.

I pull the plastic card out of my pocket. One of the cops hands the guy an identical plastic card. The cops start to pull us out of the lobby.

"Wait a second," the man at the desk says, punching computer keys. "I have to highlight the credit card so nobody else ever lets them in here again."

One of the cops laughs. "You think they're ever gonna be able to come here again, after the sentence they get?" But he waits.

And so there is time for us to see three more cops getting out of the elevator, holding onto a middle-aged man and a young woman. Why are they arresting a man who is with a woman? Maybe the man or woman is married to somebody else. If you're married, fooling around with anybody else is a punishable crime.

The cops pull at us. "Come on, we're going to the station."

"Wait a minute," I say. "My motorcycle's locked up in the garage. I can't just leave it here, since I'm never coming back."

The cops look at each other again. We're now far enough away from the desk that the fat man can get the two keys from the other group.

The cop who seems to be the leader of our group, the one who's done most of the talking so far, nods at one of the other two and says, "Yeah, we need to take possession of that. Used in a crime, so it'll be police property." He winks at the other cops. "Chick, you drive the bike behind us. The homos will go with us in the car. It'll be good to have another bike at the station."

The way the cops are talking makes me feel as if we're non-persons. But then we've been non-persons for a long time, ever since we began to love each other.

They pull us outside. I can see that the traffic is starting to get nasty. It will take a while to get to the station, wherever it is. I don't know what Pan's father is going to do, but my parents could very well disown me, and refuse to help me out of this mess. If they wanted to, they probably could help me, because my mother works for the State. But I have a sinking feeling they won't. This is the end of my life, and Pan's life too.

"Where's your damn bike?"

"Over here." I lead them to the numbered cubicle where my bike is parked. It's far from the cop cars. You can't see it from the street.

"The key to unlock this place?" The one who's going to drive—and probably steal—my bike holds out his hand.

I reach into my pocket and feel the key to the parking cubicle there. I pull my hand out, empty. "It's not here. It must have fallen out of my pocket in the room."

Pan looks at me. He knows the key didn't fall out of my pocket in the room.

The cop rolls his eyes. "You dumb pervo!" he says. He turns to the other cops. "Wait here for me to go and get it." He hurries as fast as his gut will let him toward the motel entrance.

Pan and I look at each other again. I sense that he knows what I'm about to do. And he's going to try the same thing.

Suddenly I lunge at the cop who's holding my arm, hold my leg behind his legs and push, hard. He goes right down; I'm not captain of the wrestling team for nothing. I don't have time to look and see what Pan is doing, but I hear the other cop grunting at just about the same time as mine. I throw myself on top of him, feeling his fat gut against my stomach with disgust. It's their guts that might save us, though—they make them slow. I lock one arm under his chin, squeezing his neck, and punch his eyes repeatedly with my other hand. He tries to push me away, but even though he's taller than me, I'm stronger. While I'm punching his eyes I worry about Pan. He's smaller than me.

But he's strong too.

I can see my cop's eyes bleeding now. It's reached the point where he's going to have trouble seeing. I give his windpipe an extra hard squeeze, and he goes limp.

I jump to my feet to help Pan. But his cop is out on the ground too. I don't know how he did it—it must be some kind of Asian martial arts. But there's no time for me to congratulate him. I unlock the chain on the heavy plastic curtain over the entrance to the parking cubicle, push it open. I pull on the helmet, hand the other one to Pan, and jump on my bike. Pan is right behind me. I rev up and we zoom away from the motel. On the road, we weave in and out of the cars stuck in traffic. We get ahead of them without going over the speed limit. It's clear that the cops at the motel will never catch us now.

We both realize this at the same time and start to laugh. But I don't let the laughter stop me from driving as fast as I can get away with around the cars.

"Where we go?" Pan shouts at me above the noise of the motorcycle and the other cars. Daringly, he slips his arms around my waist.

"There's a place!" I scream back at him. "I've heard people whispering about it. Way out in the country across the state line. A place where things are different. More like your village where there aren't many houses. Or no skyscrapers. A place where the army and the cops aren't in control. A place where misfits hide. It's the only place for us now."

"But how can we do anything without our ID cards?" Pan yells at me.

"They're no good any more. Even if we had them they'd give us away. The cops will send our information to every computer in the state and to other states in the Alliance. But maybe at this place I hope we can find, they might not care so much about ID cards. Maybe we'll both be happier there."

Pan tightens his arms around me. Even with our helmets on, he still manages to kiss me on the back of my neck.

• • •

Four uncomfortable, hungry, mostly sleepless days later—our route took us far away from official checkpoints and paved roads—we find the woods—woods filled with living trees, covered with leaves and blossoms! We stop in front of a wooden gate across a dirt road. On either side are lush flower-beds and I can't drive the bike over the flowers.

Just beyond the gate a small group of people are having a picnic on the grass. Some of them look as if they're as young as us, and it looks as if they're eating real fried chicken and potato salad. A big chocolate cake is waiting on a plate. My mouth waters. Pan and I haven't had anything to eat for a long time.

When the people see us they jump up and open the gate, no questions asked, big smiles.

Pan meets my eyes. "Home," he murmurs.

And then the people from the other side of the gate are hugging us.

The Empty Pocket

Seth Cadin

Bus time was nothing time. They all just rode together, idly fighting or blankly staring, tired of each other but too bored and jostled to care much about anything. Omika drifted in the cloud of noise and rattle of bad roads until her stop, where she'd get off and trudge down the block to her shack and then directly on to the moldy sofa. She dropped her sagging plastic bag of sundries and stupid backpack full of chunky noisebooks wherever they happened to fall from her hands. She'd left her flat-top 3Z turned on that morning, so it was ready and rolling on through its routines for her, warm, like a fire without heat, from any angle.

Big Balloon Hour was sparkling around the wall at the moment. On the fancier sets—the ones built from wafer-thin stacks of chips and wires—the image was always pristine and could fill the room. Still, when the host rezzed in, even a cruddy desktop set would let you make eye contact with each other, or manifestations of each other, at least.

Flickering up in multiple bright dimensions from Omika's cheap rezzer, everything on the show's set was a shade of corporate lipstick, some frosted, some matte. The lady host was arranged on a boysenberry loveseat, herself all in white, with her silvery hair carved back in the shape of an iceberg. Her scarlet toenails flexed inside crimson-dyed leather sandals. The lights came up rosy pink, and the lady host rezzed out a smile, which on Omika's old 3Z made the lady's teeth so distorted by molecular static they looked like the baleen of a whale.

This effect produced a chittery sensation in her elbows and knees, something more than a reflex: a portent, an omen, or perhaps just randomly bouncing rez beams from the universe next door. Who knew anymore? Reality hadn't been the same since The Big One. Not that anyone knew what it had been. Except Big. Anything could slip through the sudden sinkholes in the roads, or the shattered windows done up in duct taped plastic and despair instead of glass—anything at all, even pieces of other people's dreams.

Her odd feeling could be coming from anywhere—it could mean everything or nothing.

Whatever it was, it'd been happening to her a lot lately. Little signs, twinges in her joints and skin, and her senses would focus tightly until they zeroed in on the source. It annoyed her. Just more crap to think about, with time eating away at her pointless life already.

But she felt it, so she hit MUTE, and heard . . . a moment or two later . . . an unpleasantly unmysterious sound: a kind of rustling and rattling which was probably made by an insect so large it was shifting the crusty dishes on the "kitchen table" (splintered up old door resting on ancient tires near the front door) as it walked over them.

This was all total garbage, all of it—a giant bag of bullcrap strapped to her back, an anchored rope dragging her between shifts at school to the rickety bus to the crumbling shack to to the school again (and it was as much a "school" as her table was a table).

After the last flood, the Last Call of Nibiru, or whatever it was—people said everything, anything, said a whole lot of nothing, but nobody tried to rebuild the world anymore. The adults messed about trading files around the signal in half-busted-up buildings, shumbling to themselves as they trolley-lined around the cinq routes. They were playing at making work. Meanwhile the walls just kept crumbling with every aftershock and strike, and half the fires weren't even out yet, because new ones started every day. Only the Signal Corporation and its production towers were relatively intact, and only the workers attached to them ever seemed cheerful, or at least manic in a useful kind of way. After all, they worked for the signal, and there wasn't much left but the signal.

And the kids—the ones old enough to be ignored, or left helplessly behind when their folks went looking for a less toxic homeland . . . most of the older kids drifted off to places Omika didn't want to go, to do stuff she didn't care about. Though they mostly took over city blocks and little towns, everybody just called their turf the Wilderness, as if the over-growth was harmless vegetation instead of the deeply rooting weed of anarchy.

The kids who stayed behind, perpetually stuck on the school-bus loop like she was, hung around and waited for each other to wake up. Weeks became months, and soon they got used to it, until it became something like normal. They were sleepwalkers in a busted landscape, and they knew it, but it was better than being meat. So they stayed, because they knew meat was what the Wilderness would end up making them, one way or another.

Omika got up and killed the skittering critter with a careful slash from her rusty bread knife, then butchered it, deftly if not precisely, intending to sell the chitin to a beetle man. But she kept the eyes in a jar on the mantle above the flat-top. She looked at them a lot. They were iridescent, empty little gems. Sometimes they caught stray beams from the rezcast, which would make them suddenly blossom in a prismatic flash.

One day, a few months later, she got up and took the jar outside and buried it. She felt better. She made a plan. She'd been trying to keep herself between, but it was time to choose. Omika would have to become part of the signal. She'd have to be careful, though, because a lot of bad things could happen when people did that, especially if they got on 3Z.

• • •

In those parts Nguze was a real gangster. He didn't shake the ground when he walked. Most guys got up to a lot of noisy business but Nguze had the ways of stepping lightly, he said, and the ways of holding ferns too—so he could shimmy up with a mouthful on those thick cracked claws, and make Ibo hoot, because Ibo had never been tickled, never been surprised. Not since another time, and nobody remembered a minute ago, five minutes ago, five years ago, not really—not like Nguze.

It is the place where the picture is alive, like nets full of fish in your belly, or some big moths drifting by—he tried to explain, and his mother never could do it but Nguze could, and so Ibo brought him around to talk about pictures and life while they ate snails and berries.

It was good to keep their minds busy. It'd be the cold season soon and they'd slow down, until they stopped—on the last thought they had. It could be a long season in there, without a name or anything, just staring.

"Make the dead picture move," Nguze urged in Ibo's ear,

wet slappy whispers rumbling down his neck. "Push one into the other."

But it didn't make sense. Ibo pushed using his body, with his magnificent shoulders, the strength of his brutal thighs. A picture couldn't be pushed, one into the other, like a boulder into a doorway to keep the wind out.

"No," Nguze said, over and over, but Ibo didn't know, only began to sense.

"Like a tree pushes a leaf out of a stem?" he guessed hopefully, and the sigh he got back was somewhat less irritable this time.

• • •

Having navigated the Signal Corp's Recruitment & Omissions labyrinth until she finally reached someone with a proper job, Omika was silent, sensing this was a moment to let Mr. Forms Guy #3 fill the space with whatever sprang into his neatly clipped head.

He waited back at her, but she won, and he spoke first: "You say there was an accident?"

"Technically, I'm, like, a . . . *Device*," she said. Making the past up was getting easier. The details just formed around a few gritty grains of reality, not so much *lies* as stories that might as well be true, or were true enough for purpose.

Life was like that now, she'd realized, finally. You could be anybody or anything, if you paid attention and figured out the rules. "My engineers were with The Monday Machine. When the accident—well, their lab—"

"And you say—"

Omika wondered at first why he used that phrase so often, but she got it now. It was how the news guy talked—not the desk one but the outside one whose job was bothering people who were way too busy to talk. *You say, they say, some say.*

Real-time narrative, stapled to the moment, running on cue, that was his deal, Omika decided. So this time *she* interrupted, keeping him off balance:

"I'm sorry, what did *you* say *your* name is?" She looked right at his face and waited, trying not to swing her torn sneakers over the metal bar under her chair, in the space between her feet and the carpet (or whatever that flat stuff was that corporations put on the floors to keep the dirt off). Technically, at her age, she wasn't even allowed to be in the Signal Corp complex, let alone to meet with its agents, but as part of her new insight she'd learned that if you looked serious and busy enough most folks would let you go anywhere, and believe whatever you wrote on their forms.

"Swift," Mr. Forms said carefully, as if answering something more complicated. "I hadn't said, in fact. Mizter Swift is my name, but Miz Omika—and I may have neglected to express my pleasure to meet you, it's just—" He gestured at his desk, almost helplessly, as if it were a dragon he had to constantly feed, or else it would eat him alive.

"Of course," she said, trying to emulate 3Z hostess-style grace, charitably absolving him of everything unnamed. She hadn't shook a hand in months, maybe years, but you didn't freaking forget, did you? It was a simple procedure. Anyway he didn't seem alarmed by anything she did. "Mr. Swift." She smiled as fake a smile as she could remember how, hiding her teeth. "Nice to meet you, too."

For the first time he smiled back. Surprisingly, he looked as if he were a toddler on an outing and that someone helpful and friendly had, just that moment, unbuckled his straps and hoisted him out of a car seat to see the duckies at a pond. (If the duckies hadn't all been coated in soot and oil.) But now he was all cheer, as if the vexation had dissipated entirely. She'd helped take care of some of the younger orphans, though, so she knew his mood could change again quickly.

This response gave Omika her next idea: "I thought I saw a courtyard with a little fountain outside—"

"Oh, yes," her apparently new best friend enthusiastically answered, gathering up his fancy pen and important papers and cradling them in his elbows. "Fresh air, yes, and the rain from this morning stopped, didn't it?"

She'd noticed he was the color of old ash, and blinked a lot when his head moved toward the light. It had last rained three days ago, but she didn't have the heart to tell him.

• • •

"It's an amazing thing to die," Nguze said.

Ibo thought about it, and about the idea of pictures coming together, and eventually he found the way to hold patterns in his mind for what he started to recognize as a series of moments.

Not too long after, the moments started to flow into a river of pattern-thinking, and so he went to the crack in the world. He took a running leap into it, died for himself, and found that what Nguze said was true, more or less. You die, the spirits in your eyes tumble like falling leaves or dropping bones, and then you get the score. Everyone likes to know where they stand. Once your scrim is in your hand, you can just wait, which makes you free, more or less.

He'd still need patience and good behavior, Ibo found, but that is not much challenge to the trained being. Every time the swinging rope stops, you calculate the odds that you'll hop off, and you're so disciplined you won't let go until it's one to one.

Ibo'd heard Nguze's story many times before, though he only now became aware of that, each time having been new before. Yet when it happened to him, all his mortal business fell away, and he saw the purpose. Something bigger than his own life, or his mother's life, or anything they had room for back on the land. A convergence. He understood. *More than planets can sometimes align.*

• • •

Outside, Miz Omika and Mizter Swift resumed their meeting on a picnic table. She watched him closely for signs of illness. Clearly, he had not been out of his office for so long that he might have developed an allergy to sunlight, or a phobia of chlorophyll. But he seemed sturdy enough, possibly because he only ever noticed the world in a small Corp-branded sphere around himself, and everything happening outside of it was a colorful but irrelevant swathe.

"We can't, in fact, get the signal out here," he admitted as they sat on the bench. He gestured at the weeds starting to creep over the edges of the protectively high courtyard walls, and the rusted pieces of pipe stacked against some flaking bricks. "So we only use the area for emergency assemblies."

"How often do those happen?" she wondered, looking at a broken table propped on its short end against a crumbling pile of cement blocks. She noticed how warped and bloated the table appeared, like a rolled-out corpse made of flimsy wood, or like a dead puppet run over by a cartoon tank.

"Officially, they can't happen," Mizter Swift replied promptly, but he was smiling a little again. He knew it wasn't credible. "Emergency procedures are activated only due to unpredictable fluctuations in the weather, or large-scale disturbances due to planetary instability, which would, obviously, eliminate the possibility of meeting outside."

She figured this out after a moment of trying to think like he did. "You mean like the earthquakes?"

"That wouldn't be an incorrect term," he said, even more carefully, and she knew he was trying to tell her something without saying it.

There was a pause while they both thought about this, and why he might decide to do it now—here and now, where they could admittedly see the sun, but only just, because of how thick and high the walls enclosing the courtyard had to be.

Then he seemed to change his mind, or maybe realized what he'd implied, because what he said next seemed unconnected. "Sometimes I come out here to work when I can't sleep."

This sudden offer of personality was interesting, and again she saw him differently—more focused—the way his nose tilted a little to the left, the stray hair pointing up from one eyebrow. He was old, probably at least twenty-five, and he was boring, but he was nice, and she could see he needed someone like who she was pretending to be, to get anywhere in his career.

"Without it?" she asked.

"You sound surprised," he said with what he probably thought was a cunning tone. "I'd think you would understand."

"I don't know much about the shows, despite the . . . incident," she said, glad for a chance to pry. "I didn't know you could get anything done without signal."

"They do still teach us how to use a pencil," he replied drily, and she had to smile at him, and he had to smile back. "I keep a little notebook in case of outage . . ."

"Don't worry, Mizter Swift, I get it," she said. She felt the size of the space around them, the too-bright sky crouching like a big dog over them. She wanted to go inside and rez something, but this had turned into a new kind of situation and she just had to deal with it, that was all.

Magic words again. "My—some people call me Asher," he offered shyly, and she knew she had an agent now, all right. He might be a stiff collar but he wasn't so bad.

"Asher Swift," she echoed. "That's catchy. Have you ever tried hosting?"

Asher laughed openly, not at her but at her daring—delighted by it. "Oh, come now," he said with real modesty.

"Why not?" she wondered. It was like the lottery, or the slots—just a switch thrown, off or on, mostly off. If the rezmods were there, and he wouldn't have the job if they weren't, however he came by them.

"I wouldn't want to embarrass myself," he admitted, and she sensed that just acknowledging the *existence* of embarrassment was uncomfortable for him. He would melt on live rez, all right, just shake himself to pieces. "I'm happy in my work. Finding talent."

She could tell this was true, though something was off again; some hesitation seemed to be wrapped around his tone.

He pushed past it, snapping shut on her. "We should finish the paperwork inside," he said firmly, brandishing his fancy pen. "The rain could start again any time."

She looked up again at the clear blue sky but said nothing.

· · ·

Ibo did once believe in a series of gods, but none of them made themselves manifest when he'd died. Instead, a shaky little monster with an air of urgent efficiency was pumping his hand the moment he landed in rebirth, or whatever this strange little nowhere room might be called.

The creature was purple, sort of, with a metallic sheen that would be pretty if it didn't look a lot like something rotten. But then, for all Ibo knew, it was sick or old or something. It was bent, awkward—it seemed taller and older than him, but it slumped in such a way—such a cartilage-heavy way—that it gave the impression of being shorter.

"We quite adore you, of course," it said, or seemed to say through some kind of eardrum-tingling vibration. "We're all large on your package." Not precise, but the sentiment, even beamed into his skull by mystic rays, was reassuring. "Yet we cannot help but feel that mistakes have been made. At your earliest convenience . . ." It hopped around, unsettled and hopeful.

Ibo felt himself cringing back from its rawness. "Are you asking me for some kind of help?" he tried. The monster wasn't trying to eat him or probe him, and it seemed friendly, so maybe this was a cosmic test or some Nguze thing like that.

"Most appreciated," the monster said, teeth akimbo. "Your enduring patience. Please come and meet my homeys, and I will leave you to your training."

Ibo found himself led through an enclosed place with stale air and strange people, and wondered. He could do that now, just like Nguze said—ideas pushing together, imagination made linear and fixed by time. But he didn't worry, just wondered where all this would lead him. He knew now that even if it were a direct line to death, for him it could only become another transition, perhaps even a return home, like what had happened when Nguze died in the place he went after death.

· · ·

Back again in Mizter Asher's office, Omika reassembled her spine and hands and waited for him to guide her through the sea of forms—clearly his calling and possible destiny. Later, she would try to remember what parts had been real or true, and find herself unsure. But then she would compare the memories of his office with those of the courtyard and, like a dream that seems real until you wake up, she could tell the difference again.

At the end of the endless meeting, he told her he'd take her to see the rezboard room, or one of them, anyway.

"There's someone to whom I must introduce you," he said. "She's called Betty, and she runs the CRZ. Don't worry about all the metal. She's perfectly decent."

Omika thought about this particular choice of words as she followed Asher through mildewed but otherwise mostly intact miles of cubicle walls—status symbols in this day and age. Once they would have been donated or trashed, worth so little you might have had to pay someone to come get them. She could remember that time, but just barely. The Big One hit when she was only three, and twelve years later the shocks hadn't stopped. *Any* standing wall was a sign of power, success— in other words, a sign you had some connection to the Corp.

So if you didn't want the implants, you could forget the sturdy walls. Or the job, for that matter. The signal needed receivers, and the Signal Corporation had its standards. But it also had plenty of available implantees, despite the risks and the permanent loss of privacy, because the workers' main concern was whether they ate old cans of baked beans, or each other.

Of course it was always cheaper to make your own, which was why Omika was scruffing around the place at all, let alone in the company of someone as firmly mid-level as Swift. If she'd been too dumb or weird-looking, even the potential free labor might be worthless to them. But she'd never been born, she'd been engineered, atom by atom—so she wasn't any of that. And she wouldn't need the implants, or any of the rigs and wires. If they could get her to talk on cue, they could rez her all night long, no loss, no decay.

There was a line at the entrance to the CRZ station, and they all had to pass one by one through the sterile security chamber. First Mizter Swift, then an odd lizard-boy introduced by the agent as Eee-bow or something like that—"Don't worry about him, he's just a recruit," Asher barely explained—and Omika went last, so she could watch what they did and copy it without having to ask.

Inside, she and the lizard-boy both stood transfixed for a moment: a field of diamond filaments, defining the space as they wrapped around each other throughout it, surrounded the row of workerbeings of all sizes and configurations, wired in various ways to their stations. Each visible string fluxed with the pressure of countless transactions in endless chains of assembly. Standing shyly beside each other, watching the flashes of workers keeping the signal alive, Ibo and Omika felt an intuitive connection to the organic configuration of this place, despite how new it was for both of them. It was all unknown, yet somehow familiar.

Asher led Omika and the lizard-boy to a station where names and handshakes were quickly exchanged, and she could tell right away—unlike herself, Betty *had* probably been born, according to her papers, but Omika bet most people doubted it when they met her. Her gleaming skull, almost obscene in its exposed metallic state, was unsettling as it winked out segments of the signal into the air—even more unsettling because Betty's round, rough-edged eye-sockets never blinked, so the sparks from her rezplants reflected in them constantly, which made the experience of looking in her eyes stroboscopic.

Omika looked down at Betty's hands instead, and the place where the polished ivory slats slid into her wrists. When she had a thirty-second break and *they* shook hands and exchanged names, Betty casually let her sleeve fall down over the exposed apparatus, but this couldn't conceal the underlying sensation of the hinging mechanism in her grip.

Still, they were better than normal hands, as far as Omika could tell. Especially in what appeared to be Betty's line of work. She plugged away at tiny silver wires with diligence, rezboarding so rapidly her hands became a metallic blur as she worked. Her ponytail swayed, swishing against her blouse and leaving bright rainbow splashes of slowly fading chromaterms over the thin black fabric.

This too was information, Omika figured—spreading out over Betty's skin and down her spine, into the chair, which quietly signaled the tower about her status, physiotech-wise, and mood stress-management-wise.

"How would you like a job, Ibo of the Valley of the Chasm?" Betty didn't stop working while she asked. "Your species seems particularly adaptable to the technology we use here, and your, uh, cousin—Nguze, was it?—chose to break his contract, so we thought perhaps—"

Before he could answer, a number of terms and ideas had to

be explained, but they all knew he would say yes. The implants, the hours, the whole bizarre experience of it wouldn't put him off at all. His whole scaly body tensed with excitement, and he was led away to the surgical area, because once they had a good rezboarder willing to work they wasted no time.

Omika—who could tell both Betty and the lizard-boy weren't much older than she was, if at all—wasn't sure it was a good deal for him. But he would take it, because what else? Go back to some jungle and know all this was here, glittering out of reach? She let herself be led to a more boring place, wondering what it felt like to get the implants, to become such an intimate part of the signal itself.

She, too, had a job offer to consider. Her own program— *Omika's Empty Pocket*, or something catchy like that.

It was unusual, but not unprecedented, that was the point, Mr. Asher Swift made it absolutely clear. Technically, Omika was abandoned IP, though because she was also a citizen, she could legally lay a claim to own her own existence. To her hidden amusement, he said this quite seriously, as if she might have slowly disappeared if they couldn't get the proper signature on a piece of paper that proved she had a right to exist.

It felt like a long time since she'd left her hovel armed with her plan, but it was working. It seemed.

· · ·

Once his implants were complete and his routine solidified, over time (now real to him in a way never possible before), Ibo found Betty's smile was not as complicated as her hands. As she trained him in the job and guided him through the implant process at the same time, and then as they lived and worked together, her hands and smile—*her*, Betty, as a whole—all became part of his life, and more. Their minds mingled and they shared synapses, including whole new ones they created together.

At 17:00 they finished their shifts. Betty flashed her uncomplicated smile brightly around the room as they hustled out, keeping it till she reached the curb where a workers' cinq was waiting on the track.

"Did you notice? Chit Nine ditched her shift again," she told him, sinking her cool metal head against his scaly shoulder as she punched in code for home. "And she knows, she just doesn't care. Drafting, I bet. She thinks they need new bookers over at . . ." Through the matted pleats of hair in his face she saw his new luminous eyes unfocus. "Ibo? Can you hear me, dear?"

He couldn't. Through the tinted visor, she could see his eyes sparking wildly, and the reflective effect made his helmet a constellation of signal crash. Her mechanical wrists flipped and turned, quickly bringing her hands to the soft leather straps holding him onto the cinq, and allowing them to fully rotate around the helix as her nimble fingers plucked the tags. The straps fell slack and she caught Ibo, sliding off the seat with her arms firmly clasped around his chest from behind.

They were halfway between HQ and home, on a landed route Betty was pretty sure stretched from the coast to the edge of the Iron. Long white rails marked off the expanse of cinq grit they'd been riding, and she couldn't tell whether the dark wavy lines making abstract patterns over the road ahead in the distance were shadows or track marks. The jagged outlines of unknown trees and the alien rustle of strange, dense undergrowth seemed to be creeping closer to the nearby rails every moment.

• • •

Omika considered the offer, remembering the lizard-boy and how obviously they'd drawn him in and hooked him hard without him even realizing. Space and time were apparently nothing to them, with the signal—which came from the *people*, through the implants, one rez-pushed batch of energy at a time. It was Asher's primary concern, beyond the legal issues— that a truly engineered host would need significant practice to avoid overblowing the signal entirely, and would have to be trained to keep their live rez energy in the same range as those working from implants.

Maybe enough was enough, she decided, and she thought of one last plan.

Asher Swift would never understand. The adults couldn't—couldn't understand that what they were perpetually keeping alive was just a dream, a temporary way of getting by, not because they'd had too much catastrophe, but too little. It would all have to go before they'd start something new.

The signal was holding them all back. Even the corporation could hold out against the rapidly expanding Wilderness for only so long. All Omika had to do now was get back to the heart of the tower, and she could blow it out like candles—like a celebration marked with darkness, and then at last they could all begin again. She'd seen enough at the rez-station to understand. All she had to do was find an empty rezcasting set—not hard, with so few hosts surviving the necessary procedures more than a few years, these days—and her body would do the rest.

• • •

Ibo stared at the curves holding him in and wished for them to disappear until he fell asleep. So this was also death—another slip into another world, though somehow, as in a dream, he recognized enough symbols to navigate without feeling lost. He found a platform going up to a room of books and machines, and ran a general search for any workers in the Betty range. The list scrolled through collapsed trees of names and numbers. He tapped a claw against the screen to stop the spill on the mark.

Betty: Discontinued. There were too many records for too many ranges to be sure, but whatever "Discontinued" meant it wasn't applied often.

Though he knew what it meant, of course. There was nothing complicated about the word discontinued, as in no longer produced, or desired, and out of service. It was another way of saying dead. Betty was even less than a dream—she was a fairy tale, a goblin in the mine. Sometimes the walls knocked and you didn't know why, so you said it was spirits, something mysterious and not quite friendly. If she had been here she was not now.

Ibo almost believed it completely, before he heard old Nguze whisper from his memory—why would they keep a record of no record? Why write it down like that—Discontinued—for anyone to see? Just in case he happened to look?

Of course they knew he would look.

Now that he knew how to make pictures move in his mind, they never seemed to stop. He thought he saw Betty waiting under a traffic light, watching for the sign to turn, and how the neon would reflect from her head. He thought he saw Omika—he'd often seen her hanging around the CRZ with her boring old agent muttering at her while pointing at things—hiding under a desk with her knees tucked up to her chin. He thought he saw them both in a dingy mirror, over his shoulder, turning away. Outside and all around him, they were listening and responding. Understanding and passing down the word. If you can dance one way, you can dance another. If you can follow the score, you can play yourself off of the page.

They worked together, moved in bands together, every day. They understood each other very well. Anyone could have stopped it but nobody would until they woke up. He wasn't dying, he was just moving up and down the line on a rope of worlds. In all of them, the story, the structure, once you could see it, hold it, was the same. They'd warned him quite clearly—if the implants failed, his body would fall away and he'd become an invisible worker, part of an endless mine of molecular assembly and collection necessary to keep the signal alive.

So Ibo decided to be like Nguze—he talked to his latest set of new fellow nano-workers, nudged them with ideas, new ways of thinking, until when Omika's surge came, they were ready to stand up from their stations together and redirect all at once, push it through until it broke.

• • •

While Betty thought it over, she dragged Ibo's unconscious body as close to the edge as she could manage, propped his legs up and pressed his chest against the rails, and hugged herself tightly into his back. The cinq itself was just too big to be moved out of the way, but hopefully anyone coming up behind them would see that it was stationary with enough time to brake and signal out for help.

She felt inadequate, but not useless. At work, her

chromatic ponytail would have already sent out five different alarms of increasing urgency, and she'd be hearing the swift whoosh of Signal Corp copters approaching on the private flight route.

Out here, there were no comforting machine sounds. There were nothing but the forest noises she could hardly identify, and hoped were mostly just the wind.

Then the ground heaved, and she knew better. She felt the shuddering, but at first she thought it was something coming from the sky, because the clouds seemed to be vibrating. She thought it was the sky itself coming to pieces, as if a long alien hand was about to reach through a crack and pull aside the curtain. But then she saw the moon, and remembered that there were rules to the galaxy, one of which was that a planet only seems to be stable on a short-term scale.

Earthquake. It was another earthquake, not an aftershock but *the* earthquake, the one she had been waiting for. The signal had been holding it all together, drawing peer-to-peer energy from implant to signal and back again, and now—it too was finally breaking apart.

She felt her mechanical feet gripping asphalt, springing her body fluidly down the tracks.

Flying along the side of the road, she reached up to free her ponytail and felt her natural hair was already starting to grow. Cogs were grinding, wires were tangling, all around inside her, the change was taking place.

The signal was dying, was almost dead, but Betty was coming to life. Her oversized steel skull would never change, because it had been installed in a womb-cave underwater by a team of nanites, but the rest of the parts of her that had never been born were falling away and new ones flowing into place.

The whole world was falling away, reassembling—the signal was blasting out, dissipating and reforming, and they'd let it become so entwined with everything, it was reshaping the world right with it.

• • •

"Do you think if you did that long enough, you'd get a callus on your head?"

The boy, still an odd shade of green but no longer scaly, swayed to keep his balance on the rickety bus. *Hey wake up I'm talking to you. Look at me if you hear me. Look at me.*

She looked. They understood. The bus trawled over loose gravel pits and bounced her leaning skull on the window like a paddle-ball game.

"No. That's stupid." *I hear you. I'm awake. I was awake the whole time.*

"Stupid is giving yourself a headache on purpose." He felt as if he were pretending to be someone he used to know, but the past was gone again. At least the future seemed intact, his mind still able to hold it together in an orderly pattern, even if there were too many blurry spots. "Stop the bus."

It came out like an order, so she laughed. "Right. I'll just do that now."

Don't you know that you can?

The prowling rumble machine continued on. The noise stood between them like a wall. Then it stopped, and ignoring the hubbub they departed. It was a long road on both sides, but *it doesn't matter anymore, right?*

Right, she answered. They were free. She lifted the road and turned it over, easily, sculpting it up into a bridge. The bus fell like an old toy, cracked open, and people tumbled out.

Hey, he said, warning, but she was already setting the scramblers lightly on their feet.

It was fun. It felt nice, as if she were a brightly painted swizzle stick dipped in a bubbly glass and swirled around. "But why can't you do it?" she wondered out loud as they floated gently over new formations.

He didn't answer for a long time and then he just said, *What's your name?* But she didn't know anymore, and he realized he'd forgotten his own as well, shaken out of his skull by the convergence of vibrating worlds.

One day he stumbled, and she grabbed him with her hands, frantic, trying to remember what hands did. *I think it's gone, the power is gone,* she said.

Yeah. I had to draw some in to shove it off, but it ran out eventually. I'm sorry.

"Why didn't you warn me?"

"I hoped . . ."

That it was just you, that I would keep it. She pulled him to his feet and brushed him off.

"You're special," he said. Last night she had made them a forest, and now it would stand for a thousand years.

"Not so much anymore, though." She didn't seem to mind about it, but he moved closer.

Forever, he said. *Always.*

Behind a flat brick wall, under a hanging tree, they fished off a rough slab of rock about twelve feet high. For poles they had curtain rods wrapped in unbreakable plastic line.

Out of the corners of their eyes they could see flashes of little animals, so fast it was like invisibility. Some of them, she was almost sure, could walk across the tide line and over the baying ebbs. She'd seen a beetle with seven legs, one of them churning along below to propel it like a curving blade.

Just keep reeling it in, and she reeled, imagining the thin clear string cutting into her palms. Wooshing back suddenly at her because he had never learned how to follow the directions.

The flood had come from the west, a high ridge of water that pulled in the landscape behind it. "Hills," she said. They made it on bicycles they had to remember how to ride.

They found a ghost camp by the side of a cliff, left, like many others they'd found, with ordinary tasks openly incomplete. She always went around and closed the books, pulled the kettles, shut the drawers. Then they used everything and kept nothing.

That was how they did it, all summer long. Hiking, sleeping in caves, lifting what they wanted to eat off the ground. Not stopping, letting the wrappers fall and drift.

She reeled in a camera that was swollen with muck and bloat. He erased the owners by opening the bay. They passed the film between them, stringing it between their hands like black-hole cartoon-steamroller fairy-lights. In the dull ribbons they saw each other flickering, like the view through a noose, or like, in an old movie, the metallic sound of a knife when you pull it out of anywhere.

It makes sense, they told each other. *In the movies there was never any such thing as an empty frame.*

They buried it all at once, shoved it all down with the camera into a pocket of mud. Bubbles and loops of it kept rising back up, but she stepped down hard until they were satisfied.

They followed the surge to the next town by holding their noses in an old floating Jeep and riding until they crashed slowly into a pile of similar vehicles. It blocked the road for miles, as if someone had made a Great Wall of cars.

This could take forever to get around, she said. *I don't think we have the supplies to make it.*

"We just have to try," he said. "Luckily, we do have forever."

He could still make her smile. Like he'd said, then and now, it didn't matter anymore. Even when time ran out, they had forever.

For Sophia and with thanks to Chane.

About the Authors

Elizabeth Bear was born on the same day as Frodo and Bilbo Baggins, but in a different year. She is the Hugo and Sturgeon Award-winning author of over a dozen novels and fifty short stories. She lives in Connecticut with a ridiculous dog and a cat who is an internet celebrity.

Steve Berman has been a finalist for the Andre Norton and Lambda Literary Awards. He regularly speaks around the United States about queer issues and themes in speculative and young-adult fiction. His novel *Vintage* is a "boy meets ghost" story. His idea of a dystopia would be a world without ice cream. He resides in southern New Jersey.

Seth Cadin is from New York and now lives in California. More of his short stories can be found in the Prime Books anthologies *Bewere the Night* and *Bandersnatch*, as well as in the annual *Three-lobed Burning Eye* anthology. He has one partner, one daughter, and too many pet mice.

Kiera Cass is the author of The Selection trilogy. She likes cake and hangs out on YouTube. You can learn more about her projects at kieracass.com.

Amanda Downum lives near Austin, Texas, in a house with a spooky attic. She can often be found climbing on books and falling off perfectly good rocks. She is the author of *The Drowning City*, *The Bone Palace*, and the forthcoming *Kingdoms of Dust*, published by Orbit Books. Her short fiction is published in *Strange Horizons*, *Realms of Fantasy*, and *Weird Tales*. For more information, visit amandadownum.com.

Jeanne DuPrau is the author of The Books of Ember, an award-winning, best-selling series. She has written fiction and non-fiction for adults and children. She lives in California.

Nina Kiriki Hoffman is the author of adult, middle-school, and young-adult novels, and many short stories. Her first novel, *The Thread that Binds the Bones*, won a Stoker award, and her short story, "Trophy Wives," won a Nebula Award. Her novel, *Fall of Light*, was published by Ace in 2009. Her latest series is Magic Next Door: *Thresholds*, published in 2010; and *Meeting*, published in 2011. Hoffman lives in Eugene, Oregon, with several cats and many strange toys and imaginary friends. For a list of her publications, see: ofearna.us/books/hoffman.html.

Jesse Karp is the author of the young-adult novel *Those That Wake* and its forthcoming sequel, as well as the non-fiction book *Graphic Novels in Your School Library*. He is a school librarian in New York City, where he lives with his wife and two daughters. His website is beyondwhereyoustand.com.

Diana Peterfreund is the author of eight novels for adults and teens, as well as several short stories and critical essays on popular children's fiction. Her work has been translated into twelve languages, and her short stories have been placed on the 2010 Locus Recommended Reading list and anthologized in *The Best Science Fiction and Fantasy of the Year, Volume 5*. She graduated from Yale University in 2001 and now lives in Washington, DC, with her family. Read more about Diana and her writing at dianapeterfreund.com

Carrie Ryan is the *New York Times* best-selling author of several critically acclaimed novels including *The Forest of Hands and Teeth*, *The Dead Tossed Waves*, and *The Dark and Hollow Places* as well as several short stories. Her first novel was chosen as a Best Books for Young Adults by the American Library Association, placed on the 2010 New York Public Library Stuff for the Teen Age List, and selected as a Best of the Best Books by the Chicago Public Library. A former litigator, Carrie now writes full-time and lives with her husband, two fat cats, and one large dog in Charlotte, North Carolina. You can find her online at carrieryan.com.

Nisi Shawl's *Filter House* won the 2008 James Tiptree, Jr. Award and was nominated for the 2009 World Fantasy Award. For five years she has taught writing as part of Centrum's Young Artists Project at Fort Worden State Park in Western Washington. She has three novels forthcoming, including *Verde*, "a touching mother-daughter story about racial identity, body image, and soul maggots." Shawl is a co-founder of the Carl Brandon Society and is co-author, with Cynthia Ward, of *Writing the Other: A Practical Approach*. She attended the Clarion West Writers Workshop and serves on its Board of Directors.

John Shirley is the award-winning author of many novels and numerous short stories. The setting for "Rooftown" first appeared in his novel *Black Glass* and he writes of a near-future disaster that is the start of a dystopia in his most recent novel, *Everything Is Broken*. As a screenwriter, he is best known for co-writing *The Crow*, but he's also written for animated series including *Batman Beyond* and *BraveStarr*. The father of three sons, he lives in the San Francisco Bay area with his wife. His website is john-shirley.com.

William Sleator has written over thirty books. They are mostly science fiction but are now veering toward fantasy. He divides his time between homes in rural Thailand near the Cambodian border and Boston, Massachusetts. His best friend is a fisherman in Thailand, named Supan, who you will find in his story, albeit it in a different guise.

Maria V. Snyder is the *New York Times* best-selling author of the fantasy Study Series (*Poison Study*, *Magic Study*, and *Fire Study*) about a young woman who becomes a poison taster. Born in Philadelphia, Pennsylvania, Maria dreamed of chasing tornados and earned a degree in meteorology from Penn State University. Unfortunately, she lacked the necessary forecasting skills. Writing, however, lets Maria control the weather, which she gleefully does in her Glass Series (*Storm Glass*, *Sea Glass*, and *Spy Glass*). Her science-fiction novels include *Inside Out* and its sequel *Outside In*, both set in the dystopian world of Inside. Maria's website is mariavsnyder.com.

Carrie Vaughn is the author of a series of best-selling novels about a werewolf named Kitty who hosts a talk-radio advice show. Her young-adult novels include *Steel* and *Voices of Dragons*, and she has also written the novels *Discord's Apple* and *After the Golden Age*, along with many short stories. She is a contributor to George R.R. Martin's Wild Cards series. When she isn't writing, she collects hobbies and lives in Colorado, where she enjoys the great outdoors. Visit her at carrievaughn.com.

About the editor

Paula Guran is the senior editor of Prime Books and edits the annual Year's Best Dark Fantasy & Horror anthology series. Her previous anthologies include *Embraces; Best New Paranormal Romance; Zombies: The Recent Dead; Vampires: The Recent Undead; New Cthulhu: The Recent Weird*, and *Halloween*. She edited the Juno Books fantasy imprint for six years from its incarnation in small press and then for Simon & Schuster's Pocket Books. Guran has been honored with two Bram Stoker Awards and two World Fantasy Award nominations. She has a daughter and three sons.

Acknowledgments

"Introduction" © 2012 by Paula Guran. First publication, original to this anthology. Printed by permission of the author.

"Hidden Ribbon" © 2012 by John Shirley. First publication, original to this anthology. Printed by permission of the author.

"The Salt Sea and the Sky" © 2012 by Elizabeth Bear. First publication, original to this anthology. Printed by permission of the author.

"In the Clearing" © 2012 by Kiera Cass. First publication, original to this anthology. Printed by permission of the author.

"Otherwise" © 2012 by Nisi Shawl. First publication, original to this anthology. Printed by permission of the author.

"Now Purple with Love's Wound" © 2012 by Carrie Vaughn LLC. First publication, original to this anthology. Printed by permission of the author.

"Berserker Eyes" © 2012 by Maria V. Snyder. First publication, original to this anthology. Printed by permission of the author.

ACKNOWLEDGMENTS

"Arose from Poetry" © 2012 by Steve Berman. First publication, original to this anthology. Printed by permission of the author.

"Red" © 2012 by Amanda Downum. First publication, original to this anthology. Printed by permission of the author.

"Foundlings" © 2012 by Diana Peterfreund. First publication, original to this anthology. Printed by permission of the author.

"Seekers in the City" © 2012 by Jeanne DuPrau. First publication, original to this anthology. Printed by permission of the author.

"The Up" © 2012 by Nina Kiriki Hoffman. First publication, original to this anthology. Printed by permission of the author.

"The Dream Eater" © 2012 by Carrie Ryan. First publication, original to this anthology. Printed by permission of the author.

"357" © 2012 by Jesse Karp. First publication, original to this anthology. Printed by permission of the author.

"Eric and Pan" © 2012 by William Sleator. First publication, original to this anthology. Printed by permission of the author.

"The Empty Pocket" © 2012 by Seth Cadin. First publication, original to this anthology. Printed by permission of the author.